She had a job to do and everything depended on it, but that didn't mean it would be easy...

She wanted to argue with him. Defy him. Let him know he wasn't going to rule her life, but her energy was draining fast. Maybe leaving the house hadn't been such a good idea. He was right, but she'd be damned if she was going to tell him that.

"I'm driving you home," Bill said. "I can feel the fever from here."

"What about my bike?"

"I'll take care of it. Get someone to drive it to the house."

She rode with her arms around Bill, her head resting on his back. Heat flamed her face. Her eyes grew heavy from the fever. When they pulled into the garage, the last of her energy slipped away. Bill helped her undress for bed and covered her with extra blankets. He brought her a couple bottles of water, opened one, and put the other on the nightstand. He handed her a couple Tylenol tablets and watched her swallow them.

"Sweat out the fever and drink the water. Get some sleep." He kissed her on the forehead. "I'll bring something for you to eat when I close up shop. What do you want?"

"Steamed rice." She squinted through her fever at the tough president of an outlaw motorcycle club. How many people could say they had a bad-ass caregiver? "Thank you, Bill."

He was treating her well, just like Orlanda said he would. Just like *he* said he would. Damn him. It was going to be one hell of a bad day when she took him down.

Joan Bowman has a need to belong to something larger than herself. A veteran trained to the point of perfection, she belonged to the US Army and then to an underground resistance group. It was when she was a member of the militia, that she first met Wild Bill Torrence, the president of the Phoenix Chapter of the Demon Brotherhood Motorcycle Club. He fell for her and, after she fled Phoenix, he had every allied and support motorcycle club west of the Mississippi look for her. A year later, with her husband arrested and tired of being on the run, Joan turned herself in to the FBI. Knowing Bill Torrence's soft spot for her, the feds jumped on the chance to make a deal to insert her in the DBMC as a confidential informant. Now all she has to do to get her husband out of jail is to gather evidence on the Demons—and not get caught.

KUDOS for *Cowards Never Start*

In *Cowards Never Start* by Janet McClintock, we are reunited with Joan Bowman Archer, who has been a fugitive from the law most of her adult life. Married to a man now in prison, Joan cuts a deal with the FBI—go undercover with the outlaw motorcycle club, the Demon Brotherhood, and get enough evidence to bring them down, and she and her husband go free. But there are rumors of a rogue federal agent who might blow her cover. Are they only rumors? And what if she can't get any evidence? After all, the Demon Brotherhood claims to have gone legit. If Joan is going to survive this, and get her husband out of jail, she needs to be on top of her game— which isn't easy when everyone is against you and you don't know who to trust. Well written, fast paced, and compelling, this story will grip you by the throat and keep you on the edge of your seat all the way through. ~ *Taylor Jones, The Review Team of Taylor Jones & Regan Murphy*

Cowards Never Start by Janet McClintock is the fourth book in her Iron Angel series. This time, our heroine, Joan Archer, has to go under cover into world of motorcycles and the Demon Brotherhood to seduce the club president and get enough evidence for the feds to bring the club down and send the members to jail. In return, the FBI agrees to release Duncan, Joan's husband, from prison and give them both immunity for past crimes. While Joan reluctantly agrees, she has some major reservations—one of which is the likelihood that, in order to get the club president to incriminate himself, Joan will have to sleep with him, and Duncan is the only man she wants to be with. She takes her marriage vows seriously and doesn't want to be disloyal to him. But since this whole idea was his in the first place, she is not left with a whole lot of options, not if she doesn't want both her and Duncan to spend the rest of their lives in prison. Can she get what she needs without having to betray her vows, and if not, exactly how far is she willing to go to fulfill her deal with the feds? *Cowards Never Starts* is a worthy addition to the series. I have always loved Joan's character—strong, independent, and totally flawed—awesome character development. Add in a solid plot, plenty of intrigue, and lots of suspenseful action, and you have a book that is very hard to put down. ~ *Regan Murphy, The Review Team of Taylor Jones & Regan Murphy*

ACKNOWLEDGMENTS

First of all, I'd like to thank my editor, Faith, for her invaluable support in the editing process through all four books of the Iron Angel Series. Lauri, the Acquisition Editor for Black Opal Books, has been continually supportive and patient with me. I cannot say enough to thank both of you for the opportunity to work with you over the past years. You have made this a positive experience, and I hope our relationship continues well into the future.

As always, my critique group garners a large amount of my praise and thanks. I work on my submission, perfecting it, then they kindly, but firmly, tell me everything that needs more work. I wouldn't be the writer I am today without them. Thank you, Denise, Doogie, Eileen, Mary Alice, Jon, Peter, and Susan.

Someone who has enabled my attendance at my critique group meetings (which are held once a month during the workday) is Shafik Saikaly. Month after month over the past four years, he has covered the office so I could break away for four hours. Thank you, Shafik.

I'd also like to thank Michael Harris for sharing his knowledge on motorcycles. He especially helped by choosing the awesome bikes for the members of the Demon Brotherhood.

COWARDS NEVER START

JANET MCCLINTOCK

A Black Opal Books Publication

GENRE: THRILLER/SUSPENSE

This is a work of fiction. Names, places, characters and incidents are either the product of the author's imagination or are used fictitiously, and any resemblance to any actual persons, living or dead, businesses, organizations, events or locales is entirely coincidental. All trademarks, service marks, registered trademarks, and registered service marks are the property of their respective owners and are used herein for identification purposes only. The publisher does not have any control over or assume any responsibility for author or third-party websites or their contents.

PREFACE

If you have read the back cover you know *Cowards Never Start* is about Joan Bowman Archer surviving undercover in the Demon Brotherhood Motorcycle Club. Her connection to Bill Torrence, the president of the club, was established in the second book of the series *Hottest Places in Hell*.

I dated bikers in my younger days, and although each was a character in his own right, all the characters in this book are fictional. I wish to point out that I was always treated with respect by my biker boyfriends, and I have endeavored to return that respect by portraying the bikers in this story in a kinder light than may be expected.

A few words before you begin:

•   We all know, or at least presume, that bikers' language is crude and colorfully filled with expletives. I have chosen to use the "F" word judiciously, as I have in my previous books. I leave it to the reader to add as many or as few curse words as they wish.

•   This book is written predominantly from Joan's point of view. It is known, and in some cases presumed, that outlaw bikers commit crimes and behave crudely. Their actions are not always witnessed by or told to their women. Therefore, I only showed what Joan would see or hear in the situations in which she finds herself. The few scenes in Bill's point of view entail only the acts that move the plot forward.

Janet McClintock

CHAPTER 1

The rumble of motorcycles announced the arrival of dusty men, who would strut into the Bottom Rocker like they owned the place. Joan checked the clock and cursed under her breath. It was only a little after six. Bikers rarely filtered in before eight, but there was a bike show at the Albuquerque Convention Center that weekend, and things were picking up already.

She got up from the stool at the end of the bar. "I hate this job," she said to Roger, the manager of the rundown biker bar.

He didn't look like an FBI agent with his thick belly, grizzled beard, and denim cut—a jacket with cut-off sleeves, therefore called a cut.

Joan didn't look like an agent either, but that was because she wasn't one, and yet, by some tragic twist of fate, she was the one being inserted into the Phoenix Chapter of the Demon Brotherhood Motorcycle Club.

The Bureau had given her a choice: A year or two in an outlaw motorcycle club or ten-to-twenty in a prison full of outlaws. In return, hers and her husband's sentences would be commuted.

Well, when the devil has something you want, you dance with the demons. She'd agreed to the deal.

"If you don't like this job," Roger said as he licked his thumb and turned a page of *Motorcycle Digest*, "you're really gonna hate the next one."

"Roger that, Roger."

He shook his head and said without looking up, "Your sense of humor's gonna get you killed."

Joan pressed her lips together and headed toward a young, muscular biker leaning on the bar. His eyes tracked from her dyed-black hair, worn in a severe angle cut, past the skimpy, black leather vest, to the tight leather pants laced down the sides, revealing two inches of skin. The outfit barely covered her scars.

Heavy blues-rock forced her to lean forward to hear over the music. "What are you drinking today?" She checked out the lettering on the front of his leather cut. The overhead lighting was dim enough to hide most illegal activities, but she made out: DBMC Phoenix. Her gaze slid past him to the two men who had come in with him. She didn't recognize them, but she had been away for a while. A lot could happen in thirteen months.

"Hey, don't I know you?" the biker in front of her said.

She brought her eyes back him. "What's your name?"

"Dagger." His eyes dropped to her upper chest where her vest bulged, revealing a poorly healed scar.

"I'm Joan. Now we know each other." She tugged the edge of the vest to straighten it. "What are you drinking?"

"I know you from somewhere." He finger-combed his stringy, blond hair and studied her. "You look familiar."

Her gut tightened. She didn't recognize him, but that didn't mean he wouldn't recognize her. She leaned on the edge of the bar and forced a bored look on her face while she waited for his order. Chatting-up bikers never ended well. She flirted with Wild Bill, the president of the Demon Brotherhood—once—a little over a year ago, and it landed her on this path to the lie of her life.

"It'll come to me," Dagger said. "A pitcher of Bud."

"Coming up." While she filled the pitcher, his stare sent chills across her shoulders. His eyes dropped to the edge of her leather vest again. She tugged on the vest, placed the pitcher in front of him, and told him the price.

"Put it on a tab," he said.

"No tabs." Joan pointed a thumb over her shoulder. "The sign says so."

He produced some bills and, when she reached for them, he grabbed her wrist. "I know who you are. You killed Blackie."

"I didn't kill Blackie." Joan wrenched her wrist out of his grasp. "Suit killed Blackie."

She snatched the money out of his hand and turned to ring up the sale. She shuddered at the irony. Blackie was probably the only man she didn't kill in that Phoenix warehouse a year ago. He had been the vice president of the motorcycle club, and if the Brotherhood held her responsible, it was a game changer.

"Hey, you know that woman you were looking for?" Dagger said behind her.

Joan looked over her shoulder. He had a phone to his ear.

"Yeah, that's the one," he continued. "She's at the Bottom Rocker."

Joan shut the cash drawer and glanced at the end of the bar, but Roger was no longer there.

She took a deep breath and turned around to give Dagger his change.

"Yeah, it's her." His smirk sent prickles across her scalp. "How far out are you?...Coupla hours?...Okay, see ya then." He shoved the phone into an inside pocket of his cut, grabbed the pitcher, and joined the other two Brothers.

Joan watched him swagger away from her. Being connected to Blackie's death would make cozying up to Wild Bill dangerous, if not impossible. If her handler was going to do any damage control, he'd have to act fast. She locked the register and headed to the office.

Roger looked up from the monitors that gave him a visual of all areas of the bar. "Who did Dagger call?"

"I think Bill Torrence because he said something about finding the woman he was looking for."

"You *think*?"

"He didn't say much."

Roger shook his head. "You can't be passive and get information."

Joan didn't answer him. She had been over this hundreds of times during the months of FBI instruction. She wasn't a trained agent. She only knew how to do things one way. Her way.

Roger scratched his beard and checked the monitors again. "Are you ready?"

"I guess I have to be," she said.

"Cowards never start."

It was a saying that had been repeated so many times during the FBI crash course that she had the urge to deck someone every time he said it.

"Yeah, and the weak die along the way," she added.

The FBI training had been intense—not for this job, but for the next one where she would have to seduce Bill and get him to give her evidence to bring down his club. After many weeks of training, she still didn't know how to get him to incriminate himself and his club, especially in a lifestyle where women were not privy to the club's dealings. Finesse was not her forte. Physical prowess, which was her strong point, could get her killed.

"The strong, the smart, and the lucky will survive," Roger said.

"Oh, yeah, that's real encouraging. I'm going to die a slow, painful death if I can't make this lie fly." She closed her eyes and shook her head at the image of a large-scale crash and burn.

"Better get back out there before they get any ideas about robbing the place," he said.

When Joan returned to the bar, one biker playing pool looked over his shoulder at her before taking his shot. She gave him a flat stare before looking up at the camera.

The late shift barmaid, another undercover FBI agent, arrived and they prepared for the rush. Bikers piled into the bar in groups and ordered drinks and food.

Joan forgot about the Brotherhood and lost track of the time until a little after midnight when there was a lull. The other barmaid had just taken a couple of food orders to the kitchen. Joan arched her back to loosen it up before wiping bottles and returning them to the shelves in the back of the bar.

"You owe me a shitload of neck massages, darlin'," a familiar voice said behind her.

She swallowed hard, said a short prayer, and turned to face Bill Torrence, who was leaning with both forearms on the bar staring at her. He wasn't a big man, but the prestige of his position as president of the Demon Brotherhood Motorcycle Club set him apart from the other bikers.

His salt-and-pepper hair, now more salt than pepper, was longer, pulled back in a ponytail. His moustache still blended into his goatee that scraped his chest. Edged with day-old stubble, it was a little whiter, but essentially the same. His brown eyes held hers.

Joan broke from the stare first and studied the tabs on the front of his cut. Bikers were proud of their tabs, and if she exhibited an interest in them, it might earn some Brownie points—or, with any luck, a Get Out of Hell Free card.

She put a coaster in front of him. "What are you drinking tonight?"

"No 'hello' or 'how are you doing?'" he asked with a crooked smile.

"I don't chat-up bikers. They get the wrong idea, and things go south."

He eyed her wedding band. "Heard your old man's on the block. What'd he get?"

"Twenty-hard." Joan shrugged one shoulder. "He's at Safford."

What else could she say? Even for someone as strong and tough as Duncan, prison life was hard. Her insides twisted into a heavy, burning ball whenever she thought about him being locked up, fighting to earn his place in the pecking order, wasting away time they could be together. He was there by choices he made. By choices she made, she would get him out.

"Medium security?" Bill asked. "How'd he manage that?"

"He had a good lawyer who got the charges reduced to weapons violations and a few other lesser felonies."

"Twenty isn't too bad."

"Yeah, but he has twenty-to-thirty waiting for him in Pennsylvania." The corners of Joan's mouth tightened. Duncan was forty-seven. It might as well have been a death sentence.

"Gonna be a very old man when he gets out…if ever."

"I'll wait," Joan said. "He's the only man I want to be with."

"Loyalty. I like that, but life can be lonely waiting for a man who may never return."

Joan didn't respond, hoping the Bureau was right about how to get inserted into the DBMC. Be resistant. Make him work to convince her to trust him.

"He'll be okay. He's strong. A natural leader." Bill looked at Joan for a second before continuing. "How are you makin' it?"

"I'm surviving." She picked up a towel and wiped the bar. "Staying under the radar."

Bill gave a hard look at the biker next to him. When the biker moved several feet away, Bill said, "Why didn't you come to me?"

She knitted her brows. "When?"

"Last year, after that warehouse fiasco. I coulda helped you."

She glanced at the nearest biker. He was intent on his own conversation, but she leaned closer to Bill anyway. "You threatened me. I know it didn't seem like it at the time, but I didn't have a death wish."

"I didn't threaten you."

"You said something about getting a pound of flesh and paying for leaving you in the desert to die. It sounded like a threat to me."

"I wouldn't have hurt you." Bill stared at her with the flat, neutral expression common to bikers. Joan didn't blink either. Her boldness must have passed a personality test because he continued, "The DBMC can provide cover for you."

"So, what then? You're gonna forget about the past, ride in here, and give me a better life? All your hard feelings are gone in a puff of smoke. And I'm supposed to trust you?"

His shoulders tightened, and his eyes narrowed. "You don't belong here, Joan. I could move you to Phoenix. The Brotherhood would protect you."

Joan leaned stiff-armed on the bar. "From the *feds*?"

Bill grinned.

"What does that smile mean?"

"You don't have a clue how powerful I am, do you?"

"You're president of an outlaw motorcycle club. You have to have some power. But enough to protect me from the feds?"

"The MC runs security in Phoenix for the Hells Angels. I know every step the local and federal agencies make. If they come sniffing around, I'd send you off to another chapter or support club out of state. They'd never find you, and you'd be taken care of. As much as I'd hate to see you go." His gaze traveled the length of her body. "Don't know how Duncan stands being separated from you."

The burning ball in her gut grew and seared the inside of her abdomen. She doubled down on her temper. "Exactly how do you get information on what the feds are doing?"

If he knew what federal agencies were doing, he could know she was a confidential informant. This could be a ruse to get her alone. Get his pound of flesh and end the threat to his club before it even started.

He leaned closer. "You're a fugitive, Joan. I have the power to help you."

"So let me get this straight." She crossed her arms. "You're offering protection and a better place to live."

"That's what I said."

"What's in this for you?" she asked, knowing bikers never did anything for nothing.

"All you have to do is take care of my house. Between starting up the new business and leading the club, I don't have time for that."

"There aren't female hang arounds to do that for you?"

"They get the wrong idea. Become pains in the asses."

"That's it? Clean your house? I don't have to fuck you?"
Might as well talk about the fire-breathing dragon in the corner.

Bill's neutral face lightened. The corners of his eyes crinkled and a smile pushed up the corners of his moustache. "You'll never *have* to fuck me, darlin'. I'll wait for you to come around. I'm not a heathen. You'll see that in time."

"You sound pretty sure of yourself."

"Didn't second-guess my way to being president."

Joan chewed the inside of her cheek to slow down the conversation.

"Harboring a fugitive is a felony." She picked up a glass and cleaned it in the soapy water. "Why would you put your club on the line for me?"

"You saved the lives of two Brothers. We owe you."

She dipped the glass in the rinse water and placed it on the drainer. "I thought we were even after that time I rescued Duncan."

"When you save the life of a Brother, we're never even. It's a lifelong debt, unless you turn on us."

'*Unless you turn on us.*' Joan stared at Bill, as if mulling over his proposition. "I want to cruise under the radar. Hooking up with one percenters doesn't sound like under the radar to me."

"The DBMC has gone legit," Bill continued. "We bought a coupla legitimate businesses and are planning a couple more. We made more money in less time with drugs and prostitution, but that money got burned up in legal fees when the feds came down hard on the club after that sting a year ago. Almost wiped us out with arrests. We're just starting to recover. Doing it the hard, honest way."

"I don't know. I can't sit around idle. What will I do there?"

"I'll ask around. Get you a job in one of the legit businesses for your spending money."

"Where would I stay?"

"With me. I have a couple extra bedrooms in my house."

This was turning out better than even the Bureau had predicted. Staying in his house gave her an immediate closeness—a presence that could be brokered into trust, a home court advantage to facilitate getting her hooks into him.

"I'm married," Joan reminded him.

Bill was moving fast. The Bureau had not planned on him pushing so hard to get her to go with him. She hoped they were light on their feet.

"You'll get tired of waiting. He'll never be a part of your life again. You're too passionate for that. Too alive."

"Do I look alive?"

Bill studied her before continuing. "You'll see the light, and who'll you turn to? Some weakling who calls himself a man? Not you, Joan Bowman. You'd get bored with anything less than a real man."

"And I suppose you're a real man?"

He didn't answer right away. Instead, he watched Joan scan his tabs: Lost Cause, One-percenter, DBMC. President. "I protect what's mine. Don't back down from trouble."

Joan moved back to lean against the lower cabinets of the back bar and crossed her arms across her burning stomach. "Should I pretend to be impressed?"

He stroked his goatee. "No. Stay the way you are. That's the way I like you."

She had to get one thing straight, even if it jeopardized her mission. "That first time I met you, you know at the party for me and Kearney? I flirted with you, but I was just messing with your head. It meant nothing. Get that through your thick, biker head. And don't forget what happened in the desert when you tried to make a pass at me."

His face hardened. He leaned forward and motioned her to come closer.

She pushed off the cabinet.

"I convinced the Brothers to overlook that," he said in a low voice. "My word is law. As long as you play along, my protection stands."

"I can protect myself."

He scowled at her for a second before the corners of his mustache twitched up. He shook his head and chuckled. "You are fucking precious."

She curbed her temper. If he didn't respect her and her abilities, she would be become merely his housekeeper and bed partner. Access to any evidence would be out of her reach, relegating her quiet, future life with Duncan to nothing more than a pipedream.

Pipedreams were not part of her plan.

"I don't know about this," she said. "I like it here. I'm my own person."

"You'll still be your own person. And you'll be closer to Safford. It's a little over an hour from Phoenix. I'm guessing you've found a way to visit your old man."

"Let me think about it." She reached behind her for a pen. "Give me your number, and I'll let you know."

Bill pulled out his wallet and thumbed out a business card. He flapped the wallet shut, but not before Joan spied a dog-eared photo of a man and a young boy on a motorcycle.

"Here's my card," he said. "Call me anytime. I'd invite you to come to the show with me, but I brought someone. I could have one of the guys bring you so we could spend some time together." Bill scratched the stubble along his jaw. "But I don't want to start off our relationship like that."

"We don't have a relationship," she said without looking up from the card. "Besides, I'm working long hours this weekend because of the show."

The card had the Harley Davidson logo. She recognized the address of the business. In the lower right-hand corner were two phone numbers.

She smiled and raised her eyebrows. "You own a Harley dealership?"

"Maybe I shoulda opened with that." He smiled back. "We're showing a bike. Came in third a couple times, but the show this weekend might be the big one."

He pointed to the card. "The bottom number is my cell. Call me by Saturday afternoon, so I can make arrangements." He motioned for someone at the table to come over.

"I'll call you, whatever I decide," she said, tucking the card into her back pocket.

"Good. Two pitchers of Bud." He turned to the Brother who had been summoned to the bar. "Take care of this." He headed toward a table where there were now eight members of the Demon Brotherhood talking among themselves.

The biker had blank, tired eyes. He paid for the beer, and, when he headed toward the table, Joan saw his prospect patch. She picked up some empty glasses and wiped the bar while she thought about how prospects were used and overworked in order to show their allegiance to the club. Becoming Wild Bill's old lady would not be as bad as being a prospect, but it was not going to be a roll in the hay. The memory of Duncan trying to get her to literally take a roll in the hay brought a rare sweetness to mind. But that had been before everything slid off the rails. Like things always did.

Roger motioned Joan to the end of the bar. "You've been here since four. Go home. Get some rest because it's game on."

"You don't think I should stay a little longer, you know…" She gestured toward Wild Bill with her eyes.

"You have to leave without further contact," Roger said. "If he took the bait, your absence will pull him in."

She grabbed her meager tips—bikers were notoriously bad tippers—and headed to the motel across the street where the FBI had established a home for her. As she crossed the dusty macadam, she thought about Duncan, waiting in prison while she was on the outside. But she wasn't free. Her freedom was an illusion.

And there was always the chance Bill knew she was planted in the bar to get his attention. If he knew what the feds were doing, he could know what she was about to do. He could be setting a trap. Get her to Phoenix. Exact retribution.

But if she wanted to spend the rest of her life with her husband, she had to do play out the charade, see what shook out. The thought of being Bill's lover sent ice trickles down her spine. She hoped she could gain his confidence without going that far, but she would do whatever it took to free Duncan.

She shouldered open the door to her room. It shook on its hinges then squeaked open, washing her with the odor of stale alcohol and bitter cigarette smoke from years of being a monthly-rentals-only motel.

Whatever Bill is offering, it has to be better than this.

CHAPTER 2

The whine of jet engines roared over Joan's head as she backed her bike into a parking space at the Hyatt Place near the Albuquerque Airport. She headed toward the entrance and before she got inside, another plane thundered overhead on its final descent.

The lobby was cool and quiet. She pushed the elevator button for the second floor, rolled her shoulders, and took some deep breaths. Roger had called this last-minute handler-CI meet, which made her uneasy. Hank was her handler. It should have been his place to make the call. The first time they met, they had clicked right away, and a one-hour meet had turned into three, cementing her trust in him as the bridge between the Bureau and her.

When the doors opened, she followed the signs to the outside lounge. After winding through a small sea of white tablecloths and colorful flower arrangements, she emerged on a sundeck to the sound of another landing plane. She looked around for Hank. On the second visual sweep of the area, she spotted Roger in the far corner waving her over to a seating area he shared with a tanned woman with dark hair, who was looking through papers in a folder.

When Joan neared the table, Roger gestured toward the woman who was now looking up at Joan. "This is Special Agent Inez Barrero. She's been assigned as your handler."

"Where's Hank?" Joan asked without offering her hand to Inez.

"His transfer authorization didn't come through," Roger said. "Budget funding. Inez stepped in. She lives and works in Phoenix. Don't worry. She's experienced in handling CIs."

"I don't like last minute changes."

"Neither do we."

Joan pushed her sunglasses to the top of her head, pulling her hair away from her face. Inez didn't wear a wedding band. Her dark hair was pulled back into a low ponytail, but tight curls stood their ground, some escaping.

"Please. Take a seat," Inez said, her lips tight, her words clipped. "Let's talk."

Joan slid onto the black rattan seating and tried to see Inez's eyes through her dark lenses. She didn't act particularly friendly, as if she didn't really want this job. Or she didn't want to work with Joan. Or…it could be anything. Time would tell.

A waiter placed a sweating glass of water in front of Joan and held out a menu.

"I'll have what she's having," Joan said, ignoring the menu and nodding toward Inez.

"A chorizo omelet with extra hot sauce and coffee?" the waiter confirmed.

Joan watched Inez, narrowing her eyes at Inez's stifled smirk. "Put the hot sauce on the side."

"I'll bring your coffee right away," the waiter said before heading inside.

Joan shrugged off her denim jacket. It was an unseasonably warm October day, and although it was only eleven a.m., the temperature was already in the high seventies. A hot breeze warmed her bare arms. Traffic sounds carried up to the sundeck, but there were no rumbles of Harley Davidson motorcycles. The high room rates and location made it an excellent spot to meet.

"I read your file," Inez said. "You've been busy."

Joan leaned to catch a glimpse of the papers. "Does it say in there that I get along better with men than with women? Especially female agents."

"I read about what happened," Inez said. "The woman who

seduced Duncan was ATF. I'm FBI. Different job. Different priorities."

"But still a female federal agent," Joan muttered, scanning the sundeck and the surrounding buildings. "How did the ATF find Duncan? He was hidden in the Ozarks, for Christ's sake."

"The ATF has not been forthcoming with information," Roger said. "But we're on it."

"So you have some leads."

The brief shared look said the agents did not.

"Did you tell Inez what Bill said about having a way of knowing what you guys are doing?" Joan asked, looking between the two federal agents and wondering how Bill got information while they could not. A lack of professional courtesy left her in a vulnerable, weak position.

"We're taking every precaution to keep your work for us a secret," Inez said.

"Oh, thank you. That's so very kind of you." Joan bit down on her anger. This meet-and-greet in the open with a handler she didn't know was going downhill fast. If her future was in Inez's hands, Joan would have to play nice. *I can be nice.* "I'm sorry, Inez. This last-minute change—and to a female agent, at that—has thrown me off my stride."

"If you can't adapt to changes, maybe you aren't cut out for this," Inez said.

The waiter arrived with Joan's coffee, saving her from saying something that could derail her only chance of living the rest of her life with Duncan.

"I'm up for this," Joan said.

"Good," Roger said. "I'll let you two get to know each other and make arrangements on how it's going to go down in Phoenix." He shook both women's hands and left.

Joan watched Roger's retreating figure and listened to another plane on its final approach, wondering why he hadn't given her a heads up about this change.

"Let's go over the terms of the deal," Inez said.

Joan slid her gaze back to Inez. "I don't need you to tell me the terms of the deal. I made it. I know what it is."

Inez flipped through the file, ignoring Joan's sharp words.

"You will be inserted into the Demon Brotherhood to be Bill's old lady—"

"If it comes to that. I think I can get evidence without sleeping with Bill." Joan clenched her jaw. She would get that evidence without letting that lout put his paws on her. The thought turned her body to cold steel.

"I like your confidence." Inez frowned and leaned on the table. "I'm not saying you have to do it. It's not the Bureau's policy to use sex to get evidence, but if you have to go that far, are you willing to have a sexual relationship with Bill?"

"Only if I have to." Duncan's touch had always turned her insides to hot liquid. His look alone could—

"I don't want a call in the middle of the night telling me you can't do this."

"I'm not a quitter," Joan said as her comforting memory of Duncan faded under Inez's long stare. "I know what you're thinking."

Inez raised one eyebrow.

"I became a state's witness against the Legion. I didn't quit. I changed teams." Joan took a sip of coffee. "I went back in. I got the evidence you guys wanted. You want to see the scars?"

"So you're saying you'll do what it takes to get the information we need, even if it involves having a sexual relationship with Bill?"

Relentless bitch. "I said I would." Joan studied Inez's tan and pictured dodging bullets while Inez made par on the sixth green. She returned Inez's hard stare.

Inez was the first to look away. "Okay," she said, looking unimpressed with Joan's answer.

Joan shifted on the rattan seating and leaned forward. "How long have you worked for the FBI?"

"Ten years."

"All ten in Phoenix?"

"No."

Joan watched a plane fly over the hotel before speaking again. "How many confidential informants have you worked with?"

"Enough."

"Roger said you live in Phoenix. Are you originally from there?

"Let's stay focused on you and this operation."

"I'm guessing California."

Inez continued as if Joan had not spoken. "Your job is to find prosecutable evidence or probable cause for us to obtain the evidence. You will stay in the group until you get the evidence to take down the club. In the event you cannot obtain any evidence, you will be pulled out at the eighteen-month mark, starting with the date you arrive in Phoenix. Are you still set for six-thirty tonight?"

"As far as I know. I'll call Bill this afternoon to confirm."

Inez nodded. "Good. Let me know if there's any change."

"I need your number."

"We'll get to that. Back to the terms: Duncan is in a medium security prison per your deal. How's he doing at Safford? Visitations going well?"

"He's doing okay..." Joan thought of Safford. It was like a dorm, but full of criminals. With guards. And locked doors. "Thank you for asking."

"And you get one conjugal visit." Inez pulled down her sunglasses, revealing dark brown eyes framed by stress lines. No makeup. "Any idea when you want to take advantage of that?"

"If it comes to the point where I have to have sex with Bill to move forward, I'll do it then. How long does it take to set up?"

"Since it's already approved, from two weeks to thirty days. So if you think it's a possibility—even a *vague* possibility—let me know as early as possible."

"Geez. You'd think renting a motel room and assigning agents would be easy."

"It's more involved than that." Inez resettled her sunglasses on the bridge of her nose. "So that's the deal. I'm impressed. You are a good negotiator."

"I was motivated." *Was that a compliment*? Joan eyed her new handler. *Probably not.*

Inez shut the folder. "As a CI, you will not have a support team like an undercover agent would. You'll be on your own. Do you understand that?"

"I work better alone."

"I'm here to assist you any way I can. Without you, we have nothing."

"If I'm all you have, we're both in a shitty place." Joan watched another plane fly past so close she could see the passengers. "Am I the first person you'll have inside the club?"

Inez repositioned the silverware for no apparent reason. "We had a couple UCs before you. We managed to get one of them out alive."

"One of them?" Joan leaned back against the bright yellow cushion. "Not very good odds."

"If you don't want this job, I'll escort you to the county jail, get you in the system." Inez waited a beat, possibly for emphasis. "Find someone else."

"If you had someone else, I wouldn't be sitting here." Joan pictured those hard eyes behind the sunglasses. It sounded like Inez either did not want this job or thought Joan couldn't do it. *If you think you can do it better...* "You think I can get evidence and get out alive when trained undercover agents couldn't?"

"We're confident this time will be different."

"How so?" Joan asked.

"They won't expect a female informant. But it'll still be an upward battle."

Joan smiled. "One step forward. Two steps back."

"Welcome to my world," Inez said, looking up at the waiter with their food.

Joan poked at the chorizo omelet and thought about Inez's professional, take-no-shit attitude. She didn't seem to be doing anything to establish a rapport. Joan had never been undercover for a federal agency, not really—going back to get evidence in the Legion didn't count—but a good bedside manner seemed important, for both parties. Yet Inez's demeanor seemed natural. No manipulation. The two women ate in silence for several minutes.

"So how do we meet in Phoenix?" Joan asked.

"I have a motorcycle—"

"Really? What kind?"

"A Sportster. And that's going to be our cover. Two chicks with bikes. We become friends. Ride together once a week or so." She looked up from her plate. "Text often."

"You don't think Bill will get suspicious?"

"We'll have code phrases. If Bill checks your phone, which he probably will—" Inez pointed her fork at Joan for emphasis. "—bikers are a suspicious group, don't forget that—he won't see anything but two chicks with a common interest."

"Maybe a female handler isn't such a bad idea."

Inez smiled for the first time. "Sometimes we FBI agents know what the hell we're doing."

CHAPTER 3

The next morning after making a cup of coffee in Bill's kitchen, Joan looked around. The work area was an efficient U-shape. The black granite countertops caught her eye. It became clear the kitchen had been recently renovated. It opened into an open-concept dining room and living room. It took uber-bucks to not only buy this house in a middle-class neighborhood, but also to upgrade with quality materials and high-end appliances. Well, they say: follow the money. She had a starting point.

Bill was not an overly messy person, but cleaning was clearly not one of his priorities. The bookshelves surrounding the television were thick with dust. The tile floors were grimy but would be easy to clean. The grease mark on the arm of the sofa might be more of a problem.

She wandered to the sliding glass doors in the dining room. They overlooked a typical desert backyard—narrow, no grass. She sipped her coffee, wondering what the hell she had gotten herself into. Being in Bill's house, in the lie of her life—now that she was here, it didn't seem as easy as she had imagined.

After a long, calming inhale, she breathed out. *For you, Duncan. All in. For you.*

An in-ground hot tub caught her eye. She shuddered at the thought of the bacteria stew waiting to swirl into life. Something else to be cleaned.

She returned to the breakfast bar and leaned back against the counter to wait for Bill. She took a sip of coffee and thought about the night before when two bikers had loaded her few belongings into the back of the truck. There had been a verbal scuffle about putting a Honda onto the trailer with the Harley Davidson show bike. Little Al had been assigned to oversee the job, and he used the intimidation of his size—he was six feet, seven inches, 280 pounds—and the power of his position as sergeant-at-arms to get her bike loaded.

Well, as Roger used to say, 'Cowards never start.' Joan raised the mug for another sip.

"You're up early," Bill said behind her.

She jumped at his voice, and some coffee spilled down her chin. *And the weak die along the way.* She wiped at the coffee spots on the front of her tee shirt and swiveled around to face him. "Good—"

"Orlanda get you settled okay?" He popped a coffee pod into the coffeemaker.

Bill's daughter had greeted Joan when she got in the night before because Bill was busy with club business. No rode-hard biker chick, Orlanda's blonde hair was glossy. Her teeth were even and white—evidently, it paid to be the president's kid. She was married to Dagger, the biker who grabbed Joan's wrist at the Bottom Rocker.

"Yeah. She was great." Joan thought of Orlanda's blonde hair. "Was her mother a Latina?"

"Her mother liked to read," Bill said, watching the coffee flow into a mug. "Her favorite book was Tai-something."

"*Tai Pan?*" Joan asked.

"Orlanda's named after one of the characters." He blew on the black coffee before taking a sip. "I'm gonna show you around today. I asked around about a job for you." A smile tugged at the corner of his bushy moustache. "Found one. It's not much, but it'll give you your own money." He winked at her. "Wouldn't want you beholdin' to me."

"Thank you?"

"You're gonna have to get that smartass tongue in check. I'll have someone explain the lifestyle to you." He took a couple gulps and dumped the rest of his coffee in the sink. "Let's go."

"Where are we going?" Joan asked, grabbing her backpack and following him to the door to the garage. "Do I need to bring anything special?"

"Just your pretty little ass," he said over his shoulder as he turned on the lights in the garage.

Joan lasered a look at the back of his head. If she had been Superman, his head would have exploded. A gleaming Harley Davidson motorcycle with stock handlebars and round headlight stopped her in place.

"What's this?" she asked, walking up to it.

"You like it?"

Joan caressed the vintage, stock gas tank.

"It's a 1950 Panhead. Mooky gave it to me when he retired from the club. I took it apart and rebuilt it from the inside out. I know every nut and bolt on this momma."

"I used to have a vintage Triumph Bonneville. An 'eighty-five."

"Yeah? What kind of engine did it have?"

The bastard thinks I don't know anything about motorcycles. "It had a six-fifty-cc parallel-twin four-stroke engine."

She must have said the right thing because he turned his admiration from the Panhead to her.

"Well, this ain't no Triumph, darlin'."

"I know, but don't you think it's weird we both like vintage motorcycles?"

Bill chuckled and walked past the vintage Harley to another, newer bike. "We're taking this one."

"Who's Mooky?" Joan asked, still admiring the Panhead motorcycle.

"You'll meet him." Bill pushed the big, bossy Harley Street Glide to the driveway and started the ignition. Joan stilled at the sight of the big, black bike. It wasn't the one she stole from him after she left him unconscious on the highway, but it was painted the same. She took a step back when visions of him tying her to the fender and dragging her through the residential area filled her head.

"What's wrong?" he asked.

"I thought you drove a Fat Boy," she mumbled.

While the bike warmed up, Bill strode toward Joan. She looked from the bike, up the tabs on the front of his leather cut, to his eyes. She could smell the coffee on his breath and oil on his cut. "It was never the same after you—It's like this, darlin': I covered your ass for what you did to me a year ago. Any other woman woulda received a righteous beating. You're lucky I have the power I have, or you wouldn't be standing here today. Understand?"

Joan nodded.

He grabbed her elbow and walked her out of the garage. "But the VP and the sergeant-at-arms have full reign to avenge anything that happens to me from now on. Got it?"

Joan nodded again.

"What do you understand? Explain it to me."

"If I ever hurt you again, I won't be safe unless I leave the planet."

"Smart woman." He straddled his bike, pulled it upright, and nodded for her to get on the back.

She put her hands on Bill's hips. Might as well get to work. The sooner she earned his confidence, the sooner she would be out of this mess, and safe in Duncan's arms. Job One was to get him to look at her as a life partner rather than a bed partner. Maggots squirmed under her skin at the thought of Bill putting his hands on her. She clenched her jaw and leaned with him through the turns until they were on the highway.

Other than cursing distracted drivers, Bill didn't talk during the ride. Ten minutes later, they pulled into a Harley Davidson dealership in a building that was once a car dealership. Big windows opened onto a sales floor. An employee wearing the blue and gold Demon Brotherhood colors looked up from his task of moving some of the inventory outside to catch the eyes of potential buyers. Bill pulled around to the side of the building and backed into a parking space across from an open maintenance bay door.

"This is jointly owned by me, Dagger, and the club," Bill said, leading the way into the building.

"This is bigger than I imagined." Her boots scraped along the cement floor. She savored the aroma of motorcycle oil.

Three mechanics were already at work. Two wore DBMC colors.

"Let me show you around. I'm in charge of service." Bill showed her his office and the shop, without introductions to the mechanics, then headed to the showroom.

When they walked into the showroom, Dagger looked up from a catalogue on the counter. He straightened up and finger-combed his dark-blond hair. He looked taller and more intimidating than she remembered from the night three days ago in the biker bar. "This is Dagger. He's in charge of sales," Bill said. "Heard you two met already."

Dagger looked down at Joan, crossed his arms, and frowned at her. The Lost Cause tab indicated he had seen a lot of trouble. That patch was earned, club president's son-in-law or not.

Joan stood her ground. "Nice showroom."

Dagger grunted and turned his attention back to the accessories catalog.

"We're gonna look at some bikes," Bill said to Dagger, guiding Joan around the counter to the showroom floor.

Dagger nodded without looking up.

"What's his problem?" Joan asked, sitting on a blue Sportster and checking out the controls.

"Blackie sponsored him."

Her eyes darted to Dagger then back to Bill. "Sponsored him?"

"To become a prospect. How does this bike feel?"

"Nice. But I'm not in the market for a new bike."

"My old lady doesn't drive a Honda."

"I'm not your old lady." Joan checked out the sales tag. The price made her jerk back in surprise. "Is this real?"

"We'll get your bike at cost."

"Oh, of course."

Bill ignored her sarcasm and pointed to another bike. "Try this one."

Joan changed bikes several times until she sat one that made her feel like she was home. It felt substantial, had a low center of gravity. It fit.

"Go wait by my bike," Bill said. "I have something to do before we go to Mooky's."

She headed outside and hung out in the front of the dealership, pretending to check out the bikes. She watched Bill and Dagger out of the corner of her eye until the biker who had moved all the bikes outside walked up to her and asked if she needed any help. She told him she was just looking and walked around the corner to wait for Bill.

When they were on Route 10, Bill was more talkative, and Joan had to lean forward to hear him explain that Mooky had retired from the Brotherhood when his health no longer allowed him to make the mandatory rides. He had been in the club longer than most of the current members had been alive, and the Brotherhood looked after him, invited him to parties, sought him out for counsel on occasion.

He sounded like someone Joan wanted to meet. He knew club secrets and was strongly connected to Wild Bill—close enough to give him his prized 1950 Panhead. She smiled and reached a little farther forward on Bill's waist.

After making a few turns in a low-income neighborhood, Bill pulled into the driveway of a small ranch at the end of a cul-de-sac. Paint peeled from the overhang support posts. Weeds reached for the sun through the cracks in the short driveway. She expected to hear chickens clucking in the backyard.

When Bill knocked on the front door, a seventy-something-year old grizzled man with a biker-belly and straggly beard opened the door.

"Uncle Mook, I brought someone to meet you." The two men embraced, and, after a couple pats on the back, Mooky stepped back to let them into his house.

"*Uncle* Mook?"

"Yeah, this is my father's brother."

"An uncle, a father, and a son—"

Bill cut her off. "I don't have a son."

Joan swallowed hard. "I'm just saying, it's quite a gene pool." Damn the feds' insistence on her reading the personnel files of the major actors in the DBMC. She had to keep a tighter rein on her words. Think before speaking.

Bill gave her a hard look.

"Who's the damn woman?" Mooky asked.

"This is Joan. I told you about her."

Mooky shook his head and flopped into his recliner.

"She's going to clean your house for you."

"I can clean my own fucking house."

Empty boxes with the Amazon logo made a messy pile in the corner. A garbage odor permeated the house. Cobwebs clung to the corners, as if they didn't want to touch the grime on the carpet. The dust on the table tops, where they weren't covered with clutter, was so thick it looked like fuzzy concertina wire.

"I'm not cleaning this house," Joan said.

Mooky's eyes fell on her for a fraction of a second before sliding past her to Bill.

"She's new to the lifestyle," Bill said. "Clue her in. I gotta get back to the dealership."

Bill smiled at Joan's discomfort and stepped onto the concrete slab porch.

"You're leaving me here?"

Bill kept walking toward his bike.

Joan hurried down the sidewalk after him and stepped back when he backed up his bike to turn it around. "When are you coming back?"

"Take good care of Uncle Mook. I'll pick you up for lunch," Bill said before taking off down the driveway and through the cul-de-sac.

Joan rubbed the back of her neck, looked at the open front door, then at Bill's brake lights at the stop sign a long block away.

She headed inside. With one last look over her shoulder, she stepped into the living room. A book flew at her. She ducked, but not in time, and it grazed her cheekbone. *What the burning hell?* A *TV Guide* sailed at her, and she batted it away. The remote control flew toward her. She caught it and tossed it back like a Frisbee. He threw it again.

She held onto it that time and pointed it at him. "Knock it off, old man, or I'm going to shove this down your throat."

After a few seconds, his jaw softened and the corners of his eyes crinkled. "Nice to meet you, Joan."

"What the hell was that all about?" Joan asked, rubbing her cheek.

"All the other damn women sent to clean my house cringed in the corner. You threw the shit back at me." He squinted one eye. "Better put some ice on your cheekbone. I'm gonna catch hell for that."

After a failed search for a clean dish towel, Joan grabbed a bag of frozen corn out of the freezer. The kitchen stunk. Food crusted the cooktop stove. The floor tiles were probably white at one time.

She stood in the doorway to the living room with the bag pressed against her cheek. "You know, if you bag up the trash, they take it away."

Mooky grunted. "You must have thrown a lot of Frisbees."

She shook her head.

"There's only one other way to learn to toss like that," he said. "Kung-fu. Am I right?"

"Maybe."

"Wing Chun?"

She shook her head. "Zuan Shu Kuan."

Mooky snorted. "Modern style."

Joan didn't answer him. She didn't have to defend her training. But his knowledge that Zuan Shu Kuan was modern interested her.

"You throw shuriken?" he asked, referring to ninja throwing stars.

She nodded. "And knives."

"I have something you might be interested in seeing," he said, wrestling his body out of the recliner. He grabbed his belt.

"If it's in your pants, I'm not interested."

He shook his head and settled his pants at his waist before lumbering down the hallway. The floorboards groaned under his weight while he muttered, "That boy can't resist a straight-talkin' woman."

He returned to the living room with two nylon drawstring bags. "Let's go out back," he said, leading the way through the foul-smelling kitchen to the backyard.

A porch spanned the middle third of the house. It had been screened in at one time, but now tattered remnants hung from the corners of the openings. A rusting dryer sat at one end. A privacy fence enclosed the long, narrow yard.

Mooky dragged a weathered, wooden table to the end of the porch and dropped the bags on it. He walked to a corner of the yard, dusted off a piece of cardboard, and braced it against a surprisingly well cared for shed about four yards away. He returned with a spark in his eyes and dumped one of the sheaths onto the table.

Four three-pointed, black shuriken tumbled out.

"Ladies first," he said.

"It's been a while," Joan said. "I'm not sure how well I'm going to do."

She threw each of the four stars. They all hit the target, but far from the center.

"My turn," he said, dumping the contents of another bag. Four shuriken shaped and painted like playing cards tumbled out. "Haven't thrown these things in years. Don't you laugh." When he picked them up, she noticed swollen knuckles. She looked up at his face, but he was concentrating on the target.

His first tosses went wide, only two sticking to the far edges of the target. He snapped his head to look at Joan.

Joan covered her mouth. "I'm not laughing, really."

"Damn woman," he muttered under his breath.

She cleared her throat as they headed toward the makeshift target. "So Bill wanted you to explain the lifestyle to me?"

"It's simple. Don't disagree with him or say anything personal to him while anyone else is around. Not just Brothers, but anyone else."

They gathered their shuriken and started back to the throwing line.

"Like when I told him I wasn't cleaning your house."

"Yep. Like that."

"But it wasn't fair to drop that on me without telling me before hand."

She tossed her stars. After he tossed his, they headed to the target to retrieve them. They continued to talk while throwing and retrieving the shuriken.

"If you don't like something he says, talk to him in private. Not in front of anyone."

"But he dropped it on me—"

"Never. In front of no one. Period." He leaned in and widened his eyes to emphasize the last word.

"That's going to be hard for me." She aimed at the target. "How should I handle him when we're alone?"

"Not my business. You're on your own for that."

He tossed two at a time. They disappeared. "He was wrong to put you on the spot like that, but the rule stands. Better learn to zip that lip. If the president's old lady gets away with talking out of turn, it'll cause trouble."

She followed him to the target. "I'm not his old lady."

Mooky had his back to her, bent over, hands braced on his knees, searching the weeds. "Talking out of turn makes him look weak," he continued. "You can't afford that. His power keeps you safe. Ah, there they are."

"Even after Kearney and I saved two Brothers that time in the desert?"

"You're lucky you didn't get a beat down for what you did to Bill."

"He was on the shoulder. And I called Little Al so you guys could go get him." She winced. Rationalizing was weak, and from the look on the old man's face, he agreed.

He frowned while he studied her. "He's thinking with the wrong head. The Brothers know that. But Prez brings you here, you're here. He says it's hands off, it's hands off."

"He has that kind of power?"

Mooky set down three of his shuriken. "He's the club president."

"Can I try one of those?" she asked.

"Be careful, they're sharp."

She picked up one of them and sliced her finger on the razor-sharp edge. "Damn it." She pressed the cut closed to stem the bleeding.

"Fuck the lifestyle lesson. You need to learn the meaning of sharp." He gathered up the shuriken, and they headed inside. "Better clean that up. I'm gonna catch hell from Bill for returning his old lady to him all fucked up."

"I'm not his old lady," Joan said, holding her finger under cold water.

"Sure you are," he said, digging around a cabinet for Band-Aids. He looked at her out of the corner of his eye. "You just don't know it yet."

"I can't be his old lady. I'm married. Didn't you see the ring?"

He stopped with a box of Band-Aids in his hand. "I saw it. Where's your old man?"

"In prison."

"What's he in for?"

"He copped a plea for weapons charges and terroristic threats."

She selected a Band-Aid and wrapped her finger.

He crossed his arms and tucked his chin. "I never knew Bill to take another man's woman—in prison or not. He's done things that'd make a rat's hair curl, but movin' in on a claimed woman is one thing he won't do."

"We're not a couple. So…" She hunted for another Band-Aid. Blood was already oozing through the first one.

He narrowed his eyes. "What's in this for you?"

"I get a place to live and protection."

"What kinda protection?"

"From the feds."

"Aiding and abetting. That boy better know what he's doing."

Mooky's cell phone rang. "Hey. When are you picking up your damn woman?"

He listened for a while. After he hung up, he said, "Bill's sending a prospect for you."

"He said he was picking me up for lunch," she said, picking up the wrappers and looking for a garbage can.

"Got tied up. He's a busy man. Get used to it."

"What's the protocol? Can I talk to the prospect?"

"Nothing personal. No flirting—if you flirt with any of the Brothers, they *will* act on it, and you won't have anything to say about it—'cept, for a whole lot of explaining to Bill. And I suspect Bill will beat the shit outta the guy." He hesitated. "Then you."

Joan snorted. "I'd like to see him try."

"Don't underestimate him."

The warning was as clear as a glacial lake. Joan shook off the icy trickle down her back. "I better do something before my ride gets here," she said to change the air between her and Mooky.

During the next five minutes, she broke down the Amazon boxes. It was a high-return task that gave the appearance she had worked for hours. When she packed the last flattened box into a box that held the others, she wiped her hands on her jeans.

A Harley Davidson engine rumbled in the distance.

"Don't know what the deal is between you and Bill." Mooky followed her when she dragged the box of flattened boxes onto the front porch. "He isn't like men you're used to. He's strapped with responsibilities, running two businesses and the club—not to mention riding herd on support MCs in the area. He has the president of the Arizona Chapter of the Hells Angels on speed dial. Catch my drift?"

"I'll be okay."

"Be sure of what you're doin'. That's all I'm sayin'."

"Why are you telling me this?" She had never heard a biker speak so frankly, especially about other club brothers.

"You're a tough nut. That can get you in trouble. But you're a good woman. Prob'ly too good for that crazy-ass nephew of mine."

The prospect pulled up in front of the house.

"I see they sent Youngblood," Mooky said.

"Is there anything I should know?"

"Don't know much about him. He was patched-over from The Strikers. You know what patching-over is?"

"When a club merges with a larger club?"

"Close enough. Your group brought the feds down on us. Hard. Almost destroyed the DBMC after you hightailed it out of here. The Strikers were growin' fast, and it was better to patch 'em over than fight 'em as rivals a few years down the road."

"That explains all the strange faces."

"You gonna tell Bill I clocked you with that book?" Mooky asked.

"What book? I banged my cheek on the edge of your kitchen table when I bent over to pick up a knife." She glanced at Youngblood then back at Mooky. "You gonna tell Bill I didn't really clean anything today?"

He put a disfigured knuckle under her chin and squinted at the bruise on her cheek. "How often do you think I need you to come and clean my house?"

She did a mental fist pump. "Twice a week?"

"Tuesdays and Fridays. Bring your throwing knives next time." He chin nodded toward the prospect at the end of his short drive. "Better catch your ride."

Joan climbed on the back of the bike, and other than a cursory "hello," Youngblood didn't say anything during the fast and scary ride. He didn't slow down until he pulled into a strip club parking lot. A bright LED sign above the door advertised Leather and Lace—A Gentleman's Club. Four pickups and a ten-year-old Chrysler lined the back of the lot. Three motorcycles were lined up in front of the club. A muscled, middle-aged biker with a flattened mohawk watched over them.

She thought of Bill's smile when he said he had a job for her. *I'm not stripping if that's the plan.*

CHAPTER 4

Joan dismounted and turned on Youngblood. "If this is some kind of prank, I don't think it's funny."

"No prank," he said. "Prez don't pull pranks."

She followed him toward the Brother who took one last drag on his cigarette before flicking the butt into the parking lot.

"Prez said to drop her off here," Youngblood said.

The other biker nodded and watched Youngblood get on his bike and drive away. He looked at Joan. "Settle in okay?"

He didn't deign to introducing himself, but from the FBI briefings, she knew he was Mark "Blaze" Whitman, the Vice President of the DBMC—Blackie's replacement. Dread prickled up her spine at Bill's warning that morning. She resisted the urge to bolt. Besides, where would she go and how would she get there? Stealing a biker's motorcycle again would be suicide.

"Yeah, everything's great."

Blaze motioned Joan toward the club entrance.

Loud music thumped though a solid, black door. When Blaze opened it, the music was so loud it thrummed through her chest. She followed him to the far end of an eight-by-ten-foot vestibule guarded by a pudgy biker with a shaved head and fat rolling over his collar. Joan knew better than to think he was a flabby weakling. She had seen men like him lift phenomenal weights in a gym.

While Blaze talked to the bouncer, she peered into a large, dimly-lit room where a skinny brunette, with a tattoo on her left butt cheek and bored look on her face, twirled half-heartedly around a pole. Joan counted seven men scattered around the club. Several looked like bikers, though none wore colors.

The music stopped, and the DJ filled the air with babble.

"This is Joan. She's gonna wait here for Prez," Blaze said by way of introduction. He turned to Joan. "This is Garbage."

Garbage nodded at Joan. More of an I-Got-The-Name than a greeting, and definitely not acceptance of her. In this world, she was a woman, nothing more than the chairs or the tables in the other room. That would change.

Blaze motioned for her to follow him through the bar. The DJ's voice rose in introduction, and the music started up again. The air was thick with the stench of old wood and musky men. The shadowy room was lit only by the backlight behind the bar, a few sconces on the walls, and a few spotlights over the runway, a far cry from the blinding sunshine outside. He led her down a hallway hidden behind a free-standing wall that held flyers advertising upcoming events motioned her through a door where a brass plate read *Club Manager*.

Camouflage netting covered one wall. The rest of the dé-cor, if you wanted to call it that, was military tan and shades of green. Clean and dust-free. Thankfully, there were no posters of nude women on the walls. Joan chose a leather chair in front of the desk, hoping it wasn't contaminated with body fluids.

With muffled bass pounding through the wall, Blaze walked around the desk to his chair. He had the chiseled cheekbones and jaw of a man who had kept his weight in check all his life. An elastic band held the flattened Mohawk in place. Silver streaks indicated age. His manner radiated prestige. The hair trailing down the back of his head said he had game.

His dead, hard eyes said he had seen more than any human should see in a lifetime. "So, Bill says you're looking for a job."

She wondered if her eyes had that same look. "Not dancing."

His face remained neutral as he took in the athletic look of her body. His dark eyes locked onto hers as if to test her fortitude.

She wanted to get away from the whumping music, the uncomfortable office, and this cigarette smoke-soaked lecher, but she sat still and waited. However bad it was, it was better than ten years of wearing an orange jumpsuit in a large, echoing common area and a room that locked at night.

His gaze passed over her swollen cheekbone and settled on her bandaged finger. "What happened?"

She looked down at her finger. A little blood had soaked through the second Band-Aid. "I cut it on a knife cleaning up Mooky's place." No sense whining over a couple minor injuries to a man who didn't care.

The corners of Blaze's mouth curled up. "Did he try to chase you out?"

"Yeah, but I told him to knock it off, or I'd shove the remote down his throat."

His eyes caught hers. "I bet you did."

"What does that mean?"

"You're a legend, Joan Bowman."

Her name was now Joan Archer, but it was a small point and, she guessed, of little significance to Blaze.

"You can't believe everything you hear," she said.

"Copy that."

The FBI briefing said Blaze was a former marine. That explained the decorating style. But how would a veteran wind up here?

"I'd love to see you dance," he said. "But Bill would shit daggers. We talked about something else for you."

"Like what? I tended bar in Albuquerque."

"Didn't tell me that." He rubbed the stubble on his jawline, as if that fact was something to consider. "We talked about your other skills."

"Other skills?"

He stood and walked around the desk. He didn't wear a

shirt under his cut, which exposed his perfect six-pack and a tribal tattoo that stretched from his neck, across his midsection, and down past his waistband. He looked bigger and more intimidating up close.

A motion with his hand indicated they were leaving. "I'll show you around."

She stood and walked around the opposite side of the chair from him to put an obstacle between them, if necessary.

He watched her with interest then reached for the doorknob. She smelled his smoky breath when he spoke. "We've had some trouble with boyfriend wannabes going into the dancers' dressing room."

When they reached the main room, he guided her around the runway and toward the back. He leaned in close to be heard over the music. She resisted covering her nose to avoid his repulsive breath. "We thought you could sit outside the dressing room and control who goes in. Can you do that without killing anyone?"

She turned and looked hard at him but saw no sign of the sarcasm or condescension she had seen in the eyes of the Brothers who had packed up her things and brought her to Phoenix. If he was baiting her, she refused to bite.

He opened a blacked-out door that blended into the back wall. It led to a short hallway lined with six doors, much like a motel.

"What are all these rooms for?" Joan asked.

"Private lap dances. When the girls use the rooms, you time them. Ten minutes. You stay right here, in case they need help. But most guys know they'll have to deal with one of the Brothers if they get outta line." He steered her in the opposite direction toward the back of the stage. "The dressing room is this way."

After showing her the dressing room, introducing her to the dancer waiting her turn on stage, and going over the rules of who gets in and who doesn't, Blaze showed her to a seat at the bar. He introduced her to the bartender, Kelly, who had a sweet, Meg Ryan smile, curly dyed-blonde hair, and big boobs.

Joan ordered a tequila and Diet Coke. Kelly handed Blaze a drink without being told what he wanted.

Before he took his first sip, he asked Joan, "Whattaya think?"

Joan stirred her tequila and Diet Coke and thought about this job that seemed too good to be true. "Sounds interesting and easy. When would I work? Days or nights?"

"You'd work four to nine—for the after-work crowd. By nine, the customers are getting drunk. I want a man back there then."

"You don't trust my skills? I can handle drunk men," she said before taking a sip.

Blaze smiled. A short scar at the outside corner of his left eye gave him an ominous, lopsided look when he smiled.

She resisted a shudder. It took a lot to scare her. *Must be the sense of being powerless.* "Is Bill okay with those hours?"

Blaze studied her for a few seconds before answering. "Those are the hours we thought would be best for you."

"For me?" she asked. "What about for the club? This isn't pity work, is it?"

"He warned me about your smartass mouth." Blaze finished his drink and put it on the far side of the bar to indicate a refill. "I don't spend any money here I don't have to. Opened six months ago and have bills out the ass. Everybody wants a cut. Brotherhood gets theirs off the top." He grabbed his fresh drink. "Let's talk pay."

Joan picked up her drink and followed him back to his office.

After sitting behind his desk, he took a couple sips and watched her as if she were a model and he were an artist deliberating how to portray her.

"So you're a veteran," Blaze said out of the blue.

"You know about that?"

"I'm a marine. First Gulf War."

"I was in Iraq," Joan said. "I didn't see much action."

He rocked his chair and studied her.

"What days would I work?" she said to break the silence.

"Monday through Thursday. That would give you week-ends free. I assume you visit your old man on Saturdays."

"You know about that, too?"

"Brothers don't have secrets. How do you get in without gettin' snagged?"

"I have a fake ID. It's worked so far."

She sipped her drink and wondered why Blaze and Bill were being so accommodating. These were take-no-shit men in a world they controlled with ruthless rigor. She slipped up earlier when she mentioned Bill's son before she should have known about him. Damn briefings. She had told the agents she didn't want to know anything beforehand. If Bill hadn't known she was undercover, he could now.

Brothers don't have secrets.

Blaze could be toying with her or doing his own investigative work. Trying to get her to reveal why she was there. Who she was reporting to.

Not knowing is worse than knowing. She clamped down on her imagination and looked up from her drink.

His gaze was fixed on her. "Is something wrong?"

"I was just wondering why you were being so nice to me." She made a mental note to pay special attention to body language and facial expressions around bikers.

He rocked in his chair and studied her. "You'll get twenty dollars an hour."

She choked on the drink. "That's a hundred dollars a night for sitting on a stool."

"Four hundred a week. Payday is every Friday."

"It'll be cash, right? I can't have a paper trail. I mean, I have the fake ID, but no social security number I can use."

"We'll get one for you."

"Isn't that illegal?"

"We're harboring a fugitive. Doesn't get more illegal than that." He ran a hand over the side of his shaved head. "Cash would be easier. I wouldn't have to hire someone to do the payroll and compute the taxes. But Prez says the business has to be legit. So it is."

Except for the fake social security number. "I can do some bookkeeping. I could probably figure out how to do payroll. It might save you some money."

He leaned his forearms on the desk. His eyes bored into her. "I'm not letting a fugitive into my books."

"You don't know me. I get that," she said, leaning forward a little. "Just keep it in mind for when you know me better and trust me."

"You want the security gig or not?"

"I can use the money."

"Start tomorrow at four. Report to Garbage when you come in. He's in charge of day security."

After a light knock, the door opened. The brunette who had been dancing when Joan arrived stuck her head in the door. "Sapphire says she's gonna be late. I'm not covering for her again."

"I'll let you get back to business," Joan said, starting to get up.

"No. Stay put," Blaze said, his eyes forcing her back into her chair. He looked at the dancer. "Cover for her, Maya."

"Why do I get stuck covering for her?" Maya whined. "This is the third time this week she's late."

"I'll take care of it."

"How come she gets away with this? Just because she's screwing—"

"I'll take care of it." Blaze's voice had a sharp don't-fuck-with-me tone. His eyes darkened, and his jaw muscles flexed.

Maya took the hint and retreated from the room.

"I thought this was a dream gig." Blaze exhaled loudly and ran his hand over his flattened mohawk. "But I've dealt with more drama in the last six months than any man should have to take. You wouldn't want a management job would you?"

Joan knew he wasn't serious. "I've learned if someone offers to give away something, turn it down."

He smiled his lopsided smile and nodded.

With nothing else to say, she stood to leave. "I guess I'll wait for Bill at the bar?"

Blaze looked up at her. His dark eyes traveled her body. "I still think you'd be a great dancer. Your body is toned, you're light on your feet. No drama."

"I can't show my body."

"Sure you can. It's easy."

"No. I mean, I have scars, lots of them. It's not pretty under these clothes."

He frowned. "Scars from what?"

"Torture." Might as well get it out. Splash cold water on any crude ideas he might have.

"From—"

"No. Not over there," she said, meaning not while overseas.

His frown expanded to furrows in his forehead. "Go see Kelly and have another drink. When Bill gets here, ask him to come see me."

She spent the time talking to Kelly, who was friendly and upbeat. Joan watched men order drinks, never looking up from Kelly's cleavage into her dark blue eyes. But she didn't seem to mind. She used her assets to rake in tips. Can't blame a woman for that.

A new customer wandered up to the bar, and Kelly approached him. Joan got lost in thought. Mentioning Bill's son earlier was a major slip up. She went over her conversation with Blaze. Any slip ups? Anything there that might get him wondering?

A woman with a baby on her hip poked Joan in the arm. "What the hell are you doing here?"

Three drinks on an empty stomach had fogged Joan's brain, and she didn't see the woman come in. At first, Joan didn't recognize her. Did Bill have a girlfriend the Bureau didn't warn her about? She scanned the woman's face. The empty piercing holes caught her attention. Recognition hit her like a blinding light.

"Flora! Holy shit you look great."

Gone were the piercings and the heavy Goth make-up. Her once-wild hair was tied back in a low ponytail—the blue streak was history. Motherhood looked good on Flora.

If the Demon Brotherhood had an aristocracy, Flora would have been a member of the royal family. Her grandfather founded the Demon Brotherhood, growing it from a small band of men to a powerful outlaw motorcycle club. When Flora's parents died in an accident, her grandmother—and thirty-some members of the DBMC—raised her.

"You don't call? Ruby's pissed," Flora said, referring to her grandmother.

"How do you even know I'm here? I just got in last night."

"Girl, everybody knows you're here," Flora said, hiking her baby higher on her hip. "You've been the talk of the DBMC since you left."

"I—what?"

"When you disappeared, Bill contacted every MC west of the Mississippi and had them lookin' for you. He was so hell-bent on finding you, the national president of the Hells Angels called him to find out what the fuck was going on."

"That's news to me." So Joan hadn't been the cunning negotiator she thought she'd been, after all. The Bureau had known she would get in like no one else could, like a seal slides into the sea. This set-up was more than the feds would do to get the goods on a simple illegal operation. What the hell *was* she doing here? And how would Flora know the president of the Hells Angels called Bill? Someone was talking. She had to find out who.

"Well, believe it." Flora scowled at Joan and poked her again. "And Duncan's in prison, and you're living with Bill? What's up with that?"

ဇ၁ဇ၁

Bill slapped Sapphire on her backside and watched her sweet ass disappear into the strip club to go to work. *She'll be history soon as Joan takes care of the complication with her husband.* He asked Garbage how things were going but didn't hear his reply because club business clouded his attention. He headed into the main room and picked up the pace when he saw Flora and Joan in a heated discussion. Flora had been contentious since giving birth. *This could be trouble. Better put a lid on it.*

But Joan's body language suppressed his urge to take control of the situation. She was on top of it. The president's old lady had to be able to handle the club's women. Diffuse drama. This relationship was gonna work. First, divert attention then clear up something Joan said.

"Hey, lookey here," he said, letting Flora's baby grab his finger. "Let me see my little future club president."

"Blaze said he'd like to see you," Joan said.

He nodded at her and took the baby from Flora. Children were the future of the club and deserved his attention. He raised the baby high and gently lowered him several times. The baby giggled. Good. A risk lover already. Bill took the small hand in his and lifted it. "Say 'Ass-up, men. Own the road.'"

The infant smiled and kicked his feet. Bill couldn't fight his smile at the baby's enjoyment. He rocked the baby to settle him, and when the small hand reached for his beard, he raised the hand to his lips and kissed the small fingers of this newest addition to the Demon Brotherhood family.

After a caress on the baby's head, Bill handed the infant back to Flora. "Gimme a minute with Joan."

"How was your day?" Joan asked, watching Flora head to the far end of the bar.

"Any day I make money is a good day." He eyed her swollen cheek. His eyes tracked down her body, stopping at her bandaged finger. "How was *your* day?"

"I think Mooky and I have come to an understanding."

"Yeah?"

"He won't call me damn woman, and I won't beat the shit out of him."

"Any woman who can handle Uncle Mooky is my kinda woman."

Joan's lack of whining or complaining drained away the day's tension. This relationship was gonna succeed.

But first…

He narrowed his eyes and put a hand behind her neck. "How the fuck did you know I had a son?"

When he first met Orlanda's mother, he had hidden his coarser side, and she never adjusted to the Demon Brotherhood lifestyle. It'd be different this time around. No misunderstandings about him. Or the MC lifestyle. Or about Joan's place in it.

Her neck and shoulder muscles tightened under his hand. He was right there. Within reach. His eyes, his throat, his groin, but she didn't act. Musta learned some control while on the run.

"I saw…" She hesitated as if weighing her words.

He hardened his gaze. Her hesitation was short enough for a struggle with anxiety. Long enough to prepare a lie.

"When you gave me your business card, I saw the photo of you with a young boy on a motorcycle. I just assumed—"

"You assumed?" He swore he felt her skin go cold. Would she run or stand up to him? He leaned back and studied her face. "Don't assume anything. You see something you don't understand, ask me about it. Got it?"

"Yeah. Got it."

This cautious, compliant woman wasn't the Joan he remembered. That woman had been strong, straight forward, feisty. That woman would have his back if things got dirty. He wasn't so sure about that with this new Joan. But he knew men on the run. Constant defensiveness took its toll. Wore a person down. *She'll adjust. She just needs time.*

"I don't want us to start off on the wrong foot," he said. "I'll give you time to get used to me."

"I'm married, Bill."

"I respect loyalty. Took me a long time to get over Orlanda's mother. For years, I drove past her house, even after she remarried. Told myself it was just to make sure she was okay. I couldn't let her go."

"But you did?" Joan asked.

"When I had a reason to move on."

"What happened to change your mind?"

"You walked into Colors."

"Me?"

"When the club honored you and Kearney…" Her beauty and confidence the night he first saw her plagued his memory. "The second I saw you, I had to have you. The heroic Iron

Angel." Bill half-smiled and shook his head. "Didn't know you were Duncan's old lady. Then you flirted with me. And from—"

"But—"

He continued, talking over her objections, "My gut said you were my woman." He clenched his jaw. He never told anyone, but he'd claimed her in that moment. "When Duncan kissed you, pulled you into his arms, I wanted to knock him off the stool. Beat the crap out of him. Get his hands off you." Bill leaned in and gave her a peck on her swollen cheek—a protective gesture to a self-reliant woman who didn't need his protection. She tensed under his touch. *I'll figure out what she needs and use that to reel her in.* "Time'll come when you don't tense up when I touch you," he whispered in her ear.

"Didn't she tell you I wanted to see you?" Blaze said from behind him.

Bill didn't respond right away. He lingered to inhale her scent, show her the status of his position in the club, how it allowed him to respond in his own time. The power to disregard the code of "club first," this once.

"Hey, Brother," Bill said when he leaned back. "She told me, but I wanted a word with her first."

"Come on back," Blaze said.

Bill frowned and stroked his moustache. Sounded like a problem.

"You gonna be okay here for another few minutes?" he asked Joan.

"Sure. Take as long as you like."

He slid his hand down her arm, not wanting to leave the unfinished conversation, then led the way to Blaze's office. He switched gears and got his head into the meeting.

ᘓᘔᘓ

Joan's tension refused to flow out of her. This subservient bullshit was worse than the fear of getting caught in the lie. She had to get the goods on the Demon Brotherhood and get out before she lost her soul.

Flora appeared as if out of nowhere. "So? What the hell's going on? I saw the way he looked at you."

"It's not what it looks like."

"I think it's exactly what it looks like. I'm not stupid, Joan."

"Being on the run is exhausting. Bill offered the MC's protection and a place to live for a while. I'm not responsible for him or his actions."

"Do you even hear yourself? You better straighten him out right away, or you'll lose what little control you have. He could've put you up anywhere. Hell, Ruby and I would have taken you in. But he put you in his house." Flora jabbed her finger into Joan's arm again. "That says something. And, girl, you better be listening. I thought you were smarter than that."

Joan rubbed her arm, but the words hurt more. She considered telling Flora what was really going on. She had saved Flora's life, but suspected it was not enough for her to be more loyal to Joan than to the club—

Bill's words, "my little future club president," interrupted her thoughts. *His* little club president?

"Is this Bill's baby?" Joan asked.

"What? No!" Flora's face flushed from anger. "He's like twice my age."

Joan cringed inwardly at her brusque question and Flora's heated answer. She was alienating possibly the only friend she had in this underworld. She clamped her mouth shut before she said anything else off base.

"This is J.J.," Flora said, with an edge to her voice. "Short for Jason Junior."

Joan's eyes darted up to Flora's. "This is Jason's baby? How—then you must have been..."

"Pregnant before you left," Flora said, finishing Joan's sentence.

Joan did the arithmetic. "So, he's about four months old?"

"Five in two weeks."

Joan looked at the black peach fuzz on J.J.'s head. "He's a cutie."

"Like his daddy."

"He doesn't have that little womb-broom on his chin, though."

Flora rolled her eyes. "Thank God for that."

Both women laughed. The mood had lifted, and it was like old times.

"I'm sorry, Flora. I didn't mean to insult you. You know, about you and...." Joan nodded toward Blaze's office.

"Forget it. Wanna hold him?"

Joan stepped back and put up her hands. "All I know about babies is when they cry, give them back to their parents."

"He'll be fine." Flora foisted J.J. on Joan.

After making eyes and cooing at the baby, Joan got him to smile. She bounced him on her hip, checking out the perfect little fingers, thinking how innocent he was in the midst of a violent club. Melancholy crept through her. Why would anyone bring a baby into this subculture? At what point would that innocence end?

"How's Ruby?" Joan asked before the undiluted alcohol in her system clamped onto the sadness and thrust her into a nosedive.

"Not so good. Her cough is worse. She won't go to a doctor. The club would cover it, but..."

Ruby's hard drinking pickled her temperament. Her addiction to cigarettes left her with smoked vocal chords and polluted lungs. She now lived the dreadful outcome of the biker lifestyle over the long term.

Flora thought for a few seconds and shrugged. "She's a tough biker chick."

"Yes, she is. She still tend bar at Colors II?"

"We're not there no more. The feds confiscated the building as part of their investigation. Said it was bought with 'illegally gained funds.'" She gestured air quotes for the last three words.

"But Duncan owns half."

"Didn't matter to them, the fucking bastards. It was meant to break the club. The guys moved the clubhouse into an abandoned factory near the original Colors. They nicknamed it Up Yours." J.J. started to fuss and Flora took him back before continuing. "Ruby still tends bar, but doesn't work the parties anymore. Did Bill tell you about the DBMC family day? The Sunday before Halloween?"

"Not yet."

"Well, if he gets a bug up his ass and doesn't invite you, you can come as my guest."

"I'm sure he'll ask. I just got in last night so..."

Flora nodded and tended to her baby.

Joan bit her lip and tried to quiet her buzzing nerves. She wanted to ask about Jason, but agonized over the wording. The FBI told her he was in a maximum security prison. Should she act like she knew or not? She'd already made one mistake that day, and couldn't afford another one. She muddied the waters with Flora earlier, possibly making her sensitive to careless words. There was no need for more emotion or suspicion.

Flora saved Joan by saying, "Jason could be home in two and a half years, with time off for good behavior. J.J.'ll still be young enough that he won't be aware of his daddy's absence."

"Jason's in prison?"

"Yeah. You didn't know?"

Joan shook her head. "I wasn't sure what happened after I lost communication with him in that warehouse a year ago."

"Bill assured me he'd be safe. There're a couple Angels on the block with him. They're protecting him, even though he's not a member of the Demon Brotherhood."

Joan's thoughts slowed to a low hum. Flora had unwittingly saved her from possibly saying the wrong thing. The Brotherhood wasn't required to protect non-members. That spoke to Bill's loyalty and a depth of caring.

"Jason's thinking about joining the MC when he gets out," Flora continued "Get the prospecting done while J.J. is still young."

"I always liked Jason," Joan said. "He was the first person I met when I started down this path three-plus years ago—when I joined the Constitution Defense Legion. He was there when I rescued Duncan."

"And when you got stuck in the desert that time with that spook. What was his name?"

"Kearney. Yeah, don't remind me." Joan shook her head and thought about that messed up night. "I could always count on Jason."

"I know. He liked and trusted you, too. Let me see your phone."

Joan pulled it from the outer pocket of her backpack. Flora punched in several numbers, deftly taking care of it with one hand. Joan had always been in awe of what mothers could accomplish with one hand while balancing a baby on their hip with the other.

Flora pointed the phone at Joan. "I put in mine and Ruby's cell phone numbers. Now you have no excuse for not calling."

J.J. started to cry.

"Hey, I gotta go feed my little man. You call Ruby, got it?"

Joan raised her phone and smiled. She plopped onto the nearest stool and asked Kelly for a Diet Coke. No more alcohol until she ate something.

Before she could make the call to Ruby, a short brunette walked up to the bar and ordered a ginger ale with a mild southern accent. She wore a gold satin robe over her dancing outfit, opened just enough to reveal glitter across her chest and into her cleavage. Even through the robe, Joan could tell she wasn't skinny like the other dancers. The old-fashioned word, buxom, came to mind.

Joan introduced herself and said, "What's your name?"

"I haven't seen you here before," the dancer said with a slight lisp. She checked out Joan's build and clothes. "You want a private dance? We have rooms in the back."

Joan swallowed her shock. "I don't swing that way."

"Oh. I didn't mean no offense."

"None taken. You're a woman makin' a buck. Nothing wrong with that."

"Are you a dancer?"

"No. I just got hired for security. I start tomorrow night. I didn't catch your name…"

"Sapphire."

CHAPTER 5

Two weeks later, Joan downshifted on the exit ramp to the Burnt Well Rest Area on the eastbound side of Route 10. The first meet with Inez had been in the Desert Sky Mall parking lot, which was too public for Joan's taste. Inez had suggested this place. Forty minutes from downtown Phoenix seemed like overkill, but it was a beautiful fall day, a perfect day for a ride and for thinking about the whatever-it-was between Bill and Sapphire...affair, booty call. Since the discovery, she had fretted over a plan to put an end to it. It was forcing her hand, creating a situation that would be difficult to navigate without violating her vows.

She couldn't blame Sapphire for making a play for the president of the DBMC. It would give her a status she would never have as a stripper. And, with Joan's claims that she was a platonic roommate, Bill was technically available.

Joan had to mark her territory. Soon.

She spotted Inez sitting at a picnic table in a round cement area girded by a block wall, probably adobe. A pergola provided shade from the late morning sun. A warm, dry breeze sent a candy wrapper skittering across the cement mall between the parking area and the restrooms. When Joan walked up, Inez was stuffing the last of a burrito into her mouth.

"Today's food truck special is burritos," Inez said, forking heap of Spanish rice into her mouth. "Want some?"

Joan shrugged off her leather jacket and checked their surroundings. "Nah. I'll get something later."

To the south, beyond the picnic areas and the building that housed the information center and restrooms, lay a flat, open expanse skirted by scrub brush that extended to low mountains in the distance. The westbound rest area on the far side of the four-lane highway looked empty. Past that, a rocky hillock rose out of the heat four miles away, maybe more—distance was difficult to estimate in the desert. Other than a truck driver checking the block and tackle on his flatbed, no one else was around.

Inez nodded and wiped her mouth with a napkin. "Anything new to report?"

Their cover was two women who had the same interest in riding motorcycles. Joan texted Inez every day as friends would do, but it was only to let Inez know she was okay. Intel was only passed face to face. So far, there wasn't much to report. Mooky was turning out to be a bust. He was no longer a member of the club, so was not privy to inside dealings. But that didn't exclude knowledge of deals going on outside the club. She still stopped by twice a week because the newly painted shed behind his neglected house piqued her interest. Meanwhile, he kept up her spirits and helped her navigate the lifestyle.

Joan said the same thing each time they met so far. "Nothing new. I'm still building rapport."

"Still no trouble breaking away?"

Joan shrugged. "I'm free to come and go as I please. He leaves the house at eight-thirty every morning. We talk a little before he leaves, nothing heavy. Then he's gone until late, sometimes after midnight. I went through every scrap of paper and his computer in his office, checked behind and under every drawer. Nothing."

"No tails?"

Joan rescanned the hills to the north and the rest area on the eastbound side of Route 10. "Not that I can tell."

"Where does he go, what's he doing so late at night?"

"I think he goes to his custom body shop and works there. It's over on West Durango. He took me once. He builds custom cars as well as bikes."

"Know what he does there so late at night?"

Joan shrugged. "Works?"

"Passivity won't get information. You have to get closer to Bill. Exhibit some interest. Get him to spend time with you. Can't talk to you if he's not home."

Joan tensed at Inez telling her how to do her job. Getting close without setting off alarms in Bill's head was tricky. And doing so with an absent man was nearly impossible. She thought about following him, but her position in Bill's life was still too precarious to survive getting caught. She regretted telling Inez about Bill's late hours. It only made her push harder.

"I can do this without having sex with him," Joan said, rubbing the prickles off her neck.

A young couple walked past, arm in arm, and separated at the entrances to the men's and women's rooms. Nothing out of the ordinary. She chalked it up to nerves, but she'd have to get a handle on her suspicions. She didn't want another paranoia meltdown like she had when she was in the Legion.

"I know you don't want to hear this, but you'll never be his confidante, not 'til you become his lover. That's not the official stand of the Bureau, of course. Adultery is not part of our playbook, but that's the way it is." She dug into the front pocket of her jeans and pulled out a crumpled, square slip of paper and held it out to Joan.

"What's this?" Joan looked at a doctor's pharmacy script. "A prescription for a birth control patch? Am I reading this right?"

"It's just to keep you safe."

She handed it back to Inez. "I don't need it."

Inez made no move to take it.

"What am I supposed to do with this?" Joan flapped the script at Inez.

"Fill it. Wear it."

Joan stuffed the paper into her back pocket. No way was she going to fill it. She was not going to have sex with Bill just to get information. She could get him to open up to her without that.

"There's something you should be aware of," Inez said. "There's a rumor going around that there's an undercover agent in the Brotherhood."

The expansive desert closed in on Joan crushing her breath in her chest. "They found out about me?"

"No. Not you. Another agent."

"Then why am I here, if there's already a UC in the club?"

"We think the UC slipped the tether."

"Why are you telling me this?" Joan suppressed a shudder. She would not hunt him down, if that's what the Bureau was thinking. The last time she had gone after a rogue agent, she got her hands broken and the Constitution Defense Legion tattoo carved off her chest.

"Just stay alert," Inez said, eyeing Joan rubbing the backs of her hands. "Let me know if you suspect anybody."

"What agency does he work for?" Joan asked.

"Don't know. Possibly the ATF."

"The ATF won't tell you who he is?" This stunk. The ATF wouldn't share information with the FBI? While the two agencies had a pissing match, she was in the middle of the stream. This would not work out well for her. It never did.

"They won't admit they have an undercover in the MC. It's just a rumor."

"That's just great." Now Joan had to worry about some dumbass UC obtaining the evidence she needed to get her and Duncan's sentences commuted. That meant she had to turn up the heat on her relationship with Bill before this mystery agent stumbled into her investigation.

"Don't act on any suspicions," Inez said. "Bring any intel to me. No matter who. Anything else?"

"I'll try to have more next time."

"Be proactive," Inez said. "And fill the script."

"Easy for you to say."

"You have it easy, compared to other women we've inserted into an op. They had to start from square one. Bill's already leaning. Push him over. Knock his socks off."

"Yeah. Okay." Joan watched as the man came out of the men's room, looked around and, evidently not seeing his girlfriend, walked to a shaded area to enjoy the view.

"Next Thursday we'll meet at Skyline National Park," Inez said. "Great view of the city from there."

Joan didn't say anything, watching the man waiting for his girlfriend.

"Obscure enough for you?" Inez asked.

"You still riding along with me to visit Duncan Saturday morning?" Joan asked, ignoring Inez's sarcasm.

"Usual time? Chevron station at the junction to Route Sixty?"

"Yeah. See you then."

While Inez disappeared into the horizon, Joan wondered about the UC in the Brotherhood. And about Inez. She wasn't as supportive or helpful as Joan thought a handler should be. When she had gone undercover for the Legion, Duncan had been on top of everything. Keeping her calm. On point. Safe. And just as she was trying to find a way to push Sapphire out of Bill's life, Inez showed up with a prescription for birth control. So much for the original plan of taking her time to build up trust. Yet, if she gave in too soon, and things slid into the weeds—as things around her always did—Bill would begin to doubt her. Doubt was poison.

Damn Iron Angel Bad Karma.

It seemed Bill was attracted to intelligent women, the complete opposite of biker chicks hanging around the club. She could use that knowledge to drive a wedge between him and Sapphire, who wasn't intelligent by any stretch of the imagination. That little liaison had run its course. The president of the DBMC would fall for her, not Sapphire. He just didn't know it yet.

She liked being around a strong male figure—coarse and wild though Bill was. Mooky had warned her about Bill. But she had been warned off Duncan, and he turned out to be the best thing that ever happened to her. Maybe Inez was right. It was time to set the groundwork to make her move. But she needed something first. After one last scan of the parking lot, she reached for her phone.

It was not in the outer pocket of her backpack where she

always put it. She rummaged through the inside of the bag. No phone. Her insides condensed into a hard ball.

She dumped the bag on the picnic table.

No. No, no, no. Her arms and back prickled. She didn't carry much, but it became terrifyingly clear that her phone was gone. All she had been through over the past three years: Firefights. Brawls. Accidents. She never lost her phone. But she lost this one, the one with the FBI GPS tracker app.

She looked up at the sound of a Harley downshifting as it slowed in the rest area parking lot. Joan recognized the muffled double backfire of Little Al's bike. *I'm in the middle of nowhere. I lose my phone. And now, Little Al shows up. Can't anything be easy?* She told the hairs on the back her neck to stand down. This biker was a friend.

The tension must have shown on her face because Little Al skipped pleasantries. "Something wrong?"

"I can't find my phone."

"When'd you have it last?"

"This morning. I'm sure I took it off the charger and put it…" That morning a police chase ended one block over, sirens were blaring, cops searching everywhere. Evidently, the driver had jumped out of the car. The whole scene kicked her into a bout of hyper-defensiveness, which may have caused her to overlook her phone.

"Why are you way out here?" she asked him to change the subject.

"Had business in Quartzite," he said, mentioning a town further west. "What brings you this far out of town?"

"I drove out to the taco stand we met at that time, but—"

"It's not there anymore."

"No shit. My butt is still vibrating from having to backtrack without a break. I stopped to rest and discovered the taco truck is here on Thursdays."

"Eaten yet?" he asked.

"No. I just got here."

"Let me drain the beast, then I'll buy you lunch. We haven't had a chance to talk since you got to town."

"Sounds great," Joan said. "You always had a way of calming me down."

∽∾∾

A few hours later, Joan breezed into Leather and Lace.

"Anything wrong?" Garbage asked. Bikers were a perceptive group.

"Lost my phone."

"Bummer."

"Might be at home," she said as she passed him.

She headed across the main room toward the cleverly-disguised door that led to the back hallway. After setting her backpack down next to the stool, she took up her post outside the dancers' dressing room.

Loud music pommeled the walls. The evening dancers arrived, arrogant and bitter as usual. None of the women had a good word, suggesting they thought Joan was judging them.

Little did they know that whatever they had done, she had outdone them twenty times worse.

After Maya headed toward the back of the stage, two good ol' boys walked through the door. One was tall, tan with a light-colored, straw cowboy hat. The other was shorter and wore a faded tee shirt and a backward ball cap.

"Hey, sweetheart, I'm Chrystal's boyfriend," Straw Hat slurred with a Texan accent, taking a sidestep to maintain his balance.

Joan stood and blocked his path. "No, you're not. I know Chrystal's boyfriend. Go back out to the bar and watch the show."

Straw Hat sidestepped again, and Joan moved to block him. Ball Cap slipped by. Joan grabbed his arm.

"That's quite a grip for a girl," Ball Cap said.

"I also have quite a left hook for a girl," Joan said. She pushed him back and activated the mic in her ear bud. "Garbage, I have two assholes back here."

Straw Hat slipped past her and got to the dressing room door before she could stop him. Maya saw the commotion, took off a shoe, and hit Straw Hat in the head with the spiked heel.

He grabbed his head. Joan kicked the back of his knee, reached over his head, planted her fingertips in his eye sockets, then dropped to one knee. The back of his head slammed onto the floor.

Ball Cap closed in behind her. As she stood, she swung her arm backward, striking with a knife hand at his throat. It was a miss, hitting him in the sternum, but he fell to one knee. Straw Hat grabbed her leg, and Maya beat the heel of her shoe on his back. Joan kicked his arm. Garbage burst through the door, grabbed Ball Cap by the belt, and tossed him head first into the wall. He crumpled to the floor.

Meanwhile, Straw Hat staggered to his feet. Joan helped him up then pushed him toward Garbage, who manhandled both men through the door. When the door shut behind Garbage, Maya and Joan slapped a high-five.

Garbage leaned his pudgy head back into the hallway. "You girls okay?"

"Yeah, fine. Lucky for me, the little guy is a wimp. He went down with only a half-ass shot."

"You did good. Handling two men."

"They were sloppy drunk." Joan caught Maya's eye. "And Maya had my back. She's deadly with those shoes."

He gave her a nod of approval and disappeared into the bar area.

Joan paced the hallway, shaking out her hands, trying to burn off the adrenaline. She'd been at Leather and Lace for three weeks, and nobody had tried to get backstage. Cops running through the neighborhood, phone missing, Little Al appearing out of nowhere, now these jerks. Seven days in a week, and everything had to happen on one day. Life had its quirks.

Forty minutes later, the door to the main room opened, and the music carried through on the pale, pulsing light, creating an arc on the wall and floor. Bill walked toward her with a drink in each hand.

"I hear you pounded two men."

"Couldn't have done it without Maya. Garbage did the heavy lifting."

"You okay?"

"I'm fine." She nodded toward the drinks in his hands. "Thirsty much?"

"Here," he said, offering one of the sweating glasses. "This one's for you."

"I can't drink. I'm working."

"Go ahead. You earned it."

"I don't drink on the job."

A half-smile poked up one corner of his moustache. "Since when do you follow the rules?"

"If I learned nothing else on the run, I learned the lanes are my friends," she said. "Staying in my lane keeps me under the radar."

Sapphire walked out of the dressing room, saw Bill, and sashayed toward him.

Bill frowned. "Go dance, Sapphire."

With a sniff and a long stare at Joan, Sapphire walked off toward the back of the stage.

Joan laughed off the hard stare. She kept her knowledge of their booty calls on a close hold. Instead of making accusations, she'd move past the situation. Flank Bill. He wouldn't see her coming.

"I think she likes you," Joan teased.

"I think I like you." He tucked her hair behind one ear. "Been meaning to tell you, I like the new color. That black hair did nothing for you." He finished his drink in one long pull and started on the one Joan turned down. He leaned on the wall next to her, claiming her space.

"I want you to be you," he said.

"Well, I want you to be happy."

"Really?" he asked, moving closer. "How happy?"

When Joan didn't answer, he said, "I tried calling you today, but you didn't answer."

"I must have left my phone at home." She and Little Al had gotten lost in conversation, and by the time she realized what time it was, she didn't have time to fight traffic to get to the house to look for her phone.

"You sure?" Bill asked, thumbing his phone.

"It's always in the outer pocket of my backpack, and it—"

Her phone rang. She looked up at Bill, mouth open, numb. She wiped her lips with the back of her hand. The muffled ringtone continued. *How the hell...*

"Wanna tell me why you weren't answering your phone?"

Her freedom disappeared like a wisp of smoke. She'd have a tail now. No doubt about that, unless she could come up with a plausible explanation. This was going to be hard to cover, especially since she didn't even know what the hell was going on. The phone had not been in her backpack. Yet, here it was. Her instincts fired to life—this smelled like a set-up, but by whom? And more importantly, how? *Say something. You look guilty.*

"It wasn't in my backpack. Ask Little Al. He saw all my...I saw him at the—"

"He told me he crossed paths with you this afternoon, but didn't say anything about you losing your phone. Is there something you need to tell me?"

"No. I don't know how I could have missed it."

"What's going on, Joan? You seeing someone?"

Joan's mouth dried. She pried her tongue off the roof of her mouth. This was not happening. "Call Little Al. Ask him."

"If you're seeing someone after all I've done..." He thumbed a call into his phone and held it close to his ear.

"He saw everything dumped out on the picnic table when I was looking for it," she said while the phone rang in Bill's ear.

"Hey, Al. When you saw Joan this morning, did she have her phone?" He listened. "Yep. Later."

Bill frowned and put the phone in the inside pocket of his cut. "Give me your phone."

Joan reached into her backpack and pulled it out. She watched Bill thumb through her contacts and messages. The FBI said the tracker app was almost impossible to find, whatever "almost" meant. The temptation to escape out the back door was overpowering, but she sat on the stool, wondering how to play this. *They say the best defense is a good offense, but controlling the conversation with a domineering man will be impossible.* Acting like he scared her would work, and it would be easy, too. *No acting there.* Or she could throw the submissive crap to the wind and be Iron Angel. She rubbed her palms on her thighs. *Act like he's getting to me or be myself? Cowards never start.*

"Who's Inez?" he asked.

"I told you about her. She drives a Sportster. She goes with me to Safford when I visit Duncan. Remember?" Joan wracked her brain going over every text she could remember between her and Inez. They were innocuous: *What are you doing today? Exercising and going to work...Want to meet for lunch?...Going with me to Safford tomorrow?*

"You have lunch with her?"

He's checking your honesty. All good lies have a kernel of truth. "Yeah. Sometimes we go for a ride."

"Where to?"

"Different places. Canyon Lake. Sometimes west of town." Joan shrugged. "She likes hiking, so once I skipped exercise and we went to the Peoria Preserve and hiked the trail."

"Why does she go to Safford with you?"

Joan shrugged. "For moral support. But mostly for the ride."

"You never asked me to go with you." He scowled at her. "What do you do on Saturday nights out there?"

"We go to a local bar. Eat nachos. Drink beer. We don't pick up men, if that's what you're getting at."

Bill's face softened into a grin. "I know."

"What's that mean?" She snatched her phone out of his hands. "Did you send someone to check up on me?"

"Mighta sent a couple guys from a support club out in the area."

Joan crossed her arms. "I think I remember them. Side-winders. Am I right?"

Bill smiled again. "That was one time."

Stand up to him. Mooky said he likes a challenge. "And just what did they tell you?"

"Said you told 'em to pound salt."

"Damn straight. What kind of woman do you think I am, going around picking up men?"

"I think you're an honest woman." He put his hand on the back of her neck. "But in case you were thinking about it. Don't do it. I'll find out. It won't end well for the guy stupid enough to make a play for you."

"You don't own me." She got up off the stool and pointed a finger at him for emphasis. "Even if I were inclined to cheat on Duncan, you can't say who I can, or cannot see."

"Don't test me, darlin'."

She kept her face hard, but relaxed inside. "Yeah? Well, don't test *me*." Maybe she pulled it off. She got his mind off the mysterious missing phone and Inez.

"There's she is," he said, his eyes coming to life.

"Who?"

"The woman I remember."

"Don't patronize me, Bill Torrence." She stuffed her phone in her backpack.

He stroked his beard. "Wanna check out the new clubhouse when you get off work?"

What? Not working till midnight? "Are women allowed there?"

"If you're with me." He traced the length of Joan's arm with the back of his hand.

The light touch turned the squirming in Joan's stomach to a heaviness eight inches below. She hadn't been with a man in a long time. Too long. And the drama over the past few hours only heightened the need. His checking up on her, though infuriating, was a little endearing, almost romantic, and smacked of jealousy. Her breathing softened. She smiled at Bill. *I can do this.*

He pulled his hand away to check his watch, leaving a coolness in the vacuum. "I have some business to take care of."

"What kind of business?"

Bill's face hardened into stone. He put a hand on the wall next to Joan's head and leaned in to her, his icy eyes freezing hers. "It's not for you to know club business. Don't mistake my niceness as weakness."

"Whoa, there, big guy." She pressed her fingertips against his chest, but he didn't budge. "I'm just making conversation. If it's club business, all you have to do is say so."

Like water draining from a watercooler, the harshness fell from his face. When he spoke, his voice was gentle again, but his eyes remained cool. "Just mind your own business and take care of my house. That's all you have to do." He raised his eyebrows as if to say, "Okay?"

"Till later then," she said, hoping to break the bad mood he had slipped into so quickly. "Meet at the house at nine-fifteen? I'll drop off my bike, and we can ride over together?"

He turned and walked into the pale light and loud music without looking back.

After work, Joan waited for Bill at the house. When his Harley's headlights flowed across the living room wall and ceiling, she dumped her drink in the sink. He came up behind her. She turned to face him in time for him to back her to the door between the kitchen and his office, leaning his hands on both side of her head, trapping her with his body. The familiar smell of his leather cut draped around them.

He had put his hands on her before, nothing lewd, just indications of his growing interest. He was different this time. More intense. Stealing her personal space.

"I thought I'd find you packing your shit," he said, his face inches from hers.

"Why?" She gave him a gentle push to get a little space between them. He was so close she could smell the whiskey on his breath.

He stood his ground and traced the line of her jaw. His intense scrutiny was unsettling.

"Because you checked up on me?" she asked.

"You didn't take kindly to being checked up on, or your integrity being doubted."

"I understand. You have responsibilities. And I can be a handful at times."

"Don't be like this, Joan."

She knitted her brow. "Like what?"

"Weak. I got a glimpse of that strong woman in the hallway today." He placed his forehead on hers. "Call me out when I'm out of line."

"But I thought—" She wasn't quite sure what he was saying. If she could get some space between them, she'd have room to think. Space to breath. His closeness sparked an unwanted physical response. She had to keep that in check. And keep her head clear.

"Not in front of others," he continued. "When we're alone. I need you to—" He leaned back and cupped her face with one hand and looked into her eyes. "I need you."

Oh, shit. The unfilled script in her back pocket stung her. She put her hands on his hips. He pressed in closer.

"Joan," he breathed her name as he moved his hand from the side of her face to the back of her neck. He pressed the side of his head against hers. "Cut ties with you husband." His beard grazed her cheek as he whispered the words.

"It doesn't feel right. He's all alone, locked up. I'm free. I can't."

Bill shook his head against hers. "I want to tear your clothes off, take you to my bed, take you for a slow ride."

"On the bike?" She knew what he meant, but wanted to derail this conversation before it picked up momentum.

"No." He chuckled and grabbed her crotch. "Take this for a slow ride."

She jumped and sucked in a breath. *So much for slowing things down*. No one had ever grabbed her sexually and got away with it. She stifled the urge to pound a half-fist to his throat or knee him.

"Never been grabbed there, have you?" he said, sliding his hand up her abdomen to her hip.

"No one has ever been that bold."

"I am bold. And crude. And ruthless—when I have to be. I am not a nice guy, Joan. I don't make excuses for who I am. But I take care of and protect what's mine." He slid his hand up her ribs. "And if you haven't figured it out yet, I want to own you. Every part of you. I want to see your scars. Own them, too."

"I—" His thumb grazed her breast, sending hot blood coursing through her body, sucking the air from her lungs. He had never been this close before. This strong. This forward. She swallowed her desire. "I can't."

"I don't need divorce papers," he continued. "If you told him or sent him a note telling him to cut you loose, it would be enough for me. I could claim you."

She pushed harder, but he didn't move. It would be easy to give in. He was a strong, healthy alpha male. She was a strong, healthy alpha female. It'd be purely physical. Convenient. Nature taking its course. Was this how it had been when Duncan met Lucinda-Mae?

Joan's breath caught in her throat. *I can't do this.* She shoved Bill.

He allowed some space between them, lowered his hand to her waist. "This is where you tell me I'm out of line."

"Give me some space," she whispered.

His moustache pricked up in a smile. His eyes locked on hers as he nodded and pushed off her.

His sudden absence left her hot inside, but her cool skin heightened her awareness of him—that he seemed to have come to some conclusion. While he filled a glass with water, she swallowed her unwelcome emotions and said, "I'm beginning to see your point about not waiting for Duncan. But it just doesn't feel right, yet."

Bill leaned against the sink, glass in hand. The intensity of his gaze suggested he might pounce on her at any moment, tossing to the wind the one moral code he had.

"You can understand that, right?" she asked.

"I do." He chugged the water. "Still want to go to the club?"

"Not really."

"Me either." He placed the glass on the counter. "Come here."

She hesitated.

He opened his arms and gestured for her to come to him. "I'm being a Boy Scout, darlin'. If you were any other woman…"

His strong arms and unspoken words wrapped around her.

CHAPTER 6

That Saturday after her visitation with Duncan, Joan raced back to Phoenix in a huff. If she pushed her bike hard enough, she could outrun the dead feeling. But it followed her like a massive tail swooping along the curving mountain road, threatening to overtake her. Inez had kept up through the small towns, telling Joan at every light to pull over to the side of the road and get herself together before tackling the mountains. But now, with no more towns between her and Phoenix, Joan opened the throttle. Her larger engine left Inez behind. The eighty-five mile-per-hour wind blew the tears out of her eyes and the word "divorce" out of her ears.

Duncan's words had hit her like loose gravel on a curve, stealing her traction, threatening to shoot her off a cliff. Joan didn't remember leaving the prison's visitor parking lot because Duncan's voice asking for a divorce filled her head, drowning out the sound of her 1300-cc engine. Nothing was ever easy—if it were easy, it wouldn't be happening to her.

Divorce had been looming in the periphery, closing in on her, but hearing the word sucked the life out of her. She should have psyched herself up for this moment, and if the timing had been her choice, she could have prepared for the gut shot.

And fucking Inez knew.

Joan should have suspected something when Inez actually accompanied her to the prison. Inez always registered at the motel and waited there while Joan visited Duncan. And when Joan had charged across the visitor waiting area, Inez didn't look surprised. She didn't even ask what was wrong. She was supposed to be supportive, not the instigator of trouble—not the wet leaves on the road, causing Joan to fishtail. All the way across the parking lot, Inez had kept saying it was a good thing.

In whose world?

Joan sped past a sign that read: *Phoenix 20 miles*. Chancing a traffic stop, imagining Inez pushing her bike to catch up, Joan full-throttled it to Phoenix. Only then, alone and on familiar territory, would she work through her emotions. But where to go? Bill's house? A motel for privacy? How much privacy would she have with Inez hot on her tail? Fucking Inez. Where would she hesitate to go?

City traffic slowed Joan's flight. She got antsy at stoplights, looking over her shoulder for Inez, who was now only one traffic light behind—*the bitch can drive a bike, I'll grant her that*. Joan was first at the light and sped off the line, skipping a gear, abusing her bike to get away from Inez. Where to go? Her destination crystalized in her mind. She sped up, splitting lanes, weaving around slow drivers, blowing through yellow lights. The entrance to the Harley Davidson dealership came up on her fast—too fast. Only one way to make this turn. She applied the front brake. Turned the handlebars. And prayed.

Shit. This is not going to be pretty.

∽∾∽

The service shop was slow, and Bill leaned on the wall just inside Orlanda's office. They caught up with each other while she finished up the day's bookkeeping. He heard voices in the showroom and leaned out to watch a young woman check out Dagger while he talked to her boyfriend about the bike in front of them. Women had two reactions to hardcore bikers: fearful or flirtatious. Although this chick might have a certain amount of fear, she was interested in Dagger. Bill wondered what she was doing with the clean-cut businessman type.

Honking horns, screeching tires, and a screaming motorcycle engine made him lift his gaze past the mismatched couple in the showroom. A motorcyclist slid sideways fifteen feet to stop less than a foot from a line of parked All-Terrain Vehicles.

"Hey, Bill," Dagger said, looking over his shoulder with a shit-eating grin. "Your girlfriend's here."

"Jesus H. Christ," Bill said weaving around the counter. "What the hell's gotten into her?"

Before he reached the front doors, a woman on a Sportster barreled up behind Joan. He slowed to see what would happen next. Joan looked over shoulder and hurtled toward the woman, yelling and pointing at her. The woman was off her bike in an instant. Joan grabbed the woman's jacket, yelling something. The woman stood firm, yelling back. Joan shoved her to the ground.

Bill crossed his arms and smiled. His woman was the scarier of the two. This could be good. Orlanda appeared at his side.

Not one to interfere in another person's fight, he planted his feet and watched through the plate glass window. A small part of him liked watching women fight. And his woman was the better of the two, pushing back. Not backing down. Pissed as hell about something. He glanced over at Dagger.

"You gonna do anything?" Dagger asked.

Bill shook his head and checked his daughter out of the corner of his eye.

"Not unless you want to get your asses kicked," she said.

She was right. Many a Brother got his ass wiped stepping into a catfight too early. "I'll step in if it looks like someone's gonna get hurt," Bill said.

ᏆᎧᏆᎧ

Joan stomped toward Inez, pointing her finger at her. "You knew about this, didn't you?"

"No." Inez stood her ground. "Stop a sec and think. This is a good thing."

"For who?" Joan glared at Inez, grabbing the collar of her leather jacket. "You and your precious operation? What about me?"

"Be careful what you say," Inez said in a lowered voice. "Don't forget where you are and what you're doing. It's not about you anymore. It's all about the operation. And don't forget Duncan."

"*What*?" Joan released Inez's jacket and shoved her hard, sending her onto her ass. Joan looked down at Inez, fists clenched. "You convince him to divorce me then throw his name in my face?"

"I knew you couldn't hold it together for this op," Inez said in a lowered voice as she got back up onto her feet.

Joan ran her fingers through her hair and glanced toward the building.

A row of faces lined the showroom window. Mechanics stood at the corner of the dealership.

"Get out of here before I do something I'll regret," she growled.

Inez brushed off the seat of her pants and swung a leg over her bike. "You aren't cut out for this. I have to report this incident to my supervisor." She revved her bike's engine. "Divorce may be the least of your problems. Hope your husband likes his maximum security prison." She eased her bike toward the lot entrance.

"Oh, no you don't." Joan raced after Inez, grabbed her collar, and yanked her off her bike. The bike slid along its side into the street.

Inez's helmet hit the ground with a loud crack.

Cars skidded to a halt. Drivers yelled out their windows. Horns honked.

Joan leaned over Inez and said, "This isn't over until me and Duncan are free."

Inez moaned and pushed herself to a sitting position. She pressed her hands against her helmet.

"You think you're moaning now—"

Strong arms slammed around Joan, pinning her arms to her side. Bill spun her away from Inez.

Joan continued her threat. "This isn't over, you fucking bitch."

Dagger reached down and pulled Inez to a standing position. Another biker rushed past to get the bike out of the street. The sight of Demon Brotherhood Motorcycle Club colors cooled the epithets of the drivers, and they pulled away without incident.

"Bring her inside until she's able to ride," Bill said to Dagger. "Get someone to check out her bike."

"That bitch doesn't come inside," Joan said, struggling to loosen Bill's grip. "She belongs in the street with her bike."

"Go to my office," Bill said, releasing Joan.

"You can't order me around," she said, getting into his face. "I'm not your friggin' dog."

Inez's mouth gaped at Joan's insolence. Dagger looked up, his gaze sliding past Joan to Bill.

"You said what to me?" Bill grabbed Joan's arm and yanked her toward the building.

She knew she had overstepped the bounds. He couldn't allow her to backtalk in public. Even in her rage, she understood that much. But her growing hate for Inez, fueled by her unresolved hate for federal agents in general, spun her out of control.

And then there was the divorce.

Bill muscled Joan around the counter. "My office. Now."

"Take it easy," Orlanda said.

Bill guided Joan past Orlanda.

"Dad," Orlanda called out.

He stopped to look at her.

"Think before you say or do anything, is all I'm saying."

Joan knocked Bill's hands away. When she got to his office, she tried to slam the door, but he was right behind her.

He stepped into the office and kicked the door shut behind him. "What the fuck's gotten into you?"

The dead feeling caught up to her. She blinked back her tears. Not only did she lose Duncan, but Bill treated Inez like some VIP.

"Wanna tell me who that bitch is?" he asked.

"Inez. I told you about her. We go for rides sometimes. She rides with me to Safford every Saturday."

Bill crossed his arms. "Anger or not, I couldn't let—"

"I know." Joan wiped her lower lids. "I got angry. I forgot. It won't happen again."

"What did I tell you about that mealy-mouth shit?"

Joan hovered in the middle of the small office not sure what to do with herself. She walked up to Bill and put her hands on her hips. It was time to speak up.

"Okay. You don't want mealy-mouth shit? Here it is. That bitch pissed me off, and you guys are hovering around helping her like she's somebody important. When two brothers were kidnapped and about to be executed, I saved them. I didn't know them, but I stepped up. Remember that? A year or so ago? Anything I'm saying ring a bell?"

"Yes. I remember. It gives you some leeway in your behavior. But what's that gotta do with today?"

"I had their backs. I didn't know them, but I had their backs." She stabbed Bill's chest with her finger. "You know me, but you don't have mine. That's the problem here."

"We couldn't put her on her bike and let her drive out of here dazed and fucked up. She could sue. It wasn't anything personal."

"It was just business," Joan said, sarcasm spiking her tone. "Like when Kearney interrogated me."

Her promise to let what happened three years ago stay in the past stopped her. She turned her back to Bill to gather her thoughts. The past, the present—they kept bumping into each other, overlapping, squeezing out her enjoyment of life. She wiped her cheeks with her hands. Her makeup must be a mess, unlike how she had primped to look her best for Duncan before he opened up an abyss and threw her into it. She looked at Bill. Again, in Duncan's absence, the most undesirable man in her world was all she had—Kearney a year ago, Bill today. *This is one hell of a pattern.*

"Tell me what happened to make you so crazy." He leaned forward to get a peek at her face.

"It's simple." Forming the words made her eyes prick. "Duncan asked me for a divorce."

"Duncan asked for a divorce?"

She nodded.

"What does that have to do with Inez?" he asked.

Everything. Joan sniffled and swallowed the mucous in her throat to give her time to think of an answer. "Nothing. I just lashed out at the nearest person. I was coming unglued. She should have given me time to work through it, but she followed me all the way from Safford. It just made me crazier."

"I've been divorced twice. Both times I was blindsided. Didn't see it coming."

"Then you know how it feels."

"It's like riding down the highway. Sun at your back. Wind in your face. Engine humming. Beautiful day. Something goes wrong so fast, you don't even know what happened, and you're scraping along the pavement, rolling and bumping along. And you want it to stop, but you don't want to hit anything solid, because that's a game changer."

"You mean like the time I—"

"Work with me, Joan. I'm metaphor-challenged."

"You know what a metaphor is?" The surprise softened her sobs.

"Not really." Bill wiped Joan's cheeks. "But I do know this: Duncan pulling the trigger first saves you from doing it."

Joan pushed away from him. "You think this is a good thing, too? For who? You?"

"He's locked up. You're not. He's telling you to move on." Bill grasped a hand before she got too far away from him.

Joan wrenched her hand away and opened the door. "Why don't you—" A mechanic was cleaning up, putting away tools, pretending he wasn't listening. She closed the door to keep her personal conversation private. "Why don't you go suck up to Inez? You two could talk about what a great and wonderful thing this is for me."

She strode away. A part of her wanted him to come after her. Plead with her to not part on such nasty words. But, when he didn't, she got on her bike and headed home.

 හ⁣ශ⁣ශ

Bill pulled into the garage a half hour later not sure what he was walking into. Joan had said something about needing time to think about what happened, and when she didn't get it, she took it out on the person closest to her. Not wanting that to happen to him, he had waited before heading home. He grabbed a twelve-pack out of the refrigerator in the garage and headed into the house, hoping he wouldn't say the wrong thing and set her off again.

She was on the couch in the living room, sitting with bent knees, heels tucked against her butt, arms wrapped around her shins. He had never seen her look so small. So vulnerable. He was glad he didn't rumble off to the clubhouse and write her off for the evening. She closed her eyes and lay her head on her knees.

"I bet everybody already knows all about me and Duncan." She winced. "And the fight. You'll probably make me walk around Phoenix wearing a sandwich board sign that reads: I R an idiot, with a backward 'R.'"

"I'm sure half the club knows by now. Dagger was on the phone when I headed out of the dealership." Bill picked up the jug of pale yellow liquid. "What's this?"

"Lemonade," she said through her legs.

"You're hitting it pretty hard. Drinking straight from the bottle."

"I'm drinking away my sorrows. It takes a lot of lemonade to do that."

"Want a beer?" he asked, raising the cardboard box.

"Sure. Beer works, too."

Bill opened two beers and handed one to Joan. "You want to talk about what happened today?"

"Not really."

He settled deep in the chair across from her and waited, stroking his beard. *Let her talk in her own time. Prodding could wake up the inner wild woman.*

After several swigs of beer, Joan said, "It hurts. I'm being so loyal to him. To our marriage vows." She looked up.

He didn't react. *Let her talk it through.*

"And I know you wanted me to cut ties with him, but I just couldn't. And now he's done it." She swallowed hard and wiped her nose on her shirttail. "It never seemed right to abandon him."

Bill took a sip and watched her. *Never knew how to handle a crying woman.* Some wanted to be held. Some would kick your ass if you put a hand on their arm. He didn't know which Joan was. Didn't want to do the wrong thing. *Not with this woman who killed every man she put her hands on in anger— except me. That's one thing in my favor.*

"Say something, goddammit," she said.

He leaned forward and rested his forearms on his thighs. "I stand by what I said at the dealership. Cutting ties is difficult for you. I get it. Duncan did, too. He took that burden off you."

"But what about what I want?" Her eyes were red and glassy, and her voice was thick with emotion.

"What do you want?" Bill asked. "Do you want to live all alone? Without male companionship? I know you want a man in your life. I can feel it when I touch you."

"Does this mean you're going to jump my bones now that Duncan has asked for a divorce?"

Bill frowned. "I can't believe you. I've been a fucking Boy Scout. I could have taken you any time, but didn't."

"Yeah, like you could take me down."

"You just don't get it." He leaned farther forward and pointed to the world outside. "Those men will do anything I tell them to do. And if it was to gang up on you and hold you down so I could take you, they'd do it. Don't think you are unbeatable."

"You would do that?"

"Fuck no." He moved to the couch next to her. "Damn, Joan, I've told you, I'm doing this right. I want you to want me. Freely. And free from ties to another man. Otherwise, I won't claim you—can't claim you." He leaned back and rubbed his forehead. Her words had sliced him to the core.

He'd been nothing but good to her, what had he done to her to make her think he'd abuse her?

She wiped her eyes and nose. "I'm not usually this emotional."

"Divorce is emotional. You wouldn't be human if you didn't feel it."

"Let's talk about this tomorrow when my emotions have run their course," she said. "Then we can—"

Her phone rang. She checked the Caller ID and put the phone down.

"We can discuss this more rationally then," she continued. "I'll have time to rethink—"

"Aren't you going to answer that?"

She connected the call. "Yes. I'll accept the charges...You have something else to say to destroy my heart?...Divorce papers. Oh, yeah. That's what I wanted to hear from you. Good-bye, Duncan...Okay, say whatever it is you have to say."

She looked over at Bill. He got the hint and headed to the kitchen.

"Make it quick," she said to Duncan. "...you don't want to divorce me? Then what—" She stood and wiped away the last of her tears. "Really? I don't want to divorce you either."

Bill watched Joan walk away toward her bedroom. It sounded like now Duncan didn't want a divorce. *What the hell? He asks her for divorce. She races to me at breakneck speed, almost kills herself broad-sliding into my parking lot, then he calls saying it was a mistake? And she wants that cocksucker? Over me? This bullshit ends right now.*

He pulled out his phone and called Blaze. "Clear your calendar for tomorrow. We're going for a ride."

"Where to?"

"Safford."

CHAPTER 7

"Bill Torrence to visit Duncan Archer," Bill said to the corrections officer at the Visitors Desk.

The officer eyed the tabs on the front of Bill and Blaze's cuts before checking her computer monitor. She looked up at Bill and said, "We have no inmate named Duncan Archer."

Bill looked at Blaze. "Isn't that some fucking shit."

"I have to ask you to watch your language in the Visitors Area, sir."

Bill ignored the officer at the desk and walked outside. "What kinda bullshit is this?"

Blaze lit a cigarette and took a long pull. "Guys we sent to watch Joan said she visited the jail."

"Who's she visitin', if it ain't her old man?"

Blaze took another drag and thought a moment. "After that fiasco last year, I remember a different name in the news," Blaze said, flicking ash off his cigarette. "It was David or…Dennis. Dennis Archer. That's his real name."

After giving the officer Duncan's real name and their names, she pulled up Archer's visitor list on her computer. "You aren't on his Approved Visitors List."

Bill felt the heat rise up his neck to his face. He leaned both hands on the counter. "I don't give a flying—"

Blaze pulled him back. "Let me take care of this, Prez."

Bill frowned at his friend but stepped back. His knuckles cracked as he clenched and unclenched his fists. After an hour and a half drive, he wasn't going home without words with Duncan.

Blaze leaned his elbows on the desk and spoke as if he was telling a secret. "We wouldn't be doing this if it didn't mean so much to a mutual friend." He smiled. "How do we get on the list?"

"I'm sorry, sir, changes have to come from the inmate."

"I didn't ride all the way over here to get a runaround," Bill muttered. He pressed his lips together at Blaze's frown. Bill crossed his arms and checked out the families waiting their turn. The mothers noticed him and pulled their children in closer. The childless women returned his look before returning to their own thoughts, evidently, a tough, angry man was business as usual. He turned his attention back to Blaze.

"Can someone ask Archer if he'll put us on the list?" Blaze asked. "Is there, like, a one-time visit option. We only need once."

"It needs to be approved."

"Is there a supervisor I can talk to?" Blaze raised his brows and looked past her. "It would mean so much to our friend."

"Have a seat. I'll see what I can do."

Bill followed Blaze to the molded-plastic chairs farthest from the families with children. "When'd you get so friggin' charming?"

"Workin' at Leather and Lace. Taught me that sometimes charm works better than force."

"Yeah," Bill snorted. "Charmed your old lady outa the house."

"She's comin' back."

"How'd you manage that?"

Blaze smiled. "Charm."

Bill tried to fight a smile, but lost.

Talking club business in public was off limits, but, lately, he hadn't had much one-on-one time with his VP. "Talked to Little Al's old lady the other day. Seemed uptight about something."

"Copy that. What do you think it is? Kids on the run getting to her?"

"Maybe." Bill crossed his arms and watched a mother with a child in tow sign in at the desk. "Let's keep an eye on her."

"Should I talk to Little Al about it?"

Bill shook his head. "Personal business. Let him sort it out."

"Think he's cheating again? I hear he's missed a lot of time at the shop. Guys say he comes in late morning-noon most days."

When Bill invested in the Harley Davidson dealership, Al was the best man to take over his custom auto and bike shop. He thought things were going well there, but he made a mental note to keep a closer eye on it. *One more thing on my plate.*

"Any ideas?" Bill asked.

"Late nights'll do it."

"If it looks like it'll affect the club, we'll act." Bill's chin nodded toward the corrections officer at the sign-in desk. "Your girlfriend's motioning to you."

Forty-five minutes later, Bill and Blaze were ushered into a large room. People talked quietly at tables. Kids sat across from fathers, some jabbering away, some sullen and detached. Three guards, spaced around the perimeter of the room, kept watch.

"You can shake hands, but no other contact," the officer, who had escorted them to the visiting area, said.

Bill nodded and strode toward the table where Duncan sat, looking up at a fourth guard, talking quietly.

The guard walked away when Bill and Blaze approached the table. They all shook hands with brief, terse greetings before taking their seats. Bill waited for Duncan to speak first, but he seemed to be waiting for Bill to break the ice. Blaze slouched in the chair, looking around at the other inmates and visitors.

Duncan sat back and relaxed. He looked fit and healthy. His red hair and beard were neatly trimmed, his skin freckled and tanned.

Must get a lot of outside time. He still carries himself like the leader of a militia with an alliance with the DBMC. He's acting like a partner waiting to hear what I'm going to do for him. I'm about to do something all right.

"I'm guessing this isn't about how things are going for me here," Duncan said.

Bill leaned his forearms on the table. "How *are* things going for you?"

"Good." Duncan looked around the room. "It's all in your attitude. I accepted this is my home from now on. That makes it easier." His clear, blue eyes pinned Bill's. "How's my wife?"

"Not interested in how I'm doing?"

"I'm assuming she's still living with you?"

Bill nodded. *Let him talk. Let him think he's taking the lead. Whatever he says, he's not in charge of this conversation. He'll find that out in short order.*

"Then my guess is things are going well," Duncan continued. "If they weren't, you would have kicked her out, or she would've hit the road." Duncan smiled. "Or you'd be dead."

Blaze's eyes darted to Duncan, no longer interested in their surroundings. He pulled himself up straighter in the chair. "Things are not well," he said. "Did she tell you that you put her life in danger?"

Duncan tucked his chin. "No. How so?"

Bill smiled inwardly at the first crack in Duncan's bravado. "When you told her you wanted a divorce, she flew over the mountains. All it would have taken was a patch of loose sand and…" Bill let the weight of possible outcomes hang in the air.

"I thought she'd stay the night. Take time to calm down."

"She didn't. She left Safford and raced to me. To me." Bill used his forefinger for emphasis. "Then you called saying you made a mistake. You made her risk death and serious injury for nothing."

"She didn't say anything about that when I talked to her last night."

"Yeah, well…she was coming unglued. But you wouldn't know that because you weren't there."

"She's my wife, my responsibility."

"I didn't make it to where I am by beating around the bush." Bill stroked his moustache. "I'm just going to say it: she's better off with me."

"Really? An outlaw biker?"

"I can give her what she needs: a home, protection, companionship."

"Companionship? Is that all?" Duncan's sarcasm sliced the air.

"No, it's not all," Bill said through clenched teeth. He leaned forward. "I'm trying to have a civilized conversation about what's best for Joan."

"Best for Joan? Or you?"

"Don't tell me you think you're best for her?" Bill pointedly looked around the room, taking in the guards and locked doors. "You aren't exactly speaking from a position of power, are you?"

"If you're looking for a blessing, you won't get it from me."

"I don't need your fucking blessing. I need you to tell her your marriage is over. For good."

"I'm in here. She makes her own decisions." Duncan looked at his hands. "I can't tell her what to do."

"She's hung up on her vows—and you," Bill said, watching Duncan's body language. He was at the tipping point.

"Vows to you." Blaze gave Duncan a searing look, going in for the kill. "I can't see why she clings to you. You can't give her what she needs. Not from behind bars."

"You mind your own business," Duncan yelled at Blaze, pointing his finger at him. "This doesn't have anything to do with you. I don't even know why you're here. Bill can't handle this on his own?"

A guard appeared at Duncan's shoulder. "Keep it down, or you'll have to go back to your tier."

"Yes, sir." Duncan calmed down outwardly, but his neck and face were flushed. "I'm calm. Everything's okay, sir."

The guard looked from Blaze to Bill. "Same thing goes for you. I don't want any trouble from you two."

Bill sat back and crossed his arms.

Blaze nodded to the guard, who seemed satisfied and walked away.

"Get to the point, Bill," Duncan said. "Why are you here?"

"I'm going to claim Joan."

"Good luck getting her to do something she doesn't want to do."

"How do you know she doesn't want it?" Blaze sneered.

"I know my wife a whole lot better than you do."

"When was the last time—" Blaze said.

Bill put a hand on Blaze's arm to silence him. "She'll accept it if she knows you cut the ties for good. No going back."

"How can you be so sure?" Duncan asked.

Bill looked at Duncan, trying to judge how harsh he needed to be to close the deal. He leaned forward, his hard eyes capturing Duncan's. "I know."

Bill smiled when Duncan made the classic giving in gesture: the dropped head into the hands, the face wipe, the exhalation. Blaze tapped Bill's leg. Bill nodded to Blaze and stroked his beard while he waited for the concession.

"I'll tell her," Duncan said from behind his hands.

"I didn't hear you," Bill said.

Duncan dropped his hands and looked at the table between him and Bill. "It takes a big man to tell me to my face he's taking my wife away from me. That's the kind of man she needs." The corners of his mouth tightened. He wiped his lips for a few seconds. "I'll tell her it's over."

"No more visits."

"One more," Duncan said. "I have to tell her face to face."

"No more visits. Call her. Tell her. Then never again."

Duncan didn't answer.

"Are we clear?"

Duncan nodded.

Bill stood in preparation to leave.

"There is one thing you should know about Joan," Duncan said.

"What's that?" Bill asked.

"It never ends with her."

"Meaning?"

"She tends to take action without thinking first. Might wanna hone your problem-solving skills."

"I'll keep that in mind." Bill turned to leave.

"Can't say I didn't warn you," Duncan said to Bill's back.

Blaze followed Bill out of the room. When they were standing next to their bikes, Blaze lit one last cigarette before the ride back to Phoenix.

"What d'ya think?" Bill asked.

"Got him to cave." Blaze took a drag. "Did a good job, Prez, convincing a man he was no good for his own wife." He shook his head and smiled.

"Duncan's a tough man. Didn't think he'd give in that easy." Bill leaned on his bike. "Think he was bluffing?"

"Coulda been, but about what? What's it matter?" Blaze nodded toward the building. "He's in there. You're out here. Unless you're afraid of Joan."

"Think he'll make that call?"

"Who cares? If she wasn't interested, she'da split. Just claim her and take her."

"Long as he makes that call."

"Badass, pussy-whipped biker." Blaze smiled, shook his head, and flicked away the cigarette. "Ass-up, Prez. Let's get home. Check for that phone call."

CHAPTER 8

The fall Arizona sun warmed Joan's skin, but a different warmth radiated through her body as she drove her bike to the clubhouse for the MC's family day. She was going to be in Duncan's arms again. Inez had promised soon—maybe as early as next weekend. Duncan had called to reinstate his request for a divorce, but now Joan understood the papers were a sham. The singular cold spot in her inner glow was that sex with Bill was imminent.

She backed her motorcycle into an empty space at the end of a long line of Harley Davidsons and, to get control of her excitement, busied herself wiping the road dust off her mirrors and fenders.

After releasing the bungee cords that held the food containers in place, she checked the area. The clubhouse was protected by a double barrier of chain link fences. The first one separated the parking area from the road. The second had a closed gate that protected the building and paved area inside. She scanned the rooftops. Cameras looked on from every corner of the building, placed for overlapping fields of vision. Impressive.

A short prospect with tattoo sleeves walked up to her. He looked like he hadn't slept in months. Probably missed several meals, by the look of the jeans sagging at his hips.

"I was invited by Bill," she said to him.

"She's okay," Youngblood called over from where he manned the closed gate.

I'll bet any female would be okay, Joan thought as she stacked the food containers. She walked toward Youngblood, and when he looked past her and smiled, she looked over her shoulder at the other prospect. He was staring at the back of her jeans.

Bill had disappeared on a ride with Blaze the day after the broad slide stop at the dealership. That was when Duncan called and told her about Bill's visit. Duncan had basically given Bill the go-ahead last Sunday, but all week Bill had been surly, sometimes staying overnight at the clubhouse. Just as her plan was coming together, something of great importance must have happened in the club that prevented Bill from acting on the reason he brought her to Phoenix.

She had to get Bill back on track, which called for something sexy to regain his attention. She had opted for a skimpy leather vest over a tee shirt that showed a little cleavage and hid the birth control patch on her upper arm. Her faded jeans had a large brass zipper down the back of each leg. It caught the prospect's attention—a good sign Bill would notice, too.

She was in a good mood, and these bikers' leers would not bring her down. While she was enjoying family day, Inez was finalizing the plans for the conjugal visit with Duncan. Balancing on the tightrope between Bill and Duncan was draining, but she had survived tougher situations. The balancing act would end when she tipped toward Bill. She could only hope the Bureau had the safety net in place and that Duncan would still be there for her when this ordeal was over.

"Still riding that girlie bike?" Youngblood asked, bringing her thoughts back to reality and opening the gate for her.

She smiled at him. "I'm a girl, so…"

He smiled back and pointed to a door in an alcove on the right. "The women are through that door. Turn left. Kitchen is straight back."

"Thanks." Joan headed for the door conscious of the prospects' stares following her.

On family day, the men partied, and the women provided the food. The teenagers watched the children. The children were cut loose, safe inside the compound. This was the Sunday before Halloween, so there would be a costume contest, a piñata, and tons of candy. Or at least that was how Flora had described the activities.

After one step inside, she stopped short when Spiderman, Batman, and Princess Leia ran past.

She continued straight toward the back of the building, as Youngblood had directed.

Double doors opened into a large room that looked like it had been the cafeteria in a previous life. Several more children played tag in the room. A few pre-teen boys stood around looking tough.

Flora looked up from where J.J. sat in a baby carrier and waved Joan across the room. "Hey, Joan, back here."

Two teenage girls watched Joan approach, one of them rocking the baby carrier. They sat on folding chairs talking and giggling, paying more attention to the teenage boys than the kids in their charge.

"Whose teenagers?" Joan asked, indicating the two girls.

"They're Blaze's girls. The club babysitters," Flora whispered. "This is the weekend he has them. It's all kinda new for everybody."

The kitchen still had its stainless-steel counters and ancient commercial appliances. Several women busied themselves uncovering food or checking on something in the oven. The aroma of baked beans and corn biscuits welcomed her.

"Everybody," Flora said with a loud voice to get their attention. "This is Joan."

The women looked up, and Orlanda flashed Joan a smile. "Put your stuff down here," she said. She pointed to Little Al's wife. "This is Carol."

"We've met," Carol said. She looked out of place, wearing loose jeans and a plaid cotton shirt, unlike the other women who wore clothes that looked a size too small.

Joan nodded hello. "I'm surprised to see you here. Little Al said you don't participate in the biker community."

Carol shrugged. "I'm getting used to it. With the boys gone..."

Orlanda threw an arm around Carol's shoulders. "We've

been nagging her and nagging her to come. She finally gave in. Right, Carol?"

Orlanda flashed a big smile at Carol and squeezed her shoulders.

Carol's mouth worked into a hesitant smile.

"How are Joe-Sam?" Joan asked.

Joseph and Samuel were Little Al and Carol's identical twin sons who had been the communications experts for the militia. It had been rare to see one without the other, and Joan had dubbed them collectively as Joe-Sam. After the sting a year ago, they took off before the authorities could arrest them.

"I haven't seen them lately." Carol busied herself removing the lid from a plastic container. "They're doing as well as can be expected."

"They'll be fine," Joan assured her. "In time, the feds will have real criminals to hunt down. No one seems to be looking for me. It won't be long before it's the same for them."

"If only things were that easy."

Joan knitted her brow at Carol's negative tone. "Well, thank you for taking care of Duncan while he was recovering in the Ozarks. It means a lot to us."

"Joseph, Samuel, and I tag teamed his care. It was touch and go at first, but when he was out of the woods, Little Al and a couple Brothers rode out and spent a week with him."

"Who went to visit him?"

"Blaze and Youngblood rode along. Maybe Slow Motion. Why?"

"No reason. Just grateful. Anyway, it's good to be back in Phoenix."

"I owe you, Joan, for what you did to keep the boys from getting arrested. It put you in a tough spot."

"You don't owe me anything. Joe-Sam saved my ass, too." Joan touched Carol's arm. She looked like she was barely holding it together. "One hand washes the other."

"Glad you're back," Carol said, picking up a bowl of potato salad, and heading outside.

She almost bumped into a tall, heavy-set woman with a

ruddy complexion and red hair pulled back tight into a pony-tail.

"Almost had a friggin' collision. Use your blinkers. Put that tater salad on the far end of the table." She spied Joan. "Who the hell is this? You ain't no hang around, I'll bet my fat ass on that."

"This is Joan," Orlanda said. "Joan, this is—"

The Amazon flew across the kitchen and wrapped her big, flabby arms around Joan, hitting so hard it almost knocked the wind out of her.

Joan blinked and froze in place from the unexpected bear hug.

"I'm Lizzie," the big woman said. "You saved my old man. I can never thank you enough."

"Okay." Joan patted Lizzie on the back. "It was nothing. Really."

"No. It wasn't nothin'. It was friggin' heroic. If you'da walked away instead of—"

Lizzie loosened her grip, and Joan stepped back. Lizzie's mouth worked, lips tightening and loosening. Her eyes looked glassy.

"If you don't mind my asking, who's your old man?" Joan asked.

"Yeah, that's right," Lizzie said. "You saved so many people you're like a friggin' guardian angel."

"I just did what anyone else would've done."

Lizzie stepped in for another bone crushing hug, but Joan stiff armed her. She couldn't afford cracked ribs before her conjugal visit.

"Her old man is Slow Motion," Orlanda said, filling in the blank for Joan. "You know the tall, skinny one."

"Oh, yeah. I remember him. He talked real slow and moved in…well, slow motion."

"Yeah, but no more," Lizzie said. "He had a rough time dealing with what happened. He was doing meth for a while. But he's much better now that he's off the drugs."

Joan looked past Lizzie at Orlanda, who shook her head and mouthed the word "No."

"Well, I'm glad to hear that, Lizzie," Joan said. "I can't wait to catch up with him later."

"He'll be friggin' glad to see you." Lizzie looked around the kitchen. "Well, ladies, let's get this friggin' food outside before the men finish their goddamn meeting."

Everyone jumped into gear, grabbing bowls, condiments, serving utensils and headed out back. The former factory had been built in an L-shape which provided an ample compound for outdoor activities. A privacy fence blocked the street on the other two sides. The smoky aroma of grilled meat filled the air from two fifty-gallon barrels converted into grills. They were manned by another prospect. That made three—that she knew of—indicating Bill was aggressively increasing the number of members in the DBMC. Another prospect with a Tucson patch strung orange lights.

Three long tables had been placed end to end and covered with a festive red-and-white checkered oil cloth. The table quickly filled up with containers of food.

On her second trip, Joan gathered a stack of paper plates and a container of plastic utensils. She used her chin to secure two oblong packages of napkins on top and headed outside.

"Tits up, girls," Lizzie said, giving her breasts a quick up-push. "Church is over."

Joan looked over her shoulder in time to see Bill and Blaze strut into the compound. Blaze elbowed Bill and chin nodded toward Joan. Bill strode toward her. The stack in her hands bobbled, and she reached the table just in time to prevent the whole stack from falling onto the ground. Her load spilled on-to the stack of hamburger buns, scattering them into the stack of hotdog buns. She reached to re-organize everything and didn't see Bill walk up behind her.

"Hello, darlin'." In a gesture of ownership, he put his arm around her waist and pulled her into him. "What are those zippers for?" he murmured in her ear.

"For you to come up to me and ask about them," she said, turning at the waist enough to make eye contact.

"They worked. Come with me. I want to show you around."

"I'll get this," Carol said, restacking the hamburger buns.

Joan headed off with Bill. At the base of a short flight of metal stairs, Dagger and Blaze stood talking to a tall, thin biker with an arm draped over Lizzie's shoulder. Bill guided her toward the group of men.

"Slo Mo, this is Joan. Remember her?"

Slow Motion looked at Joan with unfocused, watery eyes. He blinked. "Yeah, man. You saved my life. Thank you…"

After those words, he wandered off into a world of broken sentences, describing a dis-jointed reality only he saw.

Bill clapped him on the shoulder. "We'll talk again later. I'm gonna show Joan around the new place."

"Oh. Yeah." Slo Mo blinked and scratched his head, leaving his hair wilder than before. "Sure, Prez."

When Bill opened the door for Joan, he leaned in to speak into her ear. "He's tweaking."

"You think?" she answered. "You should change his nickname to Fast Forward."

"Got something there," he said. "The club doesn't have the money right now for rehab. That's what we're doing on the mandatory run next weekend—fund raisin'. He has good days and bad days. On his good days, he's still a good biker."

"Lizzie seems to think he's doing great," Joan said as Bill guided her across a room with walls covered in Demon Brotherhood paraphernalia.

"Lizzie's a loyal old lady. Loves the shit outta him. This is our party room."

Bill fingered through a stack of Demon Brotherhood tee shirts. After picking up three and replacing two, he chose one and handed it to Joan. She checked the label—a size too small. Who would have guessed? He pointed out the colors of five Brothers who had died—displayed on the wall as a memorial.

"They look brand new," Joan said.

"The feds confiscated everything in their raid. Wouldn't return the colors they ripped off the wall. Said they were symbols of our law-breaking lifestyle."

She nodded. "Bastards."

"Roger that." He pointed to three more colors—two new,

one old and filthy. "These are for our retired members. Had to replace two. That one's Uncle Mooky's. He didn't turn his in before the raid. At least we have one original."

Monitors, hung high on all the walls, displayed the exterior of the building. Only one small area at the end of the line of Harley Davidsons, where she had parked her bike, wasn't covered. Bill must have seen Joan studying them. "No one gets in here that we don't know about."

"That's a lot of surveillance. Are you expecting trouble?"

"The MC has enemies. Don't want them to get the drop on us."

"Anything I should know about?"

"No." His answer was quick and definitive. He pointed the way. "Let's keep moving."

They headed back across the room toward a makeshift bar that spanned one wall. Two prospects with Tucson patches mixed drinks and drew beers. Several full-patch Tucson Brothers leaned on the bar.

Others sat at beat up tables. Several ratty couches were scattered around the room where a few men groped their girl-friends.

"Hey, the children are still here," Bill said to the men on the couches. "Go upstairs with that shit. You know the rules."

Instantly, and without comment, the bikers got up and herded their women past Bill and Joan to iron stairs at the end of a hallway.

He motioned for Joan to head down the hall. "These are the offices for the leadership." He stopped at the first door. "This is our security area. Garbage is our IT guru."

Two monitors divided into four views spanned the desk. The views changed every three seconds. The chair squeaked under Garbage's weight when he turned and nodded to Joan.

Garbage is an IT nerd? Yeah, and the club has a unicorn out back. But then again, she'd seen weirder things.

Bill pressed his hand into the small of her back to move her along to the next room. "This is the chapel—where we have our meetings."

Joan made a mental note of the rooms, their use, size, computers, security monitors. The Tucson chapter was there for a meeting, which meant something was going on. *Overlooked details can kill you*—that had been Jason's mantra.

"This is my office," Bill said when he reached the next door. He turned her and pinned her against the wall. She had been lost in thought and didn't see it coming. But now his arms were braced on either side of her head.

"You wanna go upstairs?" he asked. His voice was low. His eyes searched hers, then tracked to her lips.

"What's upstairs?"

He pressed his body against hers. "Rooms for fucking."

"Oh." She couldn't let this happen. Not yet. "There's a party going on, and you're the president hosting an out of town chapter. Shouldn't you be with your club?"

"I can do whatever the hell I want. I want to do you." He kissed her hard, pressing her lips against her teeth.

Joan kissed him back before breaking contact. "I'm not ready," she whispered.

"You're waiting for the motherfucker divorcing you," he said through his teeth. "He doesn't deserve you. You coulda been killed low-flying over those mountains. Had a meet-up with him last Sunday. Did you know that?" He didn't wait for an answer. "The divorce is back on the table. I'm done waiting."

"Prez," Blaze called down the hall. "We have to talk."

"Later," Bill said without looking away from Joan.

"Can't wait."

Bill took in a long, deep breath and exhaled loudly before pushing off the wall. "We'll finish this later," he whispered to Joan. He glared at Blaze. "This better be important."

Blaze draped an arm over Bill's shoulder and smirked. They walked into Bill's office and closed the door.

❧❧❧

Joan and Bill spent a pleasant afternoon together, but always in the presence of other bikers and their old ladies, giving no opportunity for Bill to bring up the previously aborted conversation.

After the costume contest and the piñata smashing, Joan leaned against the building watching Bill play with his grand-children.

Over the past few weeks, she had never thought of him as a grandfather. Powerful president of an outlaw motorcycle club—sure. A lusty, coarse man—absolutely. But a family man? And a playful grandfather? Never saw it coming.

She stepped into the kitchen and began rinsing bottles. A shadow fell over the door, and she looked up at Little Al.

"How's it going?" he asked.

"Good."

"Just good?"

Joan shrugged and tossed a bottle into the recycle bin.

"You rinse out bottles for recycle?"

"It's something to do."

"Mix with the members. You might like them. We're a big, happy family."

Joan didn't say anything.

"Hey, Joan. If you feel lonely. Need to talk. I'm here for you."

She looked into Little Al's sharp, blue eyes—eyes that retained some humanity—and smiled. "I liked that conversation at the rest stop. You kept me on an even keel when my day was coming unglued."

"Coming back to Phoenix took some heavy docs."

"Docks?"

"Docs. Like a driver's license or carry permit or valid VI-SA for a foreigner. Docs. Means you have balls. But since you don't have balls—"

"I have docs."

"Yeah. I'll do my best to protect you."

"Do you think I'll need it?"

"Still a fugitive?"

Joan nodded.

"I'll talk to Carol. Maybe have you over for dinner one night."

Joan looked up from rinsing the last plastic Coke bottle. "I'd like that."

Blaze walked up to the sink and filled a Solo cup with water. He nodded for Little Al to leave. The women had talked about Blaze's old lady leaving him two weeks ago when she learned of him availing himself of the women at the strip club. They had asked Joan if she saw anything. She wasn't going to dig a bigger hole for Blaze. He was a good boss, treated her well, paid on time, and kept his hands off her.

He chugged the water.

"Fuck Bill," Blaze said before refilling the cup.

She blinked. "Excuse me?"

"You heard me. Take his legs out from under him." He stepped to the door to watch the family scene unfolding in the late afternoon light. "I don't interfere in a Brother's personal life but—"

"Then don't," she said.

He chuckled and shook his head. "I see what he likes about you. You remind me of my old lady. Same smart mouth. But I—" He shook his head and sucked in a breath. "—just don't get the deal."

"The deal?" Joan's voice cracked because her mouth went dry. If he knew about the deal she made—

"You're married, yet he moved you into his house—not in his playbook. Your old man gave you up—as much as handed you over to him—but you won't move on."

"Bill told you about that?" Joan knew it was a stupid question the second the words left her mouth. Brothers didn't have secrets from each other.

"I was there." He crossed his arms, the leather cut squeaked under the pressure. "His head's screwed up. It's interfering with his decision making. He's short with everyone. I'd be shirking my duty as VP if I didn't say something."

"Shouldn't you have this conversation with him?" She raised her eyebrows for emphasis.

Blaze leaned in and captured her eyes. "For God's sake, fuck him, and get it over with. The man's worthless the way things are."

"I seem to remember you cock-blocking him earlier."

Something flickered in Blaze's eyes. A slow smile inched across his lips. "You weren't going upstairs anyway."

"How do you know?"

"If Bill's gonna take a woman upstairs, he doesn't stand around in the hallway. Talkin'."

"You mean like, Sapphire?"

"He doesn't fuck her. Never been upstairs with her. She's just for quick release. Till he has you."

"Yeah," Joan snorted. "Like I can believe that."

"Believe what you want. I took care of business today."

"What do you mean?"

"Made sure Sapphire's working tonight. Didn't want her showing up at the party. Causing heartburn for Bill. Or you."

"He can see whoever he wants. I'm married."

"A pen and two seconds can change that."

"It's complicated."

"Complications get you in trouble," he said. "Keep it simple. Do what you have to do."

Do what you have to do? Joan broke out in a sweat. She wiped the back of her hand across her upper lip. "What does that mean?"

Did he know what she was there to do? If he was the undercover agent, he could know who she was and why she was there and be urging her to take care of business.

"Don't play games." He leaned closer, and when he spoke, his voice was low. "Someone always loses." He tossed the cup into the garbage can and pushed off the counter. "Gotta go. Think about what I said."

Joan watched his departure over her shoulder, thinking about how direct bikers were. If they had something to say, they said it—a trait she especially liked. But was he talking straight or around something?

She stepped into the doorway to watch Bill. He was spinning his two-year-old grandson, Peter, like a chair swing ride at the carnival. Peter's three-year-old sister, Peri, was jumping up and down yelling, "Now me, Poppa. Now me."

Do what you have to do. Blaze could be the undercover

agent, warning her to get her ass in gear. He went away for a while—it could easily have been to Quantico rather than the marines. The VP would be in the loop. If he was the UC and didn't act on the information, why not? Could be rogue as Inez said.

She headed to a picnic table on the far side of the compound where Carol was sitting alone. They watched in silence while Bill played with his grandchildren. Peter squealed with delight. Dagger draped an arm over Orlanda and watched. Bikers were rowdy, rough men out in public, but here in the privacy of the club's fenced-in compound, she caught a glimpse of a different side, when they were relaxed. With family.

And Mooky was just plain Mooky. A grizzled, difficult man wherever he was.

But that was part of his charm for her, and evidently also for his nephew's grandchildren. All day they had climbed on his lap and all around him. He acted like they were annoying him, but Joan knew better. He loved his family—both blood and biker.

That didn't mean he didn't have a side of him he kept in check. It simmered with anger and brutishness.

Perhaps that restrained side emerged around bikers in their closed-off social group. But never around her. And not today.

When Orlanda went inside the building, Dagger headed toward Joan and Carol.

Evidently, Bill didn't pick up Peri soon enough because she yelled, "Goddammit, Poppa. Swing me around."

"You let Peri talk like that?" Joan asked as Dagger sat down next to her.

"It's our lifestyle." He watched Bill swing Peri around before continuing. "I hope you know what you're doing."

"What do you mean?" Joan braced for another Screw Bill Now conversation.

"Did you know I got Orlanda pregnant before we were married? The club president's eighteen-year-old daughter." He shook his head, thinking back. "Man, I thought I was dead meat. But I loved her and was going to do right by her. When

Bill realized that, he treated me like a son. Was the father I never had."

"Why are you telling me this?" Joan asked.

"Bill can be a decent guy, long as you lay it on the line. All in or get out."

"Meaning?"

"Give him the green light, or get outta Dodge."

Joan looked up at his profile. A lock of hair had fallen forward, softening the hard line of his cheekbones and jaw.

Dagger finger-combed his hair back. "Be careful. Don't do anything that'll bring the club down on you." He finally looked dead straight at Joan. "Because that would be ugly. And painful."

"I won't cross Bill. He's giving me a place to stay."

"Don't play clueless. You know what I'm talkin' about."

"Okay. Point taken."

That was two warnings. Both sounded like UCs giving her advice—or she could be seeing rogue agents where there were none. Or did both men see through her lie? Bikers were hyperperceptive, able to size up someone in a two-minute conversation, attuned to inflection and subtext. She had been in Phoenix four weeks, which was plenty of time for Dagger and Blaze to get the feeling something was not quite right. As for Bill—she could only hope love was blind.

"Oh, shit. Peter hurled on Uncle Mooky." Dagger dashed away to check on his son.

While Dagger and Orlanda cared for their kids, Joan thought about how bikers did not get caught up in the back and forth of dialogue, distracted by formulating what they wanted to say in response. They listened to the words, read facial expressions, and watched body language. If she was going to survive, she would have to master the neutral face. Her choice of words had to be precise, the same for inflection. Her stomach tightened as she rewound the day, checking for words or expressions that could be misunderstood.

"Was that a heavy warning or what?" Carol asked. "I've been wondering myself why you came back to Phoenix. I hope you know what you're doing."

"I'll be fine."

"Al and I are here for you, if you ever need help. We know you'd be there for us."

"Thanks, I appreciate that."

"Just remember: it's always 'club first.' Don't think Al will go against the club to protect you. Be careful." She studied Joan for a few seconds. "And come to dinner some night, okay?"

"Wouldn't miss it."

Joan shivered as the shadows lengthened and the air cooled. She grabbed two bottles of water and fell in with the families leaving for the day. The divorce papers niggled at her. Duncan insisted they were fake, but cutting ties with him, legal or not, was a pivotal decision. They signaled the point of no return.

"Here's water for you two," Joan said to the prospects guarding the bikes. "You've been out here all day."

Youngblood glanced at the camera on the nearest building. "We're good."

When working, prospects didn't eat or drink unless their sponsors okayed it. She wasn't a member or attached to Bill. She could defy that archaic and inhuman rule. "I noticed the cameras don't cover the area where my bike's parked. Keep an eye on it for me, will ya?"

Youngblood nodded.

"I'm going to grab my jacket off my bike. I'll just set these bottles down next to the rear tire. You know, in case you get thirsty."

Tattoo-Sleeves waved a car out of the parking area. "Thanks."

When Joan returned to the compound, Bill was no longer there. It seemed empty, now that the families had left for the day. The thought of going into the party room made her shudder, although there was plenty of rustling and moaning in the shadows to give her the creeps outside. She sat at a vacant picnic table, and her thoughts returned to Bill. If he had the same misgivings as Blaze and Dagger, it was only a matter of time before she would crash and burn. The divorce papers were a parachute, but it was too soon to pull the cord. She had to make love to Duncan one more time before stepping into Bill's life.

He walked out of the building and headed toward her. He leaned with one hand on the table, the other on her shoulder. She smiled up at him. Most people only saw his public image—powerful, ruthless, demanding. They didn't get to see this man. The one guiding his family, trying to do the right thing in this new relationship.

"You started today happy, but turned sad," he said. "Something happen?"

"What do you mean?"

All day, every time she looked at him, he had been studying her, his face flattened into the neutral expression, making him difficult to read. She couldn't tell him that Inez had come through on her request, or how bittersweet it was. Joan would feel Duncan's strong arms around her for twenty-four hours, but it was the precursor to having sex with Bill. With him, it would only be sex, certainly not making love. Nothing like she and Duncan shared.

"Thinking about your old man?" he asked.

"Did you have anything to do with him telling me to not visit him?"

"Damn straight. You won't be visitin' him again, darlin'."

"You can't make that decision for me."

"I can. And I did."

They stared into each other's eyes. She blinked first, granting him the power he needed, but not without conditions.

"I need closure. I need to see him one more time." She looked at Bill. "To say good-bye."

"No more visits."

"I hate leaving him there. That's why I always stayed overnight. I'm too bummed out to drive back."

"Except when he told you he was divorcing you."

"That was different."

"No shit, woman. You stormed into the dealership fuckin' sideways." He straddled the bench and sat next to her. "What's goin' on in that head?"

"I guess it's sinking in that he's serious about the divorce." To avoid Bill's eyes, she gathered up the trash from the table. "Thanks to you." She put as much bitterness as she could into the words.

He took the trash from her and set it on the table. "Is something wrong?"

"I don't know what's wrong with me." She brushed a non-existent piece of lint off his tee shirt. "I have a great man right here in front of me, who I can touch—more than just holding hands like in the prison visiting area."

Bill's moustache twitched above a half-smile. "Touch?" He put his hand in the small of her back, and nuzzled her neck. "I'm gonna get more than that, darlin'."

She smiled at him. "Maybe."

"Are you flirting? You know what happens when you flirt with a biker…" he said before moving his hand to the back of her neck. He turned her head enough to cover her mouth with his.

He tasted of grilled meat and beer. His lips were soft, and his moustache and beard caressed the sensitive skin around her mouth. She relaxed into the warmth that filled her. He pressed harder, but it was still sensual. He stopped, and she let out the breath she hadn't known she had been holding.

She looked into his eyes. "Please don't start something we can't finish."

"Tell me you cut your husband loose," he said.

She didn't respond.

"Say the words."

"After one more visit. I will."

Say the words. Her blood rushed to her head, making it throb in rhythm with her pounding heart. If he'd found the papers, he was playing her.

CHAPTER 9

A north wind blew hair across Joan's face as she knelt on one knee next to her bike. The oil blown back across her rear tire told the story. She sat back in resignation. Wrists on her knees, hands dangling, she stared at the broken line, cursing it. She'd never hear the end of this. In addition to the relentless teasing about owning a Honda, she'd now have to bear the taunts of poor maintenance.

The sound and breeze of a passing car brought her back to reality. She dug into backpack and pulled out her phone. She hated calling Bill. Since the Family Day four days ago, his advances had become more aggressive. But he'd stopped when she asked him to, so far.

"Hey, it's me," she said.

"What's up, darlin'?"

"I'm on Route Ten. My bike broke down. I have a blown oil line."

"Oil line? That's near impossible."

"Yeah, well…"

"Where 'bouts on Ten?"

"Just east of that rest area. Burnt Wells, I think they call it. On the eastbound side."

She heard him tell Youngblood to take the van. Grab some oil and an oil line. He came back on the line. "I'm sending Youngblood. He'll be there in a few. What are you doing way out there?"

"I came out for tacos from the taco truck that parks in the

rest area." The meeting with Inez at the Skyline National Park had gone well—they talked mostly about the conjugal visit that coming weekend. With several hours to kill before she had to go to work, Joan wanted to treat herself to some tacos.

"It's not there anymore."

"No shit,'" Joan said with an edge to her voice. It wasn't directed toward Bill. It was from exasperation about her predicament.

"You okay?" he asked.

"Yeah. I'm fine. The bike's a mess though."

He didn't answer, but she could picture him nodding his head.

"What'd you think about family day?" he asked.

"We already—"

"Just want to talk to you while you wait, darlin'. Tell me something new."

They had talked about the family day. What else was there to say? "I was told, in no uncertain terms, to have sex with you. Twice."

"No shit. By who?"

"If they want you to know, they'll tell you."

"Now you got me checkin' out my Brothers."

"That's why I'm not telling you their names. You'll start something with them."

"Start something? I'll thank 'em."

Joan smiled. She would bet her last dime he would do exactly that. "The clubhouse needs some work."

"Yeah. All in good time."

"What if I organized the women for a paint party to fix up the kitchen and cafeteria area?"

"Don't have a problem with that," he said. "You get the workers. I'll get you a key."

"Deal." The DBMC had a mandatory run planned in a couple weeks. She would be in the clubhouse without any Demon Brotherhood members around. She'd find a way to break away from the women, see if she could find anything useful.

Three motorcycles blew past, engines revving as the drivers downshifted. They slowed to a stop about ten yards away.

"Maybe help has arrived," she said, watching the men stand off their bikes.

"What kinda help?"

"Three motorcycles just pulled up and stopped."

"Bikers?"

"They aren't wearing colors."

The men projected an air of dominance, their faces in the signature neutral countenance of bikers. Two were Hispanic, one chubby with a shaved head, the other thin, wearing a black bandana. They followed a third biker who was Caucasian— maybe half-Latino. They strode toward her.

"They act like bikers."

"Ask them if they belong to a club."

"Having trouble?" Shaved Head asked.

She lowered her phone. "You guys belong to an MC?"

They looked at each other. The Caucasian with dark hair pulled back into a ponytail said, "We're Mongols."

"Did you hear that?" she asked Bill. She studied Ponytail. There was something familiar about the way he moved.

"Mongols. Not wearing colors," Bill said, as if thinking out loud. "What're they doin' in Hells Angels territory?"

"Do you really want me to ask them?"

"Who're you talkin' to?" Bandana Biker asked.

"Bill Torrence."

The men looked at each other. One chuckled.

"Let me have the phone," Ponytail said.

She turned so he couldn't get it.

"Tell them you're my old lady," Bill said.

"But—"

"Honesty's not always the best policy."

She stepped out of Ponytail's reach. "Maybe they just want to help a fellow biker stranded on the side of the road."

"Yeah. They're the fucking welcome committee. Do you have a piece?"

"No." She had carried 24/7 when she lived in Phoenix before. A year had gone by without carrying a gun. It had crossed her mind to get one, but never got around to it. Now it looked like procrastination was about to bite her in the ass.

"One's trying to take the phone." She eyed three large, tanned men fall in around her. "What should I do?"

"Do you think you can take them?"

"One. Maybe two." She ducked away from Ponytail again.

"Distract them. You know how to talk to bikers."

She heard movement in her ear, possibly Bill walking across the maintenance bay floor.

"Yeah, like that's going to work," she said.

"Do the best you can. I'm on my way."

"This is gonna suck," she said.

"I know, darlin'."

Ponytail finally got the phone away from her, but the expression on his face told her Bill had already disconnected the call.

Her conjugal visit was only one day and a wakeup away. Showing up with bruised ribs, swollen face, fractured knuckles, and maybe worse was not on her agenda. Yeah. This was going to suck in more ways than one.

"What's the problem with your ride?" Bandana Biker asked.

Joan stepped toward the rear tire. "Broken oil line. I called for help. It's on the way."

"Yeah, Bill Torrence." Ponytail smirked at the other two.

He knelt next to the bike to check out the damage as the other two bikers walked toward her from the other side.

Shaved Head stepped past Joan, scanned the horizon, then locked eyes with her. "You're out here riding alone? You should always ride with someone."

"I know that now." She took a step back to keep both bikers in view.

Bandana Biker reached out to touch her hair.

She batted his hand away. "Don't touch me. It won't turn out well for you." He was too light in the ass to take her on. He just didn't know it yet.

"You think you're tough. What you gonna do? Bill Torrence isn't here to protect your pretty ass." Bandana Biker made a show of looking at her butt. "Last I looked, there're three of us and one of you."

"Do you know who Bill Torrence is? He won't be happy if you hurt me."

"Hey, Switch," Shaved Head said to Ponytail. "She wants to know if we know who Bill Torrence is."

Switch's snort was the only answer.

"You his girlfriend or something?" Shaved Head asked.

"I'm his old lady." Saying the words didn't sting as much as she thought they would.

Shaved Head and Bandana Biker smiled at each other then turned to look at Switch.

"Hey, Switch," Shaved Head said. "Come meet your step-mother."

Switch stood, eyes on Joan, and wiped his hands on his jeans. He walked around the bike, and Shaved Head stepped back to let him past. He stopped inches from her, flexing his jaw muscles, squinting into her eyes.

Her blood turned cold. There wasn't a fleck of humanity in his eyes. She raised her hands.

"Heard Bill had a new woman in his life. You aren't what I expected." His eyes tracked down her body. "More athletic than his usual choices."

Some brave soul in a black sedan pulled off the highway.

"Friend of yours?" he asked without taking his eyes off her.

She didn't recognize the car. "No. Don't know him." As the words died in the wind, she wished she had bitten her tongue instead. If she had indicated this was her assistance, maybe these Mongols would have backed off, especially the animal in front of her.

Shaved Head leaned in with a smirk, putting one hand on Switch's shoulder, the other on hers. "We'll take care of this. You two get to know each other." He and Bandana Biker set off toward the good Samaritan.

"Let's take this jacket off," Switch said. "See what you look like."

She batted away his hands.

He grabbed her jacket. She grabbed his wrist and thrust her fingers into one of his eyes.

"Fuck." He grabbed his eye. "Fuckin' bitch." He snatched

her wrist. "Feisty. I like that. Only thing Bill and I have in common. Let's go over here. See how gutsy you are."

He pulled her toward the scrub brush on the side of the road.

She kicked the back of his knee. A knife hand to the throat sent him to the ground. "You are one lucky bastard. Bill is the only thing preventing me from taking you out."

He rose to one knee, coughing and rubbing his throat.

She stepped back out of his reach.

"Gonna pay for that," he said, getting to his feet. When he finally looked at her the corners of his mouth crinkled in a smile, but his eyes remained dead. "It's gonna be fun taking you down. Not today, I got other things to do. But if you're Bill's old lady, I'll know where to find you."

"You know him?" Shaved Head asked her, pointing to the car.

She looked at the sedan that had pulled onto the road and slowed when it was even with her bike. The driver leaned over to look back at her. They locked eyes for more than a second before he pulled away. Prickles tapped down her spine.

She shook her head. Words choked her throat. She had never seen the driver before, but she had the distinct feeling he knew her. A simple breakdown had turned into Surreal Shit City.

"Something's goin' on in that head." Switch searched Joan's eyes. "Maybe you know him. Don't matter. He's gone."

"You should call your father," she said, changing the subject to chase away the uneasy feeling settling at the base of her sternum. Youngblood and Bill couldn't be too far away. She just had to hold off these heathens until then.

Switch's mouth formed into a tight, crooked smile. "We just met, and you're already talkin' family reunion."

"He misses you."

"Yeah," he grunted. "I tried to talk to him once, and he sent me packin'. And not nice either."

"It's a tough thing for him. You choosing the Mongols over the Brotherhood." She wasn't supposed to know that, but she had to delay. And if she could do some good, why not?

"He shoulda thought about that before bootin' me and my mother out."

"It was something between your mom and Bill. I've seen him with kids. He didn't kick you out of his life."

"What did he think was gonna happen?"

"A lot of time has passed."

"Not enough."

"Call him. Give it a try. You don't have a relationship. What have you got to lose?"

"He's the dad." Switch sneered the last word. "Tell him to call. He'll get the same reception he gave me."

"It could be different."

"Bill picked a dreamer this time," Switch said to his cohorts. He turned his cold eyes back to her. "What makes you think he even thinks o' me?"

"He has a photo in his wallet. Of him with you on a motorcycle. It's faded and dog-eared."

"A photo don't mean shit."

"If he didn't take it out and look at it, it wouldn't be so creased and faded."

A motorcycle pulled off the road. Without looking up, she knew who it was from the muffled, double backfire when the driver eased up on the throttle. She relaxed. Little Al said he'd protect her, and there he was.

Bandana Biker said, "I'll talk to *El Gigante*."

Switch gestured with a nod to tell Shaved Head to go, too.

The two bikers walked away toward Little Al.

Switch pressed his lips together and turned back to Joan. "Where were we?"

"You were about to back up and save yourself."

They stared at each other.

"Were you meeting Little Al?" Switch asked.

She knitted her brow and shook her head.

He squinted toward Little Al then back at her. "How much do you know—"

"That's the prez's old lady." Little Al strode up to them, Shaved Head and Bandana Biker trailing him. He stepped into Switch's space. "Family's off limits. You know that."

Switch stood his ground, evidently unafraid of Grizzly Adams, Biker Version.

"We were just getting acquainted," Switch said, finally taking a step back. "Weren't we…what was your name?"

Joan resettled her jacket and glared at him.

"You okay, Joan?" Little Al asked.

"I'm fine."

"Go wait by your bikes," Little Al ordered the three Mongols.

"I don't take orders from you," Switch said. "Be careful."

Little Al bristled. Switch put up his hands. He hit Shaved Head's upper arm with the back of his hand, motioned to Bandana Biker, and they walked away—Switch with a slight limp, much to Joan's satisfaction.

Little Al turned back to Joan. "What's wrong with your bike?"

"Broken oil line."

Little Al squatted and picked up the line. He looked at it, turning it over in his hand. He looked up and hesitated, as if deciding whether to say something.

"What?"

"Let's see what Bill thinks," Little Al said, scooping up some dirt to wipe the oil off his hands.

"You came along at the right time."

"I was just a mile or so up the road. On my way to the shop when Bill called."

"Thank God for that."

"Thank God for Bluetooth. Wait here," Little Al said. "I want to have a word with these fuckers."

He talked to the bikers for several seconds. They were too far away for Joan to hear the words. Their body language was relaxed in spite of Little Al pointing at them, making some point.

The growl of a Harley Davidson, throttle open and getting louder, filled the distance. The Mongols straddled their bikes. Bill stopped on the shoulder of the westbound side of Route 10 and was off the bike the second the kickstand hit the ground.

The dealership van slid to a stop in a swirl of dust a few yards beyond Bill. Both men rushed across the sandy median.

The Mongols raced off toward Phoenix.

"You okay?" Bill asked, putting an arm around Joan's shoulders and watching the bikes disappear in the distance.

"I—" She looked past him at the same black sedan as before. It slowed then sped away westbound. "Yeah. I'm fine. I think they believed I was your old lady."

"Good."

"They claim they got permission to ride through," Little Al said.

"From who? Not like Fitz not to tell me," Bill said, checking his phone for missed calls from the president of the Hells Angels Phoenix Chapter. "I'll check with him later."

"Thank God you called Little Al when you did," Joan said. "He got here just in time."

Bill's eyes flashed at Little Al before his face fell into a neutral expression.

"I don't doubt they called Fitz," Little Al said.

"Trusting Mongols. Never thought I'd hear that from you." Bill turned to Youngblood and the task at hand. "Can you fix her bike here, or should we take it back to the shop?"

"I don't like this." Youngblood looked up at Bill, glanced at Joan, then said, "Since we have the muscle to get it into the van, I say take it back to the shop."

"Prez, I have a couple things to run by you," Little Al said.

"I got something for you," Bill said. "We'll ride back together."

After several grunts and curses, Joan's bike was loaded, and she climbed into the front of the van. Youngblood pulled out onto the highway, and the rocking motion hypnotized her. Scattered thoughts of the broken oil line, Mongols, Little Al showing up floated through her consciousness. She smiled at Bandana Biker calling Little Al *El Gigante*, The Giant.

Thoughts crystallized around the image of the face of the man in the black sedan. She was positive she didn't know him, but she couldn't shake the feeling that he knew her. And he showed up as if he knew where she would be. She didn't have a tail. She was sure of it. Could Stillwater be tracking her electronically? She had asked them for help with an exit plan, if it ever came to that. They were contract covert operators, specialists in security, recon, and exfiltration—and other less honorable actions. They even owned their own satellite. Tracking her would be a snap for them. But surely, they would have contacted her to get details. She shook off her thoughts. If there was anything she had learned over the past three years, it was that time, left unhindered, had a way of revealing details and unraveling mysteries.

"I hear congratulations are in order. You got your full patch last Sunday," she said, reaching to turn down the volume of the blaring blues-rock music. "I hear being a prospect is tough."

"Monday night I got my first full night's sleep in ten months. Felt good." He glanced at her, then back at the road. "Did you know those Mongols?"

Joan thought for a moment. "What are the chances of Mongols riding by—outside their territory, not wearing colors—when I was broken down on the side of the road, to say nothing about one of them being Bill's son."

"One was Bill's son?" Youngblood shook his head and thought for a moment. "What are they doing in Phoenix? Damn good thing they rode off before Bill got there."

"Do you think there would've been trouble? I think deep inside, Bill misses his son."

"Or misses the idea of having a son," Youngblood said. After a pause, he continued. "You need to maintain your bike better."

There it was, taunting right on cue. "I check everything before I ride, while it's warming up. I don't know how I missed that."

"Was your bike out of your sight any time since you checked it?"

"No." His question sounded like a TSA question at the airport. She shrugged it off. Bikers were a suspicious group. She watched the desert give way to the outskirts of Phoenix. "Now that I think of it, I stopped at that rest area to use the bath-room."

They looked at each other.

"You think it was sabotage?" she asked.

"Anything look different?" he asked. "Did you check it again?"

"Do you re-check your bike every time you take a piss?"

He leaned forward to check for pedestrians as he palmed the steering wheel, turning onto West Durango Street. "Motor-cycle maintenance has to be priority one. Bad things can hap-pen when you're stranded on the road, especially out here where there can be lotsa nothin' around you."

They pulled into Bill's original and main source of income, a bike and auto body shop where vintage cars were rebuilt and custom-designed motorcycles were created. "Why are we go-ing to Sun Valley Custom Rides?"

Youngblood chuckled. "You have to ask?"

"He doesn't want a Honda in the Harley Davidson dealer-ship." It was a statement, not a question. Bikers were incurable Harley snobs.

"That's something I don't see very often," he said, pulling up to the maintenance bay door.

"What's that?"

"Bill here during the day."

"What's so unusual about that? It's his shop."

"Yeah, but since buying into the dealership, he's only here when he has a reason to be."

"He brought me here once to show it to me. Wait. You work here, too?"

Youngblood smiled at her before jumping out of the truck, telling someone to get a ramp.

のの

Bill slouched in the chair in the shop office, waiting for Lit-tle Al to tell him what was so damn important that he had to send Joan home alone. He shrugged off the strangeness of sit-ting in a chair for visitors or employees, while Al sat behind the desk. When he invested in the dealership, he had put his shop, the one true love of his life, into Al's hands to manage. He had made a choice. He hoped it had been the right one.

"The rumor about Mongols treading on our territory is true," Bill said, stroking his beard and looking around the office. Not much had changed, maybe messier. "What are they up to?"

"They said they were riding through to Albuquerque. Got permission from Fitz."

Bill checked his phone again for a return call from Fitz. "Don't sound right. What's in Albuquerque? That's Angels' territory, too."

"I only know what they told me."

Bill eyed his sergeant-at-arms. He didn't have to remind Al that security of the Phoenix area had been passed to them by the Hells Angels. Ultimately, the Angels ran their own territory, but the Demon Brotherhood had been tagged to be their eyes and ears, and axe-men if necessary, for a cut in any business dealings. That money was instrumental in rebuilding the DBMC.

Bill got up and looked through the window between the office and the shop floor, watching his crew working in the auto shop area—he still thought of them as *his* crew. *Something's going on with Little Al. He's been distracted for a while now. Couldn't have anything to do with Joan.* It started before then, but it got worse after she arrived. He was friendly with her, but something about her presence made him edgy.

Bill had been preoccupied with the hunt to find her. Blaze had pointed it out. Couldn't blame him—just being a good VP. Blaze and Dagger could've conspired to find Joan and get her into his life. But she had been at the Bottom Rocker for months before Dagger noticed her. Why not just abduct her and bring her to him in Phoenix? No. She was not a hang-around who could be forced to do something she didn't want to do. He couldn't recall whose idea it had been to enter a bike in the Albuquerque Bike Show. Maybe they found her and arranged a chance meeting to improve his focus on club business—or as a distraction.

Bill turned to face Little Al. "Why'd Joan say I called you about her being broke down?" Bill wasn't a micro-manager. If Little Al was out on Route 10 when he should have been managing the shop, he had his reason. But her comment could not go unquestioned.

"Prez, there's something you need to know."

Bill leaned against the window sill and crossed his arms. "What?"

"It's about Joan." Little Al scratched his jaw. "You're not gonna like it."

CHAPTER 10

Two days later, Joan stood looking out the window at the Economy Inn in Safford, fighting the sinking feeling of having screwed up her life, and at the same time embracing the anticipation of someday overcoming it all. She rubbed the birth control patch on her arm. This was certainly not a time to get pregnant, immersed in the biker culture, separated from Duncan, and facing jail time if she failed. Her experience taught her no matter how bad things were, they could always get worse. Her Iron Angel Bad Karma practically demanded it. She had to do whatever she could to mitigate "worse."

She paced past the pint-sized refrigerator, where she had stashed cold cuts, condiments for sandwiches, and milk for coffee that could be made in the four-cup pot on the desk. Any requests for food deliveries had to go through the feds, and she wanted as little contact with them as possible once Duncan was with her. No alcohol was permitted, so Joan had brought plenty of bottled water. The two queen-size beds, bureau, and desk took up most of the room, leaving a path to the bathroom, but a tent in the desert with Duncan would have been more than enough.

Back at the window, she looked down at the parking lot one story below. This two-star motel was not chosen for its amenities. It was chosen because all the rooms had exterior doors in front and no window in the rear, making it easier for the feds to keep watch from a parked car.

She dropped the curtain and looked at the clock bolted to the nightstand. One more hour and the agents would bring Duncan to her. Then they'd pick him up twenty-four hours later to return him to prison. It wasn't forever like she wanted, but it would have to do until she could arrange forever.

After a light knock, Inez breezed into the room. Joan had jumped through hoops of fire to convince Inez to hold off telling her supervisor about the fight in the dealership parking lot. She had capitulated, warning Joan she would not overlook an assault again. Since then, they developed a tighter relationship. But a close relationship with Inez might not be the asset it appeared. Joan compared it to a binary star, actually two stars in different orbits circling a central point. The problem with close binaries was that one star often destroyed the other.

"How are you doing?" Inez asked.

"The better question is what am I doing? Is anything I'm doing right?"

"I don't know. Is it?" Inez grabbed a bottle of water out of the refrigerator and raised it for permission.

Joan nodded.

"Want one?" Inez asked.

"No, thanks."

"Take one. You have to stay hydrated." Inez winked and tossed a bottle to Joan. "Are you having second thoughts about going forward from here? Once you're in Bill's bed, you're in. No going back."

"If I back out, I go to jail," Joan said, setting the unopened bottle on the table. "All the time we've known each other, Duncan did everything he could to keep me out of jail. If that happens, it would make all his efforts for nothing."

"You're going into a dangerous situation. This can't be about Duncan. It has to be what you want. Do you know what that is?"

"When the devil has something you want, you dance with his demons, right?"

"Meaning?" Inez leaned on the bureau.

"To spend the rest of my life with Duncan, I have to do my time in hell."

Inez nodded and took a long swallow of water.

"Any advice?" Joan asked.

"Enjoy these few hours with your handsome husband. Don't think ahead. When I meet you tomorrow morning to drive you home, don't look back."

An hour later, teeth brushed for the third time, shaking with excitement, Joan was more than ready. Three car doors slammed. She rushed to the door.

Inez waved her back. "Don't screw this up. Arizona doesn't allow conjugal visits. We had to pull strings, call this a family reunion. Our asses are on the line here. So remember the rules I gave you—and follow them. Stand over there and wait. Let us go through the protocol."

Joan moved to the center of the room. Her heart beat so hard it constricted her breathing. The room felt smaller, yet the door seemed farther away. She wiped her sweating palms on her thighs. What would Duncan do? Rush to her? He never liked this deal, and he'd had time to think about it. Would he reject her? Maybe she was nothing more to him than twenty-four hours out of prison.

After three light raps on the door, Inez opened it to two male agents flanking Duncan. Her breath caught in her throat. Transport restraints secured his wrist cuffs to ankle cuffs. The chain was short and made him hunch forward, making him appear worn down and weak. His flexing jaw muscles meant he was concerned or anxious about something.

He held a brown paper bag and a smaller plastic bag with the Dollar Store logo. He looked down at them and nodded while the agents recited his instructions.

One agent told Duncan to face away from the door. The other agent then unlocked the restraints. They told him not to move until the door closed behind them. Inez gave Joan a supportive nod.

And they were alone.

Duncan rubbed his wrists—first one, then the other. He stood tall, looking more like himself, powerful and fit. Freckles covered his face along his neatly-edged beard.

He didn't look at her. Words jammed up in her throat. Her expectations for a blissful twenty-four hours vaporized. Rejection became too real.

She swallowed hard and said, "What do you want to do?"

He looked at her out of the corners of his eyes. A grin spread across his face. "I want to do something different. I want a bubble bath."

"I didn't know," she said. She knit her brow at this unusual request. "I didn't bring any—"

He raised the plastic bag. "I did." He clamped his arms around her and kissed her hard and long.

His touch heated her blood, and it surged through her veins. He was there, in her arms. Pressed against each other wasn't close enough. She wanted him inside her. He broke from the kiss and tracked smaller kisses across her jaw and down her neck, stealing her breath.

"How did you get bubble bath in prison?" The words came out in a whisper.

"I had the agents stop at a Dollar Store on the way and buy some," he said between kisses.

She cupped his face in her hands, the wiry beard exciting the nerve endings in her fingers. "You got them to stop during transport? To buy bubble bath? You could charm the venom out of a snake."

"I have my moments."

"I want to make hot, sweaty love to you before our bath," she said, unbuttoning his shirt.

"Our bath?" He fought a smile. "Who said you'd be in there with me?"

Joan tilted her head. "I'll wrestle you for it."

He picked her up and threw her onto the bed, pinning her with his weight. "I win."

"Best two out of three?"

"I think you're talking a different kind of wrestling," he said, running his hand the length of her thigh.

She locked her legs around him.

"I'll take that challenge," he said. "Maybe I'll let you win."

"Smart man." She untucked his shirt and ran her hands over his bare skin. "Where did you get these clothes?"

"Inez brought them when she—"

Joan scuttled backward on the bed. "Inez visited you?"

Duncan followed her. "What the hell? You knew she stopped in."

"You two are in collusion." She stiff-armed him. "I knew it."

He finally pinned her against the headboard. "We're all in collusion, Joan. The feds, you, me, Bill, Inez. You knew that," he said, trying to keep her from getting away. "You knew she visited me, planned the sham divorce."

"She didn't tell me."

"She didn't tell you? Stop pulling away from me. If something's going on, we need to figure it out. Together."

Joan stopped struggling but remained on edge.

He gave her a peck on the forehead. "Man, you're wound tight."

The gentle gesture calmed her.

"You okay?"

She nodded.

He sat with his back to the headboard and wrapped her in his arms.

She snuggled into the embrace. "She denied being in on the divorce thing. But I knew she was."

"Let me get this straight," he said. "She visits me, tells me I have to break ties so you can move forward. To you, she denies having anything to do with it, yet she tells me she told you."

"Sounds right."

"Question is: why?"

Joan thought for a moment. Her brow relaxed. "We have twenty-four hours to figure it out. Let's do what we came here to do."

"And that is?" he asked, sliding a finger along the edge of her tee shirt and under the waistband of her jeans.

She slid a hand over his thigh. "Let me show you."

There was no foreplay. No teasing. No exploring. Pure enjoyment and quick physical release. That didn't mean there wasn't an afterglow. Joan stretched and reveled in the familiarity, pleasure, and comfort of Duncan's presence.

"That was fast. I'm sorry," he said. "That probably wasn't how you pictured this. Next time'll be better."

"I miss you, Duncan."

"I miss you, too, *nena*."

They lay together, breath synchronizing, heartbeats settling into a slower rhythm.

"That bubble bath sounds good right about now," Joan said, tracing his collarbone.

"Yes, ma'am. Coming right up." After a long kiss, Duncan slid out of bed and headed to the bathroom.

When the bathwater was ready, he sat in the tub and motioned to Joan. She slid through the layer of bubbles to the warm water and sat with her back to him. She rested her head on his shoulder.

The soapy water made their skin silky. The bubbles foamed and fizzed around them. The intimacy reaffirmed their bond.

"Once again you thought of the perfect plan," she said.

He ran his hands over her body. "You have no idea how good this feels."

"I might have an inkling."

They enjoyed being together in silence for several minutes.

"Your boyfriend came to visit me," Duncan said.

"I know. But why?" she asked, ignoring the boyfriend remark, not wanting to ruin her first moments of relaxation in a month.

"He didn't tell you?"

"He mentioned it at the family day last Sunday, that was all. He's not talkative, like you." She looked over her shoulder at Duncan. "What did he want?"

"Told me to back off. Go through with the divorce."

"He has balls telling a married man to divorce his wife."

"He claims you were out of control driving over the mountains to Phoenix. Is that true?"

"No..." She dunked a washcloth and wrung it out. "...well, maybe. I don't remember much of the ride. I was so hurt and…" She shrugged one shoulder. "…surprised."

"He said when I called you to say I didn't want a divorce, it pissed him off."

"It's not his place."

"Said he was concerned with your welfare. He seemed sincere." Duncan rested his chin in the crook of her neck. "If I'm going to hand off your safety to anyone, it would be Bill."

"Hand me off?" She twisted to look at him. "Like a puppy? Really?"

"You go through life, leaving a path of scorched earth. Someone has to follow you, replanting the trees."

"Very funny." She pinched his thigh. "You didn't say that when you were kidnapped and I rescued you."

"That time was more like mass extinction." He settled her back against his chest. "I didn't say I *want* you to be with him. But you'll be safe with him. Until we're together again."

"I've always trusted you, but I don't know about this."

"He cussed me out with pure hatred," Duncan said. "When the conversation turned to you, he changed."

"How?"

"I don't know…his voice lowered. His face softened."

"He showed you emotion? He never shows me any emotion."

"Use that. Get him to open up to you."

"I don't know," she said. "He's a tough biker. The real thing."

"If he thinks he's going to lose you, he'll open up. I think he's in love with you."

"I'm just a conquest."

"Even more important to keep him sure of where you stand. He has to feel like he's in control, and part of that is controlling you."

Duncan was right. Bill had shown his interest in her in bold, lusty ways and in small, gentle ways over the past month, but she hadn't known what to do about it—a perfect example of how Duncan's strategy and her instincts were a deadly combination. After today, she would have to step up and play both parts.

She ran the washcloth down her leg, thinking through the meaning of Duncan's revelation. "If you're right, and he loves me, it makes my job easier...and harder."

"How so?" he whispered.

His breath tickled her ear, sending a wave of longing through her body.

"A man in love is easy to manipulate, but it'll make it difficult to turn him over to the authorities."

"You aren't falling for him, are you?"

She turned slightly to look into Duncan's eyes. "Hell, no."

"Toughen up that soft spot," Duncan said, tapping her over her heart.

"Why is everything so difficult?"

"If it was easy—"

"I know, it wouldn't be happening to me."

He nuzzled her and inhaled deeply. "I forgot how good you smell. Like flowers and vanilla."

"I forgot how good you feel," she murmured.

Resting his chin on her shoulder, he thumbed the birth control patch on her arm. "Have you had sex with him yet?"

"He's not my boyfriend," she said.

Duncan wasn't jealous by nature, but his question hinted that their separation had weakened his confidence in their relationship. She couldn't let that happen. Not now.

"You didn't answer my question."

"No." She glanced over her shoulder at him. "I wanted to make love to you before I did."

He tightened his arms around her.

"It goes against our vows and everything I believe. If I could succeed any other way..." Her voice trailed off, getting lost in the understanding that wishes weren't reality.

"I know how you are with oaths. You're an honorable woman, Mrs. Archer."

"I'm not." She winced at a flashback of firefights, the men she killed—some with her bare hands—and the deal she made in a desperate attempt to weasel out of jail time.

"You *are* honorable. It's what I love most about you. Remember to always keep your goal in mind. Honor is lost when it becomes self-interest." His chin poked into her shoulder as he spoke. "What you do has to be done for the greater good to maintain the honor in what you do."

"Hmm, that's nice. Who said that?"

"I just did. Didn't you hear me?" He splashed water at her.

She splashed him back. And they splashed each other until he grabbed her and pulled her into his arms. She settled into his embrace, acutely aware of his chest against her shoulders. She stroked his hands resting on her belly.

"Just one more thing," he said. "Humor me so I can relax in lock-up."

"We have plenty of time to talk. I just want to mellow out with you."

"This is nice, isn't it?"

"Mmmm." The silence got to her, and, after a minute she asked, "What did you want to talk about?"

"Did you set up your exit plan, like I told you to?"

"I contacted Stillwater," she said. "They assured me they would do what they could to support me. Send protection if I needed it. Run interference. You know, stuff like that."

"Seen any operators?"

"You said I wouldn't see them." The memory of the black sedan on Route 10 popped into her head. "Maybe I saw one of them."

"When?"

"I broke down on Route Ten. Some Mongols stopped. A man drove by. I got the distinct feeling he was there because of me. If it was Stillwater, how did they know where I was?"

"Tracking app probably."

"They never came for my phone."

"Was there a time when your phone was missing?"

"Yes. There *was* a time." And it had miraculously reappeared in her backpack. "Shit."

"What?"

"There was this time when two men wandered backstage at Leather and Lace. After that, my phone showed up. Maya and I may have roughed up a couple Stillwater operators."

"Maya?"

"One of the dancers. She hit him in the head with one of her stiletto heels."

"Tough dancers at that club. Would've liked to have seen that. Back to Stillwater. What did they say exactly?"

"No details. I think things are dicey since the feds raided the Stillwater headquarters in Yonkers."

"I'll send a secure email."

"From prison?"

Duncan put his lips next to her ear. "Venom from a snake, remember?"

"Now I remember why I love you."

"*Now* you remember? Not when I made love to you a few minutes ago?"

"I was too far gone in mind-blowing physical bliss to think about love."

"Still a smartass, I see. Mind-blowing physical bliss is on the agenda for the next go-round."

She slid the washcloth up his thigh. "In that case, I can't wait."

"I might make you seduce me," he said, followed by a nip on her ear.

"It's not seduction if the other person is willing and anxious."

"Water's getting cold." He kissed her neck. "We have to make a move soon."

"Okay." She stood and stepped out of the tub. The slippery bath soap helped her slip from his grasp before he could stop her. "Here's me seducing you: get out of the tub and onto the bed."

Duncan grinned and sprang out of the tub wet and naked. And virile. "Yes, ma'am."

಄಄಄

When her phone rang in the morning, it incorporated itself into her dream. She snuggled against Duncan, and he hugged her tighter. The ringing phone became real.

She reached for it.

"We'll be there in an hour," Inez said. "This is how it's going to work. Two agents will cuff Duncan and take him out of the room. When they are in the car, you and I can leave. Do you understand these instructions?"

Joan dropped her head onto Duncan's muscular arm. "Yes."

"One more hour," Inez added.

"Thanks." Joan dropped the phone onto the bed. She sunk into Duncan's arms. "They'll be here in an hour for you."

"Wanna make love again?" he asked.

"I'm too sore."

"Okay. Let's just spend our last few minutes holding each other." They shared each other's warmth for several seconds before Duncan said, "Is there anybody you trust?"

"Trust. In what way?"

"Life or death kinda way."

"Maybe Little Al and Carol. Flora and Ruby. And I have to trust Inez, right?"

"You don't have to do anything."

"You're scaring me," she said. "What if I can't pull this off?"

"Trust your instincts. You'll do fine."

"I'm afraid I'll say something that'll get me killed."

"Don't worry, *nena*. Challenge sharpens your instincts. Focuses your skills."

She snorted. "If it doesn't kill me, it'll make me stronger?"

He nuzzled her neck. "You being any stronger than you are scares the shit out of me."

She would miss his scratchy, coarse beard. "I don't feel strong."

"You're like Dumbo," he murmured.

"Are you saying my ears are big?"

"Wise ass. You know what I'm saying. Dumbo thought he couldn't fly unless he had the magic feather. There was no magic. He could fly without it."

He tickled her until she giggled and turned to face him. His face got serious. "Come back to me, *nena*."

"What if I'm not the same person when this is over?"

"Come to me, whoever you are."

"Evil has a way of weakening us. Scarring us," she said. "Remaking us until we're unrecognizable."

"Okay, Negative Nellie. I promise, if I don't like you, I'll toss you out on your beautiful butt. Feel better?"

Joan draped a leg over his hip and held on tight.

Exactly an hour later Inez and two other agents arrived.

"One last kiss?" Duncan asked the agents.

"You had twenty-four hours," Inez said.

"Okay," one of the other agents said. "Make it quick."

Duncan put his arms around Joan and squeezed. After a long, passionate kiss, his lips brushed her ear when he whispered, "Trust your instincts."

"Time's up," one of the agents said. "Hands on the wall, Archer."

After frisking Duncan, the agents cuffed him and escorted him out of her sight.

"Don't watch him leave," Inez said. "It's better that way."

Joan watched anyway, wanting to see him to the last second, knowing there would be no more visits until this ordeal was over. When he got into the car, she turned from the window.

"Got everything?" Inez asked.

Joan nodded and followed her into the morning light.

ↁↁↁ

The return trip to Phoenix was quiet. As Inez drove the car around the arid, barren mountain curves and through the rock cuts, Joan did as Inez said, she didn't look back, spending the better part of the trip laying plans to make headway in her relationship with Bill. In time, Inez dropped her off at Bill's house a little later than past visits. Joan didn't worry about the time. Bill was on a run to Prescott and wasn't expected until later. She unlocked the front door, anticipating some time alone to unwind and go over her plans.

She tossed her house key on the table inside the front door, lost in thought, not paying attention to her surroundings. She looked up from her thoughts and stopped short. Bill sat with both hands resting on the dining room table, backlit by the sun beaming through sliding glass door. As she approached him and could see his face more clearly, the day-old stubble around the edges of his beard and the dark rings under his eyes spoke of trouble. His lips were pressed together, eyes hard and staring. The neutral expression was gone. He was openly showing emotion—anger.

"What happened?" she asked.

"Everyone blows smoke at one time or another," he said. "Hell, I've done it myself in the course of business."

Her gaze slid to a bulge under his leather cut. He never wore a holstered gun around the house. Her eyes caught his.

"I can deal with blowing smoke," he continued. "I just don't like it when my woman blows it up my ass."

Her lifeblood drained out of her face. "What do you mean?" Her voice sounded hollow in her inner emptiness. Her head reeled from a dozen thoughts flashing through her mind in a millisecond. He knew she was a confidential informant. Or about the conjugal visit. Or the truth about Inez. Or the deal with the feds. Shit, how many secrets did she have?

"You have something to tell me." His eyes narrowed. "If you tell me now, I won't have to drag it out of you. Believe me, darlin', neither of us wants that."

She moved forward, carefully choosing her steps and her words. "I don't know what you're talking about."

A beautiful night turned into a horror show. There was no way to contact Inez. Tell her things were sliding off the rails. Joan was on her own.

"By now you shoulda realized I'm a big player in the biker community. I'm not some half-ass president of a club of wannabes. I'm a heavy hitter with influence across this whole area."

"I never thought you were small time."

He slammed his fist on the table. "Then don't treat me that way."

She jumped at the noise. Each heartbeat pressed against her eardrum. She inched closer.

Bill's glare followed her and held her eyes as she slid into the chair to his left.

"Tell me what's gotten you so worked up," she said in a softened tone. Duncan's words: '*I think he loves you*' calmed her. Her nervous energy eased, leaving enough to keep her focused. Confidence swelled through her.

"Let's start with what went down on Route Ten." Bill tapped his fingers on the table. "If you tell the truth, things will go better for you."

"That happened three days ago. What happened since then?"

"Better start talkin', darlin'."

"I broke down. Three Mongols stopped. Little Al got there just in time. That's it."

"Why'd you say I called Little Al?"

"Al said you did."

"Stop lying, Joan."

"Then what was he doing out there on Route Ten?"

"His business is not your business. Let's get back to the meeting on the side of the road. That *does* concern you. Al said you had a long conversation with Brock."

"Who's Brock?" She knew Switch's real name from her briefings, but she had to tread carefully. Bill's bullshit antenna was way up and functioning.

"My fucking son, damn it."

"He said his name was Switch. I was trying to get him to call you. Maybe enough time had passed—"

"Not that, 'bout how he happened to stop while you were broke down."

"It was by chance. Why? What did Little Al say?"

"What's going on between you and Brock?"

"Nothing. He—"

"You never met him before?"

"No. Never." She got up and paced away a few steps before turning around, her hands on her hips. "Whatever you have to say, Bill, spit it the fuck out."

Bill glared at her for several seconds. Either it was a response to her insolence, or he wasn't as sure of himself, switching gears, changing his approach. She hoped for the latter.

"Al says he heard rumors about you working with the Mongols. Then he rolls up on you in a tight conversation with Brock. Too close for strangers."

"Close? I thought he was going to attack me. I jabbed my fingers in his eye to get him to back off."

"He put his hands on you?"

"Yes, and if Little Al hadn't come along when he did, Switch would be dead now."

"By you?" Bill asked.

"By you." She leaned on the table across from him. "At least I hope you'd defend my honor. Even from your son."

The silence was unbearable, full of unspoken words. Joan stood firm. She would *not* speak first. If Bill had something to say, he'd better speak up.

"You're good," Bill said with a derisive chuckle. "Takes balls to stand there and lie to my face."

"I can only tell the truth," she said. "The onus is on you." She walked past him to look out the glass doors. The move brought her closer to him. Close enough to defend herself if he reached for his gun.

Bill drummed his fingers on the table. "You don't have any business dealings with Brock? Nothin' that goes against the Demon Brotherhood."

"No, Bill. I do not. Never met him before last Thursday."

"If you think I'm gonna believe you over a Brother, you're delusional."

"When I see Little Al, I'm going to give him a piece of my mind."

"Not your place."

"He lied. He owes me an explanation."

"Not a word. I catch you talkin' to him about this, it won't end well for you."

Bill's face was hard, unyielding. She decided to let it go for now. Choose her battles. Let this situation play out, save her strength to act on something more threatening. He had used the plural—lies. This wasn't over. The next one might be the big one, the one that spelled terminal trouble.

Bill studied her for several long, uncomfortable seconds. "Anything else to tell me?" It was stated like a question, but he wasn't asking.

She relaxed a little. He didn't know why she was in Phoenix. He would have said it outright, with other Brothers around to take her down. She looked past him. The house was deadly silent.

"No one else is here," Bill said. "It's just you and me."

You, me, and the gun under your cut. He said he knew what the federal agencies were doing. The conjugal visit had entailed several agents. One must have leaked information.

He reached inside his cut.

She braced herself. She only had to beat his finger on the trigger and his inner command to pull it. But he was no amateur. If he pulled his piece, he wouldn't hesitate to shoot.

He brought out papers with a blue cover sheet. "Look familiar?"

She stared at the divorce papers, unable to believe this was the other lie. Disbelief mixed with relief made her breaths short and shallow. If this wasn't about the conjugal visit or her being a confidential informant, she might get out of this alive. She controlled her breathing. It was no time to get ahead of herself. "You went through my things?" she asked, hoping indignation would sidetrack him.

"Does this look familiar?" he asked again.

"Yes." She knelt on one knee next to him. "I wanted to make sure it was what I really wanted before telling you." She kept her eyes on his, avoiding the bulge in his cut. "You understand that, don't you?"

"You signed them. That's 'bout as final as it gets, darlin'."

"I could have ripped them up if I changed my mind."

"When were you gonna tell me? Didn't need a legal filing, just some indication you were cutting your old man loose." He slapped the papers on the table. "This is more than I needed, 'cept you didn't see fit to tell me."

She touched his arm. "I wanted to be sure."

He looked at her hand then at her, but he didn't pull away.

Joan looked away from his gaze first. "You wouldn't want me to give you the 'go' signal then back out, would you?"

"All I want is honesty. Sharing things like couples do."

"We aren't a couple," she said. "Not really. Not yet."

"I was honest with you. You knew where this was heading."

"That's bullshit, and you know it," she said, standing and pointing down at him. "You're out almost every night until after midnight. I don't know where you go, who you're with, or what you do."

He glared into her eyes for several seconds until he looked away to check his phone for the time. "Gotta go. Waitin' for you made me late for an important meeting with Fitz." He stood and walked past her, bumping her with his shoulder.

She ignored the belligerent gesture. "Just like that. You're gonna walk out?"

"My ass is grass." Bill grabbed his keys. "Fitz is death on lateness."

Before she could say anything, the door to the garage slammed. While his Harley rumbled to life and faded as he drove out of the residential area, she rubbed her shoulder. Fucking Little Al. He came on like a friend, even inviting her to his house for dinner. Saying he'd be there for her. Protect her. Then lied. Right when she was ready to set her hooks in Bill. Little Al's timing was perfect—if his purpose was to trip her up. She would confront him and find out why he lied. No doubt about that.

First, she had to reel in Bill.

Joan texted Inez: *Need to talk. Meet for coffee?*

She flopped backward on her bed, legs hanging over the side. Two minutes passed. Then five. No response. *Fucking Inez. She's a pain in the ass, and when I need her she's not answering her phone.* Joan curled up on the bed and tried to doze, but the last of the adrenaline kept her thoughts racing.

Now that Bill found the divorce papers, would he ever trust her? He accused her of working with the Mongols. It wouldn't be long before he realized how close he came to the truth. He walked out on her, but she wasn't in the clear. Through her thoughts, she listened for the growl of distant Harleys approaching the house—several Brothers coming to drag her away to a painful death. There was time to get away, but there was too much riding on her success to pack her stuff and get out while she had the chance.

By walking out, he gave her a chance to run. A Brother could be waiting to follow her. See where she went, or who she ran to. Kearney had taught her how to shake a tail. Any tail the bikers set up would be easy to beat, almost unfair. But running would do no good unless she went far and fast. The Bureau would pull out the stops to locate her to send her to jail. And Bill was right when he said he wasn't a low-level president of a half-ass club. These guys were highly respected and trusted by the Hells Angels, who were everywhere. Besides, if she left, she'd never learn how Bill got his information or obtain evidence of his club's illegitimate business. She had to play this out, regain Bill's trust, and gather enough evidence to put him away. It was the only way to tie this up and get home free.

In time, the adrenaline drained from her system, leaving her fatigued. She shuffled through the empty house that seemed darker and quieter without Bill. Even his threatening demeanor or his anger would be better than the hollowness. She grabbed a bottle of water out of the fridge and rolled it across her forehead. The brain fog lifted enough to overcome her paranoia.

Stillwater was an option, but she didn't want to pull that trigger if she didn't have to. Mooky was a possible ally. They seemed to have hit it off, but, although retired from the club, DBMC blood still ran through his veins.

She was stuck with Inez.

When Inez finally called at five-thirty, her words were clipped, her sentences abrupt, as if Joan's operation-threatening event had imposed on her plans. They agreed to meet at a Mexican cantina in South Mountain Village, hoping no one spoke English well enough to understand their conversation.

Energized by something to do, Joan rushed to the garage. She opened the door and remembered her bike was still at the shop where Bill's mechanics were dragging their feet repairing it. How long does it take to replace a broken oil line? Bill's precious Harley Davidson Panhead sat there teasing her. It was off limits. Only Bill drove it and only if the forecast called for severe sunshine, and only for short distances. But the bike's vintage beauty tantalized her, tempting her to go against her better judgment. How would he know? She plucked the keys off their hook and turned them over in her hand. *If anything happens to this bike...well, I'm already on the expressway to hell. It's a one-way trip. I can only go there once.*

The aroma of cilantro and mesquite-scented smoke greeted Joan when she arrived at the cantina. The walls, once bright yellow and turquois, were faded and water spotted. Several plants clung to life in the scorching storefront window.

Inez was already there, seated at a table placed against the wall in the back of the cantina. She popped several fried tortilla chips into her mouth when Joan pulled out a rickety bentwood chair opposite her, turned it so her back would be to the wall, and sat down. She looked past Joan.

"No. I wasn't followed," Joan said. She started to talk about Bill, but Inez shook her head to indicate no talking yet.

A dark-haired waitress appeared. Joan eyed Inez's Corona, thinking how much she could use a drink, but after thinking about Bill's motorcycle parked out front, she opted for coffee. She placed the order in Spanish, which brought a brief smile to the waitress' face before leaving to retrieve the drink.

When the coffee came, and they were finally alone, Inez said, "So tell me what happened."

"I came home to find Bill seated at the dining room table, a gun under his cut—he never carries around the house. I knew something was up. He tried to get me to tell him what was going on, but I didn't want to say anything until I figured out what he knew."

"Good. Go on."

"He started with a minor lie, about something I said, which wasn't a lie. Then he moved on to something Little Al told him, which was a lie, and dangerously close to the truth."

Inez leaned her forearms on the table and studied Joan. The corners of her mouth tightened. "Start with the lie that wasn't a lie."

"Little Al said Bill called him to tell him I broke down on the side of the road. You know last Thursday when the three Mongols stopped?"

"What about it?"

"When I said that to Bill, he looked at Al then closed down. Put on that damn neutral face. At the time, I thought it was odd. Turns out I was right. Bill didn't call him."

"Why would he lie about that?" Inez asked, dipping a tortilla chip in salsa.

"Good question." Joan sipped the sweet, cinnamon-flavored coffee and thought about Inez's reaction—her voice pattern changed slightly, indicating deception, or that Joan's nerves were still on edge. "I think something's going on with Little Al."

Inez's eyes flashed up to Joan's. "Any ideas?"

That was not the response Joan expected. She scrutinized Inez's face when she answered. "No. But I'm going to find out."

"Keep me updated."

"Will do." Joan moved on, all senses on high alert. "Then Bill said Little Al accused me of working for the Mongols, being inserted into the DBMC. Can you believe that? How close is that to the truth?"

"What did Little Al say exactly?"

"He heard rumors, and said I stood too close to Switch for it to be a chance meeting. Talking too intense, or some shit like that."

"Were you?"

Again, Inez's tone was off. This time too abrupt.

"Switch was all over me," Joan said. "But it wasn't about business. I finger-jabbed him in the eye to get him to back off."

Inez winced. "Bet that didn't go over well."

"He threatened revenge." Joan thought about the time Bill

told her he wanted his pound of flesh. She raised her cup, and before taking a sip, she added, "Like father, like son, right?"

"These boys play for keeps," Inez said. "Watch yourself around them."

"Anyway, Bill reached into his cut. I thought he knew everything and was gonna take me out. But he pulled out the divorce papers and asked why I didn't tell him about them. I couldn't believe that was it—what pissed him off. You should have seen him." Joan looked around at the other patrons before continuing. "I think he was upset about me not being open and honest with him, maybe even more than the lie he thought I told him. What an idiot I am to have signed those papers already."

Inez shrugged. "Maybe, but not necessarily bad."

"How so?"

"You have two options in a situation like this," Inez said after a short pause. "You can back out. It'll void your deal, but you don't have that much time hanging over your head. And you'll be safe. Or, you can invest more fully in the part you're playing. The danger ramps up, but you'll get what you got into this deal for."

"Backing out isn't an option." Joan turned the cup in the saucer, knowing there was only one option for her. "First, I have to get Bill back on track and get him to trust me. Get him to take me to bed, which is going to be more difficult after this fiasco—or if he finds out I drove his Panhead here."

"Your file said you were a chance-taker. If anything happens to that bike…" Inez shook her head. "Do you purposely do things to compromise your safety?"

"When have I been safe since I left Albuquerque?" Joan asked, glancing up as two Mexicans sat at a table near the front of the cantina. One stared at her, the Gringo woman. She held their gaze until they pulled out menus.

"Go on," Inez said.

Joan returned her attention to Inez. "Second, from here on out, I'm gonna have to be open and honest with him. Tell him everything. Without telling him *everything*."

"That's a slim path. Did he tell you to leave?"

"No, thank God. That's a good sign."

"Maybe yes." Inez took a sip of her beer. "Or maybe he's going to have you killed. Stay alert. Have your phone ready to call for help. I'll post an agent nearby, but you're going to have to be ready to fend them off for a couple minutes until he can get there."

Joan snorted. "When seconds count, help is minutes away?"

"Yeah, something like that."

Joan poked her thumbnail at a chip in the cup handle. This ordeal sure got shitty in a hurry. She'd known from the start it wouldn't be easy, but she expected to get her hooks into Bill before things slid sideways. Now she had to get to work and pull him back in.

"Let him cool down," Inez said, leaning forward. "Play it cool. Wait for him to come to you."

"Sitting around waiting for the phone to ring like a teenager doesn't sound right to me," Joan said.

"If I was the one undercover, I'd play it cool. Not push him. But you're so fucking smart, go ahead and call him. Tell him you want him, can't live without him. See how that works for you."

"If I don't talk to him, I can't know what's going on in that thick biker head of his." Joan turned her chair to face Inez— screw watching the door. She'd have to learn to trust Inez sometime. "And he'll know I want to make things right. And if he doesn't take my calls, just maybe I can tell what's going on by how the Brothers respond to my calls."

"You have it all figured out, don't you?" Inez said, leaning back in her chair. She took another swig of beer. "Make the damn calls, if you think that's what will work."

Joan picked up her phone and thumbed in a number. She shook her head to indicate to Inez it went to voicemail. "Hey, Bill, call me. Please. Let's talk this through. Come home to me."

"'Come home to me.' Nice touch," Inez said.

Joan thought back to Duncan's words that morning—it seemed so long ago now—when he had said, "Come back to me, *nena.*" Those five words had been powerful enough to strengthen her resolve to get this deal done. But would they speak to Bill? She thumbed in Dagger's number. He didn't know where Bill was, but he'd tell him she called.

Joan looked at Inez. "It sounded like Bill wasn't at the clubhouse. Dagger didn't sound evasive."

"These guys are good at covering for each other. So you never know."

"But the word will get to Bill that I'm searching for him." Joan thumbed another number into the phone.

"Who're you calling now?"

While the phone rang, Joan mouthed Blaze's name. "Hey, it's me. You seen Bill?...No?...No, everything's not okay. There was a misunderstanding, and he walked out before I could explain myself...No, it's personal business, but I really need to talk to him. If you see him, *please* have him call me...Thanks." She hung up. "He says he'll tell Bill I called. We're both veterans. That could put him in my corner."

"Don't count on it. The DBMC bond is stronger than any other bond, even than with their kids."

"Maybe I should call Garbage? If Bill goes to Leather and Lace but sits at the bar rather than heading back to Blaze's office, Garbage would know Bill's there, but Blaze might not."

"Two calls to the strip club will look like desperation," Inez said. "But you know how to work a situation better than me."

Joan ignored Inez's sarcasm and made the call. After a short conversation, she said. "He's going to call Bill. That must mean Bill's not at Leather and Lace."

"Yeah, or he's going to walk down the hall to Blaze's office to tell him."

"Either way, I win."

"Maybe you're winning. But you're walking the edge of the sword here. Your phone calls may not sway Bill if he's planning to kill you."

"Thank you for your words of comfort and support," Joan said before finishing her coffee and motioning for another cup.

"Just keeping it real." Inez indicated she wanted another beer.

While they waited for their refills, Joan called Bill again, but didn't leave a message. He'd see her number in his missed calls list.

She dialed Mooky. "Hey, Mooky, what're you doing today? I'm at loose ends and thought I'd drop by."

"I have company."

"I understand."

"Are you in trouble? Is everything okay?" he asked.

"No, everything's not all right. Bill walked out after a misunderstanding, and he's not answering my calls."

"If I see him, I'll tell him to give you a call, darlin'."

Joan smiled across the table at Inez. "I'll let you go, then, Mook. See you Tuesday as usual."

The phone got quiet with faint, muffled talking. He came back on the line. "Make it tomorrow. Have an appointment on Tuesday."

"Tomorrow then." The line went dead. Joan locked eyes with Inez. "He's at Mooky's."

"How do you know?"

"Mooky called me darlin'. He never calls me that, but Bill does. He was telling me Bill was there, without him catching on. It's worth a try."

Joan scraped her chair back.

"Wait," Inez said. "You can't go there."

"I have to take care of this before it's too late."

"You want to string this out."

"I need to get over there."

"If you go running over to Mooky's house, you'll give away someone who's supporting you. You'll put him in a tough position. He gave up Bill, which tells me he's got one foot in your court. Don't blow that."

"Why do we want to stretch this out?"

"Remember the set-up in Albuquerque? Make Bill come to you." Inez emphasized each of the last three words. "That gives you a stronger position. There's something else going on here. Think about it. Mooky didn't invite you over, although he could have walked into another room to tell you. He hinted Bill was with family, not at the clubhouse, planning your disappearance."

They clicked bottle-to-cup in affirmation of Inez's statement.

"I better get back to the house then, before he returns." Joan took a couple gulps of the sweet, milky coffee and stood.

"I'll wait a few minutes before I leave," Inez said.

Joan leaned in and whispered, "And make plans for that backup, just in case…"

Inez flashed her brilliantly white teeth. "Of course."

❧❧❧

The sun worked its way around the house, shadows lengthening into twilight. Waiting was not Joan's strong point, and it took every ounce of her willpower to stay off Bill's bike to hunt him down. She wiped down the bike, vacuumed and dusted, cleaned her bathroom, packed up the garbage, and dragged the trash container to the curb. When another round of calls produced no new information, she started to clean the kitchen and looked out the window. The hot tub caught her eye. She grabbed the pH test kit and headed to the backyard.

Two weeks ago, she had Googled the care and maintenance of a hot tub and purchased the chemicals necessary to keep the water clean and sanitary. Bill had sent Youngblood over to clean out the debris and pump out the stagnant water before refilling it. While Youngblood read the instructions, Joan measured and poured in the chemicals. Over the past couple weeks, she'd monitored the water and adjusted the chemicals in an attempt to get the pH and chlorine at the right level.

The water was perfect, and she ran inside, stripped off all her clothes, and, lacking a bathing suit, put on a pair of spandex biking shorts and a tee shirt. If Bill was going to be a prick and stay away, that didn't mean she couldn't unwind in the soothing hot tub. As an afterthought, she put a carving knife under a towel placed just the right distance to the right of her head. She placed her phone on top of the towel.

Fifteen minutes later, she made another round of calls. All of them went straight to voicemail. They weren't going to get rid of her that easily. She dialed Ruby.

Ruby's gravelly voice answered.

"Hey, Ruby. It's me, Joan." She could picture Ruby on the stool at the end of the bar at the DBMC clubhouse.

"I was wondering when you'd finally contact me." Ruby coughed, the rattling cough of a heavy smoker, before returning to the phone. "What the hell took you so long?" A tough seventy-something ex-biker chick, she took no shit from the bikers and poured a mean drink. Joan loved her.

"Since I'm not a member of the militia anymore, I don't feel comfortable hanging out in the club's bar."

"What the hell is wrong with you, girl? You come down here and have a drink anytime you want. No one will give you a hard time long as I'm here."

"Hey, I've been calling Dagger and Blaze to get a hold of Bill, but nobody's answering their phones."

"They're all at church," Ruby said, using the biker term for a club meeting.

Joan's breath caught in her throat. "Something special going on?"

"Not that I know of—not that they tell me anything." She snorted. "Like I'd go running to the ATF or FBI with the information. It's just their monthly meeting. They're gonna patch-over a club in Huachuca City, but they been talking about that for months like a buncha old biddies."

"I gotta go, Ruby. Tell Bill I called."

"Get your ass down here."

"You got it." Joan disconnected the call, climbed out of the tub, and shivered from the cool November air. A couple shots of Avion would warm her, but she wanted to stay clear-headed and steady just in case Bill sent a couple of bikers to execute her. But from the way Ruby talked, it sounded like things were okay. All she needed was for him to come home so they could straighten things out.

She grabbed a bottle of water to dilute the two shots of Avion. After observing the quiet neighborhood beyond Bill's front window for several minutes, she slipped back into the warm, bubbling hot tub. It chased away the shivers. *Make Bill come to you.* Joan closed her eyes and hoped Inez wasn't misleading her.

꿍

The chair squeaked as Bill rocked in it and thought about the meeting that just adjourned. He was pleased with how far the Brotherhood had come in the last year. It was on the road to increasing its ranks. The patched-over clubs needed guidance, but that was to be expected. The move to owning legitimate businesses turned out to be a good one, and the MC was on the cusp of buying another. The resulting stability encouraged the Angels to entrust the Brotherhood with more responsibilities, which meant increased shares in the Angels' dealings. Bigger numbers, better revenue, the DBMC was on the rise.

On the downside, growing dissension in the leadership was troublesome.

"You were quiet in the meeting," Bill said to Blaze. "Didn't voice your opinion on the Mongols encroaching on our territory. Think I'm chasin' shadows?"

"Not sure the Mongols have their eyes on our area," Blaze said. "They'd have to take on the Angels. It'd be messy."

"Can't deny they're here," Bill said.

"Copy that. Question is: what're they up to?"

"Wish I knew." Bill thought about Little Al's uneasiness. "Little Al's been edgy lately. Think he'll come around. Loop us in?"

"He woulda done it already."

"Any other Brothers backin' Al?" Bill asked. Discord was new to the Brotherhood. He had felt the shift but ignored it, attributing it to the aftermath of the federal investigation a year ago. He now found himself behind the curve, forced to walk a hard line.

"Heard some grumblings. Not enough to break ranks." Blaze ran a hand over his flattened mohawk. "Gotta nip it quick, Prez. Be ready to make some examples if we have to."

"Think it has anything to do with Joan?"

"Still think it started before she got here. Her being here seems to've put him on edge, though."

"I agree. Thought I knew him," Bill said. "He's the last Brother I'd suspect of goin' against the MC."

"Copy that."

Blaze had just returned from a meet-up with the president of the San Bernardino chapter of the Mongols Motorcycle Club. The information he learned suggested a troubled future for the Brotherhood if Bill didn't get Little Al back into the fold. Switch was putting family before the Mongols. Not a good move in any biker club.

"Why'd he lie about her?" Bill asked. His decision to bring Joan to Phoenix was still the right one. Given another chance, he'd do the same thing.

"Gotta ask *him* that."

The expected knock came at the door.

"There's your chance," Blaze added.

"You ready?" Bill asked.

Blaze nodded.

"Come," Bill said.

"What did you just do?" Little Al asked, crossing his arms.

"Close the door and sit down," Bill said, indicating the chair next to Blaze.

Little Al squeezed into the chair. "After what I told you about Joan, you still claimed her. She's in tight now."

"That's family business," Bill said. "Don't have anything to do with the club."

"Wanna clue me in as to what you told Bill?" Blaze asked.

"Already told *him*," Al said, gesturing toward Bill with a nod.

"I want to hear it from you."

Little Al scratched his beard, as if taking time to choose the right tone. "Word is: she's been inserted into the DBMC. The Mongols would have the most to gain, and 'cos of Bill's all-out search for her over the past year, she's the best choice to get inside. Sorry, Prez, but you set yourself up."

Bill tucked his chin, stroked his beard, and frowned at Little Al, wondering if the Mongols told him about Blaze's meet-up with Gabo, their president. Either he was holding that information to use later, or he wasn't in the Mongols' loop.

Little Al stared back at Bill.

Bill waited, relaxed and confident in his authority. Voices and laughter of Brothers in the hallway intruded on the silence in the office. The voices faded, leaving the faint thump of blues-rock music in the party room down the hall.

Al continued to stare at Bill for several seconds before breaking the silence. "Look, Prez, my job's club security. If the feds find we're harboring a fugitive, it'll be a death blow for the club. She's toxic." He leaned forward. "That's my call. You know I'm right."

Bill motioned for Blaze to tell Little Al about his trip to San Bernardino.

"I met-up with Gabo," Blaze began. "Says he doesn't know Joan. Never heard of her till Switch reported back that he met her."

"They wouldn't out their snitch," Little Al said. "They're notorious liars. You believe Gabo over a Brother?"

"Wanna explain where you got your intel?" Blaze asked.

Little Al stood. The combination of his size and anger shrink-wrapped the room around them. "It's your call, Prez. I had my say. I'm not responsible for any fallout from this."

Bill traced his moustache where it met his goatee and thought about Joan interacting with the low-life Mongols. He didn't like the vision of her with them, or the idea of her working with them. What would be her motive? What would come of her living with him, but working for them? Keep him distracted? But from what?

He looked up at Little Al. "Where'd you get your information?"

Little Al put a hand on the doorknob and turned to face Bill. "Didn't want to meddle with your personal life. It was for the good of the club."

When they were alone, Bill asked, "Think she's a snitch?"

"We don't know where she was over the past year. Coulda

been in Southern Cal with the Mongols. Would explain why we couldn't find her."

"Didn't answer my question about his source, did he?"

"Roger that," Blaze said.

Bill rocked in his chair, mulling over the short conversation with Little Al. "Do you think he knew about your meeting with Gabo?"

"Couldn't tell, but if I had to guess, I'd say no."

"Tells me he's not cozy with the Mongols." Bill thought about Little Al's waning attention to the management of Sun Valley Custom Rides. The first couple of months, he did well. But a few months ago, Bill noticed things going wrong. No attention to ordering parts, invoicing, payroll. Late to work. Out on Route 10 when he should have been at the shop managing it.

"Ideas?" Bill asked Blaze.

"Youngblood's close to Al. He's full-patch and looking for responsibilities."

Bill shook his head. "He came from the Strykers. Hasn't been around long enough to investigate someone in leadership. Send him to Albuquerque. Ask around about Joan."

"I'll send Slo Mo with him," Blaze said.

Bill ran a finger across his upper lip, pushing aside his moustache while he thought about the original DBMC members, checking off who would investigate Little Al without tipping him off. He looked at Blaze, fighting a smile. "You're gonna think I'm crazy."

"Try me."

"Joan was close with Little Al before going on the run. Task her with finding out what's going on with him."

Blaze thought about it for a minute. "You might be right. Test 'em by what they say about each other. But this could be trouble, not only in the club but at home."

"A battle's brewing anyway." Bill stood, indicating the discussion was over.

"Gonna stay for a coupla drinks?" Blaze asked, getting up and stretching his legs.

Bill thought about Joan—his feelings for her and Little

Al's accusation. "Better get home. Tell Joan the news."

"Remember what happened the last time you tried to make her do something she didn't want to do?"

"This time'll be different," Bill said, rubbing his neck, thinking about the time he drove her into the desert. After that, his neck muscles were tight for months. Even now, when under stress, they'd tighten up.

Blaze grinned and put a hand on Bill's shoulder. "Good luck, Brother. But if it goes bad, can I have the Panhead?"

CHAPTER 11

The moan of the garage door snapped Joan's eyes open. She got out of the hot tub and listened. The door in the hallway opened and closed. She took a couple steps toward the house, inhaled deeply to steady her nerves, and readied herself for a confrontation.

Bill walked around the corner into the living room. The darkness of the house as seen from the patio made him look bigger than life.

Over the past month, she had seen him tired, energized, tense, and shades in between. But at that moment he looked powerful, dangerous, feral. His eyes seared her skin as they tracked over the clinging, dripping clothes that failed to hide her nakedness underneath. He locked eyes with her as he strode toward her.

"You drove the Panhead," he said.

His gaze was so intense she couldn't blink. Her heart quickened. She glanced at the towel, but the knife was too far away. She braced herself for trouble. The scent of motorcycle oil and the leather of his cut wrapped around them like a vampire's cape. He put a hand on the back of her neck.

"Checking up on me?" he asked.

"I—"

He covered her mouth with his. The kiss was hard. Passionate. His tongue traced her lips. He backed her up to the house and pressed against her—one hand behind her neck, the other on the wall beside her head—a position of dominance.

When he broke the kiss, he said, "At the meeting tonight, I cleared up this misunderstanding of whether we're a couple or not. I claimed you."

He kissed her again. His hand moved from the wall to the small of her back. The heat of his hand sent chills up her spine and heat between her thighs.

When he pulled away from her, he said, "Do you understand?"

"Yes." That one breathy word was all she could muster.

"Because I'm a nice guy, I'm giving you one chance to say 'no.' If you—"

"I thought you said you weren't a nice guy."

He placed his forehead on hers. "At least I know you listen to me."

"Every word."

"Good. I'm giving you one chance to stop me. If you don't tell me to stop, right here right now, I'll consummate my claim on you. I'll own you."

Make Bill come to you.

He cupped her face with both hands. "Say something."

He watched her tongue lick her lips, and when his eyes returned to hers, she said, "Don't ever walk out on me again."

He groaned as he kissed her, held her, owning her mouth and her body. He pulled her in tight.

She pressed herself against him, hands under his cut, gripping his back, aware his gun was no longer there.

He guided her through the kitchen, ripping off her wet tee shirt.

"Wait. I have scars."

"Too late, darlin'." He backed her up into his office. "You had your chance outside to call this off."

"You have to see them before we go any further."

"Nothing's gonna change my mind."

She pulled off his cut.

He tugged her wet shorts. "Fuck the scars."

"In that case—" She unbuckled his belt and unbuttoned his jeans. She smiled and looked up at him through her eyelashes. "Let's free Willie."

ᐛᔥᐛ

The next morning, Joan woke with Bill spooning behind her, his hands running the length of her body, his beard and moustache brushing the nape of her neck. She moaned and leaned into him.

"Free Willie." He chuckled. "You're some piece of work."

She stiffened. During her first night with Bill, she didn't think of Duncan, not even when they took time to rest and talk. He was locked up and alone, while she was on the outside in another man's bed. Bill's dominance and eagerness to satisfy her pushed her past the roadblocks of vows and moral duty. No holding back. She gave herself over to him. *Don't look back* had been Inez's words of advice, and Joan had subconsciously followed them.

She was lying in the arms of another man. Did that tarnish her honor? Was honor now merely something seen on the rear-camera video on the dashboard? Duncan's words came back to her, '*Actions have to be for the greater good to maintain the honor in what you do.*'

Duncan was her greater good.

"What's wrong?" he asked.

She'd have to think through the implications on her self-worth later. "Yesterday you were so upset about me accusing Little Al of lying and about the divorce papers. What changed?"

"I thought about what you said. How you wanted to be sure before you said anything. I decided I was sure enough for both of us."

"What about the Little Al thing?"

"A misunderstanding. It's being resolved." He kissed her neck. "Tell me about your scars."

"You saw them? In the dark?"

"I memorized every inch of your body," he said, rubbing the four-inch square scar above her left breast. "Start with this one."

"It was a Constitution Defense Legion tattoo. When I double-crossed them, they carved it off."

Bill turned her to face him. "Thought only bikers did shit like that."

Joan shrugged. "I don't like talking about my scars."

His face hardened. "Tell me about the ugly one on your stomach."

"That one and the ones on my thighs—also from the Legion. Enhanced interrogation."

"Blaze mentioned something about that. No wonder you have nightmares," he said, caressing the side of her face. "Kearney's work?"

"It doesn't matter."

"Matters to me."

Joan didn't answer. Talking about her scars dredged up memories she had stowed away, revisited only when she slept and was helpless to fend them off. She was finally past the resentment, and she wanted to keep it that way.

"The one on your ass?" he asked.

"That one's yours, from the time I made you lay down your bike."

"They're all mine now, darlin'." His hand slid down her thigh. "What about the two small ones on your leg?"

"That's where Duncan shot me."

"He shot you?"

"There was a firefight. A thousand bullets flying everywhere. The only round that hit me came from his gun. I—" She pictured the man she choked to death with the barrel of an M-16. Cross grip. Her knee in his back. She closed her eyes and swallowed. "—was busy. He shot a guy, and the bullet went through the guy and hit me. In his defense, he did tell me to move."

"Movin' target's harder to hit."

"Speaking of moving targets. You don't think the feds will look for me here?"

"No one's looking for you, darlin'."

"How can you be sure?"

"I'd know if anyone was askin' around about you." He looked straight into her eyes. "You're safe here. With me."

She didn't respond.

"Told you in Albuquerque I'd provide a safe place for you. Take care of you."

"I don't like being taken care of." But she knew, going into this relationship, that this might be part of the deal. Damn him, he turned out to be more considerate and generous—and passionate—than she imagined. The more he did for her, the harder it would be to take him down. "With Duncan I was more or less on my own," she continued. "He only stepped in when I really needed his help."

A half-smile pushed up one side of Bill's moustache.

Joan narrowed her eyes. "What's that smile about?"

"Never mind." His face flattened into a deadpan expression. He looked past her toward the clock. "It's seven-fifty. Gotta get ready for work."

"Dagger was at the meeting last night right?"

"Mmhmm," Bill said, caressing Joan's body.

"Then he knows where you are and what you're doing. A few minutes won't matter, right?"

"You're tempting, darlin', but I really need to get going." He gave her a quick kiss on the lips and shifted his weight to get up. "We'll have a cup of coffee together before I leave."

Fifteen minutes later, Joan's breath caught when Bill walked into the kitchen. He appeared more commanding than any previous morning, the presence of a man confident in his world.

"You're a keeper," he said, snaking an arm around her waist. "Sure you weren't a biker's old lady before?"

"I think I'd remember. Why?"

"When you took my colors off me—all that passion last night—you didn't throw 'em on the floor. Draped 'em over the back of the chair." He gave her a peck on the lips. "That's old lady material right there."

"I…uh…thank you?"

Bill laughed, released her, and took the mug of coffee she had made for him.

She leaned back against the cabinet. "You said you treat your old ladies well. It seemed like an important point to you."

Bill leaned back on the cabinet across the small kitchen from her. He took a sip and studied her for a few seconds. "I grew up in the lifestyle. I saw lots of Brothers go to jail. Some old ladies were loyal. Some turned on their men. Why's that?"

Joan shrugged.

"Some bikers would rather be feared than revered," he continued. "If a biker rules by fear, when he goes away, all the cops have to do is convince his old lady she's better off trusting them than her old man."

"How do they do that?"

"Stop by every other day or so bringing food or something for her kids, if there are any. Her old man is locked up, not able to provide for her and her kids, and the cops have all the time in the world to turn her, get her to tell them anything she knows."

"Seems underhanded."

He pushed off the cabinet and put an arm around her waist. "Bikers who earn the respect of their old ladies, don't worry about their women stabbing them in the back when they're locked up. No sweet-talking or manipulation will make them turn on their men."

"I guess you're aiming to earn my respect."

"I'm hopin' I already have."

"Bill, there's something you should know."

"What's that?"

She bit her lip. "I don't love you." Being honest upfront seemed the best choice regardless of the outcome. She steadied herself for an outburst. But it didn't come.

"I know, darlin'." He paused. "Since we're doin' true confessions, I have one."

Joan raised an eyebrow.

"Remember last year when you made that big apology to me in front of the leadership?"

"Yeah…" She wondered where this was going.

"Duncan had already smoothed everything over with the club."

She pushed him away. "What? Then why'd I have to do that? It was awful. Stressful…demeaning."

"I don't know why he did it. I just wanted to hear an apology from you personally."

"You wanted to see me squirm? Publicly?"

"Hell no. I just wanted to see you again. You were so beautiful and strong and capable. You fascinated me. Still do."

She rubbed her forehead. Duncan had taken care of everything then agreed to put her on the hot seat? She looked at Bill. She shouldn't have heard it from him. Duncan should have stepped up and told her. "Why are you telling me this?"

"Sometimes things go on behind the scenes. I want you to trust me even if you don't understand why I do certain things. Respect me and my position in the club." He pulled her in tight and planted a kiss on the side of her head. "Love's overrated. You respect me, right?"

She pulled away from him and walked around the end of the breakfast bar to sit down. Her paradigm had shifted—not 180 degrees, but enough to look at Bill in a different light. She had an honesty pact with Duncan, but Bill seemed to be more honest.

"I respect you," she said, worrying how many more incidents like this floated in an arc, like a boomerang, ready to circle back and hit her.

"That's all that matters," he said. He leaned both arms on the counter, eyes on the countertop, as if weighing his words. He looked up at her. "I have a favor to ask you."

"What's that?"

"Make up with Little Al. Talk to him."

She almost choked on her coffee. "Didn't you say *not* to talk to him?"

"Been thinking it over. Something's been bothering him lately," he said. "Might be why he lied."

"Now you believe he lied? I don't know…" It was what she wanted, but it seemed wrong. Way too soon. She searched his eyes for trickery, but he had been open and genuine about her apology—her needless apology—which could have set her off and gone badly for him.

"Don't know what?" He walked around the counter and fingered back a strand of hair and kissed her neck.

"You didn't ask him about it?" she asked. His whiskers tickled, and she curled her neck. "Isn't this club business?"

"We tried to get him talk. Wouldn't tell us nothin'. We thought you could use your previous friendship with him to get him to open up."

"We?"

"Me and Blaze." He nibbled her ear. "Talk to him. Maybe Carol, too. See if she'll spill. Even a hint might help us figure out what's going on."

She slid from the stool into his arms. "Don't you have to leave for work soon?"

"Soon." He smiled. "So what are you doing today?"

She knew he knew. He'd been at Mooky's, but she would play along. "Going to Mooky's today, rather than tomorrow, and then to work. What about you?"

"Workin' at the custom shop today. We're about finished with a bike for a special client. Test drive today."

"Want me to stop by before I go to Mooky's? Maybe we could do lunch." She smacked her head with her palm. "Shit. I need a ride."

"I'll send a prospect to take you to Uncle Mook's."

"I could cancel if it's a problem." She hated adding to the endless tasks the prospects were given.

"Uncle Mook likes your company," Bill said. "Not that you actually clean his house."

"I clean his house." She winced. He had just been there the day before and knew cleaning was not a priority for either her or Mooky. She quickly added, "At least now you can eat in his kitchen without getting food poisoning." She straightened Bill's collar and traced her fingers along the edge of his cut. "Why can't you meet me for lunch? You have a date with someone else?"

He grabbed his bike keys, kissed her, and said, "Jealousy. I like that. Means you care."

"I'm not jealous."

"Pick you up at two, darlin'." He looked at her left hand then pinned her with his gaze. "Ditch the ring."

While his Harley rumbled out of the garage and faded into

the distance, she toyed with her wedding band, turning it around her finger, sliding it up over the knuckle and back down. She went to her room and opened the hand carved, rosewood box that held her throwing knives.

I'm sorry, Duncan. She placed her ring under one of the knives then re-nestled the knife on the velvet lining. *The next time I see you, we'll be free, and I'll be wearing it.* She rested her hand on the box that held the few valuable things she owned.

Don't look back.

She thumbed the daily text to Inez to let her know all was well, telling her about the new arrangement with Bill, then spent the morning moving her few clothes into Bill's bedroom and her personal hygiene items to the bathroom between his bedroom and his office. After everything was moved, she did her morning workout, which was interrupted by a text from Mooky.

Just before noon, with the prospect's bike echoing his retreat, she rapped on Mooky's front door. When she let herself in, he was sitting in his recliner watching a World War II documentary.

"Did you bring the food?" he asked.

"Yes," Joan hissed in mock agitation. Mooky had turned out to be a friend. She was more than happy to bring him food and fix his lunch.

"Good. I'm hungry." He thumped down the foot rest and struggled to get his overweight body out of the chair. He followed her into the kitchen. "Did you get the salt-cured bacon instead of the stuff with nitrates?"

Joan looked at his big belly. "I think you have more to worry about than nitrates." She took the frying pan out of the drainer and turned on the burner.

Mooky shook handfuls of his belly. "A man's gotta start somewhere on the road to a healthy, fit body."

"You're an ass."

"I'd say something back, but I hear that'd get me in a pile of shit since you're now the president's old lady."

Joan turned around with strips of raw bacon in her hands.

"You know that already?" She flapped the bacon at him. "Ruby was right. You guys are a bunch of old biddies."

"We've been called worse." He slid out a chair and sat. "Did you get the iceberg lettuce? Not that floppy shit you brought last time. I hate that on my sandwich."

"That floppy shit has more nutrition."

"Still working on the nitrates. I'll get to nutrition later."

She shook her head at him.

When the bacon was cooked and the BLTs were made, Joan put a plate with two sandwiches in front of Mooky, and sat opposite him with her sandwich.

"Just two?" he asked.

She gave him a don't-go-there look. "So tell me, Mooky, if I had said 'no' to Bill last night, what would have happened?"

"You don't get to say 'no,'" Mooky said with a mouthful of sandwich.

"Bill said I did. What if I had?"

"Must be getting soft in his old age." Mooky wiped crumbs from his scraggly moustache with the back of his hand. At her hard look, he plucked several napkins from the napkin holder. "Or maybe he didn't want to end up unconscious on the side of the road again."

"At least he respects my abilities," she said. "What if I had said 'no'?"

"You'd be one lonely woman. No man in Phoenix would have anything to do with you. The smart ones know claimed women are off limits."

"What about the dumb ones?"

He grabbed more napkins and wiped mayonnaise that had dripped onto the front of his shirt. "They're all dead."

"Bill would kill them, even if I didn't agree to it?"

"If a Brother claims you, you're claimed."

"And you guys would risk going down for murder over some dumb schlub who makes a pass at a claimed woman? Really?"

"We take our women seriously."

Joan snorted. "I guess that's why we don't have a say in anything."

"*Exacta mundo.*"

"I don't get it." It was Joan's turn to talk with her mouth full.

"The club is for the men. The women are there to support the men."

Joan picked at her lettuce. "Like a ladies auxiliary?"

"Look, Joan, we're not exactly whatcha'd call law-abiding citizens. If our women aren't part of that, they don't go down for anything the club does. It's to protect them."

Joan stood to get a pitcher of iced tea out of the fridge. Insulating the women from the fallout of club business had crossed her mind, but she hadn't dwelled on it. It was thoughtful—in a misogynistic way.

She poured two glasses of iced tea and gave one to Mooky. "Do the men ever share club stuff with their women?"

His eyes flashed up to hers and narrowed. "Some do. Some don't."

She busied herself with opening a Splenda packet to break eye contact. "Does Bill?"

"I don't know. Why?"

"Well, if I'm in this with him, how can I support him if I don't know what's going on?"

"You'll find a way."

"I don't know...he's closed up tighter than a locking lug nut."

"Shit, woman, you got me usin' napkins. You can rule Bill's world."

She smiled in agreement and rested her arms on the table. "Can I ask you about the runs the MC goes on?"

"No."

"Why not?"

"What happens on the road, stays on the road."

"Yeah, except STDs," she muttered.

He looked at her for a few seconds before responding. "Never seen Bill cheat on his old lady. Not at home. Not on a run. That's all I gotta say."

"So I shouldn't worry about what he's doing when he's on these runs?"

"Talk to Bill."

She took the hint, and they finished their lunch in silence.

"So what's on the agenda today?" Mooky asked, when she started cleaning up. "Shuriken? Air guitar?"

"Cleaning your house isn't on the agenda?"

"Is it ever?" He stood and brushed the crumbs off the front of his shirt.

"It's part of my payment for room and board."

He leaned in to her as if telling her a secret. "You're his old lady now. You're on for the ride, Momma." He winked and headed toward the living room.

"Okay, then, I choose air guitar." She headed to the rows of CDs on built-in shelves around the television. She loved Joe Bonamassa's throaty voice that seemed to sing directly to her about Bill. She looked over her shoulder at Mooky. "Bonamassa?" The CD player sucked in the disc.

"A woman after my own heart," he said, plopping into his chair. "If Bill hadn't claimed ya, I would have."

"You wouldn't have made it through the first night," Joan said, turning up the volume.

"Yup, but what a way to go."

"You're a pig, Mooky."

"Fuck yeah," he said, eyes closed, nodding in time to the music, and air-picking the opening chords of "Bridge to Better Days." When he didn't know the lyrics, he added his own words. During the final chords, he glanced toward the front window.

She followed his gaze, jumped back, and said, "Oh, shit," as she turned down the stereo.

Bill stood hulking in the picture window, arms crossed, legs wide, chin to chest. Hard eyes unblinking.

Mooky laughed at her, but kept picking his invisible guitar.

When Bill walked through the door, he asked, "So this is what you do twice a week? Play air guitar?"

"It's not all we do," Joan said over the opening chords to "Walk in My Shadows."

Bill wiped a swath of dust off the end table and displayed the dust on his finger. "I know you aren't cleaning."

"We also toss shuriken." Mooky looked over his shoulder at his nephew. "Joan's real good."

"I shoulda known better than leave two ninjas alone together."

"It's Kung Fu, not Ninjitsu." Joan tensed as Bill approached her. "They're two separate styles."

His glare sucked any force out of her words.

"Two different styles, huh?" He softly bumped her shoulder with his and reached past her to turn up the stereo. He air picked the opening guitar riff.

Joan bumped shoulders back and played air guitar with him until the line about getting you in the shadows and giving you what for. When he sang it, he looked Joan in the eyes and sang it to her.

Blood flooded her head, making it pound in sync with her heartbeat. Prickles raced down her spine. If that meant he found out what her real mission was and she was about to pay the price, she was in trouble. She had to find a way to text Inez.

Before she could do or say anything, Bill put his arm around her and kissed her. "I have something for you. Hey, Uncle Mook, I'm stealing Joan."

"You're the prez," Mooky said with a mischievous smile. "Your call."

Bill herded her toward the door and walked her toward his bike with his arm around her shoulders—a gesture of possession that felt awkward and controlling.

She'd have to play it by ear. Everything seemed okay, but bikers were good at bluffing. Good enough to bluff a bluffer? Time would tell. "Did you drive out here to prove to me you didn't have a lunch date?" she asked, putting an arm around his waist.

"I won't ever prove anything to you. You're my old lady. I expect you to trust me and believe in me." He gave her a quick peck on the side of the head. "And if I do anything that makes you doubt me, I expect you to speak up. Got it?"

She stopped where the walkway met the drive. "You drove the Panhead?" Her mouth went dry. It felt like a taunt.

"I know how much you like it." He grinned and gave her a hefty squeeze.

"Then…" She smiled. "Can I drive?"

"Don't push it, darlin'."

This was not the Bill she knew over the past month. This Bill was possessive, borderline threatening, and, if she wasn't mistaken, saying one thing that hinted at something else. When he had asked her to check on Little Al, did she act too anxious? Too hesitant? Should she have said "No"? It could have been a test. She wished she had been more focused, but he had put her off her guard that morning, telling her something she should have known. She needed some time to think this through. Time to get her feet under her.

When they reached the beautifully rebuilt Harley, Bill pulled her around to face him and dropped his hands to her waist. "That was fun," he said.

"What?"

"In there," he gestured with his head. "Playing air guitar. That was…" He pressed his lips together and shook his head. "You make me feel like a kid. No responsibilities. No hard decisions."

If he was saying he was falling in love with her, she wasn't sure how to handle it. He was keeping her off her stride, playing with her. Her paranoia needled her to plan for a bad scenario—something that entailed a hard decision. Yet, his touch excited her. She ignored the liquid fire where his hands touched her waist. Her survival depended on staying mentally alert.

He started the bike. "Climb on, darlin'."

"But it has a solo seat."

"Guess you're gonna hafta snuggle up real close." He revved the engine. It wasn't the intense, throaty growl of his Harley Street Glide, but it was unmistakably a Harley.

She straddled the bike, intensely aware of the crotch-to-butt contact. After he showed her where to put her feet, she wrapped her arms around him and pressed herself against his back. If he was falling for her, he was equally off his stride.

On the ride to the shop, she asked him why he showed up

at Mooky's himself. His ambiguous answers indicated this was meant to be a surprise. His actions said this was important. Nothing he said or did suggested a threat, but if she was in danger, staying calm meant a quicker reaction time. She relaxed into the rumble of the big engine between her legs, the heat of the man in her arms, and the gentle weaving as Bill maneuvered the bike through the afternoon traffic.

After the final lean into the Sun Valley Custom Rides' parking lot, he slowed the bike and drove around to the side of the building to his parking space. When he heeled down the kickstand, she leaned to get off, but he held her hands where they were during the ride.

He turned his head to speak over his shoulder. "I love the feel of you riding on the back of my bike."

"Me, too."

"Good."

When he got off the bike, he again wrapped his arm around Joan's shoulders and led her out of the bright, early-November sun into the shade of the reception area. This was her new life, and she embraced it the way she held tight to Bill on the way to the shop. That one word, "good" eased her fears. When they walked past the mechanics building motorcycles, each one looked up and watched them go by. Nothing seemed out of place, no tension, no ambiguous looks.

She breathed in the now-familiar scent of his Bill's colors. The pride of being the club president's old lady swelled in her chest. He guided her to the far corner of the shop toward a bike with a metallic-black and gray paint job. The curved tank flowed into the solo seat that spilled into the stylized saddlebags and rear fender.

"Whaddya think?" Bill asked.

"This is the bike for your special client?" She was honored he wanted to show her his work and get her opinion.

"Yep."

"It's stunning. The paint job is primo." Her eyes swept from one end of the bike to the other. The pattern on the tank and saddlebags hinted of feathers. The line from the curve of the tank to the projections off the saddlebags looked like the curvature of wings. "You did this?"

"With Youngblood's help."

"If your client doesn't like it, he's a fool," she said.

"Then you're no fool. It's yours."

Joan's mouth fell open. "Shut up." She playfully shoved him away from her. "This isn't funny."

"It's yours. Remember the Pro Street Breakout you picked the first day you were here?" He pulled his hand out of his pocket and dangled a ring with two keys. "Here you go." He motioned to Youngblood. "Roll this out for my old lady."

"On it," Youngblood said, jumping up and pushing the bike out of the shop.

Just short of the line between shadow and sun, she stopped. "Oh my God. This is what you were doing all those nights when you came home late." Her body sagged into him. "I thought you were…I didn't know what you were doing."

"I know. And you didn't harass me about it. Definitely old lady material."

"I am so sorry to think that of you," she said, cradling his face in her hands. "Especially now, seeing what you were doing for me."

"Don't apologize. It's a sign of weakness." He nuzzled her neck. "Just trust me."

She pulled his face toward her and kissed him. "You're a good man."

He put one hand on the back of her head, the other on her back, and pulled her in tight against him, kissing her hard and long. His hand drifted lower.

She pulled away. "Bill, not in front of everybody."

He laughed softly. "Get used to it, darlin'. Brothers don't have secrets from each other." He slapped her ass. "Go sit on your bike. Let's see how the handlebars feel."

She didn't have to overreach to work the levers for the front brake and the clutch. Both feet were flat on the ground with a slight bend in the knee. It was as if he had measured her arms and legs and built the bike to those specifications.

"No one has ever given me anything like this before," she said.

"Fire it up. Drive it around the parking lot. Get the feel of it," he said.

Joan slid the key into the ignition. It rumbled to life between her legs. She leaned forward to check out the chromed-out engine. Every beat of the pistons sent vibrations through the seat and down her legs. She revved the engine several times to keep it from stalling out, but mostly to hear the powerful engine respond to her command. The handlebars vibrated, hiding her shaking hands.

She dropped her head back. Her eyes rolled. "Oh, my God, if there's anything greater than heaven, this is it."

"Told you she'd like it." Youngblood said to Bill, grinning.

She smiled and looked at Youngblood out of the corner of her eye to let him know she heard him. She toed it into first gear, feathered the throttle, and eased out the clutch. The bike glided forward. She gave it more gas and drove it in figure eights in the parking lot before pulling up in front of Bill and Youngblood.

"I have three hours before I have to go to work at the club." She raised her eyebrows and nodded her head toward Bill's bike. "Ass-up, Prez. Share my maiden run with me."

When he pulled up beside her, he took the lead. She was sure it never crossed his mind to think, "Ladies first." He was the DBMC president, and, when it came to riding with someone else on a bike, he led the pack. When the traffic cleared, he led the way onto the street. They stopped at a light, and she pulled up next to him, beaming her gratitude at his generous gift.

"I told you in the beginning that my old lady would not drive a Honda."

"Yes, you did. I can never thank you enough."

"You can get a start on thanking me tonight, darlin'." He winked at her.

The light turned green and he roared off before she could answer.

When they got to the eastern edge of town where the traffic

thinned, Bill yelled over the engines, "Let's open it up. See what it'll do. Canyon Lake?"

She nodded.

He took off north on Route 88. He traveled fast, over eighty miles per hour on the winding mountain roads. She opened the throttle and hung close to him—out riding her was not going to happen. Her bike's engine rumbled beneath her. The sound of both engines produced an earsplitting roar. The cooler mountain air raised goose bumps on her arms.

At one point, he slowed and motioned for her to pull up beside him. "About a half mile ahead, we'll cross a metal bridge. Just beyond that, there's a pull-off on the left."

When they fired down their engines, she said, "Thought you were going to outrun me?"

"That was nothing. When the club goes on a run, we do ninety miles per hour plus on roads like these."

She shook her head and reached for his hand. "I always thought you guys were crazy. Now I know."

He pulled her toward the rocks on a small point that jutted out into the lake. "When you ride with me, we'll be out front. Blaze'll be a little over a foot to our right. You won't have to worry about the pack riding close to each other trailing dust and exhaust."

"One of the perks of being the president's old lady."

"One of 'em," Bill said, releasing her hand and picking up several pebbles. He skipped them across the water.

"How did Blaze get his nickname?"

"Me and him were prospects at the same time."

"You grew up with a father and uncle in the club and you had to prospect?"

"Everyone has to be a prospect before getting a full patch. No exceptions." He skimmed the last pebble and sat on a sandstone rock. "And my father was club president when I was a prospect."

"That could go one of two ways."

"Yep. And it went the worst way. My dad didn't want anyone thinking I had it easy because I was the president's kid." He shook his head. "Don't think I slept more than two hours any one time during my nine months of hell. But I made it. Made my dad proud."

Joan sifted sandy loam through her hands. "What about Blaze?"

"Yeah, Blaze." He shook his head. "The number-one rule of a biker is his bike has to be in topnotch condition at all times."

"Uh-oh, I think I see where this is going," she said, dropping the sand and wiping her hands on her pants.

"We were on a run to Needles, and his bike broke down. Soon as he pulled onto the shoulder, it burst into flames."

"What did the club do to him?"

"What didn't they do to him? They stripped him of his prospect patch and demoted him to a hang around, but ramped up the intensity of the demands on him. After a month o' that, they bumped him back up to prospect, but didn't ease up. Took the heat off me those last couple months before they made us full-patch members."

"And now you're president and vice-president together," she said distractedly, shading her eyes and looking across the lake.

"Only 'cos Blackie got killed."

She snapped around to look at Bill. He brought her out here, away from prying eyes. Cars passed by, but not often enough to deter him if he had something planned. Who would suspect a man of murder who just gave the victim a bike? He gave it to her in front of witnesses, but now they were alone.

"You don't believe I had anything to do with that, do you?"

"Don't worry, darlin'. I was there. Is that what you've been so antsy about?"

Joan slid her hands under his cut and around his waist. She leaned against his chest. "I'm really sorry about Blackie."

"Heard you killed a lot of people that day. Blackie wasn't one of them."

She stepped back to look into his face.

The plan had been to kill Bill while Suit took out Blackie, but her plan was interrupted. The only other person who knew that was Suit, but he was dead. What Bill didn't know would not come back to haunt her.

A car flew by, young men hooting out the window. Bill flipped them the bird. Joan smiled at him. He took no shit from anybody. Unafraid, even when separated from the support of his club.

"So you think you're a tough guy, huh?" she said, tugging lightly at his goatee.

"The real deal, darlin'." He kissed her long and hard, pressing her hard against him, filling her mouth with his tongue. When his lips left hers, she reeled back against his strong arms.

He checked his watch. "We have to start back—"

She planted her lips on his, loosened his belt, and grabbed the button on the front of his pants. He popped open the button of her fly and pulled her down between two boulders. After wrestling with boots and jeans, they had quick, hot sex on the edge of Canyon Lake.

He had pulled on one of his boots when gravel crunched from the pull-off. He looked over the boulder that shielded them from the road. "Get dressed," he said, pulling on his other boot.

She pulled up her pants, and, when she heard three car doors slam, she looked over the boulder. She scrambled for her boots and pulled them on. "Are those the guys you flipped off?"

"Don't know. Stay here. I'll take care of this."

She zipped and buttoned her jeans. "Like hell."

Bill stepped out from behind the boulder. "I don't have any beef with you," he said to the three men.

"Come over here and give us the finger again, motherfucker," the taller man said.

Joan stood behind Bill and a little to his right. Two of the men wore haskies—a combination of a hoodie and a mask—with a green and brown camouflage pattern. The one speaking to Bill slapped a bat in an open hand, trying to look dangerous, but even with the bat, he was no match for Bill. The other stepped to Bill's right in a flanking move. The third guy stood back, hunched at the shoulders. His watery, darting eyes took in everything and nothing.

Joan zeroed in on the masked men. The one with the bat was well-built and tall. The other was shorter with a lean, muscular physique, like a gymnast.

Bill rubbed his knuckles, displaying the silver on six of his fingers—rings by day, weapons by fight. His demeanor was calm, his gaze steady. She couldn't see his eyes, but she was sure they were a fatal combination of fire and ice.

"My old lady and I are having a pleasant day out on our bikes. You go your way, and we'll go ours. No harm. No foul."

"You're not so brave now that we're here in your face," Bat Man said.

"You may outnumber me now, but I guarantee you, if this doesn't end peaceably, more bikers than you can imagine will rain hell down on you."

Short Guy was the first to register indecision. "Let's go. We've made our point."

"No. We have to teach this old man a lesson," Bat Man said. He swung.

Bill didn't flinch. The bat wasn't close enough to hit him.

Bat Man brought back his arm to swing again. Bill stepped in and grabbed his arm. Short Guy descended on Bill. Striking him with glancing blows. Joan side-kicked Doper, and he fell backward against the car, hitting his head on the fender. Bill took out Bat Man's legs and pounded him into the ground. Short Guy hit Bill from behind. Joan kicked the back of Short Guy's leg. He turned and swung. She ducked and thrust a palm heel upward into his ribs. A light crack. Short Guy fell to one knee. She pulled on Bill to get him off the limp Bat Man, haskie torn and bloody around his neck. Blood dripped from the gashes Bill's rings gouged into his face.

Bill got to his feet and looked around. "You okay?" he asked Joan.

"Yeah, fine."

He pulled a bandana out of his back pocket and wiped the blood off his knuckles. "You didn't have to get involved."

"Yeah, I did. We're a team."

Bill pulled her into him and hugged her hard. "Start your bike. I'll get the license plate number. Then let's beat it back to town."

Bat Man moaned, probably wondering what had happened to him.

"We have your tag number," Bill said. "If the cops show up, the Brotherhood will hunt you down. Got it?"

Bat Man nodded.

Bill turned to the other guy. "You're getting' off light. Be happy with that. Don't want to see your faces again."

"Think they'll call the cops?" Joan asked Bill before he started his bike.

"Let's hope not."

CHAPTER 12

After a restless night waiting for the "police knock" on the door, Joan leaned on the kitchen counter, looking out the window, nursing a mug of coffee. Where had that impulsive initiation of sex come from?

Bill wasn't the ogre the Bureau had made him out to be. Instead, he was sexy and strong in all the ways she liked. And brave, not backing down from three misguided thugs. Taking him down would be heart-wrenching. If only there was a way around it...

She heard Bill shuffling around in his office, probably putting on his boots. She popped a pod in the coffeemaker then resumed watching the birds in the backyard. Having Bill's back in the fight cemented their relationship, creating a strong bond. Breaking it would be betrayal—the cardinal sin they both believed in—disloyalty.

He walked up behind her and wrapped his arms around her. "Yesterday was great. I haven't fucked in the open in a long time."

"It was exhilarating, wasn't it?" she said, turning around and pulling him in for a kiss.

"I made a good choice this time." He kissed her before grabbing his cup of coffee.

"What does that mean? 'This time?'"

"My first wife was the daughter of one of the Brothers. Had already lived too hard and loose. Hassled me about late nights. Never trusted me."

"What happened?"

"She left me. Took my son with her. Moved in with a half-sister in California."

"Switch seems to think you booted his mom out."

Bill snorted. "That's what she poisoned his mind with. Coupla weeks in the summer wasn't enough time to undo her badmouthing."

He leaned on the counter next to her, took a sip of coffee, and frowned at a spot halfway across the kitchen. When he looked up at her, the corners of his eyes tightened. His jaw hardened. "When he joined the Mongols, he turned his back on the Brotherhood. I disowned him."

She extended her arms to hug him. "But he's your son."

He turned away from her and dumped his coffee in the sink. "Don't talk about it again."

"Have you tried to talk about this with him?"

Bill spun around and glared at her. "What did I just say?"

She put her hands on his arm. "Okay. Got it."

He raised his arm as if to throw off her hands, but instead shook her off to put his arm around her shoulders. Anger still steamed in his eyes.

She ducked from his embrace and put another pod in the coffeemaker. "Tell me about Orlanda's mother."

He glared at her, visibly fighting his anger. For a few seconds, she thought he might leave. Then his eyes softened. He must have remembered his promise to not walk out on her again.

He caressed her neck. "I went the other way. I fell for a beautiful woman who had no connection to bikers. I didn't catch the signs. She didn't like bikes, guns, partying. She was a great mother, but not old lady material. When she couldn't stand the lifestyle any more, she moved out, taking Orlanda with her."

"But Orlanda is with Dagger."

"Her mother never fought visitations." He took the offered mug. "Everyone adored Orlanda and, for her, it was like having dozens of big brothers. She met Dagger and fell in love. At least one of my kids is in the DBMC family." He set down his coffee and hugged Joan. "You're my Goldilocks old lady. Not from within the lifestyle, but not a stranger to the things I love. And you'll have my back, no matter what. Perfect."

"Yeah, until I wake up in the middle of the night screaming."

"I heard it. Seen you pacing the house in the dark. Killed me that I couldn't comfort you. I'll be there from now on, darlin'."

"Except when you're away on a run." Joan hesitated before asking, "Are there other women on these runs?"

He eased his embrace and leaned back to look in her eyes. "I'm a grown man. I can go four days without getting my dick wet." He kissed her lightly on the lips and picked up his coffee. "Speaking of the run. I need you to help out at the dealership while Dagger and I are out of town this weekend."

"Doing what?"

"You can help Lance—did you meet Lance?"

She shook her head.

"He's the other salesman. You can do the bookkeeping, run the register, help people pick out accessories. You know, shit like that. It'd free up Lance to handle sales."

"What about my job at Leather and Lace?"

"I'll talk to Blaze. Have him get someone to cover for you."

"Where's Orlanda?"

"The kids have some kind of stomach bug. We need you to cover through Saturday, starting Thursday. Stop in tomorrow and get a quick run through."

He took gulp of coffee. "Still wanna paint at the club house?"

"Yeah, sure."

"Pick up a key tomorrow when Dagger's showing you around. I'll even buy you lunch." He finished his coffee in big swallows and handed her the cup. "Be there at eleven-thirty."

In just five weeks she had gained an opportunity to move the investigation forward. That must be a new record—not that hard-ass Inez would be impressed. Joan replayed the conversation with Bill. Did she say anything out of line? Other than pushing him about his relationship with his son, it seemed okay, natural.

Was she too excited about this opportunity? Too reticent? The short conversation played over and over in her head until she called Inez to tell her the news. Inez talked her down, giving her a sense of calm and confidence. By the time Joan parked her bike at the dealership, she was on top of her game and up to speed on what to look for.

When she walked into the showroom, the aroma of new bikes washed over her. Dagger was at the counter with a customer, and when he saw he motioned her over. "Might as well learn this now."

Joan greeted the customer and absorbed the details of ringing up a sale and what to do with the paperwork afterward. She complimented the customer on the choice. It seemed straight forward, and her confidence grew.

"You greeted the customer. Didn't just focus on the details of ringing up the purchase. You got people skills," Dagger said before jumping into how the cash register worked: how to unlock it, ring up a purchase, take care of a return.

Her confidence faltered. "This is a lot to learn in one day."

"If you get stuck, call Orlanda. She'll walk you through anything you can't figure out. Prob'ly be glad to have someone to talk to." He motioned for her to follow him. "I'll introduce you to Lance."

"How are the kids?" she asked, following closed behind him.

"Didn't think those little bodies held so much puke."

"How's she holding up?"

"Can't wait to get outta the house Friday night." He stopped at a decent-sized office with family photos of Orlanda, Dagger, and their kids. He said to the man at the desk, "Lance, this is Joan. She's going to help out while Orlanda's home with the kids. Watch the floor while I explain QuickBooks to her."

Lance welcomed Joan and headed out to the showroom, leaving her with the biker, the potted plant on the corner of the desk, and the computer.

"Lance'll be able to help you if you get stuck." Dagger sat in the chair behind a desk. "Pull up that chair."

"If Lance can do this, why am I here?"

"If it gets busy, he can make the sale then leave the customer with you so he can handle the next sale. Wish I had more time to train you up, but short of reformatting the hard drive, there isn't much you can do that Orlanda can't undo when she comes back."

Fifteen minutes later, Bill walked past the office window that looked out over the showroom. He leaned into the office. "How's she doing?"

"She's a winner."

"Good. When you're done, can I steal her for lunch?"

"I think we're done here. She's a quick learner." Dagger looked back at Joan and continued his instructions. "We decided to close on Sunday. Give you guys a break. The shop closes at six all three days. But plan on being here a little later to cash out the registers and finish up paperwork."

Her eyes flashed up to Dagger's. "Cash out the registers?"

Dagger crossed his arms and looked at Bill. "She can take out an army of fighters. But balks at a cash register."

❧❧❧

Early the next day, while Lance arranged financing for a customer, Joan plopped her backpack in the corner, watered Orlanda's plant, and eyed the computer. Trusting her with all the financial information of the dealership no longer seemed like an opportunity. It had all the hallmarks of a test. If she snooped around, Dagger may have a way of knowing it. If she didn't make the attempt, Inez would come down hard on her, maybe even think she was incapable of getting evidence. Getting pulled from the investigation meant she would go to jail and Duncan would never get out.

Freedom damn sure wasn't free.

She looked at the opened mail on the desk, then studied the QuickBooks shortcut on the desktop screen. Resisting the urge to check the showroom through the window, she double-clicked on the icon.

The QuickBooks side menu opened, and the bottom menu item captured her attention and wouldn't let go. Apps. Dagger could check every move she made from the road. Would he know when she downloaded information onto the thumb drive she'd brought with her? Definitely not, if she didn't put it into the USB port. She slid her hand into the front pocket of her jeans.

"You look confused," Lance said, stepping around the desk. "You've only gotten as far as opening QuickBooks?"

She pulled an empty hand from her pocket. "Can Dagger use the app to check what I'm doing? What if I make a mistake?"

"He can see any changes you make. But, trust me, he'll be too busy with club business and partying to check the app." She must have looked dubious because he added, "Don't worry. You can't do anything that'll bring on the apocalypse."

"It depends on your definition of 'apocalypse.'" Joan toyed with the mouse. "Stay here while I do this invoice?"

"Sure." Lance leaned one hand on the desk, his other on the chair back, his head close to hers. "Which screen are you going to open?"

"Vendors?" She put up a hand. "Back off. You're making me nervous."

"Sorry," he said, moving back a little. "Go ahead. Click on Vendors."

Inputting the information was easy, but Joan feigned a lack of confidence. Hoping she wasn't laying it on too thick, she worked through another invoice.

"I have some phone calls to make," he said, putting a hand on her shoulder. "Will you be okay now?"

She looked as his hand. "I think so." *He's just being friendly*. No one would be stupid enough to make a move on the club president's old lady. That would be just plain dumb, and like Mooky said, all the dumb men were dead.

Lance headed out of the office. "I'm right next door if anything…"

The rest of the day was dead with short spurts of activity. She input invoices and watched for an opening to put the thumb drive in the computer, although nothing in the program seemed important enough to chance getting caught. It looked like the day would be a bust until five-fifteen when a man came in and wandered around the showroom floor. Lance walked out to greet him.

If she didn't act now, the opportunity would be lost. She inserted the tiny thumb drive into the USB port. It was only three-quarters of an inch in length and, when inserted into the port, stuck out only a quarter of an inch—but it might as well have jutted out a foot. It wasn't eye-catching, just a small black, plastic instrument of execution. She stiffened as the download progressed. Rolling her shoulders did nothing. She flicked off the screen.

"Can you help this guy?" Lance asked.

Her heart raced. Had he seen her put in the thumb drive?

"He's looking for a lighting package," he continued. "While you do that, I'll cash out the other register. Maybe we can get out early tonight."

"Sure thing. I'll see what I can do."

Lance headed back to the showroom, and, with a last glance at the thumb drive, she followed him.

The customer didn't know what he wanted, and she went over the different packages available for his model Sportster. Her mouth dried up. Purposely avoiding looking at the office, she managed to narrow the choices to three, but the customer continued to waffle. While he debated the pros and cons of the different options, the thumb drive niggled at her. Her heart raced and the memories of the stress of undercover work for the Legion flooded through her. Lance walked behind her and went into the office. Her mind raced, trying to find a reason to leave the customer and distract Lance. The customer made his choice at that time, and she couldn't break away.

She filled out the paperwork and fumbled through ringing it up. Lance saw her struggling and stepped in to finish. By that time, it was ten minutes to closing, and the mechanics were pushing the outside display bikes around to the service bay.

She slipped into the office and checked the download. It had finished long before. She pulled out the thumb drive and put it into her pocket. She shut down the computer before going outside to help Lance bring in the bikes to be stored in the showroom overnight.

After he locked the front door, he said, "You did good today." He pocketed the keys and studied her. "You look a little shaken. Can I buy you a drink?"

"No," she said over her shoulder, heading to Orlanda's office for her backpack.

"You sure?" he called after her.

"No thanks," she said, slinging the backpack strap over one shoulder. "I rode my bike today, and I don't like to drink when I'm riding."

"Good thinking," he said, holding the door open for her. "See you tomorrow."

"Good night," she said, slipping past him. "Thanks again for being so patient."

She started her bike and nursed the throttle to make a slow exit. Every muscle wanted to race out of the parking lot, leaving tire tracks behind her, but acting like she had all the time in the world seemed like a better idea.

A mechanic pulled up next to her. "How do you like your new bike?" he yelled over the sound of the engines.

She gave him a thumbs-up. When the traffic cleared, he pulled out and quickly shifted through the gears. She followed at a more sedate pace. Her nerves, held in check all day, started to thrum. At the second light, she stalled her bike. The driver behind her honked his horn. Fighting the urge to give him the finger, she pulled into the next fast food restaurant parking lot. If Lance had seen the thumb drive, he had remained cool and relaxed. Or he could have been cool and relaxed because he didn't see anything. Not knowing was worse than knowing. She drew in a deep, cleansing breath and exhaled. Tomorrow would be easier—no prying or sneaking around. That part of her job was done.

The message tone sounded on her phone.

ORLANDA: *Painting party still on for 7.00 tomorrow night?*

JOAN: *What are we doing for food and booze?*

ORLANDA: *It's BYOB. You provide food.*

JOAN: *OK.*

She checked the time and headed to Potpourri, a trendy bistro closer to downtown, for a dinner meeting with Inez. Joan would be early, but it would give her time to settle her nerves and prepare to deal with Inez in a calm, self-assured manner. Inez picked up on any tiny crack in Joan's self-confidence and didn't hesitate to use it to threaten to pull the plug on the op.

Joan opted for a table on the patio behind the bistro, thinking the locals wouldn't be prepared to sit outdoors in the cool air. As expected, the patio was empty. She requested the round table in the far corner and ordered a glass of red wine. Chinese lanterns along the fenced perimeter gave the area a soothing coziness. Her leather jacket provided a barrier to the sixty-degree winter evening, and she was sure Inez would ride her bike and be dressed the same.

Right on time, Inez appeared on the patio, caught Joan's eye, and headed toward her. To Joan's surprise, Inez she wore a red floral maxi dress with a white denim jacket. A big departure from her riding clothes.

"What's the occasion?" Joan asked.

"I'm meeting someone after we're done here," Inez said, pulling out a chair where she would also be able to keep an eye on the patio.

"I never thought of you with a personal life."

"Like I don't have family?"

"I pictured you golfing and sunbathing next to a pool," Joan muttered, feeling the sting of wrong decisions and lost opportunities.

"Let it go." Inez studied Joan's face before adding, "Keep your head in the game."

The waitress came at that moment, handed out menus, and chattered about the specials. They both ordered wine, and when the waitress left, Inez said, "How did it go today?"

"Good. I downloaded QuickBooks onto the thumb drive."
She finished the wine in her glass. "Doesn't getting this information without a warrant taint the evidence?"

"Let me worry about that."

Joan frowned.

"Nothing on QuickBooks will be sufficient to stand up in court," Inez said. "But it may lead us in a direction where we can get solid evidence."

"I thought if the source is tainted, the rest of the evidence is inadmissible."

"Give the computer forensics team a chance to check over what you found. We can develop a plan from there."

"You're the expert. I'm just the CI with her neck on the line. I just don't want it to be for nothing."

Inez had always seemed a by-the-book person. This departure from her professional attitude was not like her. Joan chewed the inside of her cheek.

"It's not for nothing." Inez took the thumb drive that Joan slid across the table and dropped it in her purse. "What was the big thing Bill asked you to do?"

"Oh, yeah, get this," Joan said. "He thinks Little Al might be up to something."

Inez swirled the ice in her water goblet. "Really?"

Her lack of curiosity made Joan take a longer look at her. Working Little Al could answer a lot of their questions. Inez should know that and be full of suggestions for Joan to be successful.

"You aren't very excited about this."

Inez sipped her water. "I just don't think there's anything there."

"He might be the rogue agent."

Inez quickly swallowed the water. "Anything point to him?"

"Don't know yet."

The waitress brought their wine and Joan waited for her to leave before continuing.

"Bill said since I used to be close to Little Al, I should make amends and renew our friendship. See what I can find out."

"Doesn't it strike you as odd that he'd ask you and not a Brother?"

"Odd? It's a flagrant violation of club rules," Joan said. "Do you think he's setting me up?"

"For what?"

"Could be anything. Testing my loyalty, keeping me busy, or maybe just what it is—investigating Little Al. The only way I'm going to find out is do what he asks."

"Stay on your toes. These guys don't overlook missteps," Inez said. "And keep me in the loop."

The conversation stopped when the waitress brought their food. Over dinner, Inez whined about how little lower-level agents made. Joan guessed it was better than living with a dangerous man who, if he discovered what she was really up to, wouldn't think twice about killing her—slowly and painfully. Joan had scored a rich husband, but they would never live that lifestyle. Even after this operation was in the bag, Witness Protection Services would relocate them, moving them several times. And they'd end up in an average neighborhood leading average lives.

She didn't know if there was anyone in Inez's life, but Joan would have Duncan when this was over. It was worth the struggle. It had to be.

Full from a delicious dinner and buzzed from the wine, Joan stepped onto the street and headed for her bike.

"What's Bill say about me?" Inez asked.

"He seems to have accepted our cover story."

"Let's hope it stands up to scrutiny."

Joan straddled her bike. "Let's hope this whole crapshoot stands up to scrutiny."

CHAPTER 13

The next night, Joan picked up the food and painting supplies before heading to the clubhouse. She found the light switches for the hallway and the large room that was a cafeteria once upon a time. She turned on the kitchen lights and started down the hallway to the party room and the offices beyond when Orlanda arrived, looking tired but healthy.

"How are the kids?" Joan asked.

"Much better. Good thing Dani's back. Her girls are my babysitters." She raised her arms in victory. "I'm free."

"Who's Dani?" Joan asked.

"Danielle, Blaze's old lady." Orlanda cracked open a bottle of white whiskey and free-poured two shots into two Dixie cups. "I hope she at least makes him squirm for cheating on her."

They had just swallowed the shot when Flora arrived.

"Who else is coming?" Joan asked through the whiskey burn.

"Lizzie said was coming," Flora said. "And Carol."

"Hey, all." Lizzie's voice boomed from the big room.

"Back here," Orlanda said.

The walking, talking Amazon filled the doorway, ball cap on backward, hands on her hips. The picture of what tomboys grew up to be. "Where're the shot glasses? Or you pussies been nursing the liquor?" She looked at Joan. "What're you drinkin', newbie?"

"Tequila," Joan answered.

"Then pour a friggin' round for everybody and let's get the hell started with this painting gig. I didn't clear my calendar to prittle-prattle in the kitchen."

Joan broke out laughing and spilled as much tequila as she poured.

"Where's the friggin' salt and lime?"

"Only pussies need friggin' salt and lime," Joan said before throwing back her shot.

Lizzie chugged her shot and wrapped Joan in a muscular arm covered in layers of flab. "You're all right, newbie." She released Joan and broke the seal on her bottle of Jim Beam. "Thank you for throwin' us an old ladies a party—even if we have to work. 'Cos you know our old men are partying their friggin' asses off." She leaned in until she was a few inches from Joan's face. "Am I right or what?"

"Let's get started," Orlanda said, saving Joan from Lizzie's over-zealous friendship. "Paint and brushes and shit are in the big room."

"Are we drinking or painting?"

Joan spun around at the new female voice.

"I'm Blaze's old lady," a fit, athletic woman said. "Everyone calls me Dani."

"I hear you gave Blaze another chance," Joan said.

"I can't make a go of our marriage if I'm not here. I'll be damned if some whore is gonna make me throw away seventeen years." Dani had short, spiked hair dyed platinum blonde. She was a natural brunette, which made a striking contrast between her eyebrows and hair color—but not as eye-catching as her turquois eyes. By her looks alone, Blaze became a bigger jerk. What man in his right mind would do something to lose this beauty?

"Let's crank up the music and get started," Joan said. "Everyone grab a roller and a pan. And a wall. Dani, why don't we take the bigger wall. I'll roll, you cut in?"

They laughed, talked, and drank, sharing stories. Joan poured half the shots into a paint rag. She had to keep her head clear to gather information. As the evening wore on, she learned Blaze and Slow Motion shared some club business with Dani and Lizzie. If Dagger shared information with Orlanda, she wasn't letting on, but the fact that Blaze shared club business with his wife kindled hope that Joan could get Bill to confide in her.

Two and a half hours later, her stomach growled, reminding her there was food in the kitchen. Other than cleaning up, they were done. "Anyone hungry?"

"Hell, yeah," Lizzie said, wiping her hands.

Everyone was high from drinking alcohol on empty stomachs, and they sloppily dished out food. The women were hungry, distracted, and partying, which gave Joan the opportunity to sneak away and check around for something of use to the Bureau. She excused herself with the ruse of looking for a jacket she left the last time she had been in the clubhouse. She turned down offers for help, and encouraged the women to eat. She'd only be a minute.

She crossed the darkened party room and headed for the admin wing. The room where they held club meetings was locked, as was the telecommunications center with the monitors.

She could pick the locks, but it would take too long. Bill's office was the next one down. The door was unlocked, and she crept inside. The desk drawers held nothing of interest. The flag behind his desk didn't cover a safe. The filing cabinets were locked, but she remembered seeing a key in the center drawer. She reached for the drawer.

Carol's voice stopped her. "Looking for something?"

"When you didn't show up earlier, I thought you changed your mind," Joan said.

Carol stepped into the room. "I had to run some errands. They took me longer than I thought."

Joan walked from behind the desk to leave.

Carol blocked her path.

"Is everything okay with you and Little Al?" Joan asked. "You seem...tense."

"Were you looking for anything in particular?" Carol asked.

"I thought I left a jacket in here." Joan shrugged. "Must've left it someplace else. Let's see if there's any food left."

Carol hesitated, locked eyes with Joan, then stepped aside.

Joan led the way into the hallway, hoping Carol wouldn't tell her husband she caught Joan snooping around Bill's office. The "new" Little Al would jump at the chance to tell Bill. She could probably talk her way out of it, but it would work out better if she didn't have to. That little tête-à-tête with Little Al had to come soon.

"How are Joe-Sam doing?" Joan asked.

"Haven't seen them," she said.

"Like I told you before, the feds have more dangerous criminals in their sights to keep them occupied."

"Then they need to catch them," Carol said.

Joan looked at Carol out of the corner of her eye. Carol's brusque tone hinted of a pressing situation. One she wasn't ready to discuss. Food was good at loosening tongues.

"Let's get together for lunch some time," Joan said.

Carol's eyes remained on the floor, her shoulders tight. "I'd like that."

Afraid if she pushed, Carol would shut down, Joan walked the rest of the way in silence. When they reached the kitchen, the other women were sitting on the counters finishing their dinners. Carol and Joan grabbed plates and dished themselves some food.

Dani said to Joan, "I see you have the patch."

Joan reflexively looked at the back of her arm then up at Dani. "Yeah. What do you use?"

"Did you check the lot number?" Dani asked.

"Why?"

"Didn't you hear?" Flora said. "There was an announcement on the evening news a couple nights ago. Certain lot numbers were recalled. They won't prevent pregnancy."

The food in Joan's mouth turned bitter. She choked it down. "I'm sure mine's okay." *Of all the bullshit that could happen, I do not need this.*

"I'm sure you're fine," Orlanda said. "What are the chances?"

"Yeah, right?" Joan said, thinking about her Iron Angel Bad Karma. What are the chances? Excellent. "Let's clean up and get out of here."

The clean-up was a haze of movement and snippets of conversation that faded in and out through her thoughts. Scenarios of how Bill and Inez would respond to a pregnancy churned in Joan's mind. She startled when Orlanda put an arm around her shoulders.

"I'll go to the house with you to check your box," she said in a low voice.

Joan raised her eyebrows. "My box? I don't swing that way."

Orlanda giggled and shoved Joan playfully. "I meant your lot number."

"Thank you, but I'm sure I'm okay.

"Just in case."

They piled all the paint supplies in a corner and grabbed the bag of garbage. On the way to the dumpster, Joan tried to count back to her fertile days. Between the women gabbing and, giggling—and her anxiety—she couldn't concentrate and finally gave up. She barely heard the women say they had to get together again.

When she got home, Joan headed directly to the bedroom and grabbed her box of patches.

Orlanda was right behind her, thumbing her phone to bring up the website with the lot number. "Ready?" she asked.

Joan nodded.

Orlanda rubbed her belly. "Damn. I hope I'm not coming down with what the kids had." She read off the lot number.

The numbers on the box got bright and bold, then blurred. Joan looked up. "It's the same. That doesn't mean my patch isn't working, right?"

"It says here to remove the patch if you have this lot number," Orlanda said. "If you're pregnant, it might harm the fetus."

Joan shook her head and stared at the box in her hand. "No...no...this is not the time to get pregnant." She pressed her lips together to regroup into her lie. "Bill and I just got together. He's going to think I did this on purpose."

"My dad won't think you did this to trap him."

"But Lizzie said he's mean to women."

"He's not like that—not with his old ladies. Has he been mean to you?"

Joan shook her head.

Orlanda gently peeled off the patch. "Did you know that you're the first woman to spend more than one night here since my mom moved out ten-plus years ago? He *moved you in*. Dagger couldn't believe it."

"What does Dagger think of me?"

"At first, he wasn't sure about the whole situation, but Dad's more relaxed now and—"

"Bill's relaxed?"

"For him...yes." Orlanda rubbed her stomach again. "I'm not feeling so good. Maybe I better head home."

"You're warm," Joan said, pressing the back of her hand against Orlanda's forehead. "You gonna be okay driving?

"I'll be fine. It's a short ride."

"Text me if you need anything," Joan said, putting an arm around Orlanda's shoulders.

CHAPTER 14

Six days later, Joan pulled into the Desert Sky Mall parking lot, saw Inez sitting back on her bike, legs casually out in front of her. Inez hated waiting, and Joan steeled herself for the inevitable backhanded put down.

The best defense is a good offense. "Did you pick this place on purpose? You know meeting in these open places makes me nervous." Joan looked around the parking lot for anything out of the ordinary. If she didn't know better, she'd suspect Inez wanted them to get caught.

"As long as Bill buys our cover story, we're fine," Inez said. "If he thinks we're friends, how would it look if we snuck around, meeting behind deserted warehouses?"

"We wouldn't be seen if we met in out of the way places."

"If you were on time, I wouldn't be sitting here in the open waiting for you."

Joan ran her fingers through her hair. "Do you mind if we don't go for a ride today?" Low level, nagging nausea distracted her from being on top of her game.

Inez looked Joan over. "You look like shit. Is that why you're so negative?"

"I'm actually better than I was. Today's the first day out of the house." Between bouts of vomiting, she had debated about telling Inez about the patch. She had a stomach virus, but if Inez knew about the defective patch, she would jump to the wrong conclusion.

"Still the flu?"

"Some kind of stomach bug. I think I got it from Orlanda. Her kids had it all last week."

"You're wearing the patch, right?" Inez crossed her arms and eyed Joan. "Because if you're pregnant, this op will be closed down."

"You'd love that, wouldn't you?" Joan bit back her anger and rubbed her stomach.

"Get a test before out next meeting."

"I'm not pregnant." Joan crossed her arms to mirror Inez. "I'm wearing the damn patch. Do you think I'd want to get pregnant? Now?" If she was pregnant, she'd be pulled from the operation. The baby would be born in prison and go into the system as a ward of the state. The stomach virus was a fact, and facts were all that Inez needed.

"The Bureau will not want to be responsible for putting a pregnant woman in harm's way."

"Jesus, Inez. I'll buy a damn test. Want to see the stick next week?"

"Don't cop an attitude," Inez said. "I have people I have to report to, and if I didn't push to get the facts, I'd be in deep shit. All I'm saying is take care of yourself. Stress can make you vulnerable to all kinds of things, and we need you at one hundred percent." She un-crossed her arms. "Do you have anything for me?"

"I got the wives to talk about club business. Nothing important came up, but I learned Blaze and Slow Motion talk to Dani and Lizzie. I don't think Dagger does, or at least Orlanda doesn't tell stories out of school."

"That's not enough, Joan."

She had been sick for six days. What did Inez want from her? She was still weak from the illness, and dealing with Inez was draining what little energy she had. She gathered her strength before answering. "I don't know, Inez. I don't think Bill is up to anything illegal."

"That's only because you haven't worked hard enough. This investigation was opened because of a strong indication of something illegal. Look for drug transport. The MC did that before."

Joan didn't answer. There was something going on, but her gut told her Bill wasn't involved. What was the Bureau really after? Going after a biker for some vague illegal business—*maybe* drug delivery and transportation—didn't pass the sniff test. Didn't the DEA have undercovers to get that information? Fingering the rogue agent seemed more imperative, but Inez hadn't brought that up in a while and even seemed uninterested when Joan suggested it might be Little Al. She was beginning to think this whole mess had more to do with Inez than with anything else she was sent to do. Inez was chosen as Joan's handler at the last minute. Where did she fit into the obscure, directionless operation? Everything looked too messy for the Bureau.

"You aren't falling for Bill, are you?" Inez said. "Don't get sucked in. These guys can be charming, but don't be fooled. It's 'club first—no exceptions.' Don't forget that."

"If there's something, I'll find it."

"Start working Bill. Get him to talk about small, insignificant things. That might lead to bigger things."

Joan bristled at being told how to do her job, but she played along. The sooner this meeting was over, the sooner she could relax and regain some strength. The illness had sapped her strength, leaving an opening for insidious paranoia to seep in.

She pressed on her stomach. "Did your guys get anything useful off the thumb drive I gave you?"

"No. It's basic, everyday entries. We need the user ID and password for the bank."

"You think they might be laundering money?"

"We need access to the account to find that out," Inez said. "You know what they say: 'follow the money.'"

"Can't the Bureau pull up the financials?" Access to the dealership bank account without a warrant? Joan wasn't sure she liked the idea.

"You watch too many TV shows," Inez answered. "Without a warrant, we can't 'pull up' anything. But if information is discovered during an undercover OP, it's a new ballgame."

"Can this wait until after Thanksgiving?" Joan asked. The delay would give her a chance to regain her health. "The next mandatory run is the first weekend in December—a toy drive with the Huachuca City Chapter or something. I'll offer to cover for Orlanda so she can go Christmas shopping while Dagger is out of town."

"Can't you get it sooner?"

"Christ, Inez, I got this far in five weeks. The run is only two weeks away. And that'll be the next time I'll have access to anything without triggering alarms."

"The clock is ticking."

"What's the rush?" Joan asked. When Inez didn't answer, she added, "I'll work Bill in the meantime."

"Still think Little Al might be the rogue UC?" Inez asked.

"I don't know. Maybe," Joan said, trying to read Inez's face. Since Nine/Eleven the federal agencies were supposed to be sharing information. Either this was real deep, or it was being used to sidetrack her. If so, from what?

"Anyone else on your radar?"

"I'm not saying anything until I'm sure."

"Remember," Inez said, leaning in. "If you have anything, no matter what it is, bring it to me, and I'll run with it. Don't cowboy up and do something stupid."

The look in her eyes made Joan stop and think through Inez's words. It was almost as if she was trying to hint at something. All that was missing was the wink. The stomach bug had weakened Joan, so she shrugged it off as a mind game, unwilling to expend faltering energy on a nebulous rogue agent at this point of the investigation.

"Anything else?" Inez said.

"Can't think of anything."

"Stay in touch. Daily." Inez started her bike. "And take care of yourself. We'll meet again the Thursday after Thanksgiving."

"Wow. You're trusting me on my own for two weeks?" Joan said with a hint of sarcasm.

"You aren't going anywhere without your hubby."

Joan wanted to drag Inez off the bike and pound her into the pavement for that remark. *Who is she to even mention my husband?* Instead, Joan watched Inez drive out of the parking lot before heading toward the food court in the mall. Two weeks. It was a strange feeling knowing she was on her own for fourteen days. It was liberating and scary at the same time.

She had four hours to kill before she had to be at work. She had not exercised or eaten much of anything for six days, which left her feeling drained. Wonton soup and steamed rice sounded like a good recipe for getting better. Inez and the operations nipped at Joan's heels as she crossed the parking lot to the food court—the sensation of sinking in quicksand. Not sure how that triggered a memory of Kearney, she decided to email him soon. Give him a heads-up. If it came to needing him, she'd need him fast.

She finished the last of the soup and looked up to see Youngblood walking into the food court. Had he followed her there? Worse yet, had Bill sent him to follow her? He almost breezed past without looking her way. She waved him over.

"Hey, what are you doing here?" he asked, standing over her.

"I was going to go for a ride with Inez, but didn't feel up to it. What are you doing here?"

"Prez wanted a mocha frappe."

"McDonalds sells frappes." She narrowed her eyes. "I thought you got your patch. Why are you sent on errands?"

"The other prospects were busy with something else. I'm the lowest man on the totem pole. It fell to me."

"Then I better let you get to it," she said.

"I heard you were sick," he said. "How're you doin'?"

"How did you hear that?"

"Overheard Bill talking to Dagger."

"I'm hoping this soup and rice will give me some strength."

"Hang in there. I gotta get going. Hope you feel better." He strode off toward the coffee shop.

There were places closer to the dealership to get a mocha frappe. She watched him for a few seconds. Nothing felt right about crossing paths with him. She had been in the house for several days, and the first day out, she crossed paths with a Brother. She fluffed the rice with her plastic fork. Was it a fluke, or had Bill tasked him to follow her to find out what she was doing? She went over her actions since she left the house. Did she talk to Inez too long? Or too short? If he had watched them before, was today out of the ordinary? If he was following her, coming into the mall was brazen. He may have been sending her a message. Letting her know she was being followed. Or paranoia could be sinking its yellow teeth into her like when she worked for the Legion.

She didn't know much about Youngblood. He had patched over with the Strykers, and she wondered how much Bill knew about him. She looked at Youngblood again. He was leaning with his elbows on the counter, talking on his phone. He looked over his shoulder and his gaze fell on her, sending prickles up her neck and over her scalp.

When he left without saying anything, she finished her rice and headed to the dealership to see if Bill was enjoying his mocha frappe.

When she walked into the service area a few minutes later, Youngblood gave her a chin-nod greeting before going back to his work. Bill wasn't in his office, but the frappe sat sweating on his desk. Movement caught her eye, and she smiled at Bill as he strode toward her.

"I saw you drive in," he said. "No ride today? You okay?"

"I just wanted to see you for a few minutes before I went to work."

He guided her into his office. "You aren't going to work tonight, darlin'. I called Blaze and told him to find someone else to take you shift."

"Now you're telling me when I can work, and when I can't?"

"Yes, I am. You haven't been exercising and you're off your feed."

"I had some soup and rice at the mall." It was a dumb statement. She wanted to argue with him. Defy him. Let him know he wasn't going to rule her life, but her energy was draining fast. Maybe leaving the house hadn't been such a good idea. He was right, but she'd be damned if she was going to tell him that.

"I'm driving you home," Bill said. "I can feel the fever from here."

"What about my bike?"

"I'll take care of it. Get someone to drive it to the house."

She rode with her arms around Bill, her head resting on his back. Heat flamed her face. Her eyes grew heavy from the fever. When they pulled into the garage, the last of her energy slipped away. Bill helped her undress for bed and covered her with extra blankets. He brought her a couple bottles of water, opened one, and put the other on the nightstand. He handed her a couple Tylenol tablets and watched her swallow them.

"Sweat out the fever and drink the water. Get some sleep." He kissed her on the forehead. "I'll bring something for you to eat when I close up shop. What do you want?"

"Steamed rice." She squinted through her fever at the tough president of an outlaw motorcycle club. How many people could say they had a bad-ass caregiver? "Thank you, Bill."

He was treating her well, just like Orlanda said he would. Just like *he* said he would. Damn him. It was going to be one hell of a bad day when she took him down.

"Anything for you, darlin'. Get some sleep."

Her eyes were heavy. He stopped in the doorway and pointed at her. "And stay in bed."

When she woke up, the room was dark. The clock on the nightstand said seven. She had slept so soundly she wasn't sure if it was seven in the morning or seven at night. The fever broke sometime during her nap, and she felt cool and alert. She headed to the bathroom to relieve her bladder.

After she flushed the toilet, she washed her hands and checked out her reflection in the mirror. She looked disheveled, but her eyes were clear. She heard cartoons on the television and headed to the living room. Orlanda was curled up on the couch. Her children, Peri and Peter, were kneeling on the floor next to the coffee table, intent on coloring in their coloring books, tongues out, concentrating on staying inside the lines.

Orlanda must have heard Joan because she looked over her shoulder and asked, "How're you feeling?"

"Much better. I think the fever broke," Joan said. "Where's Bill?"

"Emergency meeting with the Angels."

"About what?"

Orlanda shrugged. "Something about a snitch. Dad pulled Dagger and Blaze from their jobs to go with him."

"That doesn't sound good." Joan's stomach flopped at the word "snitch." If it was about her, he put up a good show of support a couple hours ago.

"Doesn't involve us." Orlanda stood, folded the afghan, and draped it across the back of the couch. "Leadership stuff. Hungry? Dad told me to pick up some steamed rice."

"I'm starved."

"Take a quick shower while I heat it up."

"I sweated my ass off. I'll have to change the sheets before Bill gets home."

"I'll get it," Orlanda said, heading to the kitchen. "Get your shower. Take it from one who knows, it'll make you feel a hundred times better."

"I'm sorry you had to drag your kids out of the house to play nursemaid to me."

"Don't be silly. You'd take care of me and my kids if we needed help."

CHAPTER 15

Bill took Saturday and Sunday off from the dealership and spent it with Joan, watching movies, going for a ride, eating out. It felt great to be healthy again, get out of the house, and spend time alone with Bill. But tonight, the start of a new week, he was up to his old tricks staying out late. She awakened at two-o-eight a.m. to an empty bed. She paced the house until she couldn't take it any longer. She grabbed her keys. It was time to find out what he did late at night.

She wasn't sure where he'd be, but Sun Valley Custom Rides was the first stop. After parking a block away, she hugged the shadows cast by the trees between her and the security spotlights. Spiky, icy fingers crept down her back. She looked over her shoulder, but everything outside the shop was quiet in the cool desert night. Inez said check around, find out what was going on, so here she was sneaking into his parking lot on a gloomy night.

The first raindrops of the storm plinked around her. She zigzagged around glistening bikes parked haphazardly in the front lot—an unusual lack of order. She slinked closer and saw Mongols MC decals on most of the gas tanks. Hunkering down between two bikes, she stilled, watched, and listened. No guards prowled the lot to protect the bikes. She looked around for anything else out of place.

The parking lot wasn't full, but it held more vehicles than anyone would expect to be there in the middle of the night.

The only motorcycle she recognized was Little Al's monster-bike. This was where Bill told her he would be, but his bike was not there, or at least not parked outside. If only she could see what was going on inside.

Loud blues rock music filled the air. She shook her head. Bikers loved their Allman Brothers. A man shouted orders, but she couldn't make out what he was saying. She waffled between backing off, lying low, or moving closer.

Cowards never start.

The rain picked up, spattering around her. She wiped her face and stole toward the open bay door, skirting a pile of tires and a rusting motorcycle frame. She stopped next to a windowless van parked at the edge of the shadows and strained her ears, focusing on the shop. Voices raised over the music were cracking jokes. One louder voice barked orders. But nothing indicated what was really going on.

The soft rustle of clothing caught her attention but too late for her to respond to it. A gloved hand clapped across her mouth. A powerful arm wound around her ribs and dragged her backward into deeper shadows. She fought with back elbows, kicked back at her attacker's legs, but the man was moving fast, keeping her off balance.

"Settle down," he whispered in her ear. "I'm from Stillwater."

Stillwater? She stopped struggling and let him lead her to the curb beside a black panel truck. Stillwater was an umbrella organization for a consortium of covert security companies. She had contacted them, as Duncan had directed, but hadn't heard anything back about their plans, if there were any, to help her. As far as she knew, they didn't have assets in Arizona.

The man squatted in the truck's shadow and motioned for her to follow suit.

"What are you doing here?" she asked in a hoarse whisper.

"Saving you," he said in a lowered voice, lifting the black facemask.

Joan scanned the area. "From what?"

"Yourself."

"Very funny. You guys aren't anywhere around me, but you show up now when I'm on the verge of discovering something. And why the hell are you here?" She closed her eyes and relaxed in realization that Duncan must have made good on his promise to call them.

He nodded toward the shop thirty yards away. "Is that why you're undercover in an outlaw motorcycle club?"

"I'm not sure what I'm looking for, but this looks like something of interest." She thought a moment. "You wouldn't know where Bill is, would you?"

"We only follow you."

"You don't follow me…" Her voice trailed off at the vision of the man in the black sedan when she had the run-in with the Mongols. Duncan had been right. At the thought of her husband, a sharp pang of regret pierced through her. She missed being with him. Didn't feel alive when she wasn't. As good as Bill was to her, he wasn't Duncan. She set her jaw. There was only one way to be with Duncan. "I never saw you tailing me," she said. "I'm obsessive about tails."

"We don't have the resources to tail you, but you don't go anywhere we don't know about." His teeth flashed in the dim light. "We even know every text and phone call you make. You lead a boring life."

"Boring. I wish. How do you do that?"

His smile broadened. "Ever have a time when your phone was missing? Maybe some kind of app could have been installed?"

"That was you? Man, I took some heat for that." She thought for a moment. "You got my phone during that police chase in the neighborhood?"

"That was us."

"That was one hell of an elaborate diversion. And the two drunk guys at Leather and Lace? They returned my phone, didn't they?"

"The guy whose head you slammed into the floor still has headaches."

It was exactly what Duncan had suggested to her during their conjugal visit. Stillwater was masterful at covert ops, employing elaborate diversions when needed. "But tonight. Why are you here…in sight?"

"Your tracker said you were moving at two-eighteen a.m. Out of the norm for you. You're too predictable—you really need to shake up your routine, by the way. It triggered a response for us, at least check out what you were up to."

"Us?"

"There're two guys on over watch."

"All this just for me?" She didn't need all this protection. She could take care of herself, and if she couldn't, Bill had her back.

"Word is you aren't 'just' anybody."

She didn't know what to say to that. Duncan must have dropped a hammer on these people. "What's your name?" she asked, shaking the rain from her jacket.

"Chaz." He put up a finger to wait and pressed on his ear bud with the other hand. "Roger that." He looked at Joan. "Why don't you let us find out what's going on inside here? We'll check it out and get back to you."

"I really need to see it firsthand if I'm going to report it to my handler."

"Okay to send pictures to your phone?"

She shook her head. "Better to give them to me in person."

"Let's go." He stood and motioned for Joan to stand, too. He guided her toward her bike. "Meet me at Milagro Café on Mariposa at two p.m. on Wednesday."

"Wednesday? Then I'm going with you." She turned away from her bike. "I'm not waiting till then."

He studied her and must have seen her resolve. "Okay. Tomorrow. You leave the house at eleven on Tuesdays. Meet me at the café at ten-thirty a.m. tomorrow. I'll pass along whatever info we obtain then."

He melted into the shadows, leaving Joan alone next to her bike. She pulled out onto the street thinking about what just happened. In years past, she would have resisted any interference by an outside group, but experience told her to defer to the operator. Stillwater only hired the best, and if Bill was into something serious, that was what she needed. She turned her attention to finding him.

At the first traffic light, she checked her silenced phone for a missed call and saw a voicemail from Bill. Her heart raced. If he was home, he knew she wasn't there. How would she explain her absence? The truth. She couldn't sleep and went looking for him. They were a couple, they should be together. She should be confident he was where he said he was going to be.

Bill's voicemail said he had drunk too much and was spending the night at the club.

"Oh, no, you don't. You are not cheating on me," she said to the phone. She raced to the club house.

She downshifted and stopped in front of a rain-soaked pro- spect standing guard behind a line of motorcycles. The shower had stopped during the ride to the clubhouse, but the prospect still had his chin tucked inside his cut, the collar of his leather jacket pulled up over his neck and ears. She scanned the bikes and located Bill's motorcycle as well as Blaze's.

"Bill called and told me to come and be with him," she said over the rumble of her bike's engine.

"No old ladies," he said. "That's the order."

"Except if the president called me down here."

"Didn't tell me." He pulled out his phone and thumbed in a number. "Joan's at the gate to see Bill." After listening, he put his phone away. "Go home."

"Who was that?" she asked, trying to keep her anger in check. There better be a good reason for Bill refusing to let her inside.

"Sergeant-at-arms. He says who gets in and who doesn't."

She relaxed a little, knowing it had been Little Al's deci- sion, and Bill hadn't turned her away. "But Little Al isn't here," she said to the prospect.

"Don't matter. His word is law. Go home. I'll tell Bill you were here."

She sighed. "Don't bother. This is between him and me."

She opened her throttle. Her tires spun on the wet pave- ment. She manhandled it to keep it upright and raced out of the parking lot, quickly shifted through each gear, and roared off into the night. When she was out of earshot, she slowed down and changed direction. Driving in low gear to muffle the sound of her engine, she found a place to park two blocks from the clubhouse.

She turned off the engine and sat on the bike, her thoughts heavy enough to prevent her from getting off her ride. She was wrapped around the axle about Bill cheating on her, but she wasn't much better. Duncan was her husband, and wasn't she in effect cheating on him? Sure, it was for a greater purpose, even in a convoluted way for their future together. Cheating on him for their future together. How did she ever think this was a good idea? Was she that much better than Bill that she had the standing to sneak into the compound and call him to task—for something she herself was doing?

The rain dripped off her hair and down her neck. She pulled up the collar of her leather jacket, and chastised herself for forgetting Duncan's words: '*Honor is lost when it becomes self-interest. Actions have to be for the greater good to maintain the honor in what you do.*'

Everything she did was to get Duncan out of jail. She dismounted and headed for the Demon Brotherhood compound.

She walked up to the privacy fence and pulled herself up to peek inside. The compound looked empty. Quiet as a church. Hoping no one was manning the security monitors, she slipped over the fence and dropped into the compound. She waited in the shadow of the dumpster, listening and peering into the darkness. She caught her breath and held it when the prospect at the front gate turned and took a few steps toward the dumpster where she crouched. Water droplets falling from the leaves plopped around her.

He took a few more steps, stopped, and listened. Evidently assured what he heard was the raindrops hitting the ground, he headed back to his post.

Inching through the darkness in a crouch, she snuck up the stairs to the party room. After one last look for the prospect, she opened the door far enough to slip inside and let it click behind her. Snoring greeted her, along with the stench of vomit, stale alcohol, and musty sex. Bikers slept slouched over tables. Naked women slept in the arms of bikers on the couches and floor. No longer afraid of being stopped, she strode across the party room toward the hallway that led to Bill's office. Her blood boiled.

She swung open door to the security office where Garbage slept in the chair in front of the monitors. Bill's office was the next door down the hall. She braced herself outside before going in. Her gaze slid around the room and stopped on Blaze, stripped to the waist. He lay with a tattooed arm over a naked Dani, his hand cupping an ample breast. Blaze's old lady could be here, but not her? She clenched her fists. Bill had some serious explaining to do.

"Blaze." He didn't respond. She kicked his foot. "Blaze."

He snorted and pulled Dani into him. "What?" he asked, his voice hoarse and thick with sleep.

"Where's Bill?"

"Upstairs." He snuggled against his woman. "Last door on the left."

Upstairs. That fucking bastard. Every step down the hallway heightened her anger. Adrenaline flooded her veins, increasing with every step up the cement stairs. Last door on the left—she saw it down a black tunnel of anger. Everything else faded into the background until she tripped over a biker sleeping with his back against the wall, legs across the hallway. He sleepily grabbed for her. She caught herself, smacked away his hands, and resumed tracking down Bill—following the scent of blood in the water.

The surging adrenaline made her hands shake as she reached for the door knob. This was about to become a bad day for somebody. After a brief hesitation, she entered the room. It was dark, and she blinked at what looked like a lone figure on the bed. She turned on the light to find Bill lying face down fully clothed. His hair hung loose, covering his face and beard. He hadn't even taken off his colors.

Joan looked behind the door, still expecting to find a woman hiding. She scanned the room, furnished with only a small wooden desk and chair. No closet to hide in. The single bed was pushed against the wall. No curtain at the window. The magazines strewn on the floor and clothes in the corner told her this room was reserved for him.

She nudged his arm. "Bill."

"Go away." He looked around, wiping the sleep from his eyes. They focused on her. "What's wrong? Why are you here?"

"I got your voicemail. I wanted to make sure you were all right."

He finger-combed his loose, silver-streaked hair and scratched his beard. "You thought I was cheating on you."

"I didn't know what to think. You never stayed out all night before."

He turned on his side and made room for her. "Come here. Lay with me, darlin'."

"Let's go home."

He checked the clock on his phone. "I have to get ready for work in four hours. If we leave now, I'll be wide awake."

She traced the edge of his goatee. "I know a way to make you sleepy."

"We can do that right here, darlin'." He pulled her down toward the bed. "We'll leave in time to get ready for work. Maybe shower together."

She gave in, but not before tugging on his cut. "Let's get this off you." She slid it off his shoulders and draped it over the back of a chair.

"You're a good woman." He nuzzled her neck when she snuggled up to him. "I'm gonna fucking kill that prospect."

She wrinkled her nose at the whiskey odor on his breath. "He did his job. He called Little Al and sent me away."

"How'd you get past him?"

"I climbed over the fence."

"That's my girl," Bill said sleepily. "Garbage didn't see you?"

She thought of Garbage sleeping in the chair. "He must have gone to get a cup of coffee. It only took two seconds to get over the fence. And, hey." She nudged him with her elbow. "How come Dani was invited, but I wasn't?"

He hugged her tighter, pinning her arms to her side, and sleepily replied, "She mighta called Blaze, and he let her in. I'da let you in, if you called me."

His breathing evened out and became shallow.

Joan's thoughts kept her awake. If Bill was at the club-house, could it be an alibi? Who was running his shop in the early-morning hours? Men arduously working. Supervisor barking orders. It wasn't Little Al's voice. Was it Switch? She only met him once, not enough to make a positive voice comparison. But Little Al was there. He was part of it—whatever it was. The Stillwater operator might have that information. Bill tasked her with chumming up to Little Al to find out what was going on with him. She had put it off, but thoughts of Duncan waiting in jail gave her a jolt of motivation. Her health had returned, and it was time to do her job. Obtain the evidence. Free her husband. And get on with her life.

She would confront Little Al right after she met with the Stillwater operator and learned what he found in the shop. Talking to Little Al next seemed like the better idea. Keep Bill in the dark until she turned over the evidence to Inez. Maybe even be out of the picture already, by the time the arrest went down. She shook her head thinking how earlier that day she had told Inez she didn't think Bill was doing anything illegal. Not knowing was worse than knowing.

Time to stop vacillating and find out what was really going on. Duncan had trusted Little Al with his life when Al took him to the Ozarks to recover from his gunshot wounds. She wanted to trust Al, too. If their friendship could be revived, it would give her an advantage she might not have with Bill. But she had to tread carefully. Not only were bikers wary and dangerous, but she had believed Al was a trusted friend when he lied to Bill about her.

That was something else she needed to address.

CHAPTER 16

Joan pulled out of the Milagro Café parking lot after the informative conversation with the Stillwater operator. He had explained his team's findings while he downloaded the information to her phone. She had expected photos, but he provided a short video of the activities inside Bill's custom shop. The stacks of packaged white powder—ostensibly heroin, or worse fentanyl, indicated this was a vast, high-revenue distribution operation.

The closer she got to Sun Valley Custom Rides the harder her heart beat against the inside of her chest. Would Little Al push it off onto Bill, or explain why he was a part of a drug cartel? He'd always been honest with her in the past. She hoped he'd be honest with her today. She drove past the motorcycle part of the shop to the automotive side. The sight of Little Al's motorcycle stopped the pounding in her chest. Dread replaced it with icy fingernails scratching across her shoulders.

She fought back the nagging nausea. Over the last couple days, nausea had hit her about mid-morning after her morning workout, continuing in waves until early evening. The ride across town had quelled it, but it was back in force. She pulled some soda crackers out of her bike's saddlebag and nibbled one.

No one had seen her. She could turn around and leave. But the Stillwater operators had risked a lot to get the video. If she didn't use it, not only would their effort have been for nothing, but she would lose the one chance to get Duncan out of jail—maybe before Christmas. She shook off the apprehension settling in her legs, turning her bones to water. After dropping the baggie of crackers into the saddlebag, she squared her shoulders and strode toward the building.

She recognized the inside of shop from the video. A mechanic did a double take at her leonine confident stride. He stopped work and asked if he could help her.

"Al's office?" she asked.

"Through the double doors. First door on the left," he said, wiping his wrench with a shop rag. "Sure there ain't something I can do for you?"

She turned him down with a tight smile and a quick shake of her head before walking across the shop floor, aware of the pressure of the .380 semi-automatic in the small of her back. The usual spear point dagger was sheathed in her boot. A shorter Ka-Bar knife chafed her wrist, hidden by her shirt sleeve. Little Al was a gentle giant, but this conversation could go bad in a hurry.

A worker rushed through one of the double doors, saw her at the last minute, and held it for her. She nodded thanks and stepped into the hallway. Her pace slowed when she heard Little Al in a conversation.

"Hey, Switch," Little Al said.

"What's up?" Switch asked. His voice had a distant, metallic tone.

Must be on speaker, Joan thought as she hugged the wall and quieted her breathing.

"'Bout Joan snooping around," Little Al said. "Hear you're planning to scare her into giving it up."

"That's right."

"How far you plan to go?"

"Far enough till we're ready. Why?" Switch asked.

"Let me take care of it."

"She has to be stopped."

"I'll stop her," Little Al said. "I know her better than anyone else and—"

"That's what I'm worried about."

"No need to worry," Little Al said. "My old lady says she might be pregnant. Makes her easier to control."

"Why does she think that?" Switch said.

"Something about a bad batch of birth control," Little Al said.

Light tapping on a computer keyboard filled the silence.

Little Al must be working while talking. She ignored the "pregnant" remark and strained to hear if anything else could tell her what was going on.

"Pregnant," Switch finally said. "This shit gets better and better."

"Who's that, Babe?" Sapphire's slight lisp with a hint of southern accent was faint but unmistakable.

There was rustling and muffled voices.

"Hi, Al," she said.

"Go to the bedroom." Switch's voice was lowered. "I'll be there soon."

Kissing sounds filled the silence. "Real soon," Switch said in answer to Sapphire's inaudible question. "Soon as I take care of some business." After a long silence, possibly to be sure she was out of earshot, Switch said, "I can depend on you to take care of this?"

Little Al didn't answer. He had stopped typing. Joan could feel the tension radiating into the hallway.

"How are your kids?" Switch asked. "Hate to see any-thing—"

"I said I'll take care of it."

Joan sensed more than agitation, but she couldn't be sure without being in the room. Besides the overt threat to her wel-fare, there was a wealth of knowledge there, but she couldn't zero in on exactly what was passing between the two men. Whatever it was, it didn't sound good.

"We're done here?" Switch asked.

"Yeah, we're done," Little Al said.

"Good. I got Bill's sweet pussy waitin' for me in the bed-room."

Joan leaned her head against the wall and rubbed her stom-ach. She was in no shape to handle this today, but she was here

now. Could she play Little Al without taking on the whole
Demon Brotherhood? And the Mongols? Duncan had told her
to trust her instincts, but logic said Little Al was the opening
gig. If she was about to take down Bill, she couldn't take him
head on. She had to work the field until she cornered him.

She clenched her jaw. Little Al was not going to get rid of
her. Not today. Not ever.

Weigh each word.

He's your friend. Use that.

She looked around the wall into the office. Little Al sat
with elbows on the desk, holding his head. She rapped on the
doorjamb.

"What?" Little Al asked brusquely before he looked up.

She expected agitation, but his eyebrows were tensed with
worry. He sat back, rubbed his face, and assumed a neutral
expression.

She rolled her shoulders to relax. Wishing she had told Inez
what she was doing and hoping Stillwater was tracking her,
she walked into Little Al's office.

"What's up?" he asked. "Something wrong with your
bike?"

"My bike is fine. We need to talk."

He motioned for her to sit down.

She looked around the office. A motorcycle gas tank with
an intricate paint job sat on a side table. Stacked invoices and
bills filled the space next to the computer. A parts catalog lay
open in front of Little Al. Everything looked normal, no indication of the tense conversation she just overheard.

"I thought we were friends—" she started.

"Is this about that lie I told Bill?"

Joan blinked. "You admit you lied to him?"

"Seemed like the right thing at the time. What're you doing
here?"

"I came to bury the hatchet."

"Yeah," he snorted. "In a shallow grave so you can get to it
in a hurry."

She opened her mouth to speak and shut it, thinking of the
time Kearney had said similar words to her. The yearning for a

friendly voice almost overwhelmed her. The last time she decided to email Kearney, she had relapsed and wound up in bed fighting a fever. If she made it out of this confrontation alive, she would contact him without delay. She just might need that lifeline.

"We were always friendly before," she finally said. "But something's different. You're different."

"A lot can change in a year." He rocked back in his chair and studied her. "Why are you here?"

"In your office?"

"In Phoenix."

"Being on the run was exhausting. Bill offered protection. I took him up on it."

"I like you, Joan. That's why I'm warning you to be careful."

"Careful? Of what?"

He leaned forward, propping his arms on the desk. "Just watch your back."

"Okay, let me get this straight," she said. "You lie to Bill about me, not knowing what he'd do. And now you tell me I need to watch my back. I don't get a sense of friendship here."

Little Al didn't respond.

She resisted the urge to look through the window at the shop. Pneumatic tools brrr-ed. The Lynyrd Skynyrd tune "Gimme Three Steps" blared above the noise. Just minutes before, he told Switch he would get rid of her. Was that a lie, too? Why had he lied to Bill? A calm settled over her. She knew why.

"You wanted Bill to get rid of me."

"If he got pissed enough and sent you packin', he wouldn't search for you. Keep his head where it belongs—on club business."

"Some friend you are," she said.

"Club first."

"Friendship doesn't play into the equation? Not at all?"

He rocked in his chair, watching her. Thinking. "Never saw Bill take a woman's word over a Brother's before."

"Maybe the truth was more convincing," she said, leaning forward, hoping the nausea held off until this confrontation was over.

Little Al's countenance was neutral, but his eyes narrowed.

"Why can't we be friends, like last year, before I had to leave?" she asked.

He raised his gaze from her hand pressing on her stomach then tapped his thumb on a tab on the front of his cut. "What's this say?"

"Sergeant-at-arms."

"Means I'm responsible for club security. Harboring a fugitive will take down the club. Friendship doesn't make you any less of a risk."

"Bill swears no one is looking for me anymore." If it was such a big deal, more pressure would have been put on Bill to get rid of her. This was something else. She looked into the shop, swallowing the bile working its way up the back of her throat. When she looked back at Little Al, he was looking at her more closely than before.

She need to gain control of the conversation.

"You blew off my safety. Bill could've done more than send me away."

"He didn't."

"And now, here you are warning me to be careful. Careful of what?"

"You haven't changed." He shook his head. "Still relentless."

Her stomach churned. "Do you have anything to eat?"

"I might." After rummaging through the top desk drawer, he said, "I have a protein bar."

Joan ripped open the package and took a bite.

"Does Bill know you're here?" he asked.

She gagged down a mouthful of protein bar that tasted like liquid vitamins in sawdust. She couldn't tell him that Bill sent her. She didn't know how he would respond. And if he told Bill another lie, this time a more convincing one, she couldn't rely on Bill to take her side again. There would be no telling which way it would go for her. Playing one Brother against the other was a dangerous game. And she thought this was a good idea because—

Bile filled the back of her throat. "Where's the bathroom?" She pressed her hand across her mouth.

"Left out the door. Turn right before the reception area."

Joan rushed out of the office.

"Keep going straight," he said behind her.

She barely made it in time. *I'm probably the strongest woman west of the Mississippi, and I can't get through a conversation without emptying my stomach.* She rinsed her mouth, but her stomach wasn't done. *This better be a relapse and not…*She couldn't bear to finish the thought. After rinsing her mouth again and blowing her nose, she opened the door to find Little Al leaning on the wall, arms folded across his ample chest.

"You okay?"

"Yeah, fine. Stomach bug."

"Some women find soda crackers help."

Bastard. And she would have to have a talk with Orlanda and Carol about keeping secrets.

"You okay to ride?" he asked. "I could have one of the guys drive you home."

"I'm good," she said, anxious to get to the crackers in her saddlebag.

"Let me walk you to your bike." He guided her through the shop, past the stares of his workers. They walked in silence until the only sound was the gravel crunching under their boots. When they reached her bike, he turned to face her. He exhaled loudly before saying, "This is the only warning you're gonna get: Leave Phoenix. Do it soon."

"I can't, I…" She couldn't quit now. If only she could tell him why. "I can't leave. Bill's done so much for me."

"You disappoint me." Little Al leaned against a car and shook his head. "You used to be so good at bluffing."

"I'm not bluffing."

"There's more to consider than just yourself. Can't emphasize enough to take my advice. Leave now. While you still can."

She straddled her bike and started it. *More to consider than just yourself…leave…While you still can.* Was he warning her as a friend? Or as the rogue agent? Either way, she hoped he didn't know why she was in Phoenix.

Little Al knew where Duncan hid out during his recovery. Being a federal agent could explain how the ATF found Duncan and followed him to her. But other Brothers knew where Duncan had holed up. Carol had said Slow Motion and Blaze rode with Al to Arkansas. And most likely Bill knew. Any one of them could be the agent. And she couldn't rule out anyone outside the DBMC.

When she had discovered Duncan's affair with the ATF undercover agent, it had rocked her world. Almost caused a divorce. But that was history. The conjugal visit had renewed her conviction to do what was right for him, had proven their bond was still strong, and had deepened the importance of this lie of her life.

Joan and Little Al stared at each other for a long time. He had told Switch he would get rid of her. The warning was sincere, no question about that. But she couldn't leave Phoenix until Duncan walked through those prison doors.

She pulled her phone out of her jacket pocket. "I have something I'm hoping you can explain."

She brought up the video and handed her phone to him. He watched it, frowning. His shoulders tensed.

"What does Switch have to do with this?" she asked. "What's he up to?"

"I remember these guys coming in," Little Al said, staring at the screen. "Who are they?"

"I can't tell you that."

He stood up and loomed over her. No more threats. Just exertion of will by his presence. "Who are they?"

She slid the Ka-Bar knife from its sheath along her forearm. It glinted in the sun.

He saw it and chuckled. "So this is what our friendship has come to?" He fingered his hair back from his face and clasped the back of his head, her phone forgotten in his hand.

She put her fists on her hips, the knife in earth grip along her forearm. Hidden from his sight, it was less threatening. But still in play.

"Sheath your knife. I'm not gonna hurt you." He stared at her for several seconds then handed over her phone. "You got nothing. Snooping around can get the attention of the wrong people."

"What do you mean 'wrong people?'" she asked, tucking away the knife. "I can help you, if you let me. Talk to me, Al."

He scratched his beard and looked at her. "You came here to ask why I lied, but you think something else is going on, and you won't stop until you find out what it is. I'm telling you to stop sticking your nose where it doesn't belong. Don't be you. This one time, Joan, don't be you."

"What does that mean?"

"Remember the falcon parable I told you last year? You're a predator, not all the time, but when you see prey, you fly straight toward it and take it down. Difference is this time you won't return to the safety of the falconer's arm."

"Predator? Those days are gone." *What kind of predator am I? I can't be more than a few seconds from a barf bag.*

"I'm tellin' you. You won't make it."

"I've survived worse."

"You're out of your league."

"You have no idea what I've overcome," she said. "I can handle myself."

Brothers don't have secrets from each other.

She took the plunge. "Does Bill know what's going on here?"

"You don't know everything. And you won't." His gaze fell to her crossed arms pressing against her stomach then glared into her eyes. "There won't be any more warnings. Don't make me do something we'll both regret."

He had lied. She was living a lie. One more couldn't make things any worse. "Bill doesn't know I'm here," she said, squinting up at him in the afternoon sun. "I'm relying on our friendship to keep this between us."

"I won't tell Bill," he said. "If you leave town. I'll give you till after Thanksgiving."

Joan focused on those hard, blue eyes that said the best place to be was not there. She left the parking lot, the motion easing her nausea. She headed to the library to send an email to Kearney. Libraries had a special aroma, a delicate mix of paper, ink, and carpeting. This time the hush wasn't strong enough to comfort her. She headed for the computer banks, which were on the far side of the room. They were all occupied except for the next to the last one. She would have preferred to be on the end, but she didn't have time to wait. She checked the screens on the way past, quietly checking out each user as well. Nothing out of place.

She logged into the email account that only a select few could access. They communicated by leaving emails in the draft folder, making them difficult to hack—only the most advance computer forensics specialists could hack it. She hit the Compose button and sat looking at the empty email. What should she tell Kearney? What *could* she tell him? Conjecture was all she had, but if she was right, and she didn't act, Little Al's sons would be in danger.

Hey, K.,

I hope all is well for you. I'm back in Phoenix...it's a long story. Things are great with me, but maybe not so much for Little Al's sons. They might be in danger because of something he's into. If I'm right, it's serious, life or death. I can't do anything for them for various reasons. You know I would, if I could. Could you secure them? I know it's a lot to ask of you to chance coming back into the US, but I'm really afraid for them.

Let me know if you can take care of this for me.

Joan

She read it over several times. Not the best prose she ever wrote, but it said enough without saying too much, just in case the email account was hacked.

She retraced her path to the exit. The bright sun made her squint as she crossed the parking lot to her bike.

The traffic home was light, allowing her to think. Duncan had told her to trust her instincts and that logic could be her enemy. Logic told her to start her investigation with Little Al. Instincts assured her Little Al was still her friend. But he had just threatened her.

There was more at stake than she saw openly. But what? This whole thing was bigger than the two of them. She'd bet her throwing knives on that. He wasn't the type to be a part of anything illegal, especially behind Bill's back. And yet, that was exactly what the video, and he himself, had implied. It would take time to convince him to trust her with the truth. Thing was, she didn't know how much time she had. He may not know she was a CI, but he knew she smelled prey and was heading toward it. He'd warned her off with a threat.

Her strategy had been right. Approach one biker head-on to flank the other.

The chill dread returned—paralyzing and illuminating. There was one big flaw in her plan.

She'd started with the wrong biker.

CHAPTER 17

Joan nibbled a cracker and thought about last Tuesday when she got home after seeing Little Al. She had summoned the courage to trust Bill and tell him what she knew, but he had been too preoccupied with club business and asked if it could wait. She had jumped at the chance to delay telling him something that could set him off. Four long days had passed, one of them Thanksgiving—spending the day with his grandchildren had kept him busy and distracted. When he didn't ask about it on Friday or Saturday, she thought he had forgotten, grateful for the reprieve. And it seemed Little Al was staying true to his word. But as soon as he realized she wasn't going anywhere, she would have to tell Bill what she knew.

It was Sunday, usually a laid-back day, sometimes taking a ride to the mountains or spending a day at Orlanda and Dagger's house. Having spent Thanksgiving with them, and with a threat of rain in the forecast, Bill opted to stay home. She worked off her nervousness by cleaning. This was her chance, but when she showed him the evidence, she would become a liability—unless she could convince him to bring her into it. If he was innocent, she would be considered a nosey-broad, or worse, and no longer have the freedom to come and go unobserved like she enjoyed now.

She wrapped the cord around the pegs on the back of the vacuum cleaner. A part of her hoped he was not involved. But she still knew too much. And Little Al's threat was real and credible.

She grabbed a bottle of cleanser and wiped down the tile in the bathroom between the office and their bedroom. The smell of soap seemed to settle her stomach.

"Hey, darlin'," Bill called from the office. "Come here a sec."

She leaned on the door jamb. "What?"

"Gonna rub the shine off those tiles. Does it have anything to do with what you wanted to talk about Tuesday night?"

She picked at the fingers of her rubber gloves. "I just want to get everything clean well ahead of the Christmas."

"House was clean an hour ago." He looked over his reading glasses. "Spit it out."

He hadn't pulled his hair into a ponytail, and it hung past his shoulders. The salt-and-pepper softness accentuated the hardness of his eyes, making him look meaner than he was. She debated how to approach the delicate subject of the illegal activity at his shop. Just "spit it out" like he said, or talk around it and get him to tell her on his own. She pulled off the rubber gloves and took a deep breath. *Cowards never start.*

He reached into the bottom drawer of his desk and plopped an early pregnancy test box onto the desk, brilliant white against a yellow bill.

"Does it have anything to do with this?"

Then there was that.

Bile crept up her throat. "I'm late."

"But you wear the patch."

"There was a recall. My lot number was…defective."

He hesitated so long she steeled herself for a blow up.

He tossed his reading glasses onto the pile of bills in front of him. "How late?"

"A week."

He squinted at the wall calendar.

Oh, my God, he's checking the date. She had already counted back the days. Her fertile days fell around the conjugal visit and Bill claiming her. *He knows about the day with Duncan. He knows I've been unfaithful.* She shook her head to clear it. She had already covered the definition of faithfulness on that dark street a week ago.

"Is that unusual for you?" he finally asked.

"Sometimes, if I'm under stress. I was sick last week, so…" She rubbed the back of her neck. "But with the recall, I'm a little worried."

He pinched the corners of his eyes with his thumb and forefinger. "Why didn't you tell me about the recall?"

"If I got my period, no harm, no foul. You seemed so uptight these past few weeks, I didn't want to add to it with something that might not be a problem."

"Found this in the bottom drawer of the chest of drawers. One more thing you're hiding from me."

"You're checking up on me?"

"Nothing happens I don't know about. You know that."

Joan stared at the box, but didn't see it. *One more thing you're hiding from me.* What did he know? How much? Prickles ran across her scalp and settled on her neck. Her legs turned to water.

She tried to ignore the bile that threatened her from the back of her throat. "I've seen women spring the news on the man, and he says something all wrong, only because he's blindsided. When I thought maybe…if I thought I was…" She swallowed hard. "I figured we'd do it together."

"We're together now," Bill said, opening the box and dumping three sealed test sticks onto the desk.

She stared at the sticks. "I'm sorry, Bill, I never meant—" She rubbed her mouth and waited until her stomach settled. "I never meant to do this to us."

"You didn't make the patch." He settled his reading glasses on the end of his nose and read the back of the box. "You wore it. That's enough for me."

She took a deep breath. "Let's do this. Then we'll know." She put out her hand for a stick.

"Need any help?" Bill asked, smirking and eyeing her crotch.

"I think I can pee on a stick without assistance." His teasing suggested he didn't know about checking up on him. Or the Little Al confrontation. Or the conjugal visit. Or being a snitch. Or...Damn. She was living the real-life version of Chutes and Ladders with one foot on the longest chute. And this one didn't snake downward to Start. It led off the board.

"I could hold your hand." He held up a stick.

"Just read me the instructions," she said, taking the stick and heading to the bathroom.

The instructions said to wait two minutes. They eyed the stick a few seconds before he put an arm around her waist and pulled her in to him.

"What do you plan to do?" he asked.

"You mean whether I'm going to keep it?"

He nodded.

"I don't know. I want to keep it, but I'm not sure about bringing up a kid in this lifestyle."

"I don't like calling the baby 'it.' Let's call the baby 'him' until we know different."

She ran her fingers through his hair. "I like that."

"The MC is one big family," he said. "Lotsa kids don't have any family at all. Our kids have dozens of big brothers, uncles, and aunts. What's wrong with that?"

She shrugged, thinking of the quality of that family tree. "How can I raise a kid, when I don't know what's going on with his father?"

"You concentrate on being healthy. Leave club business to me."

"See what I mean? You won't let me in. Because of that, I can't take good care of you."

"You do just fine, darlin'."

"No. I don't. If I knew what was going on, what makes you surly one minute and loving and kind the next, I could support you more when you're down, and enjoy the good times with you."

He squinted at her. "You aren't happy in this relationship?"

"I didn't say that. At times, I'm just not...comfortable."

"And knowing the dirty deeds of the club will make you more comfortable with me?"

"I don't have to know all the gory details, but if I knew what was going on, I'd feel more like a partner to you."

"Sharing club business with you is not a good idea. Especially now that you might be pregnant."

"Something told me it was wrong to tell you till I knew for sure. You're—"

"We did the right thing."

"—going to treat me like I'm handicapped."

"Bet your ass I will. Don't want anything happening to this baby. Orlanda wants more time with her kids. You could take her job. You'll be at the dealership every day. I can keep an eye on you, not like at Leather and Lace where—"

"I might get an abortion," Joan blurted. It was not an option, but she had to find a way to put pressure on Bill to be more open with her. She cringed at using a fetus as a bargaining chip. When did she lose her moral compass?

He glared at her. Her words must have hit a nerve because he said, "I had to do some ugly things during my rise through the ranks, but killin' a baby's something I can't stomach."

"How can I provide a stable home when I don't know what's going on with you?"

"Club business is off the table. Forget it."

She was silent. The seed was planted. In any case, she may already have the information the Bureau needed.

"What's so wrong with having a baby with me?" he asked.

Other than it might not be yours and sending you to prison? She clamped her eyes shut, wondering how something as lovely as having a baby turned sour when it involved her. She thought of Inez's threats if she was pregnant. For a moment, she considered spiting Inez by withholding the information she had on her phone. But that adolescent spite-fest would come back to haunt her and ultimately Duncan.

"We're getting ahead of ourselves," she said. "It might be a false alarm."

The timer on Bill's phone beeped.

They looked at each other. Then leaned over to look at the stick.

⌘⌘⌘

Switch looked at the Caller ID and frowned. "Yeah. Whadya want?" He ran his fingers through his dark hair that hung loose. The last person he wanted to talk to right now was the woman he referred to as Tia Dragon Lady.

"Haven't heard from you. What's going on?" she asked.

"We're on schedule," he said. He thought about his conversation with Little Al and smiled. "Maybe even better than on schedule. Got some news. If true, it sweetens the deal. Hold on a sec."

He looked over at Sapphire on the couch next to him, snoring quietly. Didn't mean she was asleep. He got up and walked into the hallway to continue his conversation. "Bill's old lady might be pregnant."

"Pregnant? Are you sure?"

"I said, 'might.' Don't know for sure, but if she is, it's a damn two-fer."

"If she's pregnant, it might solve a lot of our problems with her."

"I don't give a fuck." Dragon Lady was getting weak-kneed. Not what he expected. Not from her. "She stays in play. I'm gonna get even with her."

"It matters to me. It changes a lot, legally, as well as morally," she said.

He walked into the bathroom, shut the door, and tucked the phone between his shoulder and ear. He unzipped his pants to pee. "When did the law or morals mean anything to you?"

"Call this off," she said. "I'm not losing my job over this."

"Enough o' your bullshit." The urine stream started. Didn't care if she heard it over the phone. "Shoulda thought of that before you signed on to this. I'm in charge—

"No. I call the shots. And—"

"Fuck off, Tia," he said. "This's always been my deal, 'n' you ain't takin' over now it's almost done."

He ended the call. This was not over. All his work and planning. Only days till it was time to push the button. Shoulda known that bitch would weasel in on his gig. He'd show her who's boss. Didn't care who she was. If she wasn't family, a good beat down would put her in her place. Shoulda known better than to work with family. Speaking of beat downs. He had to act on another piece of information he had received.

He walked into the living room, grabbed Sapphire by the hair, and dragged her off the couch. "Why didn't you tell me Wild Bill don't hook up with you no more?"

"I told you," she whined, eyes unfocused, looking confused about what was going on after being awakened so roughly.

He backhanded her across her face. "You shoulda been more believable. You're no use to me now."

"Sure I am, baby," she said, putting up her hands to prevent another blow. "I'm always here for you."

He shook his hand that was entangled in her hair.

She whimpered and tried to get away. He snapped her head back.

"What am I gonna do with you, you bitchin' whore?" he asked, backhanding her again.

ↄↄↄↄ

Pregnant. The pink plus sign pulsated at Joan. Then blurred.

Bill pulled her in tight against his body. A good thing, because her knees turned to water the second time in less than ten minutes.

This cannot be happening to me. Not now. Not like this. She laid her head against his shoulder. *Oh, Duncan, I am so sorry.* Couldn't anything be easy? No. Not for her.

If the Bureau found out, they'd pull her from the mission. Duncan would die in prison. Something told her Inez would gloat about sending Joan to jail after putting so much on the line. The baby would be born there. She'd never see it again.

She fingered Bill's beard. "Don't say anything to anybody, okay?"

"Why not?" he asked.

"You know how sometimes these things don't work out."

"You talkin' miscarriage or abortion? Or something else?"

Joan answered with a stronger embrace. She needed his strength now. But more importantly, she needed him to trust her and open up to her.

Bill kissed her passionately. She was slow to respond. It felt dirty using an unborn child as a pawn in her sordid deal with the feds. She recalled Duncan's supportive words during their conjugal visit. That what she did had to be for the greater good to maintain the honor in her actions. She relaxed into Bill's embrace. Everything she did was for Duncan...and now for a child that could be his.

"I have that mandatory run this weekend," Bill said. "Gonna be hard to keep this a secret."

CHAPTER 18

When Bill's Harley rumbled into the garage when he returned from Huachuca City, Joan's heart leapt in her chest. The constant anxiety over their secret made the run seem longer than three days. She turned off the TV and stood to greet him.

He came through the door looking tired and strung out from the road—bags under his eyes, stubble edged his goatee. He took her into his arms, and kissed her long and hard.

"Wow. That was some greeting." She leaned back to look at him with narrowed eyes. "What did you do?"

"Can't a man kiss his old lady without her thinking he did something wrong?"

"You never greeted me like this when you got back before."

"You weren't pregnant before."

"We have to talk."

"Yes, we do, but let me get a drink first. Want one?" He stopped and turned to her. "I won't have one long as you can't."

"It's okay. Have your drink. I'll have a glass of water."

"Sure?"

"Yeah, I'm sure." Joan smiled. He had always been considerate in his roughneck way, but this was behavior a regular, everyday Joe would exhibit. It was almost comical coming from life-worn, rugged Bill.

"Good, because I need a drink," he said. Ice cubes tinkled into a glass.

"We have to get something clear," Joan said, following him to the kitchen. "I'm pregnant, not disabled."

"Yeah, I know but—"

"Treat me as if nothing's different. Okay?"

"Not happenin', darlin'." He handed her a glass of water and took a long pull on his drink. "The long ride to and from Huachuca City gave me plenty of time to think about what you said. I'm gonna tell you whatever you need to know. Only tried to spare you because I shared club business with Orlanda's mother. It scared her away."

"I'm not Orlanda's mother."

"Exactly. You been through more than her. If anyone can handle it, it's you. Don't want you brought down by club business, but if it'll bring us closer together, that's what I'll do."

"Brought down?"

"I don't mean, like, taken down. I mean..." He stopped, as if fearing anything he said next would be wrong.

"You mean stress me out?" she asked.

"Or lose respect for me."

"What could you tell me that I'd lose respect for you?"

"Talkin' to the guys this weekend, I realized imagination can be worse than truth. If you're imaginin' me as some criminal, you won't respect me. Really respect me. 'Cos I'm not a criminal. Not anymore. When I said I went legit, I meant it."

Joan chuckled.

"What's so funny?"

"I never heard you put so many words together at one time before."

"Things have changed." He guided her toward the living room.

Joan knitted her brow.

"What's that look for?" he asked, draping his cut over the back of a chair.

"This doesn't make sense," she said, noting how fatigue and the weight of responsibilities rounded his shoulders. "You said you went legit, yet you're afraid I won't respect you."

"Only 'cos you might imagine worse things than what's really goin' on." He swallowed some whiskey, sat on the couch, and pulled her down beside him. "You have to promise something in return."

"What's that?"

"No more secrets. Something happens, I want to hear it from you. Not from someone else. Not from a box hidden in the bottom drawer. Don't want to force it out of you. Just speak up."

She didn't say anything for a while, wondering how far she should go. She decided to start easy. "What's been making you so unpredictable lately?"

"Fitz's been riding my ass about sightings of Mongols in the area."

"Is it unusual for them to be here?"

"Shouldn't ride here 'less we know what they're doin'. There's a chapter out in Quartzite, 'bout a hundred miles west of Phoenix."

Little Al had mentioned Quartzite. She tried to remember the context. "So that's why there were Mongols on the road that day I broke down."

"Yes...and no."

"Meaning?"

"There's a shaky peace between the Angels and the Mongols. If they're comin' into town, they call Fitz. Courtesy call to the Hells Angels president. That call keeps everybody up on what's going on."

"But they said they called Fitz."

"I knew they didn't. If they had, they'da been wearing their colors."

"Then you knew Little Al lied when he said they called Fitz."

"Not necessarily." He took another big swallow of whiskey. "But he chose to believe them."

"Why?"

"That's part o' what got Blaze and me wonderin' about him."

She pulled her feet up onto the couch and hugged her knees. Bill and Blaze knew something was up, too. "So that's why it was so easy to convince you I hadn't lied and that I wasn't a snitch for the Mongols."

"I'm gonna get another drink." He continued the conversation from the kitchen. "Point is, I checked with Fitz to be sure. He never got a courtesy call."

While he refreshed his drink, she wondered why all this was so important. The Mongols lied. So what? Not exactly news about bikers. Besides, it was history. And that's where it should stay.

When he finished making his drink, he returned to his place next to her and continued. "Fitz tasked the DBMC to police the area. These guys are joy riding through the area, getting me in hot water with the Angels. That's what had me tied in knots the week after I rode to Safford. I knew if I talked to you, I'd blow whatever chance I had. Kept my distance till church that Sunday."

"That's why the Tucson Chapter was in town."

"Partly. We usually invite them to our Family Day."

"What happened at the meeting?"

"Can't give you the details."

She scowled at him.

"Said I'd tell you what you need to know. You don't need to know what's discussed at club meetings."

"You know I won't say anything to anybody."

"Come here." He pulled her toward him and wrapped his arm around her shoulders. "I trust you with my life. Know that, right?"

She cuddled against him, inhaling the scent of fresh air from the long ride home. He had opened up to her—the moment she had worked toward the past couple months. It was a hard-fought victory. Telling him she had been checking up on him could ruin this fragile beginning. She weighed what she knew already against possible future information she could get from him.

"Thank you," she finally said.

"For what?"

"For trusting me enough to tell me what's going on. What you can, anyway."

He kissed her head and leaned his head back on the couch. She put an arm across his chest and rested her head on his shoulder. They sat like that for several minutes in the quiet room, comfortable in each other's arms, lost in their own thoughts.

Now was the time to tell him about what was going on in his shop after hours. He claimed he was totally legit. Telling him she knew about the transportation of drugs would bring his activities into the light, that she knew better than to believe he was legit, like he said he was. And that she knew he had just lied to her. But what if her gut was right, and he was legit and was not part of it? Did that mean it would void her deal? Was she willing to give that up for the truth? She looked up at him. His head rested on the back of the couch, eyes closed, totally relaxed. If she could prove he wasn't involved in any illegitimate business, and her deal was revoked because of it, that look on his face would make whatever happened to her worth it.

He pulled her in tighter against him and rubbed her arm. He could be waiting for her to come through on her part of the promise. He had just spent three days with Little Al. She couldn't take the chance that Al said something about her visit. If Bill knew, and she was not forthcoming, it could taint this new beginning. He had tasked her to approach Little Al, and she should have told him what happened that day, not now a week and a half later.

This moment was so tender. She hated ruining it.

She sat up, took a deep breath, and said, "In the spirit of telling you something before you hear it from someone else, I have something to tell you."

"What's that?" he asked without opening his eyes.

"I went to visit Little Al at Sun Valley Custom Rides. Like you asked me to do."

Bill's eyes remained closed. Did that tightened corner of his mouth mean Little Al told him, or he knew what she was going to say? Or that he didn't care?

"I think it went well—rebuilding bridges and all that."

Bill smiled. "I know. He told me you went to see him. Also said you got sick." He opened one eye. "We now know what that was, don't we?"

"You knew and didn't mention it to me?"

"Just checkin' your honesty, darlin'."

Little Al. That rat bastard. He said he wouldn't tell Bill. True, that agreement hinged on the condition she would leave town, but she thought he would still own up to his end of the deal. From Bill's relaxed posture, she bet he didn't know all of it. Little Al didn't even know all she had. She only showed him the short video.

She eyed her phone on the table and pictured Dagger sitting at the picnic table in the DBMC compound. His words came back to her. *All in or get out.*

"That's not all," she said.

"What else did you talk about?"

"Actually, it's what he wouldn't talk about."

"Spit it out, darlin'. It was a long ride. I'm fadin'."

"Do you know what's going on at Sun Valley Custom Rides after hours?"

His eyes snapped open. He raised his head and looked at her. "If something's goin' on, how would you know?"

She took a deep breath. "Remember the night I climbed the fence and found you passed out at the clubhouse?"

"Yeah." The word was clipped, a warning to be careful.

"I was wondering where you went at night when you weren't here."

He sat upright and pinned her eyes with his. "You've been checking up on me?"

"Just that once. But that's not where I'm going with this. Hear me out."

His gaze didn't falter. This was going to hell in a hurry. Too late to back out.

"Before I went to the club, I checked your shop, thinking that's where you were. Your bike wasn't there, but there was a lot of activity." She shrugged. "So I checked around."

"We've had a lot of business lately. Prob'ly just catching up."

She pressed her lips together and shook her head. Her insides were shaking. She took a sip and set the glass on the table. "Switch and those other Mongols on the road that day? They were in there with a couple other guys I never saw before."

"Mongols? You sure?"

"Didn't see any colors. But there were Mongol decals on some of the bikes. The rest must be associated with them in some way."

Bill sat up, fatigue gone, driven away by anger. His face was red. He pulled out his phone. "Little Al needs to know."

Joan covered his phone with her hand. "He knows. I—"

"You told him?" Bill said through clenched teeth. "When are you going to learn to mind your own business?"

"He knows because he was there."

"What is this? You tryin' to get back at him for lying to me about you? I didn't think you were this petty."

She put a hand on his arm. He brushed her off and paced around the room. If he stormed off before she finished, it would be over. Might as well call Inez and tell her to bring her handcuffs. When Bill confronted Little Al, he would deny everything. Joan would be the heavy, the scapegoat. Bill had to know what she knew. "I have proof."

He stopped and glared at her. "It better be good."

"It's in my phone. Take a look."

She queued up the video. He snatched the phone from her, took a few steps away, and watched it.

"How'd you get this?" he asked, his face distorted with rage.

"I can't tell you. Does it matter?"

He strode up to her. "Better start talkin'."

CHAPTER 19

Joan put the gas nozzle into the tank, wondering if telling Bill about Stillwater had been a good idea. He had seemed equally upset about someone other than him protecting his woman as he was about the cartel transporting drugs to his shop and his men delivering it. They had talked it over for hours. She told him what happened in Yonkers and her few jobs for Stillwater. Then finished it with her cover story of a narrow getaway, winding up in Albuquerque. The only way he let it go was for her to promise no more contact with any out-side groups.

Another lie. She wondered if she'd be able to tell the truth about anything when this ordeal was over.

She pulled up the collar of her leather jacket when a cold wind gusted from the mountains to the north—the local news station said there was snow in Prescott. While she watched the numbers on the pump, her phone rang. The Caller ID said the caller's number was blocked. She almost put it back in her pocket, but her gut urged her to take it. "Hello?"

"Joan?"

"Yeah. Who's this?"

"A friend from your past."

She recognized the voice. "Hey, Roger. Haven't heard from you for a while."

"Free to talk?"

"Yeah. What's up?"

"Thought you should know, bikers came around The Bottom Rocker asking lots of questions about you."

The distinctive double, muffled backfire of Little Al's bike came from nearby. She looked around and prayed he hadn't seen her. No such luck. He swerved into the mini-mart parking lot and pulled up next to her bike.

"Hold a sec, Rog." She pressed the phone against her jacket.

"We have to talk," Little Al shouted over his loud engine. He was not a happy biker.

"We don't have anything to talk about," she said.

"Yes, we do. Pull over to the side of the building when you're done here."

"Why? You want to lie to my face again?"

"Just do it, Joan."

"Fuck off, Al."

"Don't make me chase after you," he said, pointing at her for emphasis before pulling out of the lane between the pumps and leaning his big bike toward the far side of the building by an air compressor and the slatted fence hiding the dumpsters.

If she got into traffic before he stopped her, he would catch up to her before she made it to the dealership. She didn't know what he'd do. Kick her bike out from under her and send her reeling onto the sidewalk? Maybe cut her off and make her lay down her bike. He was bigger. His bike was bigger. It would be better to face him here with her feet on the ground.

She put the phone to her ear. "Which bikers?" she asked Roger.

"Everything okay there?"

"Yeah. Another lovely day in The Grand Canyon State. You said something about bikers asking questions."

"Yeah. DBMC. Wanted to know what I knew about you."

"DBMC, you sure?" Interesting. Bill was on a truth kick. But he must have forgotten about the inquiry into her background. Imagine that.

"Sure as I'm talking to you," Roger said.

"When?"

"Coupla weeks ago or so."

"And you're just telling me now?"

"How's your investigation going?" Roger asked.

"I found the illegal activity, but Bill's not involved. I'm trying to nail down who's responsible." She looked over her shoulder at Little Al, who was seated on his bike glowering at her. "If Bill's legit, what's that do to my deal?"

"Get whatever information you can. We'll talk about that later."

She hesitated to say more on the phone. Should she tell Roger about the rogue agent? For all she knew it could be him.

"Still there?" he asked.

Cowards never start.

"Yeah. I'm still here. I'm having trouble pinpointing the rogue agent."

"Who told you about that?" he asked.

"Inez."

"What'd she tell you?"

"Not much." Joan replaced the nozzle and put her gloves back on. "Just that the undercover might be ATF, but they're not talking."

"Didn't you think it was odd, the ATF not sharing information with the Bureau?"

"Yeah, I did, but have you told them I'm working the MC?"

"We'd pull you out if we thought you'd get scooped up in one of their ops."

"So, then, you wouldn't share the information?" *And the weak die along the way.*

"If you figure out who it is, tell me first."

"Not Inez?" Her instincts went on high alert, making the hair on the back of her neck stand up. Inez had said pretty much the same thing. Did one agent suspect the other?

"Think Inez isn't up to the task?" Joan asked. "Would have been nice to know that eight weeks ago."

"I can tell you how to handle the situation," Roger said.

Joan turned her back to a hearty gust of wind. "Can't Inez do that? She's right here."

"Me first, Joan. Got it?"

"Got it. You first."

Fuck both of you. From now on, it's me first…after the ba-by…and Duncan. Damn. This situation was getting more complicated by the second.

"I'm heading to Phoenix tomorrow," Roger said. "I'll touch base, tell you more when I get there. Gotta go. And hey…"

"Yeah?"

"Watch your back." The line went dead.

She glanced at Little Al, who was still glaring at her.

Only the strong, the smart, and the lucky survive.

She tore off the receipt and tried to act nonchalant, as if it had been a normal call from Bill, but as the conversation played, rewound, and played again in her head her shoulders tensed. A wave of nausea hit her. She leaned on her bike, breathing, hoping it would pass. Roger had relayed bad news—more than bikers checking up on her. More than questioning Inez's abilities. What exactly had he alluded to?

The nausea rolled away. Now for Little Al and more bad news.

She pulled up to where he sat on his bike. When she turned off her engine, he turned off his. He had been ready to chase her down, and she was glad she met him here instead of somewhere on the side of the road, possibly with a damaged bike, certainly injured.

She dismounted on the opposite side of the bike from him. "What do you want?"

He stood. His full six-foot-seven height loomed over her. "I'm doing all I can to protect you. Stop making things harder on yourself."

She straddled her bike and put her finger on the ignition. "We already had this conversation."

"No. When you stayed in town and snitched to Bill, you made this a new conversation." He pulled the key from the ignition and tucked it into one of his pockets. "We agreed we'd keep it between us."

She got off the bike and crossed her arms. "You mean like not telling Bill I stopped by to talk to you? You mean that kind of keeping it between us?"

Little Al's anger flared, and he reached to grab her, but instead turned and took a step away. Whether it was respect for her skills, or the fact they were in public, it didn't matter. She was Bill's old lady. And pregnant. Nothing good could come from roughing her up.

He ran his fingers through his hair several times before facing her. "You have no idea what you did. You can only hope Bill doesn't make trouble over this."

"*I* can only hope? This isn't something I did wrong."

"It's *all* about what you did wrong. Jesus, Joan, I'm into some serious shit here. I had things under control, until you started snooping around and flapping your lips."

"I'm honest. That's who I am."

"Honesty isn't a virtue in an MC. Sometimes bad things happen if you don't go along to get along."

"What kind of bad things?"

"People are gonna get hurt, especially you. I don't want to hurt you, but if I have to, I will."

"You don't want to hurt me, but you will. Do you know how schizo that sounds?"

"This whole thing is schizo," he said, rocking back on his heels and raising his arms wide.

"What other people?"

"What?"

"You said 'people are gonna get hurt.' Who are you talking about?"

"Important people."

"Who?" she asked.

"People important to me."

"Like who? Maybe I can help—"

"I've said too much already." He started his bike. "I got people crawling up my ass to silence you. And if you don't stop, you will be silenced. I'm protecting you as best I can, but you're making it impossible. Get out of town. This is your last warning."

He tossed her key at her. She caught it and watched him disappear into mid-day traffic.

He told her something veiled in threats and vague words. Bill had pulled Little Al from his custom shop, pumped up the alarm system, and set it up so the security cameras fed to his phone. Something in Little Al's actions indicated there was more to it than that. *People are gonna get hurt.* He added her after that line. Other people were threatened besides her. He would have named Bill if he was in danger. What other people? It had to be connected to the drug transportation his guys were doing, but the pieces didn't fit.

She'd caught Bill flatfooted when she showed him the video Sunday night. He didn't know what was going on under his nose. In his own shop. He told her so, and she believed him. No one could act that shocked. His plans for legitimate income for the club was purposely undermined, and by his sergeant-at-arms, the Brother entrusted with club security. What made Bill even angrier was that if there was a raid, he would go down for it. Having a kid on the way and the possibility of missing out on the upbringing of another child intensified his anger. She cringed because that was his fate if she couldn't sort out this mess.

Yet, Little Al had ridden out of the mini-market after a verbal warning. He was protecting her, but he would hurt her if necessary. What could drive a man to such contradictions? Such a conflict of interest?

Then there was the call from Roger. Did he know who the UC was but didn't want to say the name over the phone? Who the hell was it?

Her phone rang.

Inez. Damn if trouble doesn't come in threes.

"What's up?" Joan asked.

"We have to meet."

"Today?"

"Now. Meet me at the end of Northern Avenue."

"Where the hell is Northern Ave?"

"Find it." The line went dead.

After checking the navigation app on her phone, Joan pulled out into traffic. Roger's phone call had jarred her sense of living in a bubble of security—Bill protected her, her mission was as yet undiscovered, Little Al had not yet come through on his threats. Roger had been cagey about why she should talk directly to him about the rogue agent, and he was coming to Phoenix to talk to her face to face. That was never a sign of sunshine and roses. Inez was out of the loop—Roger made that clear—and it seemed the Bureau wanted to keep it that way. Another damn mystery in the middle of all the other shit flying around.

And what bug had crawled up Inez's tight, federal-agent ass? Her abrupt, harsh tone hinted something happened. She had pushed hard the past week or so—easy for her, her neck wasn't on the line. While Joan maneuvered through traffic, she went down a list of possibilities. Inez could have learned something about the illegal business in Bill's shop. Joan hadn't told her about that and had planned to keep it that way to protect Bill, but things might be different now. She mulled over how much to tell Inez. If she told her about the drug deliveries and their interstate connections, the feds would swoop in and finish the job they started a year ago. If they got their way, the DBMC would be history.

It was Bill's shop, and he'd go down the hardest for it. Who would want to frame him? The rogue agent might. Pinpointing that son of a bitch just became Job One. Rogue agent possibilities was a short list: Blaze had been absent from the MC for four years. He may have trained with the ATF instead of the marines. Little Al was in the middle of the storm, trying to cover up something or somebody. Slow Motion was too whacked—or his behavior could be a cover. He stayed on the list. Youngblood was relatively new to the MC. Just got his full patch. She didn't know much about him. How much did Bill know about him?

And what about Switch? Was she myopic, only looking inside the DBMC for the agent, instead of being open to the possibility of an agent in another MC? Switch had a chip on his shoulder. Having only crossed paths with him once, she wasn't sure if he would do something to hurt Bill. If he was bitter enough to send his father to prison, who else was in danger? If Little Al was working with Switch, and everyone he knew was threatened. Her danger was real and palpable, the same for his wife and kids.

Al warned her there were "people" who wanted to silence her. Switch and the Mongols were involved in the illegal activity she had uncovered. Was Switch her threat, or was it the Mongols in general? Dealing with the Mongols didn't sound like a fun ride at the amusement park.

There was the outside chance Inez knew the identity of the rogue agent, making Joan look incompetent. Or, maybe Inez wasn't jacked-up about the agent. The worst could have happened—she learned of Joan's pregnancy.

Joan pulled up to a light and rolled her shoulders to relax. Worrying about what cocked Inez's gun was wasted energy. The problem, whatever it was, would come to light soon enough.

She raced away from the light. If she didn't pick up the pace, she'd be late. Inez would be a bear if she waited too long. Joan mulled over Roger's warning to watch her back. Tell him first, which meant trust no one. Inez was Joan's handler, she *had* to trust her. Joan trusted Bill. But then he had conveniently overlooked telling her he sent a couple of bikers to investigate her past. She hit it off with Mooky—she wanted to trust him. And she had to consider the outside chance Roger was the rogue agent, and the phone call was an attempt to keep her off his trail and to slip a wedge between Inez and her.

Duncan had told her to trust her instincts, and at this stage of the operation, it was all she could depend on. If there was no one she could trust, she was in a world of hurt.

When she turned onto Northern Avenue, Inez was a distant, dark figure kicking at something in the dirt on the side of the road, maybe a snake. Joan snorted at the thought of two snakes playing chicken. Inez must have heard the rumble of Joan's Harley because she turned away from whatever fascination the dirt held and stood in the middle of the two-lane road, hands on hips, waiting.

"Getting a little too independent," Inez said, mouth tight, posture stiff.

Joan heeled down the kickstand. "You wanted me to get in deeper."

"Deep doesn't mean blowing me off."

"Deep means I don't have as much free time." *Fucking Inez.* "You aren't the one with your life on the line."

"You don't look so good. Anything you want to tell me?"

Joan's stomach rolled. She pressed it and breathed deeply. "I'm fine."

"Get to a doctor. If you're sick, you can't continue this op."

Nausea pushed up Joan's esophagus. She swallowed to keep it down. "All's good. The tension is a little much at times, but I have a handle on it."

"You sure?" Inez asked, her eyes tracking from Joan's stomach to her eyes.

"Yeah. I'm sure."

"Something's going on," Inez said. "You need to tell me. If I don't know what's going on, I can't help you."

"Nothing's going on." If it wasn't for the nausea, Joan would have laid into Inez.

"You have something to tell me. Spit it out."

"I do have a question about Blaze. Is the Bureau sure he was in the marines? Could he have gone to ATF training?"

"His record is clear. He was in the marines. Where are you going with this?"

"Could the ATF have doctored his records?"

"That's it?" Inez said. "That's all you want to know?"

"For now, yes."

Inez's face reddened. She glared at Joan. "Withholding information will not go well for you. You may know more about the intricate inner workings of the Demon Brotherhood, but I see the bigger picture. It was a mistake to give you this mission. You have many skills, I'll grant you that, but this is beyond your capabilities."

"And you would have done better than me?"

"I was supposed to get this assignment, build up my resume, get a promotion afterward. Then the Bureau put me in charge of you. I've done my job well, exceeding expectations, always delivering when it was needed. I was loyal, hard-working, diligent, thorough—"

"Everything you think I'm not," Joan interrupted.

"I've forgotten more about undercover work than you'll ever know."

"Oh, because you see the 'bigger picture.'" Joan made no attempt to hide her sarcasm.

"If it had been up to me, I would have pulled you before you even started." Inez took a step toward Joan, a failed attempt at intimidation. "You're just a convict getting one last breath of freedom."

Joan ignored the inflammatory comment. "Is that why you called this meeting? To tell me how incompetent I am and how great you are? Because if that's all this is about, I'm out of here." She walked toward her bike.

"Don't you walk away from me."

Joan gave Inez a dismissive look and straddled her bike to leave.

"Get back here," Inez said. "We have business to take care of."

Joan stood, walked up to Inez, and glowered at her. "What do you want to know?"

"What's the status of the dealership and custom shop banking?" Inez asked.

Joan reached into the front pocket of her jeans and pulled out a thumb drive. "Here are the bank statements for the dealership for the past twelve months. Is that enough?"

"The forensic accountants will let me know if they need more. Passwords on here?"

"No."

"We need them. Of course, if you were a trained agent, you would have known that."

Joan looked across the flat expanse of the desert. No rocky hills jutting out of the ground anywhere nearby. She had asked to meet some place a little more out of the way, not the outskirts of bum-fucked Egypt. She wasn't crazy about how open it was, but it was deserted. This meeting wouldn't take that long anyway.

She rubbed the prickles from the back of her neck. It wasn't from a sense of being watched. Something else was wrong. She locked onto Inez's cold, hard eyes. The tone of this meeting was harsh, angry, and out of line.

"Figure out who the rogue agent is yet?" Inez asked.

I wish it was you so I could turn you in. Joan pressed her lips together fighting the nausea. She was flapping in the breeze. But Inez didn't seem to care. Or worse, hoped Joan would fail.

"You have," Inez said, sliding her sunglasses up to her forehead and grinning. "You know who it is."

"It could be anyone."

"Why won't you tell me, Joan?"

"I told you, I don't know for sure."

"Who do you *think* it is?"

It was Joan's turn to kick the dirt on the side of the road. All her life she'd been told the truth would set you free, but according to Little Al that platitude rarely held true in the outlaw biker world. Hoping he was right, she looked up at Inez and made a decision.

"If I had to guess—" Joan swallowed hard and took a deep breath to control her queasy stomach. "I'd say it was Youngblood."

"Really? *Youngblood*? Why?"

The derisive tone when Inez repeated "Youngblood" set Joan's nerves on edge, but not enough to influence her decision. "First of all, he's new to the club."

"What's that have to do with anything?" Inez asked, stepping closer to Joan.

Joan stood her ground. "He's been overly friendly and helpful to me…as if he knows why I'm here."

"Friendly and helpful. That's not what you base something like this on. Evidence, Joan. I need evidence."

"You wanted speculation. I'm speculating." Joan leaned into Inez. She had endured just about enough of her shit. "You asked who I thought it was. And I told you."

Inez spun on her heel and strode to her bike. "Keep looking."

After Inez pulled away, Joan emptied the contents of her stomach on the shoulder of the road. She pulled a towel from her bike's saddlebag to wipe her mouth. The emptiness around her crawled into her bones, and the desolation of the area hung heavy on her shoulders. She had handled tougher circumstances alone before. She could do it again, only this time she had a tiny passenger clinging to her for life.

As Joan sat on her bike, Inez's figure veered onto the main road, and the identity of the rogue agent dawned, slow but insistent, like a desert sunrise. She hoped she was wrong.

CHAPTER 20

Later that night, Joan mindlessly flipped through the channels on the television, sorting through everything that had happened that day. Little Al's warning still jangled her nerves, but all the way to work and back nothing was out of the ordinary. That didn't mean Little Al's warning-slash-threat was idle. Since lying to Inez, the sinking feeling in her gut would not go away. Every instinct said she did the right thing, but common sense insisted she was wrong to lie to her handler. She had hoped Bill would stay home to talk through recent events, but he had gone out to some bar, drinking with a few of the Brothers to celebrate Blaze's birthday. She texted him at nine p.m. to ask how late he'd be, and he'd answered they were leaving the bar soon. That was two hours ago.

On top of everything else, Kearney had answered her email.

I'll see what I can do.
K.

What kind of answer was that? Was he coming or not? Men. She couldn't figure them out: A mean man was treating her well. A friend, threatened her. A mean friend was being ambivalent. Renting a hunting cabin in the wilds of Idaho—far away from people, especially men and female federal agents—suddenly sounded like a great idea.

She must have dozed off because she woke to banging at the door. Nerves on edge, her first thought was the police. Inez had been royally pissed that afternoon, possibly enough to pull her deal and turn her in to the authorities. Joan's first thought was to run, but if the locals arrested her, Inez might just leave her in jail. That was not the place to straighten out the mess and uncover what was going on with Inez.

Joan slinked to the door, staying out of direct line of sight. "Who is it?"

"Bill said to bring you to the clubhouse," Youngblood said through the door.

Her knees got weak. "Why?"

He sounded gruff and insistent. Could he have found out she fingered him as the rogue agent. If so, what did that mean? Her mind raced, searching for answers and a way to escape. She inhaled deeply and relaxed with the exhale. Her running days were gone. She'd face down Youngblood. Her hands shook with adrenaline, and she struggled to unlock and open the door.

Youngblood must have seen her shaking hands because he grabbed her elbow. "Whoa, you okay? Don't get all weak. Bill needs you."

"Needs me?" This did not sound right. Playing along might shed some light. "What happened? Is he okay?"

"There was a fight. You have a first aid kit?"

"Yeah." A first aid kit? *It could be a distraction. Stay alert.*

"Go get it," Youngblood said.

She headed to the kitchen. "I thought you guys were tough and could take care of yourselves. Why me?"

"Prez said come get you. Here I am."

Not an answer. This could be a trick to get her to the clubhouse where she would be out numbered, out muscled, and out of luck. She grabbed the first aid kit and followed Youngblood to his car.

In the front seat, she checked the kit in the growing and fading colorless light of passing store signs. "We need to stop at a drugstore. This kit is useless."

"We don't have time."

"We don't have the supplies." She looked at him and asked for the first time, "How serious is this? Anyone shot?"

"No." He pulled into a drugstore parking lot too fast and braked hard. "Get what you need. Hurry."

She grabbed rubbing alcohol, gauze pads, adhesive tape, anti-biotic cream, and butterfly-bandages. As an afterthought, she grabbed a second bottle of rubbing alcohol and a pair of medical scissors. She tapped her fingers and shifted her weight from foot to foot while the cashier painstakingly totaled her purchases. The woman glanced at Joan a couple of times but seemed too unsettled to ask if Joan had a rewards card. Joan paid for the items, not waiting for change, and rushed back to the car.

When they arrived at the clubhouse, the prospect at the gate waved them through. Only five weeks ago, it had been festive, but now it was dark, overgrown with shadows. As the car pulled into the center of the compound, bright spotlights came on, chasing the shadows to hover in the corners—lights with motion sensors was one of several new security layers. The unexpected brightness darkened Joan's expectations.

Youngblood ushered her into the party room. Six bikers sat with makeshift ice packs on their faces and hands. Bill sat on a stool at the bar, holding an ice pack on one eye that was swollen shut. Tracks of blood soaked the neckline of his tee shirt.

Relieved the call was a legit emergency, she rushed to Bill. "What happened?"

"Got hit in the head a couple times. Not that serious. You know how head wounds bleed. Take care of the guys first."

"I'll do that," Youngblood said, dumping the supplies onto the bar top. "Let Joan take care of you."

"Keep ice on that eye," Joan said, moving around to look at the back of Bill's head. She parted his hair and winced at the bloody lump on his scalp. "What the hell happened?"

"Don't know exactly. We were hangin' out at Clarissa's Roadhouse drinking and talking, and somewhere between 'fuck' and 'you' pool sticks started swinging."

"Is that what this is from?" She poured some alcohol onto a gauze pad.

"Yeah." He sucked air through his teeth when she dabbed the wound with alcohol. "I always sit separate from the guys. Keep an eye on the surroundings while they drink and unwind. Shoulda seen it coming."

"But you got distracted by what…a cute ass?"

"Big tits."

She pressed into the wound to clean it.

Bill flinched. "Take it easy, darlin'. I'm just kidding. I got caught up in the partying. Haven't been out with the guys for a night o' drinking for a while."

"Gimme that ice pack." When he handed it to her, she grabbed his hand. "Holy shit. Your knuckles."

"Do I have to follow you around to keep you out of trouble?" She put the ice pack on the wound on the back of his head. "Hold it there. Let me see that eye."

Bill looked past her.

Joan turned to see Sapphire rushing through the door. She looked ragged, with dark circles under her eyes. Make-up failed to cover a swollen cheekbone.

"What can I do?" she asked Joan.

"Get some soap and water to clean these guys up."

Sapphire took off for the kitchen.

Bill studied Joan.

"What?" she asked.

"No hard feelings 'bout calling Sapphire here to help?"

"You know what they say about many hands." She smoothed Bill's moustache before looking into his good eye. "You're my old man. I trust you. Now let me look at that eye."

While she cleaned the cut over his eyebrow and applied a butterfly bandage to it, she thought about Little Al's warning. She should tell Bill. It might be relevant. But there would be time later when she got him home. She turned her attention to the men in the room.

"Where's Little Al?" she asked Bill.

"Not invited."

She felt responsible for this rift in the Brotherhood, but she reminded herself it was Little Al who had done this by his actions. The other Brothers didn't hold it against her, or at least they didn't show it.

No hard stares. No obscene gestures.

Sapphire returned with the soap and water and began cleaning up the guys before they headed out into the night to their homes. When she finished up, she headed for the kitchen.

"Wait up," Joan said. "I'll help you."

"You don't have to. I can do this."

"It'll go faster if we do it together."

They walked down the dusky corridors to the kitchen.

"How are you doing?" Joan asked.

"What do you care?"

"I've always cared. You and the other women just never gave me a chance to show it."

"How big of you."

"What does that mean?" Joan asked.

"Never mind."

"Sapphire, I want to know," Joan said, touching her arm.

"I mean it's big of you now that Bill chose you. I was dating him, doing everything he wanted to make him happy. Then he brings you back from Albuquerque like I'm nothing. I was there with him that weekend. Did you know that?"

"No."

"Of course not, because you don't care."

Joan bumped shoulders with her. "You want him?" she asked with a half-smile. "He's still got one good eye."

"No." Sapphire fought back a smile. She dunked the bloody towels into soapy water. "I have a new boyfriend."

"What's he like?"

"He's not a biker. Well, he rides a motorcycle, but doesn't belong to a club." Sapphire talked without looking at Joan. "He lives in Southern Cal and comes out to see me two or three days each week when he has business in Phoenix."

"What kind of business?"

Sapphire shrugged one shoulder. "He delivers things."

"Does he treat you good?"

"He's real nice to me."

"Is that who gave you that shiner?" Joan took the rinsed

towels from Sapphire and started wringing them out. When she didn't answer, Joan asked, "What's his name?"

"Why? You wanna steal him from me, too?"

Joan stopped and looked at Sapphire. Was that how all the women at the club looked at her? She wrung the towels harder to work off the bad feelings. "Do any of the Brothers know him?"

"Little Al does. They get along real good."

"Little Al?" Joan must have answered too quickly, because Sapphire shot her a questioning look. Joan busied herself laying out the towels to dry.

Instead of asking Joan what she meant by that remark, Sapphire pulled the stopper and busied herself wiping down the sink.

"We'll let these towels dry here," Joan said. "I'll come back tomorrow and take them home to wash them."

"Yeah, it's getting late," Sapphire said, heading back to the party room. "My boyfriend's in Phoenix now, but he had business to take care of tonight. Even if he didn't, he'd understand that when the president of a club says to do something you have to do it."

"Only club members would understand that. Are you sure he's not a biker and just didn't tell you?"

"Why wouldn't he tell me?"

"Yeah, you're right," Joan said. "Don't mind me. I'm being nosey. I've been told that could get me into trouble."

"Especially in a motorcycle club," Sapphire said as they walked into the party room.

Everyone had left except Slow Motion, Blaze, and Bill who were in a deep conversation. Bill saw them and said, "I was gonna send Slo Mo to check on you. Thought maybe you two got into it."

"There was a lot of blood," Sapphire said with a side glance at Joan. "It took a lot of rinsing to clean out the towels."

"Let's get home," Bill said to Joan, hanging an arm over her shoulder.

"Are you okay to drive?" Joan asked. She held up two fingers. "How many fingers am I holding up?"

"Smartass. Let's get this place locked up and get out of here before I start feeling pain."

When they got home, Bill tossed his keys on the counter. "Let's go to bed. I'm getting too old for this rough housing."

"You could have a concussion. I think you should stay awake for a couple more hours."

He pulled her into his arms. "Always thinking of what's best for me. You must be tired."

"Let's sit on the couch and talk."

Bill hesitated.

"Just for a little while," she said. "There's something you should know that might be related to tonight." She put her arm around his waist and guided him into the living room.

"What is it? Been out producing more videos?"

She ignored his question. "How many club members did you tell about Little Al's side job?"

"Just Blaze. I called a special meeting for this Saturday. Why?"

"I saw Little Al this afternoon."

Bill frowned and exhaled loudly. He gave her a hard stare. "What did I tell you about interfering in club business?"

"It's not like that. I was gassing up my bike, and he pulled in and...he warned me."

"About what?" He rubbed his forehead. "Get me some aspirin. My head's pounding."

She returned with the aspirin and a glass of water.

"Warned you about what?" Bill said before downing the tablets.

"He said people wanted to silence me after I told you what was going on. Did I make a mistake?"

"Tellin' me was right. What'd he mean 'silence' you?"

"He didn't give details. I didn't ask. In his defense, he did say he was doing everything he could to protect me."

Bill snorted. "I bet he is."

"You don't think this fight tonight was somehow related to this whole problem?"

He stroked his beard. "Don't think so. The bastards were locals, flexin' beer muscles."

"There's more."

"Of course, there always is with you." He put his arm around her shoulders.

That sounds like something Duncan would say. She squelched the thought. "He said, 'people' wanted me silenced, which means there's a group, right?"

"Sounds like it."

"Do you think it's the Mongols that have been seen around Phoenix?"

"I asked Little Al. He denied it was connected to the Mongols. Denied everything."

"Some of the guys in the video were Mongols—or at least, there were bikes with Mongol MC decals in the parking lot."

"You might be right, darlin'." He thought for a moment before continuing. "He was evasive…and nervous. Tried to hide it, but I noticed. Didn't say it in so many words, but he almost begged me to back off."

"Like it seemed there was more going on than his business relationship with these guys?"

"Maybe."

"What else could it be?" she asked. "You don't think his kids are threatened, do you?"

"Don't know. Tell me more about this threat."

"He also said 'people' were going to get hurt, especially me. Could that mean there's more at stake than my safety?"

"Think he meant me?"

She shook her head. "I think he would have named you specifically, like he named me. Who else do you think is in danger?"

"Could be other club members."

"Yeah…I don't know." It wouldn't matter how far over the levee Little Al wandered, he would never threaten any Brothers.

Early morning light filtered through the windows, draping the room in an eerie half-light.

"Want some breakfast?" she asked.

"When are you gonna let me sleep? I'll be able to think through this mess better after a couple hours in the sack."

"Tell you what...if you eat and don't have projectile vomiting, I'll let you lay down. Maybe I'll lay down with you."

"That's my girl."

She started digging out the eggs and butter, put a couple slices of bread in the toaster, and ran the water for coffee. Bill followed her to the kitchen and sat at the breakfast bar.

He had just taken two more aspirin when someone banged on the door. "I'll get it," he said as he stiffly slid off the stool.

He opened the door. "Hey, Mike, how's your 'sixty-nine Camaro doin'?"

"Great, Bill, can we come in?"

Bill backed up and let two police officers in. "Don't think you're here about your car."

"You're right. Who's this?" the cop named Mike asked, indicating Joan.

She put her hands on the counter and stood stock still. No need to make anyone nervous. She stopped breathing, waiting for Bill's answer.

"This is my old lady, Angel," Bill said.

Joan exhaled and relaxed. With everything he had going on in his life, Bill had remembered her alias.

"Anyone else in the house?"

"Nope. Just us."

"Mind if we check?"

Bill gestured for them to go ahead.

While the second cop checked the house, Mike asked, "Where were you tonight about ten?"

"Me and some Brothers were at Clarissa's Roadhouse on Tenth," Bill said.

"How'd you get that swollen eye and the bloody knuckles?"

"Had a little disagreement with some locals. Thought they were tough till they messed with us. Why?"

The second cop returned to the living room and stood between Joan and Bill. "House is clear."

Mike acknowledged him and asked Bill, "Know anyone named Jarrod Kingsman?"

"No. Thought one o' the dickheads was Clark or some other preppy name. The other was Bob or Boyd or something like that. Thought we all agreed to not press charges. Jarrod Kingsman, you said?"

"He's a Mongol. Does that jog your memory?" Mike asked.

"Don't know him."

"Kingsman says you and Dagger beat him to hell and back. Almost killed him."

"Are we talkin' about the same fight? At Clarissa's?" Bill asked.

"This was behind the Come On Inn on Van Buren," Mike said.

"Wasn't there." Bill stroked his beard. "He says it was me by name?"

The two cops exchanged looks. The second cop said, "Let's talk about this at the station."

"Cops were called to Clarissa's. Check it out."

"We'll do that, at the station. Turn around. Put your hands behind your back." One of the cops cuffed Bill and yanked him toward the door.

"This is bullshit. Call Orlanda," Bill said over his shoulder. "She'll know the lawyer's number."

CHAPTER 21

Later that afternoon, fresh from the meeting with Roger, Joan sat in Mooky's dusty living room, fighting the urge to pace, and wishing the nausea would go away. But if the past week was any indication, she still had four hours before it would subside. Roger had confirmed her suspicions that the rogue agent was someone she knew and a roadblock to the completion of her mission. He assured her he was there to support her, but at this point, she wasn't sure of anything but the tiny dude clinging to life in her womb—and she wasn't sure if it was a dude or dudette, or even which alpha male was the father. One thing was clear, she was alone in quicksand with only her skills to save her.

"Do you think Bill told me he went out for Blaze's birthday, but really went after this Mongol?" she finally said.

"It'd start a war with the Mongols," Mooky said. "Bring the Angels' wrath down on the Brotherhood. Break our alliance."

"And deprive the Brotherhood of any support from them," she said.

"A biker war is vicious and bloody. Nobody wins."

"Bill's too smart to set that in motion." Joan's leg started to jiggle. She pressed her hand on her thigh to stop it and chewed the inside of her cheek instead.

Mooky watched her and scratched his beard. "Don't worry. He'll get through this."

"The guys in the bar, could they have been Mongols who weren't wearing their colors?"

"Maybe," Mooky said. "You sure the charges were for attempted murder and not conspiracy to commit?"

"Yeah. Why?"

"A club president doesn't commit acts of violence. He has guys to do that."

"Who in the Brotherhood?" The feds might be interested in this information, especially now that she had nothing on Bill.

"Not at liberty to say." Mooky studied her for a couple of seconds. "The one who pulls that duty is usually the most screwed up in the head."

"Slow Motion?" Joan asked. "Does he ever have a clear grasp of reality?"

"He's sharper than he looks."

"Could have fooled me." She thought of the time his old lady bragged about how well he was doing in his struggle with drug use. When Joan had seen him later that day, he had been tweaking.

"Bill claimed he didn't know this Jarrod Kingsman?" Mooky asked, getting back on track.

Joan nodded. "Would Bill lie to the police?"

"If he says he doesn't know the guy, and the police find out he does, he's caught in a lie—shit falls apart. This isn't Bill's first lap 'round the track."

"Wish I knew what was going on."

"I know one way to find out." Mooky picked up his phone.

"Who are you calling?" Too late. He finished punching in the number and was listening.

"Hey, Al, whatcha up to?…Uh-huh, good…"

She sliced across her neck with her fingers. And mouthed the word "stop."

Mooky glanced at her but kept talking. "Heard Bill was arrested this morning. You hear anything?…Don't sound good…She's here, safe and sound…Yep." Mooky placed the phone on the table beside him. "Seems Little Al's concerned for your welfare."

Joan snorted. "Yeah, right."

"Went to your house to check on you."

Her jaw tightened. "And now he knows to check here."

Mooky narrowed his eyes. "Thought you two were friends."

"What did he tell you?"

"Says the guy fingered Bill."

"I just can't believe…" Joan rubbed her stomach. She refused to believe she was too attached to her mark—so blind, she couldn't see the real person under the loving façade. Her gut said Bill was who he said he was, but her gut now held a baby. Could that warp her perspective?

"Killing a Mongol on Angels' territory is bad business," Mooky said.

"*Attempting* to kill…" she corrected.

"Still serious shit. Things could go bad in a hurry. What're you packin'?" Mooky asked.

Joan pulled out the corner of her jacket to expose the gun holstered at her hip. "A three-eighty."

"If trouble's brewin', you're gonna need something bigger than that," he said, struggling out of his recliner. "I might have somethin' for you."

He lumbered down the dark hallway muttering, "Can't believe that crazy-ass nephew o' mine gave you a pea shooter for protection."

She followed him to his bedroom—new territory for her. Men's magazines cluttered the floor, clothes draped from every horizontal surface or had been flung onto the bed, unpaired boots filled any empty space. A potpourri of gun oil and dirty socks floated in the air. It looked worse than the rest of the house had looked the first day Bill dropped her off. Mooky opened the farthest closet door to reveal handguns, loaded magazines, and a shitload of ammunition. Two sets of shuriken hung on hooks next to two drawstring bags on a third hook. Mooky's life priorities came into focus, neatly racked, stacked, and packed.

"Pick one," he said.

She chose a .45-caliber Glock, checked the magazine, then slid it into her waistband.

He watched her movements, seemed to come to a decision, then reached around the edge of the closet door to the inside wall and pulled out a ring of keys. "Follow me."

He led her out into the dwindling sunshine to the far end of his backyard to the shed that had held her imagination for so long. Her heart skipped a beat. Finally, she was going to see inside.

"Don't make me sorry I showed you this." He held her gaze for a couple seconds then unlocked a Master padlock then a deadbolt. The door stuck. He yanked on it, and the bottom scraped across a makeshift ramp. Three footlockers sat in the darkness. He turned on a Coleman lantern, washing his face in soupy yellow light that formed ghoulish shadows around his eyes.

"This key opens all the footlockers," he said, holding up a silver key in the pale light. He opened the first one on the right and pulled back the burlap.

Joan pressed the back of her hand to her mouth to calm her stomach. Several AR-15s were stacked inside. Across the back of the chest, rectangular ammo boxes were lined end to end.

"I only have six o' these left," Mooky said, lifting out an AR-15 and holding it in the light. "There's a coupla AK's—they're useless, but some people like 'em. Think there's an H and K carbine in there somewhere. I know you liked the Magpul FPG."

She looked at him expectantly.

"Sorry. Too rare, too expensive. Not worth the investment."

She nodded. "That's the ammunition for these rifles?"

"A gun without bullets is just a hunk of metal and plastic." He replaced the carbine and the burlap, closed the lid, and moved on to a second footlocker on the opposite side of the shed. He opened the lid and let it speak for itself. It held handguns, shiny with oil, and beneath the lift-off shelf, ammo boxes were neatly labeled and ordered according to caliber. Before he opened the footlocker along the back wall, he said, "The contents of this chest are near and dear to my heart. The last person to see inside here was Bill two years ago." He pegged her with his gaze. "Hear me?"

She nodded.

He pushed back the lid to reveal what Joan guessed were collectible, one of a kind, rifles and carbines. There was an oblong block wrapped in olive green paper.

Something else, farther down, caught her eye. "Is that a shoulder-fired rocket launcher?"

"Ain't she beautiful?" A smile of pride slid from his face. "Haven't been able to get the rockets for it, though. Feds are touchy about bikers gettin' hold of 'em."

Joan tore her eyes from the cache to Mooky. "How do you have all this stuff?" She was going to have to tell the Bureau about this. It couldn't possibly be legal to own that many assault weapons or C-4, or a rocket launcher. Damn. Mooky had been so good to her.

"Remember the dealers who sold arms to your militia?"

"Yeah."

"Where do you think they got their merchandise?" he asked.

Her jaw dropped, thinking of all the people who died in the chaos in that warehouse over a year ago. She shook her head to get it in gear. "Wish I'd known this then. We could have avoided that sting."

"Sorry, Momma. You guys were hot way before then."

One corner of her mouth twisted. She nodded in sad agreement. She had tried to warn Duncan off the arms deal, but it had been his decision, and a big price had been paid. She thought of one of the few survivors. "Kearney would love to see this."

"He was your arms guy, right? Never met him, but knew of him." He pointed the way out of the shed. "I know what he did to you."

"Know what?" she rubbed her stomach to ease the nausea. "There's nothing to know."

Mooky busied himself with the locks. "Maybe the backroom gossip was wrong." He gave her a fatherly shoulder pat. "Let's leave it at that. Hungry?"

That word made her aware of her hunger pains. "I haven't eaten much of anything since yesterday."

"Then let's see what I got to eat."

Mooky had everything needed for his favorite meal— BLTs. He handed her the package of bacon then gathered the bread, tomatoes, and lettuce. When she peeled off a strip of bacon and put it in the pan, she squelched a gag, got it under control, and managed to get four more in. But when the pan heated up and the smell of the greasy meat hit her nostrils, she covered her mouth and raced to the bathroom. Because her stomach was empty, it spasmed, bringing up green bile over and over again. Nausea was becoming a damn nuisance.

With pale skin and watery eyes, she returned to the kitchen, where Mooky had removed all signs of bacon. "We can have lettuce and tomato sandwiches," he said, slicing a tomato.

She nodded and slid into the chair across the table from him. They made their sandwiches in silence.

"How does Bill feel about you bein' pregnant?" Mooky asked before biting off a chunk of sandwich.

"What makes you think I'm pregnant?" she asked, nibbling hers.

"Had six kids. Seen my share of morning sickness."

"Bill knows, but we aren't telling anybody until…well, I'd rather not get everyone excited, then…you know."

"This stress isn't good for you." Mooky finished the first sandwich. Before starting the second one, he asked, "Wanna tell me what's really going on?"

She made a show of chewing her sandwich.

"You aren't one to get nervous," he said. "Somethin's got you spooked. And it's more than being pregnant. I'll bet all my hardware on that."

She picked at a piece of lettuce. He seemed sincere, but he was a Brother. Retired, but a Brother through and through. If she told him what was going on, he would side with Little Al. On the other hand, he was Bill's uncle. Blood family. Mooky could be a strong ally in a fight where she was alone, especially now that Bill was in jail and Inez was as good as useless. Mooky had trusted her with his arsenal. Showed her where he hung the key. She looked up to see him watching her. She took a big breath. *Cowards never start.*

She told him about meeting Switch on Route 10, discovering the drugs transport and delivery operation under Bill's nose, informing Bill, and Bill confronting Little Al. She continued with a description of Little Al's cock-eyed threats. And why Al was probably on his way over to Mooky's as they spoke.

Mooky listened, chomping on hunks of sandwich.

The heaviness of the situation got to Joan. "What am I going to do if Bill goes to prison?"

"I don't know. It'll be hard for you to find another man, since every guy you live with ends up behind bars. Not a big plus on a dating website."

"What would you know about online dating?" she teased back, grateful for his attempt to lighten her mood.

"Nothin'." He winked. "Heard talk of it."

"Seriously, if Bill goes to prison for this—I'm pregnant. I—" She shook her head and bit into her sandwich. Her concern was misplaced. Or was it? If her deal stood, Duncan would be released from prison. But if he didn't want her, Bill would be the only father for her child. But not if he also landed behind bars. How did she get herself into his quagmire?

"He isn't locked on the block yet, Momma The club has a good lawyer. He'll straighten it out."

She set down her half-eaten sandwich, stood, and started cleaning up. "Thank you, Mooky, for listening to me."

"You're family. It's what we're about."

Family. It had meant so much to her father. But through Joan's misguided choices, it had all been taken away from her. The army had filled that void. But then she joined the Legion, followed by the militia. Years of belonging to destructive counter-cultures brought nothing but pain and loneliness. Now the Demon Brotherhood was family. She watched Mooky eat like a hungry lion and reminded herself that, like the previous groups, this family was an illusion. The only family she had was the baby in her belly—and Duncan, if he'd have her after all this.

The rumble of Harleys, faint but getting louder, made Joan and Mooky stop and listen.

"Let me take care of this," he said, getting up and wiping his face with his sleeve.

"It's my problem," she said, following him to the living room. "I'll deal with them."

"Let's see who it is first."

Mooky peered through the small window in the front door.

Joan watched through the picture window, staying several feet back in the unlit room, as two Mongols pulled up in front of the house. Her bike was parked in the drive. They knew she was there, but standing where she was, they couldn't see her.

"Recognize 'em?" Mooky asked.

"Never saw them before."

He motioned for her to move away. "Go, in the kitchen." His voice was commanding. His old biker persona emerged, posture arrow-straight, crippling arthritis forgotten.

"Want one of my guns?" she asked in a hoarse whisper.

"You got 'em," Mooky said. "That's enough for me."

She took up a position next to the wall. She pulled the .45, chambered a round, and held it diagonally against her chest, ready, but not aggressive. It seemed like a long time for the bikers to walk across the small, barren front yard before they banged on the door.

Mooky opened it. "Whoa," he said, backing up into the room. "Whatdya want?"

"Wanna talk to Bill's old lady," the gun-wielding Mongol said.

"Talkin' with a gun ain't talkin'."

"Where is she, old man?"

"Put the gun down," Joan said, stepping into the living room and aiming at the biker's head.

He glanced at the side of her gun. "Might want to check the safety."

"It's a Glock, numb-nuts," she replied, tightening her grip on the gun. Just because she was a girl, it didn't mean she didn't know her shit.

"You shoot me. I shoot him," the biker said.

"You'll still be dead," she said. "And you might miss Uncle Mook."

"There were two of you when you pulled up." Mooky's gaze slid past Joan. "Where's the other guy?"

She spun around. The other Mongol must have come through the back door. He grabbed her arm holding the gun and punched her in the jaw. She slipped away from it, taking only a glancing blow. She shook it off and put him into an arm bar. She broke his elbow then kicked his knee. He went down like a rock, moaning and cursing her.

She turned her attention back to Mooky who had disarmed the other Mongol. He blocked a couple punches before landing a fist on the biker's nose, knocking him a couple of steps back. Mooky tackled him with a move worthy of a Wildcats lineman. They hit the floor with a window-rattling thud, turning over a side table. Mooky pounded his fists into the biker's face.

When the biker stopped fighting, Mooky struggled to his feet, panting and triumphant. "Get over here with your friend," he ordered the cursing biker on the floor.

"I can't. That fucking bitch broke my knee."

Mooky reached down to drag him into the center of the living room then pulled back. "Shit!" He thrust his heel into the biker's face, kicked aside a dagger, and dragged the unconscious biker into the living room next to the other one.

"That mother sliced me. I'm too old for this shit," Mooky said, putting pressure on his arm with his other hand. "Tie up these motherfuckers while I patch this up."

Drapes drawn, Mooky bandaged, intruders stripped of their colors and bound to chairs, Mooky said, "Time to get some information."

The bloody-faced biker spat out blood and looked at Mooky with one good eye. "I'm not telling you shit."

"What about you?" Mooky said, kicking the other biker's broken knee.

He wasn't in a talking mood. Pain had commandeered his vocabulary, relinquishing only expletives and spit.

A slow, wicked grin formed on Mooky's face. "You're tied up, and we're not. Looks like we're in charge. But you do have some control. Know what it is?"

The only answer was threats and more cursing. And spit.

"You determine how long this is gonna last," Mooky said, answering his own question. "Talk now. Talk later. Don't matter much to me. What about you, Joan?"

"My old man's in jail. All I have is time."

Mooky headed down the hallway, leaving her with their prisoners.

"Looks like you two are in bad shape. You need medical attention." She looked over her shoulder for Mooky. "You should talk sooner rather than later."

"Fuck you," the bloody-faced Mongol said.

She poked the other Mongol's swollen elbow. It was already turning purple. "You, my friend, should start talking. You need a paramedic."

When Mooky reappeared, Joan's breath caught in her throat. Brutishness, that she had long sensed simmered below the surface, had devoured his last speck of humanity. His actions were slow and calm, his eyes hard and focused.

"Won't need a paramedic," he said, screwing a silencer onto the barrel of a gun, "if you don't start talkin'."

❧❦❧

"What is taking them so long?" a young biker named Victor asked with a slight Mexican accent.

Switch smiled at the young biker's impatience. Victor had been with him the day they came across Joan broken down on the side of Route 10. If Switch was a believing man, he'd swear that day was a gift from God. She would pay the price for being Bill's old lady, but not before Bill knew what Switch had done to her. And there was still the matter of the payback for hitting him, embarrassing him in front of his men. He looked forward to getting to know her—every fucking inch.

"Give them a little more time." He leaned his elbows on Little Al's old desk. "Might take a little longer than planned."

"You think they ran into trouble?" Victor asked, holding up and inspecting a gas tank with a specialized paint job. "What could go wrong with a seventy-year-old man and a woman?"

"That old man is a tough motherfucker," Switch said. "Story is, he took on five Hells Angels. And won."

"He is a crippled old man," Victor said. "Can't even ride a bike no more."

Switch rocked back in the chair for several seconds. He motioned to Hernandez, the heavy-set biker who had been with him that day on Route 10. "Go check it out. Remember I want her alive."

They heard Little Al's motorcycle pull into the parking lot.

"Take someone with you," Switch said to Hernandez's retreating back. "And remember—alive."

Little Al strode across the maintenance floor to his old office. "You shouldn't be here."

"Close the door," Switch said.

"Why are you here?" Little Al didn't make a move for the door. "Bill shut us down."

Al botched the plan, and he was acting defiant. That didn't sit well with Switch. "You're right. Can't use this to frame him, but I took care of that."

"What do you mean?"

"Got him arrested for attempted murder. And his fucking son-in-law. Dagger got everything I shoulda had. They won't be causin' trouble any time soon."

"How'd you do that?"

"A club member screwed up. Jumped at the chance to show his loyalty to the club." A flat, mirthless smile crept onto Switch's face. "Let's just hope nothing got screwed up with your kids."

Little Al clenched his jaw muscles so hard they showed through his beard. "I did everything in my power—"

"Everything?" Switch let the word hang in the air, relishing the big man's unease. "If you had done everything, we wouldn't be in this mess."

"If you hurt them, I'll hunt you down. You won't be able to run far enough."

Switch overlooked Little Al's insubordination of walking up to the desk and pointing his finger at him. Little Al must have found his courage. Too bad he didn't have it sooner, before things went south.

"I'll make you sorry you ever heard my name," Little Al added.

"Shoulda stayed on top of things better." Switch savored Little Al's bluster. Everything was set in motion. Nothing Al did now would change anything.

Little Al continued to point his finger. "I know things got a little out of hand, but you—"

"A little out of hand? Bill's old lady found out about our business. How'd she do that? And why's she still able to make trouble?"

"She's the president's old lady. I can't just gun her down."

"People disappear in the desert all the time," Switch said, raising his hands palms up.

"I'll take care of it." Little Al turned to leave.

"Don't have to," Switch said. "I did your job for you. She'll be here soon. But I still have one problem."

Little Al turned to face Switch. "What's that?"

Switch crossed his arms and looked past Little Al at Victor holding a garrote. He looked back at Little Al. "What am I going to do about you?"

CHAPTER 22

As the sun closed in on the horizon, the living room darkened. Mooky stopped his relentless badgering of the two Mongols and turned down the blues-rock music used to muffle any sounds.

"Think we're gonna get any more out of them?" Joan asked.

"Don't think so." Mooky wiped the blood spatter off his silencer.

"Now what do we do?"

"Finish 'em off. No witnesses."

"We can't do that." She couldn't stand by and let this happen. The interrogation had sparked flashbacks of her own torture at the hands of the Legion. She knew death was the easy way out. "Look, Mooky, I know they're Mongols, but they're somebody's son or brother or father."

"They came here to kill you. Remember that."

"Didn't you say killing Mongols in Angels' territory was bad business?" She had to think of something to deter him. "If we kill them, won't we have to report it to the Angels?"

"Not if the Mongols don't find out what happened to their brothers."

"This—" Joan gestured to indicate the bloody Mongols, "—pushed my limits. But I have to draw the line at murder." She couldn't stand by and let him commit murder in front of her. It wouldn't play well with the feds. And with her deal weakening, adding accessory to murder charges was not something she wanted to face. She'd never see her kid grow up.

"They set up Bill and came here to kill you," Mooky said. "You better get on board—"

The front door crashed open. Three Mongols burst into the room, guns drawn.

Mooky spun and fired at them. They ducked. He charged them.

One slipped past Mooky. She pulled her .380 semi-automatic, fired, and missed. He smashed the side of his pistol against her temple. The .380 dropped from her hands. She fell to one knee, tried to shake it off, but before her vision cleared, the biker kicked her in the ribs. Thrashing and lamps breaking sounded far away as Mooky put up a fight.

She rolled to her side. When the biker kicked at her again, she grabbed the toe and heel of his boot and twisted hard. Ligaments snapped. He fell to the floor, howling in pain. She got to her knees, plowed a foot into his groin twice, and pushed off him to her feet. She staggered two steps to the side, bumped into Mooky. She stilled at a gunshot. Her eyes focused on a gun. Then on Mooky's surprised look at his chest and the blood soaking through his shirt.

Her eyes dropped to the blood spatter on her shirt. And she bolted. Tripped. Found the Glock on the arm of the recliner where she'd set it down earlier. Got off a shot and ran for cover, bouncing off the walls, trying to get her feet under her. Ears ringing. Nose filled with burnt gun powder. A bullet buried itself in the wall near her head. Another shot. The sound of Mooky hitting the floor, followed by clattering.

She reached Mooky's room, knelt, and aimed the Glock at the door.

A Mongol appeared in the dark opening. She fired. The blast blew him backward against the wall. He slid to the floor. A gun appeared around the corner, shooting wildly into the room above her head. She pulled the trigger. The gun jammed. She reached for her .380. Not there. She dove toward the closet, grabbed four shuriken. She tossed two at the biker, one slicing him above the eye.

She struggled with the slide.

Rubbing the blood from his eye, he cursed and shot several blind rounds.

She ducked and tossed the remaining stars at him.

He growled, pulling them out of his neck.

She wrestled with her gun.

His gun clicked. Empty. He lunged for her.

She squeezed the trigger.

∾∾∾

Bill and Dagger strode out of the county jail into the cool night air. His and Dagger's alibis checked out, and, after finding no other wants or warrants, the police released them with a warning to stay available for further questioning. They walked toward the black Ford pickup parked at the curb, where Blaze handed their cuts to them, and they shrugged them on.

After shoulder bumps, Blaze said, "Fitz wants you to call him."

Bill nodded. His hopes for a peaceful end to this bullshit spiraled into the dirt. Going home and holding Joan in his arms was on hold. When the president of the Hells Angels wanted to talk to him, it wasn't about the weather.

"Where's Joan?" Bill looked into the crew cab. "Thought she'd come to meet me."

"After the police left your house, she disappeared then showed up at Mooky's," Blaze said. "I called to tell her you were getting released, but no answer."

Bill pulled out his phone and dialed Joan's number. "She always answers. What d'ya think that means? She get arrested?"

"Maybe the police spooked her, and she skipped," Blaze said, lighting a cigarette.

"She's not a runner." Bill disconnected the call when it went to voicemail. She hadn't been sleeping well, waking up several times a night. She would calm down in his arms, but her sleep was still fitful. He eased her fears about being pregnant. Must be something else.

"Maybe she fell asleep." Bill tucked the phone into the inside pocket of his cut. He motioned everyone into the truck. "Let's go to Uncle Mook's."

When they rolled up to Mooky's house, Joan's bike was in the drive and three bikes he didn't recognize were parked at the curb. Mooky's pickup truck was not in the carport. Bill looked around the neighborhood. Other than a dog barking several doors down, it was quiet.

"What d'ya think?" Blaze asked.

Bill stroked his goatee. "We're here. Better check it out."

While Blaze backed into Mooky's driveway, Bill tried to shake the tension tightening his shoulders. Mooky probably went on a beer run. Light shone through all the windows in the front. Joan's bike was there. It should have been a relief, but adrenaline ramped up his heart rate and quickened his breathing. Trouble had a way of seeping through his pores, soaking into his skin. He climbed out of the front seat and headed toward the front door. His skin told him he was not going to like what was inside.

Blaze must have felt it, too, because he stopped Bill and pulled a gun from the small of his back. "Let me go first."

Bill nodded and opened the door.

Blaze rushed into the house. And dropped his arms. "Fuck the hell outta me."

Bill pushed past him, scanning the room, looking for Joan. He didn't see her, but blood spatter covered every surface. His gaze fell on Mooky with his back against the shelves, CD jewel cases scattered around him, chin resting on his bloody chest. Two bikers were tied up; they looked dead. One had a misshapen, purple elbow, and his leg slanted at an odd angle.

Mooky moaned.

"I'll look for Joan." Blaze pushed Dagger toward the kitchen. "You look out back."

Blaze took off down the hallway, kicking open each door along the way.

Mooky looked up. His eyes focused in recognition. "Get the guns...get Joan."

"Where is she?"

Blood trickled out of the corner of Mooky's mouth. Each breath gurgled. He grimaced and swallowed hard. "Make those assfuckers...pay." The last word was less than a whisper.

Bill checked for a pulse, knowing it was a useless act. *Must have died defending Joan.* He fought the emotion threatening to eliminate rational thought. Little Al would not get away with following through with his threat to hurt her. This broke the cardinal rule of the biking community—families were off limits. The Brother-bond was broken. Little Al would pay.

Bill stood and looked around the bloody, messed-up room. A more pressing concern was the two Mongols, dead or dying, in his uncle's house. Two—there were three bikes at the curb. He rubbed his good eye, trying to remember when he slept last. The wound on the back of his head throbbed. His swollen eye watered. With a little sleep, he could sort this out. The only thing keeping him going was adrenaline, and that wouldn't last much longer. He pulled out his phone. Time to call Fitz.

"Bill," Blaze groaned from the rear of the house. "You're not gonna like this."

Bill took off down the hallway with Dagger on his heels. He noted the large blood smear on the wall opposite Mooky's bedroom door then looked into the room at a Mongol lying face down on the floor. A flash of yellow caught his eye, and his insides froze.

Blaze stood in the middle of the room, a yellow, blood-soaked shirt dangling from his hand. Bill couldn't take his eyes off the faded *I ♥ New York* tee shirt Joan loved and wore a lot.

Bill scanned the room. "Is she..."

Blaze shook his head. "Not here."

"Her shirt's here, but she isn't." Bill knew he was stating the obvious, but his brain chugged through the motions until it could build up steam. The bloody tee-shirt took a bite out of his earlier resolve.

"Looks like a home invasion," Dagger said. "Mooky died fighting them off. She got back here. Shot one of them." He judged the distance between the blood-smeared wall and the dead biker. He toed a bloody star and pointed at the Mongol lying face down. "Not this guy. No exit wound. She fought this guy off. Shot him."

"Where's that guy?" Bill asked, nodding toward the bloody wall.

"Maybe it was a flesh wound," Blaze said. "Took off. Probably didn't expect push back."

Bill thought of Mooky's missing pickup. "She must've got away. Why'd she take the truck? And, dammit, why isn't she answering her phone?"

"I hate to say it," Dagger said. "But maybe she was abducted. Might be why she's not picking up."

"Call her phone." Blaze looked around the messy bedroom. "Maybe it's here somewhere."

Bill dialed her number. It rang in his ear. Nothing in the house. "Check outside," he said to Dagger. "Let's go through the place," he said, pushing Blaze out of the room. "Snag anything that points to Joan. Take it with us."

They checked the living room again.

Blaze spotted Joan's gun and slid it into the pocket of his leather jacket. "All this gunplay, and no one calls the cops?"

"Mooky's been known to fire off a shot or two now and then," Bill said. "Don't think the neighbors pay much attention anymore."

He looked up at Dagger as he returned.

"Found this in the far drive," Dagger said, holding up Joan's phone. "More bad news. Someone's been in the shed. Footlockers are mostly empty."

"Dammit," Bill said. "Now there's a bunch of heavily armed Mongols on the loose."

"We'll hunt 'em down, Prez," Blaze said, clapping Bill on the shoulder.

"Call in a clean-up crew," Bill said. He couldn't think about what might be happening to her while they stood around. "Pack up the house. Furniture, food, garbage— everything. Scrub down the rest with bleach. Put Uncle Mook in the club freezer till we get the story figured out. Get rid of the others."

He looked around the room again. "Where *is* she?"

ↄↄↄ

"The first men I sent are dead?" Switch asked. "Both of 'em?"

"They looked dead, *jefe*," Hernandez said, limping to a chair. "Mooky's dead. So's Wizard. Victor's at the ER. We barely got outta there with our lives."

"That makes three dead, and now the cops'll be called because Victor got himself shot." Switch ran his hand over his hair. Victor wouldn't talk. He was young, but he was a good biker. *I might just get this wrapped up and be back in Berdoo before the cops get their asses in gear.* "And you're sure Mooky's dead?" he asked Hernandez.

"Wizard shot him," Hernandez said. "Looked dead to me."

"It's gonna look like Joan killed them?"

Hernandez smiled. "She dropped her gun. We used it to finish Mooky off." He flexed his knee to loosen it up.

"What happened to you?" Switch asked.

"Fucking bitch twisted my knee."

Switch leaned back in the chair and studied his phone, thinking he should warn Dragon Lady. Too bad he couldn't pin any of this on her. She had become a liability. On the plus side, Bill would go to jail for attempted murder. His old lady would go up for murder. Wizard was dead. Never trusted him—another end neatly tied up.

"What about Bill's grandkids?" Switch asked.

"We got a guy on Dagger's house. Say the word, they're ice."

"Set it in motion, but spare Orlanda."

"Not Orlanda?" Hernandez asked.

"Let her live without Bill like I had to," Switch said. "But first we have to find Joan." He smiled at the thought of what he'd do to her. "I want to spend some quality time with my stepmother before they cart her off to prison."

"How are we gonna find her?" Hernandez asked.

"Ask *El Gigante*. He must have some idea where she'd go."

Switch's phone rang. He frowned at the Caller ID. Dragon Lady. He connected the call. "*Sí, Tía.*"

"Bill was released from jail," Dragon Lady said. "Turns out there's a police report for an altercation that puts him someplace else. Alibis don't get any tighter than that. Didn't you think to make sure you knew where he was before pinning something on him? You better get your act together. That's two frame-ups you've blown."

"Don't mean shit," Switch said, getting up and pacing around the office. "Did I want him in prison? Yeah, but I adjusted the plan. I got everything under control." *You'd think with all her experience, she'd know how plans change in an instant.*

"What about Joan?" Dragon Lady asked. "Where's she?"

"She got away. I got guys lookin' for her."

"She's on the loose?" Dragon Lady's voice raised an octave. "You didn't have the forethought to kill her?"

"She's alive because that's what I want."

"Her, alive, wasn't part of the plan. As long as she's loose, she can finger you…and me."

"Fuck you and your plan." Switch gloated at Hernandez, who nodded support. "Like I told you, this is my plan now."

"I'm coming there. See if you have the *cajones* to say that to my face."

"You're coming here?" Switch stopped pacing. "Am I supposed to be afraid?"

"You better be."

He disconnected the call. "Ah, if you weren't family…Fuck you," he said to the phone before laughing.

ᴄ᷍ᴐᴇ᷍ᴐ

Bill returned to his house to gather weapons and ammo, but mostly hoping Joan had found her way there. The house was quiet and felt empty without her. He looked at the clock—one-thirty a.m. In the last twenty-one hours, a shitload had happened. He got into a fight, was arrested for a fight he didn't have anything to do with, and Joan disappeared. She reappeared. And Mooky was killed, then she disappeared again.

He walked through the house, pulling handguns out of their hiding places, stacking the pitifully few boxes of ammo he had on hand, taking his time, hoping Joan would show up. He'd have to leave soon and get to the clubhouse. Where was she? What was she up against? Wherever she was, he hoped she was well and able to protect the baby.

Might be a good time to call Fitz. He thumbed his phone.

"Bill Torrence," he said into the silence at the other end of the line. Fitz never spoke first.

"Yeah, Bill, how are the Mongols treatin' ya?"

Bill ignored the touch of sarcasm in Fitz's response. He pulled an ice pack out of the freezer and put it on the back of his throbbing head. "My old lady's missing. They prob'ly have her."

"Why d'ya think that?"

"Blaze update you about what happened?"

"Yeah. Told me about your false arrest for attempted murder of a Mongol."

"When the cops hauled me away, she went to Mooky's. Went to get her when I got released. Found three dead Mongols instead."

"This is a fucking mess," Fitz said under his breath, but Bill heard it.

"She's gone." Bill clenched his jaw. He didn't care about the consequences of a biker war. His old lady was missing. "Can't find her."

"What'd Mooky say?"

"He's dead." Bill moved the ice pack to his forehead. He lost two family members in the few hours he was in jail—one missing, one dead. Emotion was catching up with him. He straightened his shoulders and shut it down. Mooky wasn't coming back, but he hoped to hell Joan was. He decided against telling Fitz about Little Al. He needed Fitz on his side. Didn't need questions about his ability to lead the Demon Brotherhood. Or how he should've been on top of this from the get go.

"They stepped over the line," Fitz said. "No matter what goes down between clubs, family's off limits."

"This might be personal," Bill said.

"You mean, 'cos of your son?"

"Yeah, that bastard better not let me catch up with him. Maybe the Berdoo chapter leadership can do something." Bill winced when he pressed the ice pack against his swollen eye.

"I'll call Gabo," Fitz said. "Tell him to get his men under control."

"I owe ya, Fitz." He rarely spoke in the singular—always club first. But more and more, this situation seemed focused on him.

"What are you gonna do?"

"Mobilize the club," Bill said. "Put the Tucson and Huachuca City chapters on alert."

"Need any Angels?" Fitz asked in a rare commitment to get involved in another club's problems. "The Brotherhood always stepped up when we called."

"This is our fight."

"Hey, Bill," Fitz said before Bill could hang up. "Something you already know, but I gotta say it: get the rest of your family under wraps. Just in case."

"Dagger's on it."

"Let me know if anything—"

"Yep." The line went dead.

Bill knew he should check the hospitals for Joan, but fatigue dragged him to a stop. Jail had been noisy. What little sleep he managed to get had been ragged. He popped a pod into the coffee maker and watched the black liquid pour into his cup.

The doorbell rang.

He rushed to the door. *Joan made her way home.*

The man outside made Bill's blood shoot through his arteries to his already pounding head. He opened the door and, without any words, grabbed the guy by the front of his jacket, and yanked him into the house. "Where's Joan?" Bill yelled in his face.

⌘⌘⌘

Joan jammed the brake pedal of Mooky's truck and skidded to a stop in front of Dagger and Orlanda's house. She jumped out of the truck and pounded on the front door. Nothing.

She turned her back to the door and glanced around the neighborhood. Her instincts screamed danger, but nothing looked out of place. She paced circles on the small front porch to relax her nerves. What went down at Mooky's must have rattled her. *Get your shit together, girl.* When she raised her fist to pound on the door again, the porch light came on. The door opened.

"Hear anything?" She rushed past Orlanda into the dark foyer.

"Shh, you'll wake the kids. Where've you been?"

"I was busy."

"Didn't you hear?" Orlanda said in a low voice. "The charges were dropped. Blaze went to pick up Dad and Dagger."

"He did? When?"

"A couple hours ago. Blaze called you, but you didn't answer."

"I lost my phone." Joan paced around the living room and recoiled when she stepped on a squeaky toy.

Orlanda's gaze traveled from the gun in Joan's waistband to the blood caked on the front of her jeans. "You look like you need a drink."

"I can't." Joan debated whether to tell Orlanda she was pregnant. *No alcohol...but I get into fights and gunplay—and it's far from over. My kid better be a tough son of a bitch.* She fingered back the curtain and glanced out the front window. Something didn't feel right. "Mooky's dead." She let go of the curtain.

"Oh, my God. How?"

"Mongols...it's a long story. I'll take a glass of water." Joan followed the soft slaps of Orlanda's flip-flops to the kitchen, and squinted when Orlanda turned on the light.

Orlanda's eyes widened and she gasped when she turned to hand Joan the water. "Holy shit. What the hell happened to you?"

"There was a fight." Joan rubbed her eyes at the memory of Mooky sitting on his floor. The jolts of pain when the gun slammed against the side of her face. The burnt gunpowder in her nose.

Orlanda grabbed Joan's arm and rushed her to the downstairs bathroom. "You need to clean up."

The blood spatter on Joan's face and neck shocked her. No wonder Orlanda had been so unnerved. Joan fingered dark purple bruise on her cheekbone. At least her stomach stopped rolling. "Good thing I didn't cross paths with anybody."

"Especially the cops." Orlanda handed Joan a washcloth and towel. "While you clean up, I'm gonna call Dad and let him know you're here." From the stairs, she called back in a loud whisper, "And I'll get you one of my tee shirts."

Another tee shirt sounded like a good idea because Mooky's was way too big. The neckline sagged and the knot at her waist didn't hide the bagginess. It was smeared with blood, but not as bad as her neck. She scrubbed her face and neck then rinsed with cold water, turning the draining water pink.

"Joan," Orlanda called from the top of the stairs.

Orlanda's loud voice sent dread crawling across Joan's arms stood up. Orlanda was not whispering.

Joan rushed to the bottom of the stairs. "What happened?"

"Help me get the kids ready."

"Ready?" Joan took the stairs two at a time. "For what?"

"Dad's phone was busy, so I called Dagger. He said to pack up the kids and get to the clubhouse."

"Why? What'd he say?" Joan pulled off Mooky's tee shirt and took the one Orlanda offered.

"He didn't say we're in danger, it's—holy shit…your ribs."

"Yeah, the boys played rough tonight." Joan yanked the clean tee shirt over her head. "Waking up kids in the middle of the night and carting them off to the clubhouse sounds a lot like danger to me."

"You get Peter and Peri ready," Orlanda said. "I'll get dressed and gather whatever we'll need."

Five minutes later, two cranky kids in tow, Orlanda and Joan stepped into the carport. They stopped short at the black silhouette of a large man blocking Orlanda's car. Though the air was cool, a sweat broke out all over Joan's body.

"Where do you think you're going?" The man stepped into the pale carport light, revealing a Mongol cut. He pulled a gun and pointed it at Orlanda.

Orlanda guided her kids behind her then put her hand into her purse, where she kept her revolver.

Joan tightened her grip on the gun held behind her thigh. Every nerve told her to raise the gun and shoot, but training told her it was all about reaction time. "We're leaving." *Wait until he speaks again…can't speak and react.*

"Over my dead—" the Mongol stated to say.

Joan raised her gun and fired.

CHAPTER 23

Bill slammed the man against the wall again. "Better start talking, Kearney."

Kearney rubbed the back of his head. "I don't know where she is. All I know is she emailed me a week ago basically saying, 'Come now. Secure Joe-Sam.'"

Bill dropped his head, trying to put the pieces together, resigning himself to still not knowing Joan's whereabouts. He glowered at Kearney, sure in his belief that he was the reason for most of Joan's ugliest scars. Joan had too much class to finger Kearney, but they only could have been the result of torture—the kind a CIA interrogator would leave. Bill gave Kearney one last shove in frustration at his inability to right a wrong this weasel perpetrated on Joan. It was their history. Nothing he could do about it now. Finding Joan was more important. Bill walked away.

Kearney followed him to the kitchen. "What'd she get herself into this time?"

"A big fucking mess."

"It never stops with her."

"I'm beginning to see that," Bill said. "Coffee?"

"Yeah, thanks. I got in town a couple of days ago and got Joseph and Samuel in a safe place," Kearney said. "I stopped by yesterday, saw the cop cars out front. Thought she got arrested."

"*That* we could handle," Bill said, pushing the coffee he had made for himself across the counter to Kearney. He grabbed another mug and started another cup.

"I was tapped out from lack of sleep and jet lag," Kearney continued. "I went to that café down the street. When I got back here, she was gone. Maybe if I stayed, things would be different."

"Maybe. Maybe not." Bill leaned on the counter. "Sorry for the rough greeting."

Kearney nodded and took a sip. "Where was she last?"

"My Uncle Mooky's, a few miles from here. Serious shit went down there. Mooky got killed. Found three dead Mongols." Bill pressed his eyes with his thumb and forefinger, trying to rub away the carnage that flooded his vision.

"I don't remember problems with the Mongols."

"There weren't." Bill stopped rubbing his eyes. "Not till lately. Coupla months ago, Mongols started riding through our territory. I foiled a set-up at my custom shop."

"What kind of set-up?"

"Drug distribution." Bill blew on his coffee. "From what I learned, the Cartel brought the shit in from Mexico in bulk. Mongols broke it up in my shop after hours and delivered to distributers. Used their bikes to move it."

"Across state lines and the border. Federal offenses."

"I trusted my guy I put in there. Shoulda checked up on him. Anyway, Joan found out about it and told me. I shut it down."

Kearney didn't respond, just looked around Bill's house. "Nice place."

"Yeah, my custom shop's a money-maker." Bill debated how much he should tell Kearney. "There's bad blood with my son. He was the leader of the shady deal at the shop."

"Then it's personal?" Kearney asked.

"Wish I knew for sure, but that's what my gut says."

"The gut never lies." Kearney sipped for several seconds before continuing. "I take it you didn't find her at Uncle Mooky's."

"All we found was her bloody tee shirt and her bike."

"She was alert enough to change her shirt, but not ride her bike. How'd she get away?"

"Uncle Mooky's truck is missing."

"Okay. What do we have?" Kearney rubbed the stubble on his jaw. "She changes her shirt and gets outta Dodge. Why take the truck and not her bike? Her bike would link her to what went down at the house. She's too well-trained to leave incriminating evidence like that behind. Might have been abducted."

"Don't even want to think that."

"Was there a tracker app on her phone?" Kearney asked.

Bill shook his head. "I trusted her. Things were peaceful…"

"Nothing's ever peaceful with Joan," Kearney said. "But what does this have to do with Little Al and his sons?"

"Little Al was in on the shady business at my shop. Don't know anything about his sons being involved."

Kearney leaned back on the stool. "Joan told me to secure them. Maybe they were being used as leverage."

Bill didn't respond. Didn't care about Joseph and Samuel. All he wanted was Joan to walk through the door.

"Back to the bloody tee shirt," Kearney said. "Say the blood was someone else's, do you know where she'd hole up?"

"Here. The clubhouse."

"Did you check hospitals?"

"That was the next thing I was going to do."

"You do that," Kearney said. "I know some people I can call."

"We have plenty of men."

"These are specialists. If anyone can find her, it's them." Kearney pulled out a sat-phone and started dialing.

"Not your CIA buddies…" Bill wasn't sure about bringing in outsiders. Would they work with the Brothers, or would they just get in the way? "If you're talking technology, we have our own tech specialist."

"Good. I'll have their tech guy hook up with yours." Kearney put the phone to his ear and said to Bill, "Joan can hold her own. But we don't know her condition, where she is, or what she's up against. Time is the point of a spear. It can stab us in the ass. But I'd rather nail them with it."

Kearney's words got Bill out of idle. He headed to his office to boot up his computer to look up local hospitals and their phone numbers. Kearney's voice drifted from the kitchen. It was mostly codes and numbers until he started speaking sentences.

"This is Kearney. Joan Archer gave me this number to call if she was in trouble...Then come to Bill Torrence's house to verify for yourself, but time is not our friend. The address is...You have it?...Right." Kearney hung up. "They have to check to see if I am who I say I am," he said, leaning on the doorjamb to Bill's office "After that, they'll send a liaison over to work with you."

"Why not with you?"

"I'm not here," Kearney said. "I'm a fugitive, too, remember?"

Kearney's phone rang back right away. "Yeah...Yeah... You do?...no...No fucking shit...And you're sure...Out."

Bill went back to Googling hospitals.

"They know where she is," Kearney said.

"They do? Where is she?" Bill turned at the sound of metal rubbing leather and a click. He was eye-to-eye with the barrel of a high caliber handgun.

"You tell me," Kearney said.

"Whoa." Bill put up his hands. His heart kicked into high gear. "I don't know what they said, but I don't know where she is."

"They say she's here."

"What? Why would they say that?"

"They put a GPS tracker on her phone."

"Who?" Bill realized why Kearney's contact thought Joan was there. "Her phone is in my jacket pocket."

"I don't give a fuck where her phone is. Where is she?"

"I don't know. We found her phone in Uncle Mooky's driveway."

"Pull it out. Slow," Kearney said, without moving the barrel of the gun.

Bill reached inside his cut and pulled out the phone with two fingers. He handed it to Kearney, who thumbed through it, still holding the gun on Bill.

"Kearney, put the gun away." Bill wasn't sure what Kearney would do—he had the reputation of being a loose cannon. "We're on the same team."

Kearney didn't answer. He checked the phone a few seconds until he stopped and stared at one screen. His face reddened and his mouth tightened. He stared at Bill while he slid the phone into his back pocket.

"Who put a tracker on her phone?" Bill asked.

"Stillwater, for starters." Kearney clicked on the safety and slid the gun into its holster. "Ever hear of them?"

"Joan told me about them. Said they helped her get the evidence on the shit going down in my shop. Why are they tracking her?"

"Maybe 'cos she's married to one of the founding members."

"She didn't tell you in one of her little emails to you? She divorced Duncan."

Kearney's face dropped. "That's a trip wire I didn't see."

"Will it make any difference to them?" Bill asked.

"Hope not."

✪✪✪

Orlanda insisted that Joan take her phone. Bill wasn't at the clubhouse, and with Orlanda and her kids safely stashed there, Joan headed out. It was time to act on the information Mooky had beaten out of the Mongols. After pulling out onto the road, she called Bill.

"Hey, it's me. I'm on my way to you."

"Are you okay?" Bill asked his voice tight.

"Mooky's dead."

"I know. I went there to look for you. Have a clean-up crew there now. Where'd you go?"

"I didn't know you were released. I went to see if Orlanda knew anything." She checked her mirror and pulled around a slowpoke. "Where are you?"

"At the house. I'm leaving now."

"Stay there. I'm just minutes away." She stopped at a traffic light. There were no other cars on the street, and after craning her neck to check for cops, she headed through the intersection.

"You didn't answer my question," he said. "Are you okay?"

"Don't worry, I'm good." She turned into the winding streets of Bill's housing development.

"Your old friend, Kearney, is here."

"He is? What's that rat bastard doing there?"

"You didn't contact him?"

"Yes, I did contact him, but he's supposed to be doing something for me. Never mind, I'll be there in a few seconds. Oh, and when the clean-up crew finishes at Mooky's, you might want to send them over to Dagger's."

"Damn, Joan. Not another shootout."

"Nothing like at Mooky's. Just one."

"A Mongol?"

"Yeah. Orlanda and I dragged him into the kitchen." Joan palmed the steering wheel and turned onto Bill's street. "I'm coming up on the house now."

When she parked in Bill's driveway, he ripped open the driver's door, pulled her out of the truck into his arms, and kissed her as if it were the last time.

"Don't do that—not pick up a phone," he said. "Any of the Brothers would take your call. You gotta let me know what's goin' on. Can't help you otherwise."

"I lost my phone. Orlanda gave me hers. I called as soon as I could."

"You scared me shitless." He stopped before going through the door. He eyed the blood on the front of her jeans and rubbed her belly. "Is everything okay?"

"We're fine." When she spotted Kearney in the doorway, she broke away from Bill and walked up to him until they

were nose-to-nose, and glared at him. "Didn't I tell you to secure Joe-Sam?"

"They're fine. They're in an undisclosed location."

"Already? Damn, K, you're good." She hugged him hard
then stepped back to look into his eyes and touch his Van
Dyke goatee. "You look great. All tanned-up. I like the chin
dribble."

"I thought it was a nice touch." He put a hand on each of
her shoulders. "Wanna tell me why I blew out one of my false
IDs and flew halfway around the world to get here?"

"We had to secure Little Al's kids first. Now we can move
forward." She brushed past him. "I have to change my jeans,"
she said over her shoulder as she headed down the hallway.

"Move forward?" Bill asked, following her. "When did you
become club president?"

She pulled off the stiff, bloody jeans and grabbed a clean
pair of cammo pants. "I'll tell you what—if you can keep up,
I'll let you lead."

"There she is—the woman I fell in love with." Bill crossed
his arms. "What are you going to do?"

"Save Little Al," she said, pulling on the pants and button-
ing them.

"He threatened you, and now you want to save him. I don't
get it."

"I'll tell you on the way." She slipped past Bill while tucking her gun into the small of her back.

"You know where he is?" Bill asked, putting a hand on her
arm to stop her.

"Yeah. Mooky's got a way of charming information out of
people."

"Gonna take days to clean up that charm." He released her
and followed her to the living room.

She grabbed Kearney's arm and dragged him with her out
the front door.

"Jesus H. Christ," Bill said after looking at the back seat of
the crew cab. "Guess I know where Mooky's arsenal went to."

"In a moment of psychic lucidity, he showed it to me. I figured that was an invitation to use it, if I ever needed it." She climbed into the front seat and slid to the center. "I need it."

Kearney turned to face front after checking out the stash of guns in the back seat. "Are we taking on the Mexican Army?"

"Close," Joan said. "Mongols from Southern Cal."

"Where to?" Bill asked, backing out of his driveway.

"Arrowhead Middle School. He's being held in the boy's locker room."

"What about students?" Kearney asked.

"Closed for renovations," Bill said. "Or at least I hope it still is."

"And you know that—how?" Kearney asked.

"Garbage's son goes there," Bill replied. At Joan and Kearney's questioning looks, he added, "I'm the president of the club. It's my job to know everything about everybody."

Kearney pulled out his cell phone. "I'll reroute the Stillwater liaison."

"Wanna tell me what happened at Uncle Mooky's?" Bill asked Joan.

She told him about the first two bikers and the information Mooky forced out of them. Then how the second invasion went down, and how she ran to Mooky's bedroom for a stronger defensive position—and access to more weapons. She tried to gloss over it, but Bill wanted more.

"How'd you get covered in blood?" he asked.

"I was kneeling on the floor trying to unjam the gun, like I said, and the second guy emptied his gun over my head. When his gun was empty, he lunged. I cleared the gun, shot him midair, and he landed on me, pinning my legs under me. The dude was big. The fucker bled out on my favorite shirt while I struggled to get out from under him. If I could've killed him again, I would have."

Kearney shook his head and looked out the window.

"What?" she asked.

"In Yonkers, you said, 'no more killing.' Now you want to kill people twice?"

She kicked him in the ankle. "So, shoot me. I'm venting."

He rubbed his ankle while Bill glared at Kearney. The look on his face suggested he would take out Kearney in an instant. Joan needed to calm Bill down before he acted without understanding the complex relationship she and Kearney had. They had a painful and tragic history, but over the past year, she had made headway in putting it behind them, forgiving Kearney—not necessarily forgetting. Before she could soothe things over, Bill pulled into a narrow lane one block past the school and parked between a baseball field and a training field. Mercury lights created pools of darkness between their poles.

While Bill, Kearney, and Joan waited for more bikers and the Stillwater liaison, they spread out for an initial recon of the area. Using the murky shadows, they crept closer to the rear area of the school, avoiding detection in case the Mongols had a patrol. Several steel outbuildings in various stages of completion were erected in what looked like a former soccer field. When Joan looked through the windows of the cubes, her suspicions were confirmed. They were temporary classrooms until renovations were complete in the main building.

They regrouped at the edge of the shadows to wait for their backup. A black sedan pulled in and stopped behind Mooky's pickup.

"He's here to see you," Kearney said to Bill.

"I'll go introduce myself," Bill said, heading toward the newcomer.

When he was out of earshot, Kearney said, "You want to tell me what went on at Bill's house? You two looked a little too chummy."

"It's not what it looks like."

"Then what is it?"

"We're together, but…it's complicated."

"I like complicated." Kearney looked up at the approaching newcomer and offered his hand. "I'm Kearney."

"I'm Chaz." He turned his gaze on Joan, eyeing her swollen cheek. "You okay, Archer?"

Her heart skipped at his use of her married name, but she kept her face neutral—something she learned from the bikers. "So far."

"Wanna tell me why we're here?" Chaz asked while he inserted an ear bud.

Bill got him up to speed.

"Give me a sec while I brief my tech team." Chaz quietly passed the information on to someone else. "Tech support is online," he said, pulling a glider out of a dark resin case he brought with him. "They'll pilot this drone and receive the video. I'll also have video feed to my phone." After fiddling with the drone, Chaz said, "Ready for flight...Copy." He threw it like the balsam gliders Joan had played with as a kid, but this "glider" was larger, sleeker, and equipped with a camera. It buzzed off toward the school building. "We're doing a quick initial sweep," he explained.

While he concentrated on the aerial video of the school, Bill draped an arm over Joan's shoulder and pulled her in to him so they both could see the screen. Kearney raised his eyebrows at Joan. She scowled back.

"The drone can only see so much. We'll have to do a window check, set up some mini-transmitters. See if we can figure out where everyone is. What they're up to." Chaz slid the phone into his pocket. "Bill, you're with me. You two," he said to Kearney and Joan, "stay here. Brief the others when they come."

Chaz turned to Bill. "How many you have coming?"

"Only three. We have assets to protect."

"Copy that."

Bill and Chaz conferred briefly then headed toward the school, hugging the shadows.

When Kearney was sure they were well out of hearing range, he asked, "Wanna tell me why there's an FBI GPS tracker on your phone?"

"My future with Duncan is on the line here, K. Just go with the flow."

"That flow I saw back at the house? It didn't look like that future included Duncan. I need more information to 'flow.'"

"I'm pregnant. Okay?" Joan whispered through her teeth. "Is that enough for you?"

"You're having Bill's kid?"

"He thinks so."

"*He* thinks so? How many others think so?"

She grabbed Kearney's collar and growled, "I'm not that kind of girl."

"You divorce Duncan while he's in jail and move in with Bill. And, oh yeah, you're pregnant, but not sure who the father is. You're not exactly standing on moral high ground here."

"Only Bill and I know…and now you." She let go of his collar with a push. "Duncan doesn't know I'm pregnant, and it might be his."

Kearney's gaze dropped to her abdomen. "Last I looked, he's in prison."

"It's a long story."

"Jesus, Joan, I leave you alone for a few months, and your whole world goes to shit."

"Yeah, like you made my life easier."

"Who'd you call when you needed help?"

She didn't answer. Why had she contacted him? She knew he'd be like this, but she'd emailed him anyway.

"You didn't answer my question about the tracker app." He rubbed his eyes. "Although after that irrational rationalization, I'm not sure I want to know any more."

"Come closer." She looked over her shoulder and scanned their surroundings.

A car whispered by on the side road they had used to enter the back of the school. Tiny feet of a nocturnal animal scuffled in the shadows.

She pulled up her collar against the cool December night air and whispered, "I made a deal with the FBI. Our sentences will be commuted if I bring down the Demon Brotherhood. Bill is—was my target."

"Was pregnancy part of the plan? If it was, great hook."

She grabbed his upper arm. "It wasn't my choice…or my mistake."

He pried off her fingers and rubbed his arm. "You've turned into quite the spinner of yarns."

"You wanna know what's going on or not?"

Kearney smiled, flashing his large front teeth. "Please proceed with the Circuitous Saga of Joan."

"Nothing changes with you, does it?" She looked around again. "Anyway, there isn't anything to bring him down. Well, there is, but it's a frame. Bill's son tried to frame him with illegal activity at his shop. When that failed, he tried to frame Bill for attempted murder."

"Let me see if I have this straight," Kearney said. "There isn't anything to bring down the president of an outlaw motorcycle club, just a son framing his father for transporting drugs across state lines and attempted murder. Move along. Nothing to see here. Do you even know how this sounds?"

"It's a frame."

"You drank the Kool-Aid, Joan. Stay objective."

"When we rescue Little Al, he'll back me up."

"How is he part of this?"

"He's part of the frame."

"Which one? The drugs or the murder?"

"The drugs. And it was attempted murder, but the charges were dropped." Joan rubbed her forehead. Kearney always had a way of making her sound crazy, even to herself. "But Little Al wasn't a willing part of this."

Kearney looked into Joan's eyes as if searching for an answer he might already know. "This have anything to do with securing Joe-Sam?"

"Everything. They threatened his kids if he didn't go along with it." She looked away from Kearney's stare. "My deal is going to be voided. Duncan will never get out of prison, I'm as good as locked up, and my kid will be a ward of the state."

"Relax. I won't let anything happen to you or your kid. Why do you think they'll void your deal?"

"Lack of evidence—since there isn't any."

"Then we'll find some."

"Not to take down Bill."

"Kool-Aid?"

Joan dropped her head and took a couple steps away before circling back. "He is *not* going to prison because of some manufactured evidence."

Kearney put an arm around her shoulders to stop the pacing. "Then we'll find something better."

"Find what better?" Bill asked, appearing out of the shadows.

Kearney dropped his arm and turned to face Bill. "Oh, she was saying that she was afraid you'd someday wind up in jail, and what kind of life would that be for her and your baby?"

"I'm not going to jail," Bill said. "I've gone legit, remember? If I get charged with that drug distribution bullshit, the charges won't stick any better than the attempted murder rap."

"Which problem you want to solve? A nebulous future one or the one staring us in the face?" Chaz asked in an obvious effort to get everyone to focus. "I'll do whatever Joan wants."

"This one," she said.

"Okay," Chaz said. "Only two roving guards on the ground, two on the roof. Must be short manpower."

"Mooky and Joan took care of that," Bill said, squeezing her shoulders.

Joan cringed inwardly at the offhanded compliment. Was he really proud of her for being a part of torture and murder? *He couldn't possibly have meant that.* She looked up to see Kearney watching her. She glared back at him. Damn psychologist—always psyching her out.

Chaz watched a guard through a monocular. "The roving guards are predictable, and concealing guns. Looks like short autos—maybe Mac-Tens. Hard to tell in the dark at this distance."

He handed his mono to Joan, who glassed the area behind the school. There was a sizeable bulge under the guard's jacket. The guard disappeared around the corner of the building. If they were up against bikers with Mac-10s, fully-auto with thirty-round magazines, it was going to be a bad day in hell. She rubbed her belly. Good thing the guard wasn't checking the back area when they did their initial recon. Having seen all she needed, she returned the monocular to Chaz.

"Unless there's a shitload of men inside we don't know about, with your other three, we'll be good to go," Chaz said to Bill.

"All that's left is to get eyes inside." Chaz opened a metal box that looked like a jeweler's ring case. He pulled out a metal object the size of a Carolina June Bug and placed it in the palm of his hand. "This is Mike-Delta."

"Mike-Delta?" Bill asked.

"Phonetics for mini-drone. When someone opens one of the doors, we'll zip this operator inside. Get a fly-on-the-wall perspective." He pulled out his phone, thumbed to an app, and plugged in a small controller. He lifted his palm, and the mini-drone hummed off into the night, quieter than an actual beetle. "Mike-Delta will transmit video to my phone, give us eyes inside. The miniature transmitters I stuck on the windows will send audio to my ear bud."

"The other drone will keep an eye on the perimeter," Joan said.

"Yes, ma'am," Chaz said. He looked up at Bill. "Does your son have any military training?"

"Not that I know of."

Chaz nodded acknowledgement. "Door opening on the east side. Copy," he said, evidently to the operator of the original drone. Chaz played with the controls, and after a few tense seconds he said, "We're in."

He turned his phone to allow Joan to watch the monitor that showed the back of the shaved head of the biker who had opened the door.

"Looks like a hallway. Junction coming up. Don't see any light from under any of these doors. Hallway to the left runs the length of the building—a death funnel." Chaz moved the mini-drone toward a wall. "Let's settle here and see where this guy goes."

The hallway was distorted by the mini-drone's fish-eye lens, wrapping the corridor both ways in an arc. The biker pushed through a door. Chaz slipped the mini-drone through the opening behind the biker's head and stopped as the biker continued through a doorway on the left.

"Good thing bikers tend to be hard of hearing," Chaz said.

"All those long rides in a close pack," Bill said.

"Copy that," Chaz said. "I'm going to land Mike-Delta on

the wall here. It seems to be a vestibule. Don't want to push my luck."

The video was hi-def and remarkably clear. It showed an open door to what looked like a coach's office with a desk, two chairs, and various sports memorabilia. A thin Mongol slouched in the desk chair. The biker who had unwittingly opened the door for the mini-drone limped to a guest chair and sank into it.

"I don't see Switch." Joan looked at Bill, but his face wore a neutral expression. Only the tightened corners of his mouth revealed his irritation. She turned back to the video. "That guy with the shaved head was there that day I broke down on Route Ten."

"Yeah, I remember him." Chaz listened as he watched the video. "The skinny guy just called him Hernandez."

"Do you think the other door is the locker room?" Joan asked.

Chaz adjusted controls. "That'd be my guess."

"That's where I'd hold him," Kearney said. "Little Al's a big man. It'd take heavy-duty restraints to control him. There's usually an equipment room or some other storage area. At the very least pipes or urinals to secure him."

"Anything helpful from the audio?" Bill asked.

"Nah, just bullshitting," Chaz said. "Something about Switch acting crazy. Wondering where he went. Who's Switch?"

"My son," Bill said through clenched teeth.

Chaz listened for a while. "Talking about how Hernandez's wife gained weight after having a baby. About the loss of a woman named Sapphire. How beautiful—"

"Loss?" Bill interrupted.

"Uh…from what I hear, she's dead." Chaz's eyes focused on the ground as he listened.

"Dead? How?" Joan asked, sensing a change in Chaz's demeanor.

"It wasn't pretty. Something about—" Chaz pressed his lips together and shook his head. His jaw muscles clenched and unclenched. "From the sounds of it, no remorse. Who are these guys?"

CHAPTER 24

Two pickup trucks pulled into the lane and parked behind Chaz's sedan.

"I'll meet 'em," Bill said, walking off toward the Brothers who had just arrived.

"Joan, you're going to stay here, work Mike-Delta," Chaz said.

"Why? Because I'm a girl?"

"Because you're pregnant."

"How do you—" She narrowed her eyes and looked over her shoulder at Bill's retreating figure. "Bill told you?"

"He's concerned about you."

"Fuck him. I will not sit on the sidelines."

"We have enough—"

"*Men?* Really?" Joan put a hand on her hip. "I've more than proved myself."

"Yes, men," Chaz said. "*Non-pregnant* men."

She looked at Kearney who made no attempt to hide his amusement. She fought the impulse to pull her gun—and kill all the men in sight—and squelched the vision that extended her anger into a rampage. "Pregnancy is not a disability." She rubbed her forehead. *Wow! Where did that come from?* "What is it with you bastards?" she asked.

Chaz nodded to indicate behind her. "Take it up with him." He went back to his controls.

She turned to see a wall of dead-serious bikers. She zeroed in on Bill. "I will not sit this out."

"You're not goin' in, darlin'. I'll be distracted, worrying about you," he said.

"I'll be all right."

"It's my call."

Joan looked at Blaze. His face showed no signs of support. Neither did Youngblood's. When she looked at Slow Motion, he crossed his arms and frowned, his ice-blue eyes uncharacteristically clear.

"You get an ear bud for communication," Chaz said.

"Well, let me twirl for joy in my pretty pink skirt," she said but immediately felt bad. He was there to help with something that had nothing to do with him—all to protect her. He didn't owe her anything, but he was willing to put his life on the line. She leveled her gaze on Bill and frowned. *I did tell him if he could keep up, I'd let him lead.* "You're the boss." She put out her hand to Chaz. "Show me how to work the controller."

After a quick roll-out of the plan, the men crept toward the building, leapfrogging between the shadows. Joan, Bill, and Chaz had ear buds. Kearney and Chaz would take out the rooftop guards and become the over-watch while the bikers took care of business. Kearney and Chaz could aid in the op, yet keep an eye on Joan. They broke off from the bikers. After that, she lost them in the dark.

"Foxtrot, do you read?" Bill's voice was quiet but strong in her ear.

Fucker was jerking her chain. He had insisted on Foxtrot as her call sign—phonetic for female. Why did she even need a call sign? This wasn't a military operation.

"Five-by-five, Delta-Whiskey," she answered.

"Delta-Whiskey?" he asked.

"Phonetic for Dickwad."

"Cut it. Maintain radio discipline," Chaz said. "Are the bad guys in the same place?"

"Same room. Hernandez just got up." Eyes glued to the screen, her heart jumped. "He's going into the locker room. Do I follow him?"

"Do not follow," Chaz said. "If Mike-Delta gets into that room, we may not get it back. Remain in place."

"Remain in place. Roger that."

If she didn't get eyes in that room, they wouldn't know for sure if Little Al was there. Mooky got the Mongols to spill information through torture. People would say anything when in pain. Mongols were no exception. If Little Al wasn't there or still alive, someone could get hurt for nothing. The door was open. Go. Stay. The opening narrowed to little more than a crack. She worked the controls and slipped the mini-drone into the room.

Big mistake. The mini-drone did not have night vision capabilities. It bumped into something and went out of control— must have run into Hernandez's head. It hit the floor, from where she saw the puke-green glow a SnapStick, which lit up one of the bathroom stalls. The light was pale, most likely near the end of its life.

She piloted the mini-drone toward the glow. The shape of a woman came into view. It was Sapphire. She was naked, sitting on the toilet, head back against the wall, feet bent inward at an awkward angle, ankles striped with dark ligature marks. Her hands rested in her lap, wrists looked dark and swollen as if from struggling against restraints.

Several flashes on the roof made Joan look up. No sound of gunshots split the night—Kearney and Chaz had the only silencers. The low crack they emitted wasn't loud enough to reach where she waited, certainly wouldn't reach the avenue beyond. Bill and his crew could now take out the roving guards and make their entry.

Joan moved the mini-drone in for a closer look. Sapphire had been strangled. The multiple tracks across her throat indicated more than once. Joan moved the mini-drone lower. And pulled the phone in tight to her chest. She gagged on bile in the back of her throat. Her stomach churned, but she kept down what little she had in it.

"You okay?" Chaz said in her ear.

"Yeah…no. I'm inside the locker room. I saw—"

"I specifically told you to stay in the vestibule." Chaz's irritation slapped against Joan's eardrum.

"Yeah...I know." When her convulsing stomach relaxed, she looked at the phone's screen.

"Why are you in the locker room?" Chaz asked.

She ignored his agitation. "I saw Sapphire. She's dead, like they said."

The scene grew on the screen. Like watching an accident in slow motion, she couldn't pull back or tear her eyes away. Sapphire had been mutilated, most likely after death because there wasn't much blood. The way she was posed suggested she had been sexually assaulted.

"Look for the package," Chaz said, breaking the gruesome scene's hold on Joan.

"'The package.' Who talks like that?" She maneuvered the mini-drone away from Sapphire.

"Can it," Chaz snapped.

"It's dark. I only saw Sapphire because there's a SnapStick near her." Joan's stomach cramped. Those assholes lit up the body? Why—to check out their handiwork? The cramping became a burning ball of hate—Mooky had not been mean enough. She pictured the violent, repulsive things she would do to them. Make them suffer like they made Sapphire suffer. Joan shook her head to get her shit together and refocus on the phone's screen. Working the controls, she wondered where her newfound meanness came from—killing someone twice, if she could. A rampage to kill all men. Torturing these pigs. *I must be*—she hated to admit it—*hormonal.*

She pushed away the vision of running into the building and killing the depraved Mongols. Instead, she turned the mini-drone in a circle to see what was around it. Another glow came into view. She stayed close to the floor and moved to-ward the light. Hernandez's feet moved. She maneuvered away from them. A door closed, returning her to darkness, but not before she saw Little Al, huge and round from the fish-eye lens. He sat slumped against a warped wall. His thick beard, plastered with blood, lay flat against his chest.

"Shit." The word slipped between her teeth before she could stop it.

"What?" Bill asked.

"Little Al's in a room off the locker room. Maybe equip-ment storage? He looks unconscious."

"Can you get out of the locker room?" Chaz asked. "The inside team needs eyes-on."

"I'm following Hernandez out." She sped after him, gritted her teeth, and stared at the dark screen. "Didn't make it. Wait-ing for your orders, Chaz."

"Why? So, you'll ignore them?" Chaz's voice crackled in her ear. "This is one fucked up mess, Archer. Stand by."

Joan's ear bud went silent. She could picture Chaz pulling the bud from his ear and cursing her three ways to hell.

After several seconds his clipped voice grated against her eardrum. "Land Mike-Delta above the exit door. And stay there. Think you can do that?"

"Affirmative."

"Out."

Joan squatted back onto her heels and stared at the screen. *'This is one fucked up mess, Archer.'* Archer—that's what the Stillwater operators called her husband. Bet no one had ever said those words to him. In the scramble for evidence against Bill, she had lost her future with Duncan. Heartache consumed her from the loss of their marriage and the spoiled grand scheme to save them both. The vision of Sapphire that had burned into her memory reproached her. *This is one fucked up mess, Archer*—a textbook summation of her past three years. She clenched her jaw and vowed to never hear those words again.

Gunshots, muffled by the thick walls, indicated Bill and his team were inside. They had "no eyes" because she had been the maverick she always was. She couldn't help them, but maybe there was something else she could do. The mini-drone responded to her command and moved toward the sickly glow. From there, she got her bearings and headed toward the band of light beneath the door where she had seen Little Al. She sized up the opening. And slipped through.

Little Al hadn't moved, but she could see his chest rise and fall. She flew toward his face. If she touched his skin, maybe he would wake up. The gunshots would tell him help was on the way. She landed above his battered right eye. Nothing. She skimmed the drone across his forehead.

He moved his head.

Her heart bounced against her ribs. She pulled back for a view of his face.

His eyes opened, unfocused, but moving.

Exhilaration made her thumb jerk the controller. She had to get him to notice the mini-drone. She rocked it in front of his eyes until they focused on it. He turned his head as if he heard something. He looked back at the mini-drone.

She piloted it up and down.

He shook his head, as if to clear it. When he nodded, she jumped to her feet.

She had to get to the wall above the exit. She flew a farewell circle in front of Little Al and headed for the space under the door.

"Foxtrot, when we get inside the locker room, you have to guide us," Bill said.

"Um…yes." Her hands trembled with excitement. After a short struggle, she wedged under the door and flew into the dark locker room.

"Guidance, Joan."

"Turn right inside the door. Then right again."

"Got it. Two rights."

The mini-drone sputtered. She lost her bearings for a couple of seconds. A bright light burst to the left, and she made a beeline for the top of the door.

Through the fish-eye lens, she saw Bill and Youngblood come into the room, crouching, hugging the wall until they disappeared from view. Where were Slow Motion and Blaze?

She landed above the door and waited for someone to retrieve the mini-drone. The right side of the screen displayed the stall around Sapphire and the corner around which Bill and Youngblood had disappeared. After several seconds, Bill and Youngblood reappeared supporting Little Al. Bill left Little Al with Youngblood and headed for Sapphire. Little Al grabbed him and held him back. It looked like they had words, but Bill gave in, turned away from Sapphire, and they all headed out of the locker room. On the way out, Bill grabbed the mini-drone.

Her job done, Joan ran toward the school. She headed around the building toward the east door, but Bill and the others crashed through the glass entrance to her right. She spun around and ran toward them, relieved to see Blaze, but he was holding his side, hunched over under Youngblood's arm. Blood oozed between his fingers.

"Youngblood, get Blaze to the hospital," Bill said as they crossed the schoolyard toward the vehicles.

"I don't need to go to the hospital," Blaze muttered through the pain.

"Go to the hospital. Call the club lawyer. Have him meet you there."

Joan slammed into Bill's side, and he put his arm around her. Chaz and Kearney rushed out of the shadows. Sirens whined, shrill and distant.

"Where's Slow Motion?" she asked.

"Won't be coming with us." Bill kissed her on the lips, hard and quick. "We gotta get outa here."

Bill opened the truck door and climbed in after her. After helping Little Al into the back seat, Kearney jumped into the passenger seat. Everyone else ran to their rides, throwing weapons into trunks or truck beds. They headed out onto the surrounding streets in different directions, fading into the night.

"What's with all these weapons?" The effort to talk must have irritated Little Al's throat because he rubbed his neck through his blood-clotted beard and produced a couple of dry coughs.

"I thought we might need them," Joan said, turning slightly to face him.

"Against some piss-ant Mongols?" he asked, his voice scratchy.

She turned to face front. "For GPs."

"There isn't anything general purpose about what you started," Bill said, adjusting the rearview mirror so he could see Little Al.

"Sorry, Prez, but they threatened my kids."

"You coulda come to me. We coulda worked through it to-gether."

Little Al didn't respond.

"Is this about you doing time on the block in my place?" Bill asked, switching between watching the road and looking at Little Al. "Was well over a year ago. Thought you were okay with that."

"Me, too," Little Al said quietly.

"We're gonna see what the club wants to do about this mess. I owe you that much."

"Thanks, Prez." Little Al sat back and cleared his throat. "My little princess must be scared shitless."

"Joe-Sam mentioned a younger half-sister." Kearney glanced over his shoulder then looked at Joan. "When you didn't mention her, I thought you took care of her."

"Tell me you secured her," Little Al rasped, grabbing the front seats and leaning forward.

Joan's world ground to a halt. Her blood stopped flowing. She had forgotten about Little Al's daughter from an extra-marital affair. She sank into herself, clamping her eyes shut, cringing from the unforgiving words, '*This is one fucked up mess, Archer.*'

CHAPTER 25

Joan kneeled on the seat to look Little Al in the eye. "I'm sorry," she said. ". I forgot about her."

Bill looked into the rearview mirror. "Where is she?"

"At Maya's, I guess," Little Al said.

"Why Maya's?" Joan asked.

"Her mother," Little Al replied.

Maya had been the other woman? It now made sense that Maya talked back to Blaze and got away with it. Tough Maya, who had helped Joan handle two drunks who had wandered backstage at the strip club—whacking them with her three-inch stilettos.

Joan thought back to that day in the park a year ago, when she had witnessed the little girl with the bouncy ponytail running into her father's giant hands, but couldn't remember the mother. Joan had been too caught up in her own problems. "We'll go get her right now. You in, Kearney?"

"That's why I'm here."

"Who made you boss?" Bill asked Joan.

She glared at him. "You have some place better to be?"

"Your ex was right," Bill said.

"Right about what?" she asked, dropping onto the seat and facing forward.

"It never ends with you, does it?"

"Oh, it's gonna to end," she said. "It's gonna end tonight."

During the ride, fatigue set in, and all Joan wanted to do was doze on Kearney's shoulder. A few minutes of sleep sounded enticing, but after being left out on the last entry, she didn't want to show any weakness. She had completed more demanding missions on less sleep and not been as tired, but, lately, things were different.

The weight of her past was catching up with her, draining her energy or...surely, pregnancy wouldn't affect her this early on, would it?

She scanned the area when Bill pulled into an apartment complex and parked near Building F. Anyone could be hiding in the shadows behind the shrubbery made darker by the pale light of the sidewalk lighting. The pre-dawn quiet only intensified her nervousness. Not even a dog barked.

"Where's she live?" Joan asked Little Al.

"Upper floor on the left."

Four apartments opened onto a common entryway that was a patio on the ground floor, a deck on the second. If someone had a shotgun on the other side of the door, there would be no way to avoid getting hit.

They piled out of the truck and stood in a circle. A black sedan pulled in two cars down from where Bill parked. Joan walked over to greet Chaz. She knew he wouldn't leave her without checking in to see if there was something else going on.

"How'd you know I was here?" Joan asked, leaning her forearms on the door and talking through the open window.

"You don't get it, do you?" Chaz said. "You don't go anywhere we don't know about."

"But how? I don't have my phone."

"Someone has it, 'cos I'm here." He turned off the engine and leaned back. "Why are *you* here?"

"To pick up Little Al's kid before Switch does."

"You going in?" Chaz asked.

"Yeah. You?"

Chaz shook his head. "We don't do illegal entries."

"It's not illegal, Little Al—"

"Joan, we're on the move," Kearney said from near the rear fender of Chaz's car.

"Catch you later," Joan said to Chaz.

"Okay," Bill said, leading the way to the building. "The only way to do this is to do it."

He stopped at the bottom of the stairs leading to the second floor. "Joan, you stay here. Signal if anybody comes."

"No." The word sounded harsh in the nighttime stillness, so she continued, "I mean, if Maya's tied up or hurt, I think a child will respond better to a woman's presence."

"Her father's here," Bill said.

"She's right," Little Al said. "If something happens to me, a woman in there would be a good idea."

"Okay, but you stay behind me. Right behind me," Bill said, pinning her with his gaze. "Kearney, you're lookout."

Little Al knocked then listened at the door for movement inside. He looked at Bill and shook his head, then unlocked the door with his spare key.

Sheer curtains turned the exterior lights into a silver eeriness. The furniture looked comfy, the living room was neat and clean, except where Barbie dolls and plastic, doll-sized wardrobes cluttered the floor. Al turned on a light as he entered each room and called to Maya and his daughter, Alyana. The brightness did nothing to raise the mood. And Little Al's voice sounded more desperate with each call to his daughter.

Little Al tapped his cut and pulled out his phone. "Yeah?" he said into the phone and held it so Bill and Joan could hear.

"Heard what happened at Arrowhead." Switch's voice was unmistakable. "I have Maya and Alyana. Better worry 'bout that."

Joan saw Bill's mouth tighten through the moustache and goatee. His face darkened. He clenched his fists. She snaked an arm around his waist.

"Where are they, motherfucker?" Little Al asked.

"Sun Valley Custom Rides."

"You worthless excuse for a son," Bill said. "Families are always kept out of any biker shit. You have a problem with me, come to me."

"This isn't biker shit," Switch said. "This is family shit."

"We're coming for my family and for you," Little Al said.

"Bring it on."

The phone went dead.

"He's on my turf," Bill said, guiding Joan toward the door. "No one knows that shop better than me.

When they reached the bottom step, Chaz was standing with Kearney. Kearney said, "I take it they're not here."

"No," Bill said, tossing the truck keys to him on the way past. "They're at my shop." He slid into the truck after Joan. "You know where to go?"

Kearney nodded and pulled out into the street. "Went there first to get some intel on where Al's sons might be."

Bill pulled out his phone. After checking on Blaze's condition, he told Youngblood where to meet up. He pulled Joan into him. She gave in without fight, taking the opportunity to rest her eyes and gather some strength.

A rocking motion stirred her awake. "Where are we?" she asked, inhaling to expand her lungs. The quick snooze had refreshed her.

"On a dirt service road behind my shop," Bill said.

It wasn't long before an SUV pulled alongside. Bill gave instructions to Youngblood across the space between the two vehicles. He pulled forward to park, leaving dust swirls in the headlights.

Joan, Bill, Kearney, and Youngblood gathered on the far side of the truck from the shop. Bill used a fast food wrapper for a hand-drawn map to lay out his plans.

Joan's heart quickened at the thought of what might lay ahead. "What about me?"

"Sorry, darlin'. Can't take a chance of something happening to you. You're more valuable as our eyes on the outside of the building." He pulled out her phone and handed it to her. "Text if anything happens we need to know about."

"This is bullshit, and you know—"

Little Al silenced her with a heavy hand on her shoulder. "Keep the perimeter safe for our exit."

He coughed to clear his throat. When he lifted his beard to rub his neck, she saw red, swollen ligature marks. For the first time, she noticed the fat lip. She guessed there were more injuries under his clothes by the way he held his side. *Even big men can be taken down.*

Chaz pulled into the service road and parked behind Mooky's truck. He got out then reached inside the car. He pulled out an HK-416 assault rifle and slung it across his chest. "What's the plan for Joan?" he asked as he walked up to the men selecting weapons and ammo from the pile in the back of the truck.

"Perimeter guard," Bill said. "You want to go in?"

Chaz shook his head. "I'm with Joan."

Bill nodded in agreement then motioned to the others to head out. They slipped through a hole in the fence. Joan climbed into the driver's seat and Chaz joined her in the passenger side. They watched the dark figures head toward the shop, avoiding the spotlights and surveillance cameras, then disappear under the trees that shaded the side of the building from the lights.

Headlights approached from the west. Joan and Chaz slid down in the seat. When the car turned into the lot, Joan texted Bill to tell him two more men showed up.

"Think we should find a more secure location?" she asked.

Chaz eyed the distance to the shop and the open space between it and the truck. "Bikers aren't known for marksmanship. We're good."

"All my years of training and I'm reduced to texting from a truck fifty yards from the action," she muttered. She reached between the seats and grabbed an AR-15. She fished around and pulled out a full magazine, slapped it into the weapon, and charged a round.

"Be thankful you're out here," Chaz said. "Nothing good's gonna happen inside."

"I never got left out before."

"You were never pregnant before."

"I know." Joan looked out the side window. "But Alyana's in there."

"You have your own kid to think about."

"I know. I'm just saying…"

She sat back and waited in silence with Chaz. A loud crack startled her. She saw a hole in the windshield then looked over at Chaz. His head was back, his eye socket torn and bloody. He moaned.

"Chaz, if you can hear me, roll out of the truck," she said with a push to get him moving. "I'm right behind you."

He fumbled for the doorknob. Another gun shot, and Chaz flopped back.

"Dammit." She reached over him for the door handle. More rounds slammed into the metal with loud clunks, barely missing her. She slithered over Chaz, opened the door, and slid to the ground. More clunks hit against the car with the sharper cracks from rounds going though glass.

The gunshots stopped. Joan looked left and right then crawled to the tail end of the truck to peek over the bed. The shooter started again. She ducked behind the rear tire, but not before she saw the muzzle flashes. When the shooter stopped to change magazines, she took several quick, deep breaths to clear her head then eased up to put the roof of the building in her gun sites. And waited. After several tense seconds, she thought, *What'd he do? Go to take a leak?*

She recoiled at a tap on her shoulder. She turned her head and looked up the dark, round hole of a rifle muzzle. Her heartrate revved to hyper-speed. The biker at the other end of the gun told her to drop hers. She thought of her baby and complied. No way the little guy would die before he had a chance to live. She slowly slid up the side of the truck, hands up, head lowered in submission. She glanced up through her lashes. The biker had made one fatal error—he was within reach.

A shot cracked the night, and the Mongol fell backward, moaning from a shot in the chest. Joan ducked and spun around to look at the roof of the building. Youngblood gave her a sloppy salute before disappearing.

She grabbed the biker's gun and shot him again, left of center in his chest. Sneaky bastard. No way would he get a second chance to surprise her.

Her location was blown. Chaz was dead. She'd heard the

tires go flat from bullets. She looked around, thought of rifling through Chaz's pockets for his car keys, but who knew how many Mongols were out there or where they might be? Running away from the shop to the nearest building was not an option—too much open space. As crazy as it sounded, the safest place was inside, find an area to defend rather than be a sitting duck out in the open. But she needed cover to get across the parking lot and inside. She rummaged around in the back of the truck, and came up with two smoke canisters. A magazine full of .223 ammo caught her eye. She snatched it, too.

Joan chose Chaz's Heckler & Koch—no doubt, the best maintained gun within reach and the least likely to jam—and slipped the sling over her shoulder. She looked down and rubbed her belly. "If you have a 'Holy Shit Handle' in there, Little Dude, hang on tight. The ride might get a little bumpy."

She popped smoke, and, while it billowed and expanded, stowed the other canister and the extra magazine in her cargo pockets. When she scrambled through the fence, the bulging pocket with the smoke canister snagged the cut links of the fence. After several muttered curses, she disentangled herself and darted toward the building, hugging the shadows until she reached the same stand of trees where the men had disappeared.

After slipping into the welcome darkness behind the shop, she exhaled. And listened. No gunshots. That could be a good sign, but knowing her Iron Angel Bad Karma, it was most likely not anything close to good. The guys went toward the back of the shop. If they were in trouble, coming from the other direction might give her the element of surprise. A back door caught her eye. She stopped and listened. The desert was quiet, except for the sounds of distant, early commuters. Nothing else stirred. Even the nocturnal creatures had gone to ground.

A volley of gunshots erupted from inside. Then stopped. She didn't know which was worse, the gunshots or the quiet. Dread squirmed from her stomach into her bones while she checked the door in front of her. It was secured only by the doorknob lock. An easy fix with her driver's license. She opened door inch by inch and froze at muffled orders shouted from somewhere farther inside the building.

The door opened into the breakroom, which looked as it should. She walked across the room on the balls of feet, clearing the area as she moved through it. Her toe snagged a chair, and it groaned across the tile floor. She darted to the cover of the coffee station and knelt, not daring to breathe. No sound of an approaching guard checking out the noise. At the threshold to the reception area, she caught her breath again. The approaching dawn made harmless items like the reception desk and advertising banners loom out of the pale light. She exhaled and did one last 360-degree check before stealing along the short hallway to the corner. She waited and listened. No sound, only the beating of her heart in her ears.

She peeked around the corner. The back of a Mongol appeared in the glassed upper half of the closed double-doors to the maintenance bay. She looked again, and he was gone. She snuck around the corner to Little Al's office. It was dark and vacant. A muffled conversation filtered through the steel doors.

She looked through the window in one of the doors and pulled back. Two bikers stood in the middle of the bay facing to her right, guns at the ready, but not aimed at anyone. If Kearney and the Brothers were captured, they must be to the right. She hoped Maya and Alyana were there too—only one area to search and protect. Crouching where the wall and doors met, she checked her six and listened for any movement in her escape route—if it came to that. Still clear. Her heart pounded against the inside of her chest.

Her hands were sweaty, forcing a tight grip on her rifle. She rubbed her palms on her thighs and took a deep breath. Now she knew why soldiers wore gloves.

Why was she doing this? She should hole up in the ladies' room, or some other easily defended place. Help would come eventually, and her baby would be safe. But what if Bill and Kearney were in danger? She was the only person in a position to do something. If she didn't act, and they were killed, she would live with that for the rest of her life.

Life. She had to consider the tiny, vulnerable life relying on her to protect him.

She leaned against the wall. Roger had not gotten back to her about her deal. She could only assume it was as useless as all her past efforts as a freedom fighter. That meant the only father her kid would know was inside that maintenance bay, in danger, she guessed, or he would be giving orders. Thoughts raced and circled through her head. Fight and endanger her baby. Run and be safe.

I'm a fighter. Fighters…

She thought back to the first day of this long journey.

Fighters…

She pressed her abdomen and whispered the words she had said that day, "Fighters stand their ground."

But more than a lifetime's-worth of events had muddied the waters since then. Joan Bowman stood her ground. Joan Archer took the fight to the enemy.

If she went in and lived, or fled to preserve a tiny life—either way she would forever be tormented by the outcome. She had to choose the action with the fewest recriminations.

She looked back at the escape route and calculated the possibilities.

Nothing good's gonna happen inside.

CHAPTER 26

Her little guy, or girl, deserved a father.

After checking again, and seeing the bay was now clear, she slowly opened one of the doors and entered low, in a duck walk. The bikers who had been in the center of the room had moved out of her sight. She braced herself against the wall and listened. Through the sounds of her breathing and the wild beating of her heart in her ears, she heard sobbing. She duck-walked two more steps and peered around a large tool chest. A moan caught in her throat.

The parts room was actually a line of shelving along one wall of the bay, cordoned off by chain link caging that formed an aisle the length of the area. Inside the caging, Little Al sat on the floor, gagged and with his arms bound behind him. Maya was tied up and sat with her back braced by the shelves, chin to chest, sobbing. Joan tried to imagine the frustration and sense of helplessness they must have felt. Next to Maya, Bill sat also bound and gagged. Kearney was not in sight.

Neither was Alyana.

A door closed. Footsteps neared her position. She dropped to one knee, steadied her weapon, and looked down the sights. Two bikers stopped in surprise and raised their weapons. Bullets smacked the wall behind Joan. She fired. The first few shots went wild then training zeroed her on target. The men went down. She changed the magazine.

She hadn't wanted to fire, at least until she got to the men and Maya, but now chaos was biting her in the ass. Joan rushed in, looking for more targets, but none came. She backed up to the caging and tried the door. It was locked

"How do I get you guys out?"

Bill motioned with his head toward a biker with a red plaid shirt under his cut.

"That guy has the keys?"

Bill nodded.

She raced across the bay, crouching, eyes focused on her surroundings, only looking down to locate his pockets. The keys were in the inside pocket of his cut and, as she hooked the keyring on her pinky and started to back away, another biker cautiously entered the bay, searching for her. She ducked behind a vintage car turned into a low-rider.

Under the car, she saw his feet approaching her. She pulled her .45 out of the small of her back, and, after a deep breath, stood, and fired. The rounds hit center mass. He went down. The door opened again. The handgun was empty. Damn. All her preparations, and she forgot to check the magazine of her handgun. *Can't worry about that now.*

Ears ringing, she retreated between the cars toward the caging and took up a defensive position behind the last car. She saw movement on her left, then more movement on the right. She might get one, but what were the chances of hitting both men closing in on opposite sides of her? The realization she might get hit slithered down her spine. The error of ignoring the odds and coming into the maintenance bay anyway screamed inside her head. She clenched her teeth. Killing the dream of a baby before he saw the world was not going to happen.

She inched toward the rear fender of the car. She'd take out the one on this side first then take out the second attacker from the cover of the rear of the car.

Sounded good. Definitely not foolproof.

Bill was signaling something with his eyes.

She changed directions, backing away from her near-fatal mistake. The attacker appeared. He fired. The bullet whistled past her head. She fired. He fell backward. She spun around. The other biker's gun jammed. He dropped behind the same tool chest she had used as cover only minutes before. She advanced toward the tool chest, shooting through it several times. The man cried out and moaned. She kicked his gun away. Another bullet whizzed by, hitting the wall behind her. The first attacker had recovered enough to fire at her. She turned, shot several three-round bursts at him, and changed magazines while approaching him. Kicked his weapon away.

After one last scan of the bay, she reached for the keyring. It wasn't on her finger. Sweat broke out over her body while she frantically searched the floor. There, next to the tire. A quick look each way and she crawled toward it. Shadow movement made her look under the car. Nothing. Must've been just heightened awareness making her see things.

She grabbed the keyring and put the key in the lock.

The hair on the back of her neck stood up.

"Hands where I can see them," Switch said.

Too late, she realized the movement hadn't been a hallucination. She put up her hands and turned to face him.

"Don't turn around," he said. "Drop your weapon."

Eyes steady on Bill, Joan slid the sling over her head and laid the rifle on the floor.

She could see the length of the parts area. No Kearney. Dread hung heavy on her shoulders. She looked at Bill but couldn't read his face. Her vision of Kearney bleeding or dead somewhere slowed her thoughts to crawl.

"Turn around," Switch ordered.

She closed her eyes, swallowed, and turned around to see Switch leaning on the hood of a car, his rifle leveled at her.

"You have been a pain in my ass since the first time we met," he said.

She braced for impact.

The double doors opened. A child's tormented screaming for her daddy echoed off the high ceilings. Both Switch and Joan looked.

Inez was aiming at Switch and holding Alyana by the back of her ballerina pajamas. Joan looked at Switch, who didn't seem bothered by it. She shifted her gaze back and forth between Switch and Inez, without moving her head.

"Let her go," Little Al said, but it had no force. His voice still suffered from his being strangled.

"Daddy!" Alyana squealed. "Daddy, make her let me go—o—o."

"Shut up," Inez said to Alyana, shaking her into silence. "I don't know which one of you to shoot first. Switch." She moved the barrel of her gun from Switch to Joan. "Or you."

"Why would you want to shoot me?" Joan asked.

"Shut up," Switch said, pointing his rifle at her. "Sit down, your back to the caging."

Joan slid down to her butt. Bill was directly behind her, Little Al and Maya to her right. Darling little Alyana would be mentally scarred for life. Another poor young soul hardened by life from events beyond her control. Joan rubbed her hands on her thighs, worrying that her own kid would be faced with shit like this, if she didn't do something—and not just at this moment. But if she—they—lived through this, she had to get free of these violent subcultures for good.

"…lost control of this a long time ago," Switch was saying.

"I had her chasing rabbits, but that mother had to go off script." Inez pointed her gun at Little Al.

"Had me chasing rabbits?" Joan's blood boiled. "What do you mean?"

Inez pointed her gun at Joan and glared her into silence. "Switch and I are related. I'm his mother's half-sister. Had many dealings in the past and, as it turns out, I owed him a favor. Didn't I, Switch?"

He didn't answer.

Joan studied Inez and remembered her advice when Bill walked out—if she had followed Inez's advice, the op would have been over. Inez's clandestine visit with Duncan, pulling the trigger on divorce before Joan was ready. Her constant threats to pull Joan out of the fray, in spite of her successes. That day on Northern Avenue, when she lost her cool and said she could have done better.

"When I learned the Bureau was sending a CI—" She looked past Joan to Bill. "Didn't know that, did you?"

Joan dropped her head back against the caging and closed her eyes. This was not how it was supposed to go down. Bill wasn't supposed to know about her dealings with the feds until this was over. Fucking Inez.

"Joan, look at me," Inez said.

Joan opened her eyes.

"I knew a CI would discover Switch's plan, so I inserted myself into the insertion." She chuckled. "The downside of irony is that it's so damn ironic." She turned her gun on Switch. "We were making good money off this business, until Switch here lost control of the key players."

"And this is how you repay me, *Tía* Inez?" Switch said. "Screwing me over when I'm gonna complete my plan?"

"Go ahead," Inez said. "Tell her your sob story so she can understand why she's going to die here, in Bill's shop, at his son's hands."

"That poor excuse of a father kicked out my mother and me—"

"He didn't kick *you* out," Joan said. "Just your—"

"Shut up, or I swear I'll kill you right now," Switch said.

"Let's get back on point," Inez said. She turned her attention back to Joan. "That day at the meeting in the middle of nowhere, when you told me about the illegitimate business that would reflect on Bill, but he was no part of. Remember that? In the sun, making me wait? Getting so damned independent?"

"I—" Joan's dry mouth made it difficult to speak. She cleared her throat. "I remember."

"I knew the time had come to bring this train wreck to a close. And I knew—that day I knew you figured out I was that rogue agent."

"I didn't know." Joan forced her parched tongue to form words. "I didn't know until you drove away. You outed yourself."

Inez snorted. "Like I believe that. But believe this, Miss I-Got-The-World-By-Its-Nuts, that was the day you died. You just didn't know it."

Alyana squirmed to get away. "Daddy! Daddy—y—ye!"

"Shut up, you little bitch." Inez yanked the little girl's hair hard enough to bend her neck. Alyana screamed in pain.

Joan jumped to her feet. A bullet hit the floor next to her. She felt a sting on her calf when a piece of shrapnel ricocheted off the floor and through the leather shaft of her boot. Too bad her sheathed knife was in the other boot.

"Sit the fuck down," Inez said, waiting until Joan complied before turning her attention to Switch. "And, sorry, Switch, my half-sister's son or not, you're a loose end I just can't leave dangling. I have to plan for retirement."

In her peripheral vision, Joan saw Kearney ease through the door.

"Let the little girl go," Kearney said.

"Okay, sure." Inez put her gun to Alyana's head.

"Drop your gun," Kearney said.

"Don't get itchy on that trigger. Don't want anything to happen to this kid."

"Don't worry about me," Kearney said, keeping her between him and Switch.

Everyone looked in the direction of gunshots in the hallway beyond the double doors. Switch headed toward the door to check it out. Joan took that as her cue to unlock the cage door. She pulled the knife from her boot, sliced the duct tape around Bill's wrists, then cut the tape on Little Al's wrists and ankles, leaving him to free Maya. She turned back to Bill who had the gag off.

"I trusted you," he said to Joan without looking up, working loose the duct tape on his ankles.

"Bill, I was going to tell you. I—"

Gunshots interrupted her.

"Everybody freeze," a new male voice bellowed.

When Joan turned toward the voice, Kearney had his hands up. A Mongol wrenched the gun from Kearney's raised hand and shoved him several steps backward, bumping into Inez.

Youngblood stumbled through the door, a growing blood spot on his chest. He fired. The bullet went through the Mongol and grazed Switch in the left arm.

Kearney wrestled the gun from Inez, shot her, then aimed at the Mongol. Fired. Dove for cover.

Switch grabbed his arm and cursed. "I'm done playing with you people." He fired at Kearney, who returned fire.

Joan scrambled out of the cage and grabbed her rifle. Before she could aim and fire, a round tore through her left shoulder, knocking her back against the caging. The rifle skittered away. She had no idea where the knife went. Breathing through the searing pain, trying to keep the blackness from clouding her vision, she crawled, groping for the gun. Found it. It blurred. She closed her fingers around the stock. Shook her head to clear it. She aimed at Switch and squeezed the trigger. The recoil from the rifle blasted waves of pain through her body.

Switch grabbed his stomach and dropped to his knees, looking at Kearney who had shot him at the same time.

Inez shot at Joan—must've had a spare.

Joan ducked. Tossed aside her empty gun. And lurched for her knife. Knelt. Threw it at Inez. Then dove toward Alyana, who stood shuddering in place, terrified into silence. Joan pulled her away from Inez and into Little Al's arms.

Joan turned back to Inez, who was lying on her back, struggling to breathe, her hands blindly fumbling for the knife sticking out of her neck.

With the back of her hand, Joan wiped the vision of Alyana's tormented future from her eyes, stumbled toward Inez, and reached for the knife hilt. Staring into Inez's eyes, Joan twisted the blade and pulled it out.

She staggered to Switch. Picked up his gun, planning a make-sure bullet. Kearney pushed the barrel up. She leaned against him, breathing through the pain, pulling herself together.

He said something she couldn't make out through the ringing in her ears. She blinked and concentrated on his mouth. It looked like he was saying, "Stop...over...gotta go."

She nodded and looked past him. Little Al knelt with his arms around Alyana, who was barely visible in his arms.

Bill was still inside the caging, flat on his back.

"Get out of here," Kearney reminded her before disappearing around the end of the nearest car.

But Joan was on auto-pilot, wiping her eyes to clear them, fighting the encroaching darkness, closing in on Bill, using a fender, an upright for the caging—anything to maintain forward momentum. She finally made it to Bill and knelt next to him.

"Don't raise your kid in this life," he said.

"Our kid."

Bill smirked weakly. "Maybe. Maybe not." He writhed and moaned. He swallowed. "Forgot how much this hurts."

She smiled through her pain. "Me, too."

"Fucking snitch." Bill's chest rattled with each breath. "Shoulda known."

Joan thumbed away the blood from the corner of his mouth. "I came to you when I had proof. I could've—"

His words came out as breath.

"What?" She leaned toward his mouth. "I couldn't hear you."

"When were you gonna—" He went limp, blank eyes staring at her. She swiped her fingers over them.

Going to...what? Joan flinched when Little Al dragged her to her feet. "Cops'll be here. We gotta go."

Maya put an arm around Joan and led her out of the parts area, following Little Al toward the rear door. Joan turned her head and looked at Bill's lifeless figure, remembering when she left an injured Duncan, believing he was dead. But he wasn't. Maybe...

Little Al pushed the button to open the towering bay door.

"Wait," Joan said. "There might be more Mongols." She fished the smoke canister out of her cargo pocket and handed it to Maya. "Do you mind? I'm kinda..." She gestured with her head toward her injured shoulder.

Maya pulled the tab and tossed the canister. It rolled away, purple smoke rising between the cars and the rising door. The influx of fresh air swirled the smoke around them. They waited, Alyana's head buried her daddy's neck, Maya steadying Joan.

"Neck's a small target," Little Al said. "You are one deadly woman with a knife."

Joan shook her head and leaned into Maya's supporting arm. "I was aiming for her heart."

When they left the swirling smoke, they walked into a wall of rifle muzzles held by black-clad men in SWAT gear, yelling repeated orders to raise their hands and get on the ground.

Pure, powerful relief overwhelmed the pain and flushed the adrenaline from Joan's system. She dropped to her knees, raising her one good arm. Maya got down on the ground next to her.

"I have a kid in my arms," Little Al said from somewhere in the smoky darkness.

Someone said, "This one's mine," and strong hands guided Joan to her back on the ground. She blinked up at Roger's face. Instead of his denim cut with biker tabs, he wore a Kevlar vest over a flannel shirt and jeans.

"Get medical over here ASAP," he yelled as Joan reached up to touch the glowing FBI letters to make sure he was real. "Sorry I didn't get back to you," he said. "Didn't know where you were till someone at Stillwater called with the information." He looked up and bellowed, "Where's medical?"

Two paramedics dropped to their knees beside her, asking Roger her name and what he knew about her condition. Ripping paper. Pressure on her shoulder. It all seemed distant, as if it was happening to someone else.

She must have looked like she felt—cutting ties and fading toward the pain-deadening darkness—because one of the paramedics said, "Stay with me, Joan."

Roger moved from her side. But before he left, he squeezed her hand. "Hang in there. Soon as the paperwork's completed, you'll be reunited with Duncan."

"If he'll have us."

"Us?" Roger asked.

"I'm pregnant," she said, not sure if it was loud enough to break through the darkness.

"Stay with me, Joan," distant voices repeated over and over. "You have a baby to live for."

She must have blacked out because the next thing she sensed was the thud of closing doors. Gentle rocking motions. A handsome face encouraging her, telling her to stay with him. But she couldn't stay with him. She was married to a different handsome man. More ripping paper. A bag with clear liquid swung on a hook above her head. Maybe a pinprick in her arm. It all seemed unreal and far away.

Everything she did, she did it for others—for the greater good. Duncan would recognize that, maybe even enough to help her build a life for her kid. And help her fight off the dancing demons that would taunt her and distract her from rebuilding her life.

Content, she withdrew into the comforting, shadowy, light-lessness that promised shelter from her pain, where she'd relax for a while, because in so many ways her life would never be the same. In so many ways.

CHAPTER 27

Ten days later:

J oan gazed out the window at the parking lot of the Safford Quality Inn where dry dirt swirled in wind gusts. As it turned out, they didn't need the Witness Security Program. The Demon Brotherhood knew she didn't take down Bill, although she could have made up evidence or altered it to her advantage. And she took out some rogue Mongols who were embarrassing their chapter. Evidently, even bad elements in the biker culture recognized good when they saw it.

A gray Uber car pulled into the parking lot and disappeared under the portico below. Nothing indicated it was Duncan, but she knew. She waited in the quiet, dark room for the scrape of the card in the lock. The moment she had wanted since their first night together was finally here, but there was no pounding heart. She was dead inside. Not a glimmer of emotion that her dream of a quiet life with Duncan was starting. She had been with another man and involved in torture. She had killed so many people, and many others died because of her. Worst of all, she had endangered her unborn child. She shuddered at the person she had become. More importantly, would Duncan see the woman for whom he had sacrificed his freedom, or the splintered woman who sold her soul for him?

When the door opened, she didn't turn away from the window. She closed her eyes at Duncan's presence that filled every room he entered. She smelled his cologne well before he was an arm's length behind her.

"The agents told me you got shot," he said.

"Yes," she said from the darkness behind her lids.

"Said the prognosis was good, maybe some residual numbness, but you should get most of your range of motion back."

She bit the inside of her cheek. "That's what they say."

A shroud of silence hung between them. When it was unbearable, Duncan turned her to face him. "Am I going to kick your ass out?"

She smiled through the tears that clung to her eyelids. He referred to his words during their conjugal visit when she had asked, "What if I'm not the same person when the op was over?" and after her persistence, he had said, "If I don't like you, I'll kick your ass out."

"I'm different," she said.

"I told you it wouldn't matter to me." He gently pulled her into his arms, careful of her arm in a sling. He held her for what seemed like forever.

His cheek against her head reminded her of better days and she wished this moment would never end. But she knew it had to. He had to know it was no longer only the two of them.

There was a baby.

"You came back to me. And I'm here for you—" Duncan leaned back to put a knuckle under her chin. "Whoever you are."

He leaned in to kiss her.

She ducked her head and swallowed hard. *Cowards never start.* "I'm pregnant."

"Oh..." He ran a hand over his curly, copper-colored hair. "The agents said you had something to tell me. Wow. Didn't expect this."

The heavy silence turned jagged. She guessed pregnancy was outside the parameters of "whoever you are."

"How are you feeling?" he finally asked. "Is the baby okay after…everything?"

"Good as gold."

"Good…I mean, that's great. How far along are you?"

"Eight weeks."

"Eight weeks..."

She saw him calculating dates in his head. "Yes, eight weeks ago was the conjugal visit, but I had sex with Bill that weekend."

His gaze held her eyes for what seemed like an eternity. When she couldn't stand it any longer and looked away, he ran his hand over her hair until it rested on the side of her face.

"Wait right here," he said. "I need a cup of coffee or...something."

She watched him head for the door. *So, this is what being helpless feels like*. She couldn't let him walk out without a saying something—anything. "You're walking out on me?"

He stopped, backlit by the hallway lighting. "I'll be back. I just need a minute to get my head into this fatherhood thing. A baby. Wow."

His exit left a vacuum in the room, no forever, no togetherness, no dreams.

And the weak die along the way.

She flopped onto the king-sized bed, and immediately regretted it. Pain shot up her neck and across her shoulders. The doctors said she was lucky the bullet hit her front to back, leaving a smaller wound in the brachial plexus, and limiting the damage to arteries and nerves. She still didn't have feeling in her left hand. She slipped off the sling and flexed her elbow. The pain increased a little without the support of the sling, but the constricted movement made her antsy. She fiddled with the top of the prescription bottle for a pain pill, dropped one in her hand, and looked at it.

Her kid had been exposed to more than any unborn child should endure. Whatever she ingested would go straight to him. She didn't care who the father was or if it was a boy or girl, as long as it was healthy. She always thought that phrase was corny—until she became a mother-to-be with the reality of a precious life that would be her responsibility for the rest of her life. She put the pill back into the bottle.

She turned on the television, and after a brief search, selected the National Geographic Channel. The narrator's voice lulled her to sleep. A knock on the door woke her, and the realization of Duncan's absence returned with the heaviness of a dentist's lead drape. Under its weight, she shuffled to the door and opened it.

"Forgot to take the key." Duncan stood in the hallway holding an ice bucket with a champagne bottle.

He held it up. "It's New Year's Eve, and we have a lot to celebrate." He gave her a quick kiss and slid past her, turning on the light on his way.

"But I can't have alcohol."

He lifted the bottle out of the ice and said, "That's why I bought sparkling grape juice."

Tears that had clung to her eyelids released their grasp and trickled down her cheeks. She hadn't expected to fall back in love with Duncan after falling for Bill. It hadn't been true love with Bill, but she couldn't shake the thought that her feelings for him would tarnish or diminish her love for Duncan. She had seen how Bill treated Flora's baby, and she was sad that he would never see this one.

But there stood Duncan. He returned like he said he would. Not only returned, but returned to celebrate. She should have been happy. Gratitude was the best she could feel at that moment.

"Hey. No crying on New Year's Eve," he said, wiping her tears with his thumbs.

"I broke our marriage vows."

"We knew that going in."

"I broke my vow of no more killing."

"You didn't murder anyone…" He hesitated, waiting for her answer.

She shook her head. They had all attacked first.

"I know you. You couldn't go on a killing spree. Only in self-defense. I can respect that. And you have to respect that, too."

She didn't answer.

"Am I right?"

"It's not just that. I feel dead inside. If it wasn't for this dull ache in my shoulder, I wouldn't feel anything." She looked up at him. "What if I can't feel anything toward the baby when it comes?"

"You will."

"How can you be so sure?"

"We'll work through it." He pecked a kiss on her forehead.

"You haven't told me how you feel about all this." She didn't want to ask the question, but she had to know the answer.

Duncan set the ice bucket on the bureau. He looked at her and rubbed his mouth. "If I were to say to you that it doesn't bother me that you were physical with Bill, I'd be lying."

Joan had expected as much. Still, hearing the words hurt. But at least she felt something.

Duncan continued. "I left the room because...yeah...I was shocked. But it tore me up that your first baby might not be mine. You wore the patch. What the hell happened?"

His words were worse than a slap in the face. "I'm sorry it turned out this way." She waited until her words wouldn't quiver. "It was a defective lot of patches. I didn't mean for it to happen."

"But it did. Look at me, Joan." When she looked up at him, he said, "There's a chance the baby is mine."

"What if it's not?"

He put his arms around her and rocked her. "One thing we do know is that it is your baby. Half you. You're my wife, which makes the baby ours."

She hugged him with her right arm. How could she not give Duncan the chance he so passionately wanted and rightfully deserved? His resolve was her resolve. His strength was her strength—always had been. His positive attitude could carry them both until she was whole.

"Things are going to be rough for a while," he said. "We have some adjustments: me adjusting to life on the outside, your physical therapy and recovery, parenthood. The worst is over, *nena*."

Nena, his pet name for her when they made love. The sound was like honeysuckle to her ears. She hadn't realized how much she missed it.

"Remember, together we can overcome anything," he continued as he opened the bottle, oblivious to her monumental first step to wholeness. "Let's toast to our future."

She watched him pour the sparkling juice into the glasses. He was there, looking better than ever—not for any reason other than simply because he was who he was—and he was there. With her. He handed her a plastic cup, and tapped his against hers.

He locked eyes with her. "Live free or die."

"Death is not the worst of all evils," was the response to their age-old toast, but their past melding with their present produced a pinpoint of light in the darkness inside her. "Thank you," were the words that slipped past her lips. She took a sip of the sweet juice, the bubbles tickling the back of her throat.

He knitted his brow. "'Thank you,' for what?"

"For not making a big deal about not knowing who the father is."

"Do you know?"

"No."

He put his hand on the side of her face. "Then it doesn't matter."

"We'll get a DNA test as soon as he—"

"Isn't it too early to know the sex?"

"Bill and I decided—" She had worried about mentioning Bill to her husband. She set down the glass and turned away.

He grabbed her elbow to stop her escape—from the reality of the situation, as well as from him. He had always held her feet to the fire, and this time wasn't any different. "It's okay, *nena*." He picked up her glass and handed it to her. "He was a part of your life. We both knew the probabilities going into this. I don't hold anything against you."

Duncan. Always on point. Always there for her. Never jealous.

She took a sip. "Bill and I didn't like referring to the baby as 'it' and decided to say 'he' until we knew the sex for sure."

Duncan held her eyes while he took a long swig of sparkling grape juice. "Like I told you. I was comfortable with Bill watching over you when I couldn't. That proves to me I wasn't wrong."

"Watching over me—like I'm a child?"

"In many ways you are," he said taking another sip. His grin lit up his eyes. "It's part of your charm."

It still hurt to think Bill was gone. The sense of betrayal stung even more. Duncan and she stood together in the flickering light of the television while the narrator's voice, telling the story of the wildebeests crossing a crocodile-infested stream with their young, softened the silence between them.

Duncan ran a hand down her ribcage and nudged her ear with his nose. "How much can you do?"

She knew he meant sex. She wasn't quite ready for that. "Not much. I still have a lot of pain. Well, not a lot, but—"

"What do you want to do?" he whispered.

"We could watch the boring New Year's Eve shows."

"Sounds good to me." He jumped onto the bed, scooted up to the headboard, and grabbed the remote. He patted the bed next to him.

She gingerly sat on the bed and scootched back to rest against the headboard next to him. He fluffed pillows, placed them, and moved them until she was comfortable. While he flipped through the channels, Joan studied his profile. Seeing him, being together, knowing they would never be apart again felt comfortable, natural. Like a therapy session, Duncan's strength, commitment, and presence allowed feelings to seep back into her life.

Together they could accomplish everything.

EPILOGUE

Two-plus years later, on a ranch outside Casper, Wyoming:

I love it up here on top of the butte that overlooks our ranch—I come as often as motherhood allows. I can look down and see my world as God must see it. Our house glimmers white between trees that are turning bright reds and yellows between the towering evergreens. It's only August, but fall comes early in Wyoming. Next to the house is a rotting barn, Duncan's work in progress. Our small, but growing, herd of cattle is out of sight on the back-forty—who thought those words would roll off the tongue of a Jersey girl? And no ranch would be complete without horses. Ours are tiny dots on the far side of the high meadow.

Yes, Duncan taught me to ride like he promised in that horse barn many years ago. It didn't take long before I could ride bareback. And he was right. Galloping across the mountain pastures and through the woods was ephemeral and powerful. He's a great teacher.

And he's a great father.

I forgot my binoculars today, but if I squint through my tears from the chilly wind, I can see our son, Maurice William Archer—we call him Mo—playing in the dirt while Duncan chops wood in the backyard. My breath catches in my throat. Mo wobbles to his feet and toddles to his dad. Duncan sees him mid-swing and stops in time. He sets down the axe and picks up our little man, whose carrot-colored hair glints in the afternoon light and outshines the changing leaves. Mo must have asked where I was because Duncan points to where I am, and Mo waves in my direction with his father. Then father and son burst into a game of tag.

Duncan burned the DNA results without looking at them. In his mind, Mo is our son. Period. We're united in our hope that Mo grows up to be an accountant or a rancher or an insurance salesman—anything but a mercenary or freedom fighter. But with our genes, who knows what he will do? We'll support him, no matter what he chooses.

I'm pregnant again—fifteen weeks. I know the sex of the baby, but again, Duncan doesn't want to know. He takes what life hands out. Deals with it, whatever it is, and moves on. That's the best thing about him, that and—he's a great husband, and an even greater father, and now he's given me two children.

"Boadie," I call to my dog, Boadicea, named after the Celtic queen who bravely fought the Roman invasion of England.

She's a Cane Corso, a courageous breed, aggressive toward strangers, but loving toward her family. We bonded instantly. She's still basically a big puppy and thinks everyone is her friend. Protective tendencies are in her genes, and maybe, as she grows into adulthood, she will share that burden with me, and I won't have to walk the house at night, watching for unseen enemies.

Boadie looks at me then returns her gaze upward, to a tree limb where I hung the rabbit I killed earlier. It's the only way I can keep it out of her powerful jaws.

"Come, Boadie. Time to go home." I pat the passenger seat in the side-by-side ATV.

I have to call her several times before she reluctantly comes to me then waits in the driver's seat while I pack up my painting supplies. I'm not the best painter in the world, not even good, but it gets me out into nature. And it's something I can do with one arm. My left arm works, but I can't raise it above my shoulder, and I still have no feeling in three fingers. Too bad I didn't get out of the violent subcultures before I was injured for life. Anyway, the art gives me a day away from being a wife and mother when I can work through the demons of my past. Duncan understands and helps wherever he can. But nothing's more therapeutic than hunting in the fresh air, standing with my face in the wind, and spending the day with Boadie.

It must bother Duncan that I was intimate with another man for seven weeks. I guess the fact that I wrapped it up so quickly counts for something. If it does trouble him, he doesn't burden me with his feelings. He loves me, and part of loving someone is overlooking past indiscretions, swallowing the hurt, and being supportive.

I secure the easel and paint box in the storage area in the back of the ATV and set my crossbow and arrows on top—guns are reserved for personal defense. In Wyoming, with grizzlies and wolves and wild cats, if you don't carry a gun, you're prey. But I prefer to hunt with a bow and arrows. Boadie is looking past me at the rabbit. And I smile. The rabbit will be the last thing to go in the ATV. My handheld crackles—we have spotty phone reception on the ranch—and Duncan asks if I'm coming home soon. We have visitors.

"I'm packing up now." I shield my eyes from the setting sun and make out a black truck between the house and barn. If asked, I will neither confirm nor deny if the frequent visitor is a former CIA interrogator I may or may not have known in my previous life as a freedom fighter. He and his bride, Elaine, recently moved to Casper and opened a real estate agency.

I key the walkie-talkie. "Feel like rabbit stew for dinner?"

After a pause Duncan comes back, "Do you ever stop hunting?"

"Maybe someday."

"Do I have to keep you barefoot and pregnant in the kitchen?"

I love Duncan's optimism. "I'd like to see you try."

"I accept your challenge." When I don't answer, he adds, "Hurry home to your menfolk."

"Roger. Out."

My men. Where would I be without them?

While I pull the slip knot to release the rabbit, I think about parenthood. Mothers always have a special place in a child's life. But fathers—they're the lucky ones. If they have a son, they have their best bud. If they have a daughter, they're a god.

I tuck away the rabbit, push Boadie to the passenger seat, and climb on board. "Let's go home, Boadie." I adjust my sidearm and start the ATV. "Let's go home to our little man and our future god."

About the Author

After twenty-two years in the army, Janet McClintock exhaled and settled down in Pittsburgh. She has completed four novels of her four-part Iron Angel action series, the first of which, *Worst of All Evils*, was published by Black Opal Books in 2014. She is also trying her hand at a paranormal novel before returning to her passion—action.

Action comes easy to McClintock. Over the years, she has owned motorcycles and horses and driven a tractor trailer across the country. She has trained in various martial arts over the past forty-two years and is currently training in Kali and Maphilindo Silat. She is also a certified Edged Weapons Combatives Instructor.

Learn more about her at her website: website:
http://www.janetmcclintock.com
or on Facebook:
Janet McClintock, Author